Kingston by Starlight

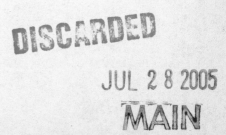

Also by Christopher John Farley

My Favorite War

 THREE RIVERS PRESS • NEW YORK

Kingston by Starlight

A NOVEL

Christopher John Farley

Published in the United States by Three Rivers Press, an imprint of the
Crown Publishing Group, a division of Random House, Inc., New York.
www.crownpublishing.com

THREE RIVERS PRESS is a registered trademark and the Three Rivers Press
colophon is a trademark of Random House, Inc.

Library of Congress Cataloging-in-Publication Data
Farley, Christopher John.
    Kingston by starlight: a novel / by Christopher John Farley.—1st ed.
    1. Bonny, Anne, b. 1700—Fiction. 2. Irish—Caribbean Area—Fiction.
  3. Kingston (Jamaica)—Fiction. 4. Passing (Identity)—Fiction.
  5. Caribbean Area—Fiction. 6. Women pirates—Fiction. I. Title.
  PS3556.A7165K56 2005
  813'.54—dc22   2004020110

ISBN 1-4000-8245-5

Printed in the United States of America

DESIGN BY BARBARA STURMAN

"View from a Fern-Tree Walk, Jamaica" (1887), by Martin Johnson Heade,
on title-page spread and part openers courtesy of Manoogian Collection.

10 9 8 7 6 5 4 3 2 1

First Edition

FOR MY FAMILY

AND FOR JAMAICA

Now we are to begin a History full of surprizing Turns and Adventures . . . Some may be tempted to think the whole Story no better than a Novel or Romance; but . . . it is supported by many thousand Witnesses, I mean the People of Jamaica, who were present at their Tryals, and heard the Story of their lives . . .

—Capt. Johnson
A General History of the Robberies and Murders
of the Most Notorious Pyrates, 1724

*Poseidon saw her passing
And loved as soon as look'd
Now suffer my desire she said
Erase my sex*

—Ovid
Metamorphoses, *Book XII*

PART THE FIRST

Under a Black Flag

chapter 1.

I believe I will begin at the end. Distemper and despondency are easier to bring into recollection than joy and all the emotions that the bright angels bring. And thus it is that the many melancholy moments of my life are still with me. The happy occurrences, however, flash and fade away, like the sun peeking its shining face between gray clouds. I recognized this bit of chicanery among memory's tricks while in my youth; it was at that time that I made a vow to myself to always hold tight to my flashes of joy. You, my darling, my loved one, will be the judge of whether my enterprise has met with success or with failure.

Ah, but the saddest days still come to me first. For I am not this bag of skin you know—this grandmother, this widow, this baker of plantain tarts and darner of breeches, this bespectacled flipper of paged things. I am closer to the tomb than the womb and there is something sepulchral in my soul now. I wake when dusty light slides through the jalousies, by way of expedition I take my lunch on the verandah, in the late evenings I lean heavily against the balustrade and dream of evenings long before. But there was a time, by my faith, when I was young, as young as you are now, my love, and all the Spanish Main, from the wild pig fields of Hispaniola to the silver mines of Peru, rang with tales of my exploits. Yes, there were deeds of infamy, to this I'll admit. But there were feats of courage, too, and acts of some ingenuity, and perhaps in these I can take some measure of pride, even now, even years after the doing. But infamy echoes longer and louder than fame, and it is on account of the actions for which I might be presumed to have some remorse that I was caught and imprison'd in Bridewell Prison in Port Royal, Jamaica, in the year of our Lord 1720. Many scores of years have passed since, but, by my faith, it seems as if only a single night's slumber separates me from those events. What delicious agony that time's ride passes so much more quickly for the old, who are so much closer to the journey's end.

It is said, by some, that members of my sex should speak softly and read lightly; I know this because when I spied it in a passage in one of the many volumes of my library, it made me laugh and curse until passersby came to check on my sanity. If I have read widely, blame it on the fact that I long ago conceded that I cannot travel as far as my fingers. If I sometimes exaggerate the exploits of my juvenescence, it is because I have, over the years, acquired the word-hoard necessary to gild the story of my adventures.

How could even the tide of time wash the stain of those days and nights from my memory? I recall it all: the dirt floor, the stone walls, the tiny barr'd window. Every soul I had loved, every one of my compatriots from my travels and adventures, had been taken to Gallows Point or were awaiting their escorted journey to that grim place. On the tips of my toes, standing before the grilled orifice to the outside, I could see the dark outline of the gallows, the cruel flamingo neck, the sad dangling rope, the heavy body of its latest victim swinging in the warm, fetid wind. The steps and the string were awaiting me as well. An admiralty court had been convened in St. Jago de la Vega to consider my case and I was perhaps but a brace of shakes away from being called before the judge to speak my peace, hear my verdict, and take my final paces down the white sands of the Palisadoes. The court was presided over by Sir Nicholas Lawes, his majesty's captain-general and governor in chief of the island of Jamaica and a close confidant of His Excellency Woodes Rogers, governor in chief of the Bahamas, the site of the bulk of my alleged crimes. And I knew, all too well, that every court proceeding with Lawes in a presiding role had resulted in a sentence of death.

My cell seemed to strangle me even before the noose. The crypt's door was made of iron, the bulwarks were of stone, and the soggy hole dug in the center of the dirt floor for my bodily relief stank as if giving vent to the odors of Old Scratch's kingdom below. Around me, perfidious shadows scampered ever closer, black spiders loosed from some witch's cauldron. I sat on the dirt floor, back against the wall, and closed my eyes, seeking to be lifted, as if by wings, out of my surroundings. I flew up over the thatched-roof huts of Port Royal, once a glorious privateer town, now broken by earthquake and malfeasance. I rode the light high above the newly constructed city of Kingston,

with its bustling harbor, and fleets of three-masted sloops pulling into port. Now I felt light as an eyelash 'gainst the cheek—
my soul moved over the face of the deep, gliding over the warm
waters of the Caribbean, only blue before me, the serrated
distance where the sky meets the sea. I was flying home.

chapter 2.

Past where the roads end, under the shadow of
the hawthorn trees, there was a wolf in the woods.
I was born near this place, a small village in Ireland, a
smattering of huts and houses too small, or perhaps too
insignificant, to have a name. Travelers, when they referred to
this region at all, would describe it not by any particular appel-
lation, but through its connection to somewhere else—it would
be called a spot fifteen miles from Kinsale, or five days' journey
by horseback from Dublin, or a short walk from a particular
bend in the River Lee, and so on. But we saw very few visitors
of any sort in my village, at least not the kind that stopped. The
local roads were too rocky for carriages, and all but the hardiest
horses had trouble with the hills, which were steep, innumerable,
and inevitable.

And then there was the wolf. He had come in November, as we pulled and clamped the last of the mangolds and turnips; by February, as we began to plow the spring crops, he became bolder, feasting on goats and even the occasional stray cat; by April, he was a full-fledged terror, and most of the inhabitants of the area, if they weren't already, took to bringing their livestock into their cabins at night—the cows, the sheep, the clucking hens—to safeguard them against the new threat. Even the dogs, when they heard the beast's howl, would scratch their claws against the door and whine to be brought indoors to safety.

There were no streetlights in our village—there was word that they had begun to install such things in Dublin—so the only illumination at night came from the moon, if he was out, and the stars, if there were no clouds. Since the wolf's arrival, the livestock in the town had taken to falling silent at dusk, and even men would grow mute over their tankards, and so the only sound echoing across the dark hills and the shadowy woods was the beast's own howls. By my faith—what a sound it was! It was a deep, sonorous roar, like a horn in its clarity, and it would climb to some fell note and hold it, letting the sound travel across the heavens. There was an utter abandon about it that made you want to both flee for safety and run into the wilderness to join with nature's creatures. The villagers, of course, chose the former. Huddled in our homes we would listen to the bays, each one, and judge the wolf's distance by the sound, much like one would hear a peal of thunder and then figure whether a storm has passed, is approaching, or is just overhead.

Ahh, I remember those days and nights well. We had the finest abode in the village then; while others slept in huts, their floors covered with rushes to soften their slumber, we had a real house, and four-post beds; while others had tiny gardens that could barely provide sustenance for their families, we had acres of land and sold off our excess food at a fair profit; while others lit smoky branch fires in the center of their cabins to ward off cold, we had a fireplace, and a chimney besides; and while others dressed in rags made from older rags sewn together, my ma, da, and I had clothes from London and Paris, and some of my ma's things were even silk.

We were rich, I suppose, or supposed to be rich, which is very nearly the same thing. In this clod of earth where little was worthy of kings or queens, we were seen as a kind of royalty. In that place, in those times, there were no means by which to acquire wealth, only to lose it; thus those who had it were viewed with a kind of unquenchable envy—the gentry were like the gods, to be imitated but never matched. We had no grand tower, no vast army, and no lofty titles, but we had a name that was known, a family history that was respected, and wealth that was assumed, and those things encircled us and held us up before our neighbors as surely as a castle on a hill ringed with high walls.

In that time of the wolf, when I was green as new leaves, we lived our lives in daylight. Men peeked out of the doors at first light and hurried home as the sun set. The wolf, which few had seen, was reckoned by its howl to be too big for arrows, and since there was no native man in our village that possessed a gun, it was deemed unhuntable. Zed, however, the old Moor who lived in a cabin not far from our house, owned a pistol, saved from, it was rumored but never proved, his days as a corsair. There were those, in days past, who had wanted Zed slain, or driven off, but over the years he had proven too elusive to capture, and later, the curative soups and potions he would mix for sick villagers proved too helpful to do without. Zed was also a storyteller of great skill (few things are more valued), and, by firelight, he would recount epics of the elder days that he had compiled during his journeys, of characters such as King Gormund the wise and Balor of the Evil Eye. One night, Zed went hunting for the wolf but his aim was not what it was when he was young and he only wounded the creature in the eye. Afterward, other men of the village, perhaps shamed by the courage of the old foreigner, placed a prohibition against any further attacks, announcing that such efforts were bound to failure and, in any case, would only inflame the wolf's rage.

The men of the town soon found a new focus. Every year, for as far back as memory, a Game of Bowls was held in the village, a match in which competitors pitched iron balls along a three-mile course in an effort to see who could do so in the fewest throws. Men from points as distant as Counties Kilkenny, Tipperarry, Leix, and Armagh would come by to test their skill and endurance in the competition. Da was a great follower of sporting endeavors and would travel many miles to find an involving event of whatever sort, and, much to Ma's distress, he was given to placing large wagers. Sports then were not so popular as they are now but Da seem'd to have a nose for finding games—he would offer bets on tennis, which was then being played in Dublin; and though hawking was then considered antique, and in any case was too expensive an affair for most people, Da was known for placing money on that as well. Most of our neighbors, hardworking farmers all, considered bull-baiting a waste of time, not to mention a good bull, and likewise cockfighting was seen as the frittering away of a good fowl, but Da nonetheless squandered fortunes on both, tho' he often claimed—with little substantiation—that he had won nearly as much as he had lost and, besides, his luck was due to change and he'd be damn'd if he got out just when his ship was coming in.

When I reached the age of ten years and two, I asked Da to enter my name as a competitor in that year's Game of Bowls. In past seasons, he had told me that I was too small—but since then I had grown until I was taller than almost any girl or boy my age and I was growing still. When I asked again, he rebuffed me once more and replied that I was too young—but this year I was older than half the competitors, and so I again deem'd myself ready and I accordingly renewed my inquiry. Da had been making wagers throughout the region on this year's race, and much of his wealth, and therefore that of our family, was tied up in the event. I had thought that he would be pleased to have me participate in an enterprise that he had been so hotly anticipating. Instead, when I asked him about the Game of Bowls, Da's face turned pale as a knuckle, and he answered thus: "You have chores to finish."

Anger flashed before my eyes, as when one looks direct at the sun and turns away, yet a blot still obscures one's vision. Gathering myself, I did not act nor say anything untoward, but instead went about my appointed tasks. And so I tended to the plot of cabbage next to our house, and, in an adjoining field, I ripped up the weeds that had been growing between the rows where we had planted potatoes and corn. Then, after washing my hands and face in a stream, I stood side by side with Ma, taking Da's clothes down from the line, sewing them where there were small tears, patching them where stitches were not enough. After that, as Ma went to fold the clothes, I stood watch as the cows grazed and I picked brambles from off the sheep.

By then, it was well after noon, and Da, who had been receiving guests and placing more bets, prepared the horse so he could go forth and watch the Game of Bowls. Herding the cows before me with a stick, I called out to him and asked to accompany him, but he replied that I had more chores to do still and, for instance, the cows needed milking.

"Besides," he added, "sport is not a thing for girls."

And so he rode off.

This time the anger was in my blood, and I felt as if my innards would fry with the fury I felt. I gathered my wooden stool and bucket and sat down to begin my milking. What frustration was in me now! So then I hatched a plan: I would be hard-pressed to finish this last chore in time, but I would do it, and I would enter the competition. I would then win the Game of Bowls and show Da what's for. Our family would lose all the money he had wagered in the competition, but it would be a small price to pay to force him to see the error of his ways. In my mind, I was as strong, at least, as some of the lesser men who had entered the game. All manner of men, boys really, participated—some corpulent of form, some short of leg, others with no strength in their arms, still more with no wind in their lungs. Why should I be barr'd, and the others enjoy the match and reap the rewards?

In my fury, and immersed in my scheming, I may have given the cow's teets too hard a tug, for she unleashed a kick that knocked me off my stool and onto my back. The milk pail was overturned, its contents spilled, and the warm froth soaked my head and the floor as well. I came to my senses from my dream of revenge and felt a throbbing pain. The blow had landed square on my thigh, and already a fierce bruise was welling up twice the size of a chicken egg. This cow would have no more milk today. I was done with my chores. Limping, I headed off to the Game of Bowls.

chapter 3.

The match had begun, and I was already behind. I could see the whole throng far in front of me, a dozen participants throwing their balls up a hill, a crowd of some fifty onlookers scattered on the sides of the paths. I saw young Aidan—blond haired, grunting as he threw; Da was sure to have bet heavily on him—leading the field. Aidan was as stout as a mug of beer and had a head filled with as much froth. He was not my better, that's for sure. The racers and onlookers moved up to the crest of a green swell and then proceeded down it, and all the people—the watched and the watchers—disappeared from my sight.

Ahh—my heart thrilled, for the game was on. There was a chance I could still catch up. Da would yet see that I could compete with the best! What did I care of the money he had wagered? A hut was as good as a house, and I did not love our chimney so much that a fire in the center of the floor would not suffice. Yes, I could catch up. A come-from-behind victory would be a thing that our whole village would talk about! I edged up to the starting line—a long deep gash in the dirt of the road—and, spinning in a circle, I then heaved my ball as far as I could hurl it. This was a technique that Zed had taught me; he said it would add more distance to my throw.

The old Moor was right! Indeed, after a few tosses, I was drawing closer to the pack. I could hear them now—a buzz had started as soon as I had been spotted. Heads turned and hats were tilted up in amazement. More than a few racers even halted in their paces and pointed at me. Ha! I would catch them and beat them all! This day would be mine! Then I saw Da, astride his horse, take off his cap and run his hand through his hair, his eyes wide with amazement at the strength of my throws, the uniqueness of my technique, and the speed at which I raced down the path.

I was deeper in the forest now, and the path turned into a ragged trail of tramped grass and undergrowth. I could catch the leaders, I knew that now. There was no fatigue in my legs and my arms felt light. I rotated in a circle to unleash what I hoped would be my longest throw yet—but just as I let go, I felt a sharp pain in my left thigh where the cow had kicked me during my chores. In my initial excitement, the injury had been forgotten. Now, the wound returned and my throw went awry, past the edges of the jagged path and into the darkness of the woods. I grabbed my leg; already it was stiffening, and my knee locked in place and I could barely bend it.

From up ahead, I heard a laugh, followed hard by guffaws. There were smiles on the faces of the spectators as they watched me bent over in pain, my ball lost among the trees. Even beer-headed Aidan, still leading the field, stopped in his paces and threw me back a smirk. Then I saw Da; lowering the brim of his cap, he turned his attention to the leaders, looking away from me and riding forward. Soon he was gone along with his horse, and all the spectators and all the racers with them.

Tears running down my cheeks, I went off the path to look for my ball. If only Da hadn't forced me to do my chores! The other racers, I knew, were excused, by long-standing tradition, from all their tasks on the day of competition in order to be fully rested and prepared for the event. Already exhausted from all I had to do around the house, the injury from the cow's kick was more than I could overcome. Now the sobs came—but I continued to search for my ball. If I could only find it, I could rejoin the race. I had lost the lead, that was certain, but I could, at the very least, finish the course.

My fingers closed 'round the ball. But by now, darkness had come. The brambles had been thick, and my injury had made the search more difficult. The sound of the crowd had faded into silence; the crickets were louder than the cheers. Returning to the path, I could see not a soul on the next hill, or the one after it. Looking back, perhaps I should have simply left the ball and gone home. I should have returned to my bed, and the safety of my house, and the certainty that the next day, I would once again tend to the fields, and the laundry and the cows. I should have set aside any thoughts of the race, and my da, and of winning or even finishing. But I was set on completing what I had begun. I was filled with rage—at the laughter, at the cow that kicked me, at fate itself for betraying me so cruelly. So I threw my ball into the darkness.

A howl split the shadows. It ripped through the quiet of night. I should have left then, but again, I made my way forward, swept my hands in front of me, secured my ball, and hurled it down the path. I was determined to finish, or perhaps I was in some way addled by the wolf's howl and thus unable to focus my thought onto a more reasonable course of action. Now was not the time for balls or sport—it was a time to seek safety and shelter! And yet I pressed on, throw after throw into the blackness. The creature's howls seemed all around me now, sounding and resounding through the black columns of the tree trunks, winding down the path, arching over the ebon sky. There's a child's game one can play, where if a word is repeated many times in succession, it loses its mooring to meaning—it becomes syllables without sense. With the wolf's incessant howl, the very opposite was taking place. What had been just a base noise now became, to my ears, a kind of wordless shout— amorphous in form, perhaps, but not without meaning. I heard hunger in that voice, not just for meat, but for other unnamed things, and I heard anger, no, more than that—rage, and perhaps a bit of loneliness, and a sadness as well. The roars entered my ears and rattled my chest and mingled with the thoughts in my own head.

Two stars from the starless night had fallen to earth. No, they were eyes, peering at me through the night. They were the color of moonlight, I could see that now. This was not the beast himself, but something else—a wolf pup? Now there was another pair beside the first. I thought I could almost discern the outlines of their forms—the small snouts, the pointed ears, the stubby legs. The eyes did not move but held their positions in the shadows, fixed like constellations.

There was another eye, but this one I did not see. I rather felt this one on my back. I did not hear the wolf's approach, so stealthy a hunter was he, but instead, in the cool of the just-fallen night, I could feel his hot breath and smell the murder on his blood-soaked tongue, and now feel the gaze of his single good eye boring into my back. But he did not move, he did not leap forward out of the shadows. Why? I had no weapon, no gun, no sword, no knife. Surely my ball was not what kept him at bay. Why didn't he spring at me, jaws wide, claws slashing? His gaze held steady as Polaris. Leaving my ball behind, I left him and the cubs there in the darkness of the forest.

*W*hy didn't he kill me?

I was in Zed's cabin. Da had locked the gates that led to my house; when I shouted for him to open them, he parted a curtain, looked out the front window, met me with eyes as hard as two knots on an oak, and would not come down the path. He held out his right hand and bade me to halt.

"You have disgraced me," he shouted. "You were not to have run that race. You were not to have been out. Now you can stay out there. Let the wolf have at you!"

I wondered if his losses in his wagers on the race upset him more than my attempts to join it. I hoped against hope that froth-faced Aidan had failed to live up to Da's faith in him, and so had squandered his wagers. In any case, wiping away tears, I went to the old Moor instead, and he took me in and made me a bowl of soup to warm me up.

"It's pepperpot soup," he said. "It's spicy—drink it slowly."

The race was long over. By the time I crossed it, there were only shadows on the finish line. The crowds had dissipated and the runners had all walked home. The festivities, I was sure, had been boisterous. The winner had no doubt sung his traditional song of victory, the spectators chanting the chorus. The losers had performed, as was customary, the dance of the defeated, laughing as they stomped their feet in a patch of mud and pelted one another with spoiled food that would be collected later, rinsed, and fed to hogs. After the dance, the winner would be escorted by the three loveliest ladies in the village to the foot of Kelly's Peak; up above, a crier would call out his name seven times, and then the number of throws it took for him to secure his victory. I had heard the cry. One hundred and seventeen! I had been on a pace to break a hundred.

I sipped my soup and told my tale to Zed. He laughed when I told him about the wolf.

"*He* is a *she*. The wolf did not kill you because she was a mother afraid for her cubs."

"*He* is a *she*?"

"*He* is a *she*."

"I still don't understand why he or she didn't . . ."

He laughed again and pulled a quilt over me.

"Ceasair, the granddaughter of Noah of the Ark, was the first person to settle Ireland," he said. "Your elders rarely speak of it, but your legends confirm it. She sailed from Egypt and landed at Dun na mBarc, right here in County Cork. But the first people to make war on this land were also from Africa— the Formorians."

"Who?"

"They were sea-pyrates, and descendants of Ham, son of Noah. They made their base on islands off the coast. They demanded that all Irish pay them, in tribute, half of their children, cattle, butter, and wheat. The Formorians were as strong and fearsome as any wolf. I see all these things in you: the spirit of the daughters of Noah, who nurtured the land, and the fire of the sons of Noah, who ravaged it. There is something special about you. There always has been."

"What? What will I ever do that's special?"

Zed leaned in close.

"You ask the wrong question. We never know our fate. We only know our selves."

But who was I? I could not find myself in the cold face of my da or the pale eye of the wolf. My father's right hand blocked my vision. Halt. Go no farther. Do not go down the path. The ire within me was so great it had become a kind of sadness, because it could not be satisfied. I felt as if I needed to say my own name, to shout it, to scream it, but I had no mouth. The great wolf had shown a strength and tenderness that I had longed for but never experienced. As sleep took me, I thought of those cubs snuggled up to their mother, and wondered if my bedding—or any bed in Ireland—was as soft and safe as the great wolf's fur.

chapter 4.

My da, being pursued by creditors and having a Commission of Bankrupt issued in his name, decided to transfer his affairs from the Old World to the New and continue his life in the Americas. His gambling debts had crushed his reputation as an attorney at law. Routinely, he owed his clients more money than they were scheduled to pay him for his services. More than infrequently, he would be unable to enter his place of work, his office having been surrounded by small parties of men looking for him to either make good on his wagers in pieces of eight or in pieces of his hide. The high walls of reputation that had set our family apart had been breached and, in fact, had utterly crumbled. We were no longer godlike gentry, but mere men, and even worse, men who owed other men money, which may be the very oppo-

site of divinity. So, after witnessing his name soiled in his original profession, Da decided to adjust his geography and focus
his attentions entirely on dirt, becoming a farmer. He left word
that he was bound for the Americas—if leaving a note buried
under a rock in a cabbage patch can properly be called leaving
word—but word was all that he left, except for debts. He
booked us, his family, no passage; passed on no specific address
where he might be found, other than a region, Carolina, and a
city, Charles Town. I thought I felt him kiss my forehead before
he crept out the door on cat's paws, but it may have simply been
a breeze, tho' the wind, at that period of year, carries with it a
little more warmth. It was autumn.

Around that time, our neighbor Zed also vanished. Ma had
shown little emotion until this event. It seemed, to me, she was
suddenly all too aware of the fact that there is an impermanence
to people; they can rule one's life entirely and yet still slip away
as if they were mere yesterdays. People are morning mist, they
are clouds, they are weather. The full import of Da leaving the
house had finally been brought home. She threw herself into
work, performing her chores as well as mine, plowing the fields,
slopping the pigs, milking the cow, remaining out of doors all
day and returning only when the dark of evening ensured her
eyes and my eyes wouldn't meet. But I could see her pain across
the shadows; the anguish of abandonment is darker than any
night. Ma and I, at the time, knew little of the details of why Da
left. I did, however, have a clear sense of his absence. In a short
time, I found it difficult to bring to mind the shape of his face,
the touch of his hand, or even the sound of his voice, but I did
see, in the corridors of my remembrance, the spot in the corner
where a chair he fancied once was, the sad rectangles on the wall
where paintings he purchased once hung, and there was a certain manly aroma that would come wafting from his skin after a

long hot day that was now missing from the air. Every mirror in our house bound the void of his image, the silence in every corner gave mute testimony to the former echoes of his footfalls. His absence filled the house.

Ma sat me down for a talk.

"Your father is gone," she said, "and—curse them all—we have many creditors."

"Doesn't the Lord teach us to forgive our creditors?"

"He teaches us to forgive our debtors," Ma said. "As for creditors, there's no hell deep enough for them."

"What must we do?"

"The truth of the matter is," Ma said, "many of our neighbors believe that I married above my station. Money protected us from such charges, but that protection is now gone. Things will be said about our family, and many of these words may hurt, because some of them will be true. Our life has been far from hard, but now things will be harder, and we will have wants. Many things will have to go."

The first thing that went was us. We sold the house and traveled to Cork, moving into a small, damp room that was rented out by the employer of a friend of a cousin. I cried as we left our home, but my ma told me to save my tears, for, given the trajectory of our lives, I would surely have need of them later. And besides, she added, when my da had slinked from the house, he had left a pillow that was cool and dry, having shed no tears of his own. He gave my ma not even a fare-thee-well. We sold almost all that we owned that my da had not taken with him— clothes, livestock, tools, and the like. But I managed, unbeknownst to Ma, to retain one thing—at least for a few nights. There was a dress coat of my father's that I loved. It was brown and trimmed with fur and hung down past my ankles when I wore it. I kept it folded beneath my covers and each evening, after saying my prayers, I would hold the coat to my face and think of my father. The coat smelled of him; I drew whiffs of his scent into my nose and thus fell asleep until the sun, and my mother, woke me up in the morning.

"This one thing you can keep," she said. "But all else must go."

I have always been taller and more mature than my years, even when I was very young, and it encouraged adults to share with me adult burdens and concerns which they may have imagined, given my seeming maturity, that I was ready and willing to bear. My precociousness, on the other hand, seem'd to confuse and anger those of my own generation, and as a result I spent many a day alone, wandering the streets or the hills or my own thoughts, heedless of the goings-on around me. When the children played Bee-Up in the alleyways, pitching half-farthings heads or harps, their light laughter sounding like chimes in the wind, I would not be there. When the girls, with wide innocent eyes, thronged to watch the older boys at the bowl matches, I was not in the watchers' company. When the other young'uns gathered behind the bakeshop for donkey's gudge, which is cheap cake made from the crust of unsold cheap cake, or when children congregated at the market off Princes Street for drisheen, which is a sausage made from dried pig's blood, I was always elsewhere, somewhere, and usually wearing my da's fur-trimmed coat.

"Hey, joulter!" called out Liam, a lanky lad, several years older, who fancied me, I think, but nonetheless treated me only with hostility, because, for boys that age, enmity is a less troubling feeling than affection. "Why're you wearing a man's coat?"

"Leave her alone," said Cormac, a neighborhood boy whom I myself fancied. He had long black hair like a girl's and thin fingers like twigs, and he would always stick up for me with the others. Cormac cried out to me: "How you doing there?"

"Stawkhawlin'!" I said, which is Cork-speak for "I'm doing fantastic," and continued on my way wherever.

"That lass is septic," I heard Liam growl to his fellow. "Her family fancied themselves so high, and now look at 'em. I'd like to cut the tripes out of her."

Our reputation had followed us. But I was already off. I recall wading in the River Lee wearing my da's coat, holding the sides of it high and spread out like a bird's wings so that my precious garment would not be soaked by the current running cold and strong around my calves and between my legs. I remember the brawny, broad-shouldered hills, green and mossy, laying like lazy giants around the edges of Cork. It was a small village, but there was much to explore. Streams and waterways ran through town winding this way and that; neighbors and strangers, some scolding, some waving hail-well-mets, peek'd their heads out of the windows of the short brown buildings constructed along the banks of the water. In the early morn, I would skip through the lanes and passageways, north down the steep and narrow byways of Barrow Street or south up the wide embrace of Barrock Place. I was looking for nothing in particular and nearly always finding amusement or misadventure or both. In the late afternoons, before the day became evening, I would run and play on the murky fields just outside of town; the ground there was soft and wet and spongy beneath my blithesome wriggling toes.

At the foot of the sloping hills and in the shadow of a grove of broad-leaved alder trees, there was a field to which I would often come, where the sod was wet and the light was silver. I loved this place, because this is where the dragonflies would alight after daylight had dimmed. Between the mud patches were tangles of long grass and the winged insects would alight on the tips of the slender green stems. There were hundreds of the creatures, and, when the dying light caught their wings, the whole field shimmered and rolled like green waves of the sea.

"Hey, joulter!"

It was Liam and Cormac again, with a pack of lads and lasses besides.

"Leave her alone then," said Cormac to Liam.

"She's septic, this one is," said Liam. "How grand m'lady once was! Now she needs to be put in her place. You know who your ma is, lass? A maid, whom your da took up with when he tired of his first wife. The whole county knows the tale. She's nothing but a common strumpet, she is."

Of course I knew it was true. The stories had been only murmurs when I was growing up; our money and status had shielded us against all scandal. Now the whispers were shouts and they found my ears. I could not move. I stood in the bog, gripping the sides of my coat in my hands to keep them from touching the ground. I watched as Liam and his gang scooped up balls of mud. The bog mud was thick and warm and tan, like handfuls of flesh.

"It's near dinnertime," Cormac said to the others. "Let's head back for some milk and odds. C'mon then!"

Liam ignored him. Now his gang faced me, a dozen of them, hands dripping mud.

A single dragonfly floated down, in search of a landing place. Liam stuck out his tongue as if he were catching a snowflake. The dragonfly landed on the tip and Liam quickly pulled it into his mouth. Baring his teeth, he chewed the creature to shreds, wings and all, and spat the parts into the air.

"C'mon then, you've had your fun," said Cormac. "Let's head back."

"Are you with all of us, or with that one?" said Liam.

Liam had a mean look in his eye, like a street dog without a master, and so did the others in his pack. Cormac met his gaze and then looked over to me and back at his fellows again. He then scooped up a handful of mud. Now he, too, had that same street-dog look.

I should have run, but I could not move. Yes, I feared the assault that was to come, but there were other emotions at work. I hated myself for not being braver. I had more disgust for myself than any of my tormentors, and it was my own self-loathing, I think, that was the hardest to bear. What makes persecution sting the most is if, in a moment of honest reflection, one comes to the conclusion that if the tables were turned, one would act like one's tormentors. Righteousness, which is so strong and sure a shield, dissipates like smoke. I fought the notion, but I knew, deep within, that I longed to be in that pack, throwing mud at myself. At that thought, my skin grew cold, cooler than the evening chill. Then I felt a warmth trickle down my thighs. A wet splotch blossomed, visible to the whole world.

"Look at this one then!" said Liam. "M'lady's done her pooley right in her dress!"

With a sweep of his twiggy fingers, Cormac brushed one of his girlish curls from off his face and then, rearing back, hurled the first ball of mud. The dragonflies buzzed up into the air.

Why couldn't I fight them or at least run away? What element was lacking in my constitution? I hated myself for what I was not, and I also despised myself for being so alone. All the things in nature, it seem'd, had their companions, the birds in their flocks, the ants in their hills, even the rivers ran to the sea and thus were intermingled with like-minded waters. I thought, too, of my old village and of the wolf. The beast had been just another mother seeking to provide for her cubs, and yet she had struck fear in all the men of the region. I thought of her eye, that single planetary glare of light. A rage grew in me then. I felt as if I had been plunged in fire.

Liam and all his fellows were ready to hurl their handfuls of filth. But as they looked up at me, they hesitated. I do not know what they saw. I only know how I felt. It seemed, at that moment, that I could have devoured the world. My skin felt hot, I could hear my blood in my ears, and a huge scream was building within me. There are some emotions you have, and there are others that have you. Love, I suppose, is one of the latter, at least according to the poets. And I've had sorrow possess me— its boundaries extend beyond the human form, it saps your limbs of power, chokes the air from your throat. There is still another feeling with such power: rage. That is what I felt. I had no plan of action, I had no weapon, but it seem'd, like Medusa, with my eyes alone I could lay waste my enemies. Chase me! Throw mud if you will! My rage felt consuming and filling as well—it filled my lungs and pumped out of my palpitating heart and pushed against my eyes. I didn't care what anybody else said, I didn't care what they did; I was lost in my own anger. I felt as if my face was aflame, burning with its own light. I did not scream, I did not shout or swear—I had no need to do so. My countenance was announcement enough.

Liam let the mud that he had scooped into his hand fall back to the earth. Slowly he and the other children backed away, and soon, one and all, they moved out of my sight.

But the first mudball had stained my da's coat beyond repair. I left the sad garment there, by the bog.

"Shhhh, my child," my ma said afterward. "We are fighters now, you and I. That is how it must be, and will be, from now on. Take these words as my gift to you."

And so passed my sixteenth birthday.

chapter 5.

It was at this time that the sea arrived to claim me for its own. Cork was home to many rivers and bodies of water. The brown currents of the River Lee flowed through the center of town, and climbing the loamy hills one could look out over the misty murk of St. George's Channel and imagine that one saw the towers of London in the distance. I was schooled more than most girls, my ma insisted on it, and ere I had reached a blooming age, I had even read some Dante and seen Shakespeare performed by traveling troupes—tho', in my learning, I was most enchanted with the poems of that great Roman, Ovid. His songs of myth and change excited my soul and I committed to memory, in Latin and in English, a number of his ancient tales: the strange, sad story of the sea nymph Salmacis and her doomed, unrequit'd love; the tragic verses devoted to Phaetheon, who steer'd the sky chariot of his father, the sun god, into the currents of the broad Eridanus, which is in Italy, and was washed ashore, lifeless; and the legend of Arethusa, who fled from her home and was transform'd, at last, into a sacred fountain. I thrilled to other poems by honey-tongued Ovid as well and let them enter my spirit. How tragic that, in our mundane, empiric lives, such wild mutations are impossible. I wondered, Would I ever embark on an adventure that boasted the magic and peril of the antique days? Would I ever gaze upon waters that ran beyond the limits of my horizon?

Both my education and my childhood in Ireland were, in the end, abort'd before their full term, and not of my untemper'd volition. Ma, having heard some rumor of my da coming into some money overseas through some business venture or another, decided to head off in pursuit of her undivorced spouse. So she booked us passage on a British ship making stops along the coast of that Dark Continent, and from thence to the Americas. We had accepted berths on a slaver, the most wretched of all vessels that sail the seas, because we lacked the funds for transportation of any higher station.

The first leg of our voyage, which was to last some few months if the winds blew in our favor, was not unpleasant, or more correctly, it was purgatory and not quite hell. We were lodged above the lower decks next to the captain's quarters. With us were two other women, the captain's sister-in-law, whom he was transporting to the Americas to be with his brother, and the lady's daughter, who was perhaps a score of years in age. Slavers did not normally transport passengers of our sex, but we were taken to keep the captain's passengers company, and also to ensure some margin of profit for the underwriters of the trip if there were some fatalities in the cargo, which there often were.

Every afternoon, the navigator—or so I assumed his position to be—would take to the deck and check the position of the sun with a device that looked like a wooden cross. At that time, the sister-in-law and her daughter, who both had silver crucifixes around their necks, would each open a Bible and conduct a service of sorts. Both women were pale and thin with big insect eyes that made them look perpetually terrified. Engaged in their prayers, clasped hands trembling, they seemed to fear God more than they felt his love. The crew had been ordered, it appeared, not to talk to any of the women on board, and the Praying Mantises had more to say to God than to us, so my mother and I let days pass by with little conversation.

"He died so that we may reach that Higher Place," they prayed. "Safeguard us, O Lord."

The early stages of the trip were uneventful—save one incident during which, late in the evening, the captain gave the order to extinguish all lights on board, cease all work, and still all tongues. There, against the stars, in the slanted and enchanted rays of a crescent moon, I saw a three-masted ship. Without words, I knew what it was—it was a pyrate craft. If it took us, our crew would be enslaved; had we taken on slaves, they would have been freed. The crew of the slaver, hard men all, looked wary and nervous. The Praying Mantises mouthed silent psalms. But I felt no menace from the shadow vessel. I could see the distant, welcoming flicker of firelights on board; I thought I could hear the faint echoes of voices raised in joyous song. Ma put an arm around me and kissed my forehead. The silhouette glided off into the larger darkness.

A few days later we reached the African coast. We never set foot on land, nor even saw a tree. We sat at anchor for a time, until the cargo arrived in small boats. The captives arrived during the night, while I was asleep in my hammock, and Ma was slumbering in hers. The sound of the shackles woke me. I rose from my hammock and, kneeling, I peeked through the planks in the walls of our cabin. At first I could see only feet—a long line of black feet, shoeless, chained two-by-two. They were clothed only in shadows. I turned away, ashamed. But I had to watch this ghastly procession, so I looked again. The women were next. They were also naked. I could see the gleam of starlight on their skin. There were perhaps thirty women and a hundred men. They were herded into the lower decks through a hatch near our cabin.

There was a flat thud. Someone or something had knocked a Bible to the floor.

The room was bathed in light. The younger Praying Mantis had lit a lamp. The elder Praying Mantis and my ma were both awake as well.

"It's a savage!" said the younger Praying Mantis.

A young African girl, naked and shivering, had somehow broken free and found her way into our cabin. This one, in appearance, was different from the others. Like all the Africans, her cheekbones were high and sharp and her lips full. But this one, this girl, had skin the color of the moon. Her hair was a pale yellow and fell in long knotty ropes. Her thin eyes glinted pink in the inconstant light. She was damp and shivering.

"We must call the captain!" said the elder Praying Mantis.

"No!" said Ma. "Do you not hear the crack of the whip outside? She's only a girl."

"We must call the captain. She's a slave."

Ma, holding a blanket, approached the girl.

The girl drew back farther into the shadows.

The younger Praying Mantis began to scream. Our door burst open. A half-dozen crewmates stood outside. One had a cat-o'-nine-tails.

"She's ours," said the one with the whip.

"Take her!" said the younger Praying Mantis.

"Stay back!" said Ma.

Ma went over to the younger Praying Mantis. With a jerk and a snap, she pulled the silver crucifix from her neck.

"She can have this back when she learns the true meaning of it," said Ma.

She draped the blanket around the slave girl's shivering body and handed her the crucifix. Then three crewmen stomped into the cabin and pulled the slave girl out. They left the blanket on the floor.

I woke late. It was afternoon; the navigator was checking the sun with his cross and the Praying Mantises were trembling before God. It was the moans that woke me up. From one side I heard the slave women crying out. Then, from another section of the lower deck, louder and deeper and greater in number, came the voices of the slave men. Together they formed a ghastly chorus that echoed through the ship. We could not see the cargo, but we could hear them. All at once their voices were everywhere, and had transformed everything, like when one awakes on a winter morning and suddenly finds that snow has covered the entire world, every house and every tree, every pathway and every field. So the calls of these Africans spread themselves over our voyage.

The Africans were to be served one meal a day—a putrid stew of ground fava beans, flour, and rat flesh that made me wretch when I saw it prepared. As some of the ship hands carried buckets of slop to them, I followed. I had to see how they were being kept. A crewman shut the hatch behind him. I opened it a bit and spied through. The smell hit me first. Sweat mixed with vomit and excrement and the aroma of that foul stew. I could see little. The darkness was too deep. Then I began to pick out shapes and movement.

The Africans were laid out on wooden planks. They were all on their sides, crammed next to one another like spoons in a silverware drawer. The mates ladled gruel into the mouth of each captive. Some swallowed, others spat out the foul mixture and let the food dribble down their closed lips. All the Africans were naked. Most had open, oozing sores on their backs, arms, faces, and legs. Their wounds would certainly grow worse as the voyage continued. Their cries were already growing louder, more insistent, and, here, in the belly of the ship, their voices seemed to coalesce into a single howl of horror.

I could see no more. I scurried back to my cabin.

*T*he next morning I awoke to music. An accordion was playing a merry tune.

I could hear the voices of the crew singing:

> *"Dance you dogs! Dance you dogs!*
> *Dance dance dance!"*

The accordion played on. The Africans had been crowded onto the main deck. The men were in one group, the women in another. The men were chained together two by two, the women, unchained, huddled together in a great mass.

"Come on now!" cried the navigator. "Dance the minuet!"

Another crew member snapped the cat-o'-nine-tails across the back of an African man.

"Bow to your partner!"

Another lash, this time across the back of an African woman.

"Curtsy! Curtsy, you bitches!"

The accordion played on. The African men, as lashes rained down, began to step to the left, and then to the right, and then spin in a circle, as the crewmates directed. Some hopped up and down, roughly in time with the music. The group of African women, still clustered together, swayed back and forth. The men and women were all murmuring now. Were they calling to their God? Or were they simply in pain?

The Praying Mantises had come out to watch the spectacle. The daughter, seeing the dancing Africans, pointed and laughed. My mother turned on her.

"Hold your tongue," she said, "or I'll feed you your Bible, every book, Old Testament as well as New, from Genesis to Revelations."

The cruel dance continued. The girl I had seen before was at the edge of the group of women. Her milky form was rippling with terror.

"Bathtime!"

A half-dozen crewmates, all holding buckets, threw the contents onto the clustered Africans. Some of the Africans screamed and clutched at their sores. The buckets had been filled with seawater.

The accordion played on.

I could smell them before I saw them. They reeked of beer and sweat. From their voices, I could tell that they were drunk. From the sounds of chains clanking, my mother and I judged that they were trying to break into the slave women's quarters. My ma rose from her hammock.

"Where are you going?" said the elder Praying Mantis.

"To help, of course."

"But it's none of our concern!"

"Maybe not yours," said Ma, "but it's mine."

"Do you think I don't know?" hissed the elder Praying Mantis. "You're just like them! You're a slave! An Irish slave! You paid for this voyage by selling your body! The minute you step off this boat, you'll be pressed into service. Your daughter may be free, but you're no better than the Africans! Go to them then!"

Ma gave the Praying Mantises a small, sad smile.

"We are all servants of God," said Ma.

Then Ma stepped out the door.

I did not want to be on this ship. I wanted no part of this trade. I wished I had the power to change what was happening, but I knew I did not. I would have prayed for pyrates to come if my prayers would have done any good but I knew that they would not. I could not stay here. I slipped outside behind Ma.

There were five men. They were unshaven. I was young, but I could not mistake, even at that age, the lust in their eyes when they looked at Ma and then at me.

"Get in your cabin, misses," said the navigator, who seemed the leader of the group.

"I have to ask you to leave," said my ma.

"We're just getting bellywarmers," said a crewman with a cat-o'-nine-tails.

"Get in your cabin, misses," said the navigator.

There was a loud crack. A crewman had kicked off the lock of the hatch that lead to the deck where the female Africans were held.

"I plan to report this to the captain," said Ma.

The crewman with the whip laughed.

"The captain's paid two trips down 'ere already," said another.

The navigator came close up to Ma and me.

"I tried asking you nice," he said. He pushed her back into her cabin with a savage shove, then stepped inside and locked the door behind him.

I ran toward the cabin, but something struck me from behind. A crewman was standing over me.

What happened next took place in a blink. From below, I saw an ivory shadow sprint up onto the deck. It was the girl with moon-colored skin. In her hand, she had something that glinted, something sharp. I could see it now—it was the crucifix, its tip filed to a deadly point. She slashed at the man standing above me. He fell back, clutching his throat. His mates took a step back, uncertain. The African girl ran to the side of the ship. She looked back at me and our eyes met again. I began to swoon. Then she leaped over the side of the ship, through the night, into the cold waters of the Atlantic. We were two weeks from land.

chapter 6.

I awoke in a feather bed. The lace curtains had been pulled open and sunlight streamed through a large window. Outside I saw a swallow fly and heard the quack of ducks. The bed on which I lay had a sturdy brass frame and enough pillows for a family of sleepers. There was a mirror that was taller than I was and almost as wide as my outstretched arms. A deep brown carpet was on the floor. A chandelier hung from the ceiling. The crystal knob to the door of the room was in the shape of a parrot's head.

I left the room and walked down a winding white staircase. The main room was even grander than the bedroom. There were more large windows and flowered curtains. In the corner of each room was a cage with a parrot—one was blue, another red, another green, the last a mix of the other colors. Silver plates hung on the walls, as well as oil paintings of stern-faced gentlemen and pale, red-cheeked ladies. Just off this grand parlor was a wood-paneled smoking room adorned with the heads of bears. I could smell breakfast cooking and followed the aroma into the kitchen. Several servants were at work. On the table were laid out biscuits and bacon and several baked hens and something I would later learn was called grits. A tall white woman in an apron turned away from the oven and smiled at me.

"Oh dear. Oh dear me!—you're on your feet! Welcome to Mount Apollo!"

I had been in a swoon for more than a fortnight. My ma was dead. I wept bitterly. The slavers had done it. But they had dropped off their cargo and their remaining passengers before any justice could be done. The Praying Mantises had saved me, begging the captain's help and seeing me safely to shore in Charles Town, South Carolina. (I could only imagine their change of heart, and their prayers: "She gave her life. Safeguard her child, O Lord.") When my name was learned in town I was brought immediately to my da's estate. My da's luck had changed. Through some business venture called the DeDanann Land Holding Company, he had engaged in real estate speculation in the Americas, thus successfully and profitably harnessing his inclination to gamble. He had established himself and his name was starting to be known around these parts. He lived just outside of Charles Town, down Broad Way in a vast mansion with tall white pillars. He was renting this abode while he searched for permanent accommodations. The woods all around were filled with tall trees and fragrant flowers. The nearby homes were grand, with high walls and drawbridges and wharves and servants' quarters. My da, I was told, had lately purchased an even grander estate elsewhere and would be leaving the area soon. He was away on that business even now, working on the final details of his expected relocation. When he came back, there would be both a welcome-home party and a going-away celebration. Surely my unexpected arrival would only add to the gaiety of the event.

My ma was gone. For some time, I kept to my room and refused all food. My ma was gone. I cared not for the curtains and the staircases, the vast lawns and the large meals. She was gone. I kept the curtains closed and remained in the dark. My ma had been a maid when she met my da but never talked about it. Her union to my da had begun in scandal, but she had draped all that history in silence. She had fought to create a space for herself, to be part of a family with a name, and she had succeeded, only to see Da squander it all away. And now, when his luck had turned, she had failed to see all the profit in it.

I recalled what my dear ma said: I should save my tears, for I would have need of them later. So I dried my cheeks and swallowed my sadness. I could not remain in my room forever. There, I was alone with my thoughts, which were miserable; on the outside, there were distractions to be found, which could be consoling. The tall white woman I had met in the kitchen was named Siobhan. She was the mistress of the house and directed all the servants.

"You and I aren't alone here," Siobhan confided. "This town has English, Scotch, Dutch, French Huguenots. But many other Irish are here also. Richard Kyrle—he was governor of Charles Town. And so was James Moore. And many of the great families—the Lynches, Barnwells, and Rutledges—they're Irish, every one of them."

Siobhan took me into the city with her as she purchased goods to prepare for my da's homecoming. The town was large and loud and hot. I begged Siobhan to pause for a sip of water, but she cautioned me that the water in Charles Town was so brackish that it was scarcely potable unless it was mixed with liquor. We passed by many shops on Broad Street and Bay Street selling drinking glasses, looking glasses, livestock, tobacco, silver-headed canes, sugar, rum, calico petticoats, bodkins, Bibles, and Africans, these last two being offered at the same store.

"Best to stock up, and not just for the party," said Siobhan. "Privateers are prowling the coast, and if one of them lays siege to the city, we ladies should not be out-of-doors."

"Privateers?" I said.

"Yea. All of the men of the town fear them, but can't do anything about them. They come from New Providence, many of them, where there are no rules and no laws. New Providence! What a cursed place! New Providence is the very opposite to Charles Town: where here we have proper families, there they respect no ties of blood; where here women have a cherished place, there all society's dictates are broken and women curse and drink like men. Where here a man's reputation may be ascertained and weighed, in New Providence, among the privateers, men cloak themselves in lies and mystery and are all the prouder for it. Mind you, I've never been, but I've heard the stories, all of them, and many more than once."

I looked out to the bay. There may have been a hundred vessels and of every shape and size and sail—sloops, schooners, canoes, scows, brigantines, and other kinds I could not name. But if a privateer's ship was among them, I could not say.

My da was due in at three o'clock. That was the traditional time to eat dinner around these parts so that one could get an early start from recovering from the heat of midday. A beautiful gown had been prepared for me. It was pink, with a low neckline, elbow-length sleeves, and a full skirt. It was made of damask silk, and beneath it I wore a matching petticoat of buckram cotton. On my feet I wore leather shoes, which were tight but made my feet appear to be pleasingly small. I twirled in front of the mirror in my bedroom and, liking what I saw, I twirled around again.

"What do you think?" I asked Siobhan.

"Oh dear," she said. "Oh dear me."

"What?"

"The sun has kissed your skin."

"We don't get sun like this in Ireland. But what do you think of the dress?"

"Perhaps you should choose another color that doesn't bring out . . ."

"There's no time! This is my color!"

Downstairs were assembled all the prominent families in their finest clothes. A magnificent feast had been prepared: spiced venison; oyster soup, okra soup, and terrapin soup; plum marmalade and loaves of rice bread; mince pies and white custard in glasses; and all varieties of wines, with especially large quantities of port and Madeira. Awaiting, too, was a long table, draped with a red tablecloth, each place set with sparkling silver cutlery, each piece's handle fashioned into the image of a parrot's head.

But around me I heard whispers and titters. As I sipped fruit punch made from lemons and limes imported from the Bahamas, a planter's daughter pointed at me from a few paces away. As I watched from the side of the room as guests danced the minuet, I could feel eyes on me. I tried to focus on the dance: the honors to the audience, the partners facing each other on the floor, the plié on the left foot, rising to the ball of the right foot, straightening both legs, heels close together.

The whispers continued: "Look at her hair . . . her eyes are . . . the color of her . . . she arrived out of nowhere . . . Charles Town is the place for it . . . there is scarcely a planter in Virginia who has not tasted a sweet black berry . . . can't tell the whites from the blacks . . . she acts as if she doesn't . . . the sun brought it out of her . . . look at her skin . . . does she know . . . does he know . . . the mother is dead . . . does the father know . . . look at her hair . . . everyone does it . . . everyone has one or a dozen in some cases . . . blood should not mix . . . the sun brings it out . . . we can sniff them out down here . . . Charles Town isn't the place for it . . . is she really his daughter?"

I knew why they gossiped. Family secrets are the closest held of all confidences. They are discerned but not discussed, they are passed down in glances, in nods, in silences. But I knew why they tittered and talked. Some seventy years ago, on June 20, 1631, Moorish corsairs had kidnapped almost all the residents of the Irish town of Baltimore; 154 souls had been stolen away to Algiers, never to return. Baltimore is in County Cork. The raiders left their mark on some of the women they left behind, but the incident had faded into local history, and then into legend, and dispersed into innuendo. But Zed, that old Moor, had filled me in on many of the details. He had even hinted that he had witnessed the events, and perhaps even participated, tho' he would never share such facts with others in my town. I knew the gossip of course, of corsair blood flowing through the veins of friends and neighbors. I chose to ignore it all, both from outsiders and from inside my own head. I didn't even care to acknowledge the question, much less search for answers. I told

Zed I didn't want to hear any more stories. I wasn't blind. But I knew who I was. I was Irish. I was like they were. I knew that in my heart. So let them talk, if they wanted to, and let them choke on their words.

But the heat of the day had been too much for me. I had not fully recovered from my earlier swoon. I found myself sweating, and my petticoat clung to my legs beneath my dress. The room shimmered and shimmied and faded in and out and rocked like the deck of a ship and I was back on the slaver again. The African men were naked and shackled on one side of the deck and the African women were on the other, clutching on to one another. The little girl who had jumped overboard now floated down from heaven. She walked toward me, her hands behind her back. Now she stuck her left arm out. She was holding a silver sword. I looked in her face and saw Ma staring back at me.

I awoke back in my feather bed. Siobhan was standing over me.

"I thought you were feeling better . . . perhaps you left your bed too soon . . . I thought he'd want to see you . . . oh dear . . . oh dear me."

"What happened? Where are the guests?"

"The guests are still here. But your father has come and gone."

I noticed then that all my things were packed.

"Da? Where is he? What did he say? Am I to go with him? Tell me! Tell me!"

"I cannot say wither he is bound. But he did see you after you swooned, and I can tell you what he said."

"What? What?"

"You must understand, he did not expect you. He did not know you or your mother were coming. He was surprised—"

"Tell me! What did he say when he saw me?"

Siobhan's voice was cold.

"He said, 'This girl is not my daughter.' "

*C*arrying a bag, I ran downstairs, my tears flowing. I was fatherless, motherless, homeless, hopeless. There is this strange power that fathers have over their daughters—the more they withhold their love, the more we desire it. And when it is withdrawn altogether, it pulls us inside out, like a gutted fish. All other men, save fathers, want women for one thing, for the secret that is between our legs. Fatherly love is therefore the purest and the most valuable of all the ardor that comes from men, and the only affection from them that is irreplaceable. But I had been cast out of the possibility of that love. I was in flight. All around me, in the halls, on the stairs, in the great rooms, were the many slaves of the estate. As I rushed out each one in their turn looked up from their labor. Strange that I had not noticed before how many there were, and how completely the happiness of this house depended on their exertions. I pushed open the front door and drew the cool evening air into my lungs. I rode a horse to the wharf and took the first ship that would take me. One thought was on my mind.

chapter 7.

So I set sail with the sickle moon as my only companion and my course fixed on New Providence, a place with not a little reputation for revels and emprise. My heart itself was a waning crescent moon, a sliver from going all dark. My da's actions were still inexplicable and hurtful. And the grief from my ma's passing was still with me; such things, like shadows, never leave; they just seem to fade for a time, only to return later. So to the sea I would go, and to New Providence, in a vain attempt to outdistance my own adumbration. I paid for my voyage with several silver spoons from my da's mansion that I filched upon my removal from that place. The captain of the vessel was at first reluctant to take on board a young woman traveling alone. But by the time I unveiled a set of stolen forks, my cutlery had won him over. And so I was bound away. In my way of thinking, an island in the Bahamas, which New Providence was, would be an ideal spot to sate my love for the far fathoms. Once there, if I applied some industry, tho' in what field I knew not, I could make my way in the world, wherever that path might take me.

I suppose my romance with the deep began, in large part, because I have always had more than some fair amount of fascination with the ways of men. My father was ever occupied with his affairs of business, and failures thereof, and, having no uncles or brothers to which to look, I found myself drawn to sailors and the like to unravel the mysteries of masculinity. Zed had his sea stories and they enthralled me. All who worked the sea— the fishermen and the boatswains, the lighthouse keepers and the captains' boys—were male. Accordingly, large bodies of water, to me, seemed to be churning cauldrons of manhood, stirred at the bottom by long-bearded Poseidon with his scepter; oceans, lakes, and rivers, in my mind, contain'd in their white-flecked crests the very sum of the rages and storms and swells of that other sex. If I could just learn the ways of water, of ships and the sea, then, by my faith, I would have something of real value in my life.

On the isle of New Providence, having established my residency by booking a small room for eight shillings a fortnight, I would stroll the dock by day, watching sailors come in from the sea and observing others as they caught the wind and blew back out into the deep. It was a world on the fringes of a world. Whilst the wan-faced landsmen wore their long waistcoats over knee breeches and white stockings, foppish hand-me-down fashions inherited from Europe, the sailors had their own style, casual, comfortable, fit for work and sweat: short blue jackets over checkered shirts, long canvas trousers and heavy-soled black boots. Only rarely had I seen a man in any form of undress, and then only by accident or surreptitiously through door cracks; the men on the docks, given the tropic heat of the region, would with regularity go about their chores stripped to the waist, their thick muscles as dark as brown leather, their chests and arms and broad backs gleaming with sweat and salty sea-spray. As white-winged gulls circumscribed the air above and green curly-tailed lizards skittered across the gray wood planks of the quay, the men would pack the holds of their ships with crates of salt and turtle shell and barrels of indigo, all destined for foreign ports. As other women breathe in the scent of periwinkle or Easter lilies given to them by some gentleman caller, I would suck in deep the reek of workingmen's musk, ship's tar, and sea water. By my faith, I must confess it smelled like it issued from some flower to me.

Ofttimes, the sound of a fiddle would dance through the air, and the men would sing as they worked, led by a crew foreman or chantey man, a call-and-response rhythm that undulated with the tides.

> *"Me bonnie bunch o' roses, O!*
> *Go down! Ye blood red roses, go down!*
> *It's time for us to roll an' go!*
> *Go down! Ye blood red roses, go down!"*

At such times, I would inch closer, straining to hear every word, every note. I wanted to rub my small hands over those muscled backs and smear the sweat from their spines onto my face. I would lose myself in the sound of the docks, forget myself entirely, only to be reminded of my sex when, noticed by the sailors, the deep-voiced work chants would change to rude, high-pitched whistles and my eyes would open to see the leering gazes of sailors running over the length of my body like those curly-tailed lizards scampering over the wooden planks of the quay.

"Ho there, you mariners!" I cried. "I am not some evening lady, but am of good stock. I seek some employment to make my way across the waters."

"Ha!" shouted one sailor. "The only industry for women quayside is performed whilst on the knees, tho' some harlots of a short stature may tend to their duties standing!"

There was much loud laughter all around.

"You make me blush, sirs!" I said.

"Your cheek is too tan for blushing," another sailor hollered. "Put away thoughts of employment, you Moorish maid, and sail with me to my bedchamber!"

"You have me mistaken for some other creature," I replied. "For tho' my skin has some shadow on it, 'tis true, I am an Irish woman born, as was my mother before me. And I would not take up with you if you were the lord of Blarney Castle!"

And so I walked off. This scene repeated itself, with some variation, and saltier language, all along the docks and throughout my search for employment and sea-passage.

Now, I had been told, by men whose intentions were, without doubt, not entirely honorable, that I was a comely lass, though I did not take such commentary to heart. Taking after my mother, who as a lass was known far and wide for her surpassing beauty, my skin is not necessarily fair, but is more correctly described as the same shade as beach sand or the flesh of almond nuts. 'Tis true that, in sunny seasons, there is a Moorish tint to my cheek, but do not even the trees, as constant as any thing that lives, change their colors as the months give sway one to another? Men have remarked in a complimentary fashion on the color of my eyes, comparing them to the green of the River

Liffey or that of Montego Bay, but I pay no mind to statements of this sort as well, since I think of my eyes as a kind of ridiculous shade of emerald, too bright and too gleamy in appearance, rather like a cat's eyes or a cheap piece of jewelry haggled for in a Sunday market. My hips, perhaps, could be described as shapely, but it is all undone, I must admit, by my height, which is comparable to that of a full-grown man; it is hard to imagine the size of the dowry that would make me acceptable to a gentleman of breeding and station.

When I walk quayside and see my reflection in the water I invariably carry in my mind's eye a picture of my self that stands in sharp contrast to the visage I see before me in real life. This has long been the case, even in the days when I skipped along the banks of the River Lee as a young girl, but, until I left my father's influence and control, I had not the spirit nor, it must be said, the thought to act on it. There had to be some way for me to escape my flesh and with it my past! Women, it seem'd to me, were prisoners of themselves. I had heard whispers, when I was in Cork, that my skin would do me in, that no dowry would make me attractive to a man of stature. I endured the whispers, suffered the sidelong glances, and ignored the slights, the mournful looks from my own kin. By my faith, I say, my coloring comes from my fair mother and it signifies nothing more than God's abundant humor and nature's capacity for infinite variety. Now here, in New Providence, I was finally free from all those who would laugh and smirk and point.

But I was running low on silverware. There was little work for an honest woman—as a female, I could not join a guild to learn a trade, I would be ridiculed for any job on the dock, and the pay for farm labor was little more than an insult. Shopkeepers laughed me out of their stores; ship captains threatened to whore me out if I returned again. Never before in my life had I actually given thought to what I was going to do with my life. It seemed every line had already been written. Either I would be married, happily or not, to a man of means or a man without, and I would bear children or else I would be barren. And if I was not taken by a man in marriage, then I would live the life of a spinster, caring for the children of others, or, if I was choleric, bitterly shooing them from my property. In any case, my life would be filled with farmwork and housework, with laundry and the teets of cows, with sewing and planting and cooking and skinning fish and making a man happy or miserable or both. Now there were real choices before me, and the prospect filled me not so much with exhilaration as with fright.

My options were not all good ones, and there were not so many of them. The life of the slammerkin was the main occupation of the women of New Providence. Harlots clustered on street corners, in taverns, and quayside. They sang bawdy songs, and showed their elbows and ankles to strangers on the street. They clawed at patrons who didn't pay and fought one another over customers who paid well. One thing I took note of: none of them were old, but neither were any of them young. The profession aged newcomers instantly, and it used them up almost as quickly. That was not the life for me. I was out of work, but not out of ideas. If I could not find work as a woman, I would take some other form, at least in appearance, since true change is relegated to myth. Thus outfitted, I would join some trade of the sea. Resolved in this matter, I needed only to put the scheme to the test. My da had his new life. I would have mine.

*L*ooking back on the matter, the first time I dressed as a man I must have looked the fool. The style of privateers, among all the men of the sea, had stood out to me the most because it was so bold and so evocative of things foreign and wild: silk shirts, felt hats, gold chains, silver crosses encrusted with all manner of precious stones. I had never seen the style's like. So, inspired by that lot, I clad myself in a crimson damask waistcoat (taken off a drunken officer), leather breeches (borrowed from a similarly inebriated sailor), and leather bucketboots (many sizes too big but purchased at a bargain price), all topped off with a purple scarf tied around my head and a red feather stuck behind my ear. My face I disguised as well, cutting my curly red hair above my ears, like a boy's, and adjusting my countenance and gait, like an actor in the theater, to take on a sterner, more decisive manner.

New Providence was a perfect breeding ground for privateers and runagates, freebooters and sea-dogs. Nassau Harbor, sheltered by Hog's Island, was deep enough for smaller ships, but too shallow for warships to wade entirely in, giving the advantage to speedy craft looking to run the edges of the law and society's rules. Food was plentiful—from the peach-fringed white flesh of conch to local sweetfruits such as dilly and tamarind—and fresh water, too, was available in abundance. The high hills around the port provided ample lookout for any approaching fleets dispatched from London, Havana, or Rotterdam, and the hundreds of neighboring islands, ranging in size from simple knolls rising only a little above the waves to large islands hundreds of miles in length, provided any number of cays and coves in which a ship on the run could take shelter until the attention of any pursuing authorities had moved on to other matters.

So all the sea scum and desperadoes who could came to New Providence, and many others of similar ill repute followed to cater to them. Taverns and gambling establishments and whore-houses, mostly wattle huts with palmetto fronds for roofs, crowded and leaned and elbowed one another for space around the bay like travelers seeking warmth 'round a fire. Vagrants and piles of garbage lay along the length of the streets and alleyways, often indistinguishable from one another either by form or by smell. There seem'd to be no silence in that place, only a constant cacophony composed of wildly disparate noises—the barking of stray dogs, the clank of swords crossing, the splash of dead bodies deposited in the water, the rude laughter of slammerkin, the patter of merchants, the drinking songs of drunks, the thump of barrels of indigo and rum and sugar being set down in storehouses, and innumerable other varieties of sounds. And yet all this discord served to make a kind of turbulent music, as a thousand braying variations combined to form a single grand theme: a city alive, inexhaustible, defiant.

The Falcon and the Bull was the first drinking establishment I entered in my new life as a man; it was, I had heard, among the toughest and randiest spots along the wharf, and that was quite a boast. It was a small, scabrous joint, burrowed into Dorchester Street off of Bay Street like a tick that had scratched its way into a scalp. No ladies ever passed through its swinging wooden doors unless the lady in question was ready to offer up her body for whoring, and at a considerable discount. No landsmen entered either, lest they were well armed and well schooled in the art of close combat; men who were not of the sea were considered easy marks, and, once identified, were quickly and continually tested by the ocean-hardened patrons that made up the bulk of the tavern's clientele. So many men, of such varying character, dress, and countenance, passed through the place each day, I figured that I would hardly be noticed.

I entered the tavern as smoothly as possible, as if I was a customer of long standing. Luckily, as I slid into a booth in the corner, my face did not betray my heart and stomach. Even as I ordered a mug of coconut water blended with sweet milk and gin, my innards seemed to fill with a hot excitement which, if it had a color, would have been bright red bordering on the white hot of metal when placed in a forge. Nonetheless, I kept my face impassive and my voice calm and low as water without wind.

The bar was as small and cramped as a coffin. The patrons, and there were many, came in all shapes and sizes and shades— some with skin as dark as well bottoms, others with cheeks as pale as clouds. I heard a variety of languages—Spanish, French, Portuguese, and other tongues that I supposed came from Arab lands. It was very loud, and the stale air sounded and resounded with boisterous oath-taking and cursing and debate over games of dice and the like. In one corner a scuffle had broken out over quoits, and as the participants began to swing at each other with the iron rings and target pins used in such matches, spectators began to take bets on which of the combatants would ultimately lose his life that night as the violence inevitably escalated. As one man struck another in the face, and thus drew blood, loud laughter erupted, and a chant rose up for the dispute to be settled with blades, since, in order to resolve an argument in an entertaining manner, gunplay was usually over too quickly and fisticuffs, in general, took too long.

I was readying my own wager, preparing to either toss a ring or pick a survivor, when a harlot, still breathless from servicing a band of British midshipmen lately put into port, came over to my booth. Acting quickly, she ordered herself a mug of Kalik, the light wheaty local brew, indicating to the barkeep that I would settle her bill. Before I could mount an effective protest, she was in my lap, her hands rubbing my neck, her lips pressed roughly against mine. Then she pulled back.

"Your Captain Johnson has not offer'd his salute," said the harlot.

"I—"

"Shhh. It matters not. Moors, Chinamen, Jews, Turks—if they sail in the company of privateers, they are welcome in the harbor of my bed. Mark you my credo—in the dark, it matters not who is atop the masthead. I earn my shillings."

"You don't—"

"Why are we still talking?" the harlot asked, drawing back slightly. "Is there some other secret you hold? Do you make your bed with Woodes Rogers' men?"

I quickly realized that, given this woman's obvious breadth of experience, any show of faintheartedness and lack of passion on my part would betray my gender not only to the harlot, but to the devil's company that comprised the bar's patronage. So I kissed the harlot's rouge-smeared lips with as much passion as I could muster for a creature of my own sex, and, after she whispered into my ear her carnal rates, I used the monetary revelation, tho' her rates were more than reasonable, as an excuse to spill her from my lap, in as rough a manner as to seem manly but not so viciously as to undermine my natural empathy for a woman making her way in this world. Then I quietly and hastily made my exit. I had dipped my toe in the waters.

A smile played on my lips as I walked down Bay Street, past the ships rocking in the shadows of the harbor, past shirtless louts relieving themselves in spattering streams on the prone forms of other shirtless louts who had fallen down, past the dark whispering promises of West Street and Queen Street, past the Iron Goat, the Blue Mermaid, and the Five Corners Drinking Hole, all the way back to my small flat on Culmer in the cheap section of the bad side of town. There is this enigmatic space between who we are and who we must be. All our lives we seek to cross it, to bridge it, to follow, apostolic, the image we see in our soul's mirror. A thousand daily distractions and derelictions keep us from our goal, from the great work, from the best self, but, in the end, we are all on a journey toward that secret soul or away from it. It stands waiting, indigenous, on the continent of our hopes. And like those explorers who first discover'd the Indies and the Orient and other far-flung places besides, I, too, had set a bold booted foot on a new land—in me.

chapter 8.

Things of value in this life are ofttimes captured by the strangest nets. There is a nigrescent substance called ambergris that washes up on tropic beaches, in particular the sands of the islands of the Bahamas. I have seen it in the mornings, quivering in piles on the surf, as if dozens of ill-disciplined children had upended bowls of black pudding. By touch, it is soft and gelatinous; by origin, it is said to issue from the intestines of those great sperm whales that navigate the blue fathoms. It would seem no more than waste, flotsam and jetsam to be paid no more mind than the poisonwood tree branches, empty crab shells, and speckled bodies of dead angelfish that similarly litter the white sands. But ambergris has proved to be a rare and valuable fixative for perfumery, as an ingredient that locks in a given fragrance, preventing sweet odors from escaping and evaporating into the surrounding air. Ambergris, which hardens into a grayish brittle substance of a pleasing redolence, can fetch up to four pounds an ounce in the salons of Paris and London, no small sum.

The taverns of New Providence were my ambergris. Their dirtiness, their fighting spirit, kept me in corporal form, and prevented me from vanishing into the breeze. Tho' hard-pressed for funds, I put aside my active search for employment for a time, feeling it best to practice my ruse among those best qualified to see through it. One establishment in particular grew to become my most familiar haunt: the Roach and Salamander. There was no sign above the door of the old R. & S., the patrons of the tavern having pilfered the marker with such persistent regularity that the owner long ago despaired of raising a nameplate ever again. Because of this, the tavern's location, indeed its very existence, was very much a secret among the lower ranks of the folk of New Providence. It was a thing spoken about softly in the ear, with the lips cupped with one hand, much as one would relay the location of a treasure key or the family shame of some close relation. Also, because the Roach and Salamander had no marker, the tavern tended to move from spot to spot, Union Street one month, Augusta Street the next, like some recurring rash or boil that no physician can salve or lance.

So I had taken to raising a pewter cup with regularity at the Roach and Salamander, having fallen into an acquaintance with the barkeep, a short, stout man named Punch whose face resembled a closed fist, but whose jocular manner belied his appearance. I was also affable with a number of the serving maids, who all doubled as harlots and slammerkin, and from whom, on occasion, I bought kisses at a shilling a piece in order to maintain my image of virility and manliness. I am of a sufficient height and with broad enough shoulders, that my secret was never guessed.

I felt more at home than I ever had in Cork or the Carolinas. Whenever the tavern would open for business, new location or no, I would take my same spot at the leftmost portion of the bar, my back against the wall to better guard my health and fortunes against the establishment's more colorful and dangerous clientele. And so the Roach beckoned.

The latest location for the tavern was as foul and dissolute as any of its former incarnations. It was currently inhabiting a shack on Charlotte Street directly across from the cemetery. A plank of wormy wood, salvaged from a recent shipwreck, was laid out to form a splintery bar counter; two granite tombstones stolen from the cemetery supported it. I recognized the name on one of the stones as that of a former patron of the bar at a previous location. I took my customary spot on the left, my back 'gainst the wall, and ordered my usual, a pewter cup full of Kalik, which I sipped slowly, as was my custom, to keep my wits about me throughout the evening.

"*B*y Pluto's damn'd lake, this I swear—you're nobody 'til somebody kills you!"

I heard his voice before I saw him. His manner of speaking was not louder or more booming than that of other men, but it carried with it an air of command. With such a throat, and with such a tongue, must fair Antony have deliver'd, in tribute, his funeral oration for murder'd Caesar! Once heard, I could only but listen to this man, and him alone. Even his laughter was direct and to the point, utterly lacking in frivolity. The sound of his voice separated itself, and made itself known, from the other voices in the air and from all the other sounds, the belches and the guffaws, the clattering of pewter and the stomping of boots. It rose above them, the sun ascending from the sea in the morn.

He was sitting on a stool at the dead center of the bar counter and all eyes were on him. He was a lodestone pulling every compass needle. He was turned not toward the barkeep, but out toward the general area of the bar, addressing no one in particular but everyone in general as if he were engaged in intimate dialogue with every soul in the bar. He cut quite a rakish figure, even among rakes. He was dress'd crown to toe in black: black scarf tied around his head, black coat with black buttons 'round his body, black leather breeches, and square-toed black boots (his footwear was of particular note, for his boots were polished as bright as gemstones). His chest, which was broad, was crisscrossed with bandoliers, each of which held a brace of pistols. Around his waist he wore a wide leather belt, also black, and tucked into it were two long, naked dirks and a sheathed cutlass the length of an arm. In his right hand he held a pewter mug filled to the brim with some dark brown brew; in his left hand he twirled in his fingers a small black die with blood red markings.

I had long considered myself a sort of connoisseur of men, and yet, I had never seen this one's like in all my studies. I had once seen a panther, brought to Cork as part of some traveling carny. This man reminded me of that creature in his sleekness, his equipoise of viciousness and serenity, of power held in reserve. One longed to stroke his side but feared it might cost a limb. This man before me, like that jungle cat, was neither too heavily muscled nor too lightly so. His visage, also, was arresting: he was not what one would describe as pretty or handsome, but rather he was in possession of a rough, dramatic grandeur, like the jagged face of a cliff. He boasted a strong chin, as solid as if he had been hewed from rock, or the heavy wood of lignum vitae. High square cheeks hung over the lower half of his face like balconies. His lips were full, his nose prominent but broken and shifted to the left, his eyes two onyx stones, deep set and penetrating, the night staring back at you. His curly black locks tumbled out of his scarf at the back as if his hair was an autonomous thing, too vibrant to be contain'd by mere fabric. In manly form, he was akin to Apollo or Adonis, save for two things. The first was that he was shorter in stature than one might presume upon first hearing him speak—his voice seem'd to issue from the throat of a taller man. The other unexpected detail was this: on his jaw was a port-wine stain, the size of an infant's palm, the color of a congealing pool of blood. I knew who this was. The spot gave birth to his nickname, which I had heard in talk throughout the town these many weeks and months: this was Calico Jack Rackam. His stratagems in things pyratical and amorous were known to be identical: no time wasted, straight up alongside, every gun brought to bear, the prize boarded quickly.

"So his majesty in England has issued a proclamation for the suppression of freebooters and scourges of the sea," Calico had said, his voice dripping scorn, speaking to everyone and no one. "That every man of the trade, if he should declare himself and renounce his profession, should receive pardon."

"'Tis an offer worthy to be entertained," said Mackinnon, a tavern regular with a Scottish brogue, eyes as thin as coin slits, and two jagged black eyebrows that struck down at his nose bridge like lightning bolts. "The halcyon days of De Graff are finished. How well I remember his fair hair and blues eyes! But De Graff is much retired, or is entombed with his fortune. Governor Rogers has been hard on the brethren of the coast since he was installed in office. There have been two score hangings in the last fortnight. And Governor Lawes in Jamaica has mounted a similar campaign. This proclamation of pardon— 'tis an offer worthy to be entertained."

"Enough!" Calico had cried, slamming down his mug at the bar. "You fear a man who should fear us! More directly, I have come to say this: my sloop sits in the harbor awaiting. In the afternoon of tomorrow, I am of the intention to sail out of New Providence, and we go under a black flag."

Silence greeted those last words and all laughter died.

"Who among you will join my crew?" Calico's voice rang out. "We give all hands a fair shake, no matter who your mother was, no matter if you arrived in the Americas in glory or in bondage."

There was much grumbling and talk among the patrons at the bar, but no answers in the affirmative.

"Come, come! This town has a reputation for breeding seadogs! Can a few hangings quell both bite and bark? Know you not what his majesty's Royal Navy provides its seamen in return for their labors? Let me offer you an education: an admiral on a ship of the line is entitled to half of all prizes taken under his command. A ship's captain, one quarter, and so on and so forth, until all the officers, from fore to aft, larboard and starboard, from lieutenant to midshipman, have dipped their beaks in the wealth that you ordinary seamen have purchased with your own sweat—forsooth, your own blood. Serve you the Governor? Serve you his majesty? Well, I've metal monarchs on my mind. And you all know that the loot we win as brethren of the confederacy of the coast is divided up in a more equitable manner. No prey, no pay. Two shares for the captain and high officers, a share for all else. Let his majesty keep his Royal Navy! I'd rather serve monarchs I can spend!"

Still, silence.

Calico coughed a bit, and his hack was thick and hoarse, as if his throat had been layer'd with phlegm as the result of the course of some long infirmity or flux. Then the wily privateer laughed, clear and strong, and he bent over, hands on his knees, with his laughter. The men in the bar, cautiously at first, joined in. Soon the whole tavern was rocking with mirth. Then Calico, pulling something from his boot, stood straight up and slammed it on the bar with a loud thud. It was a leather bag, out of which tumbled a goodly number of large doubloons. Each coin glitter'd gold.

"This is but a taste," said Calico. "A squeeze from a rag dipped in a barrel of wine. Indeed, the men that sail with me shall slake their thirst on treasure and grow drunk with wealth. De Graff never set his blue eyes on such treasure! For on my sloop we have obtained the secret routes of Spanish galleons returning from Cartagena and Portobello, laden with the riches of those gilded ports. This information was precious and much blood was spilt in its taking. But I swear to you, those who sail with me shall end their lives rich men—or else, at the least of it, you'll have coin enough to pay grim-faced Charon for your ferry ride 'cross the Styx!"

There was silence again, but it was a different kind of quietude than the first. The second was akin to the kind of uncomfortable, unbearable pause that comes at the end of conversation when two people have naught left to say to one another and yet still must spend time together. Or rather, it was akin to this: when a joke is told, if the teller but slightly trips upon his tongue in relating it, all humor is drained, and it will earn naught but polite smiles, but certainly no guffaws. After Rackam had completed his speechifying, there was a painful sense that something had been tripped up.

"Do I waste my words on an audience of drunken tinkers?" Calico roared. "Are you not men? Are you not men?"

At that, there was a kind of growling among the patrons in the bar, like when some low beast is disturbed in its sleep. After some debate, a wager was struck: several of the scoundrels at the bar agreed to go with Calico, if he would but put his manhood to the test. He was known as a man willing to take gambles, so this group challenged him to a single coin flip—if the shilling's toss showed the king's head, they would go with him, and gladly, but if it lay with the king's crest facing up, they would split Rackam's bag of doubloons among them, and send him on his way.

"Done," said Calico.

With that, he flipped a shilling into the air. All eyes watched its fall.

It landed crest side up.

The group of men who participated in the wager, with much laughter, converged on the bar to split their winnings. Mackinnon was among the group, and he turned, with a broad grin, to mock Calico.

"Your wild wagers will be the death of you, Calico," said Mackinnon.

The patrons of the bar turned away from the scene and the buzz in the room returned and grew back to its usual almost insufferable din. Calico's recruiting drive, at least at this venue, was a failure. Calico, his face betraying no emotion over his loss, paid for his drink—his bill was two shillings—but he dropped a third shilling on the floor. Falling to all fours, Calico searched for the lost coin, first near the counter, then beneath nearby tables, asking patrons to move their legs as he continued his inquest. At last he found the shilling had rolled into a puddle of Kalik that had spilled on the floor. Calico picked up the coin, wiped it off, and pocketed it.

Calico exited the bar and I followed hard after him. There is a sort of state of mind that the Greeks call *akrasia*, which is being of a disposition to know the right action and yet take the opposing course instead. Following Calico was, no doubt, a prime example of akrasia, and an error in judgment, but I was primarily ruled by the fact that I was running short of coin and was in desperate need of employment.

All through the night, and with only a little less cacophony in the daylight hours, I could hear the cries of whores in the streets of New Providence. It was the fate of all women in that town, unless they were well married, and sometimes even then, to end up in the streets, renting the space between their legs, and as of late a great fear had grown in me that I, too, could be sucked down into that hell. When I passed strumpets in the streets, their rouged cheeks rough as plowed fields, their dresses rent with holes as if by sharks, brown clay pipes tilted insolently out of their stained mouths, they seem'd to call to me, wordlessly, to join their numbers and despair. I imagined my body circumscribed by their crude, cruel eyes, and sharp fingers tearing at my clothes until I was revealed naked in the street, to be measured and bartered like a barrel of indigo. The sea's siren song seem'd less ruinous. So I followed Calico with little concern for peril.

He slipped into the shadows of an alley, and, fuddled a bit by the darkness of the night, I lost sight of him. Feeling my way against a stone wall, I came to the end of the alley, which led to another passageway, which came at last to a gutter. There, sitting in a rivulet of filth, was one of the figures I so feared: a draggletail, clad in a worn purple petticoat and a tattered gray mop cap pulled close over her face. She sucked on a long-stemmed clay pipe and, after each drag, she coughed a little, in a voice that was low and full and rather like a man's.

"Ho there, harlot," I said. "Have any passersby lately come through?"

The woman looked up.

"Calico?"

Quicker than the flick of a cat's tongue, he was on his feet and his dirk was at my throat.

"Do you have any money?"

"What?"

"If you have money for harlots, you have money for me."

"Why were you dressed . . . ?"

"When times are hard I work this ruse and it pays handsomely. Come now, give me your purse, so some profit may come of this night."

Calico had thrown off the petticoat and the mop cap and now stood before me in manly form, as he had at the bar.

"I have no money."

He pressed his blade closer to my throat.

"I saw you at the Roach and Salamander," he said. "Why were you following me?"

"I have only a question," I said.

"Speak it then!"

"I seek employment on your ship. Do you need a hand?"

Calico smiled and the fires from the torches burning along the street paths were caught in his eyes.

chapter 9.

On the west beach of Nassau Harbor there was strange commerce afoot. I had risen from my hammock in the morn with the resolution that on that very afternoon, I would go out to sea. The thought filled me with an exultation the like of which I had not previously known or experienced. My limbs and my spirit were light and free, I felt as if my tie to the earth had been loosed, that I was not merely taking to a ship, but I myself was an unanchored sloop, the wind filling my white sails. Of course I had traveled upon both the Atlantic and the Caribbean and other bodies of water as a passenger, but, with Calico's crew, for the first time I would be a woman of the waves—or, more properly, a man of the sea, given my continuing ruse.

My flat on Culmer Street was a small one, its major features being a pinewood chest, an iron trivet, and muslin netting hung over the hammock to ward off the unwanted annoyances of no-see-um's. Having no other occupation over the last few months other than pilfering through the pockets of drunks, I had fallen behind on my rent, modest as it was, so I thought it best to pack light so as to not arouse any suspicion of my leave-taking with the landlord of my abode. A trick of the shadow-life, my love, and advice to all tenants present and future: the last week's rent is always free, and never leave a forwarding address. So, living out that maxim, I gathered together, in a tidy brown leather sack, a small portion of my few belongings: a pewter washing basin, a pewter drinking cup, a toothbrush with tooth powder, a pair of red woolen socks, two pairs of brown canvas trousers, and a loose-fitting white shirt. I had long since torn my women's clothes into strips; now I used the remnants to bind my breasts tight to my body. Having not reached full womanhood in that area, there was not much to bind.

I strolled onto Bay Street to take in the sites and sounds and smells of quayside for one last time. It was a fair day in late August and because the sun was newly arisen, the full heat of the day had not yet arrived. There were no clouds and the sky was very blue. The turf was kissed here and there with shrubs of yellow buttercups, the proud stalks of red heart flowers, the mauve petals of potato bushes. Sweet melodies of doctorbirds hummed from blossom to blossom. The air was still except for a high breeze that shook the emerald crowns of the tall palm trees that grew next to the strip of sandy beach that ran alongside the wharf. Seamen were just awakening on their ships and the clustered masts of their vessels, denuded of their sails, made the harbor look like it was fringed by a forest of stripped pines. I paused for a moment to imagine the men slipping out of their sleeping places, stretching their sun-color'd bodies in the softness of the morning illumination. The thought of the private waking rituals of men, of warm lather, leather strops, and straight razors, left me breathless, and my tongue water'd as if in anticipation of sucking on a stalk of sugarcane. I longed to both touch their bodies and inhabit them.

The marketplace beside the harbor was already bustling with activity, with gray wooden booths set up to sell various goods, most stolen, many available at a substantial discount if one was a canny enough haggler. There were trays of iron cutlery, tables spread with cheap glass jewelry in hues of crimson and heliotrope and aquamarine, stands piled high with various native fruits including spiky-crown'd pineapples, smooth-complexion'd papayas, green scaly sweetsops, tanned toelike tamarind pods, and brown coconuts cover'd lightly with coarse hair like the heads of grandfathers. Having no coins of any sort in my pockets, I did as the less fortunate of the island often do, and picked my breakfast from the green clusters of sea-grapes that grow in the bushes near the beach. The sea-grapes were green and crisp and large as eyeballs and more sour than sweet. But the juice within them was cool and tasty and so I plucked a half dozen and continued my stroll down to the beach, my snack in hand.

*T*he gallows was an unexpected sight. It was located between two booths in the market, both selling overripe guineps, and commerce continued all 'round the ghastly monument, the buyers and the sellers, one and all, apparently impervious to the specter of death. The gallows, like the booths, was made of gray wood, with a large gray platform and a large gray wooden arm reaching overhead from which, suspended by a thick braided rope, dangled the corpse of a young privateer. He was dressed in brown canvas trousers and was naked from the waist up. His hair was blond and his eyes had rolled partially up in his head, greatly exposing the whites. His cheeks and chin and forehead were puffy and red, the rope 'round his neck having caused the congestion of blood in his face. I had expected the final look of a dead man to be a peaceful one, as cares are released and the soul passes, with pacific resignation, to that other place. However, the privateer's expression was the opposite: love and hate and fear and all else seemed drained out his visage, leaving only an awful void, an abeyance of humanity.

There was a sign posted near the gallows, a piece of splintery worm-infested wood with red letters crudely slathered on it: EXPULSIS PIRATIS, RESTITUTA COMMERCIA. The words were in Latin, and I knew well what they meant from my study of Ovid. This was not a poet's phrase, but a politician's, and a hard one at that.

"It was a prize of a hanging, it was," said a voice.

A boy, no older than ten, had taken a place next to me. He had full cheeks and bright eyes, this boy, and his brown hair was as tangled as a bird's nest. He conversed with me in an easy manner, as if we were of long acquaintance, and, as he talked, he sipped from time to time on a gourd of Flip, which is a mix of beer and spirit, sweetened with sugar and heated.

"It appears to me that the good citizens of New Providence have, after this man's death, made a prize of his shoes," I said.

"No—they hung him barefoot," said the boy.

"Barefoot? Why?"

"He made a speech, he did. Addressed the crowd like a pastor delivering a sermon to a Sunday congregation."

"They took his shoes because of a speech?"

"That's not the whole of it. His name, as he gave it, was Dennis McKarthy. He said that friends told him that he would die in action, that he would die in his shoes. So before they hanged him, he kicks off his shoes and he tells all those assembled: 'Some friends of mine have often said I should die in my shoes, but I would rather make them liars.' "

"And what became of the shoes?"

The boy shuffled his feet. He was wearing shoes big enough for a man twice his age.

"It was a prize of a hanging, it was," said the boy.

I turned away from the boy and walked quickly toward the meeting place.

A small band of recruits had gathered on the open space of the parade in the cooling shadow of Fort Nassau. Calico's powers of persuasion had indeed made an impact: I recognized a few of the throng from the Roach and Salamander. The largest number were unknown to me and appeared to be around my age at the time, which is to say old enough to consider one's self an adult but too young to realize one is far from a state of full maturity. A dangerous and ridiculous age. All things seem possible, all directions appear open, and life seems as endless as the open sea. Then wisdom arrives, the hair grays, the muscles ache, the waist thickens, and, perhaps blessedly, the memories of a healthier, more youthful time fade away. But I still remember my age of action. It is a time more precious than any other because only after it has passed do we realize its value. And it cannot be lived again except in imperfect recollection and in our hopes for our children. No, by my faith, not even then. We stumble through our youth like fools in blinding sunlight, and, when twilight comes, we remember the day and exult that we got even one thing right in our vast and bless'd and inexcusable ignorance.

So I stood with the new recruits, a varied lot from their looks and dress and the sound of their talk among themselves. They were Spaniards and Swedes, Welshmen and Dutchmen, Moors and mulattos. They ranged in shade, from the darkest dark to the whitest white. They were united in this: sea-dogs these were not, but mere sea-pups. I was as eager and anxious as any of them, but I knew that continuing my ruse would require a certain effort. I couldn't show myself as others could show themselves; I would have to spin an air of privacy and mystery about my person. I had taken the stage and the curtain was being pulled up. I positioned myself a bit apart from the crowd of my fellows, and I stood upright, squaring my shoulders, feigning an air of professional indifference as we waited for Calico to arrive.

"I hear he's killed two score men," said one boy, with cheeks as round and red as a baby's slapped bottom.

"I hear half that number were his own crew," said another, with a mouth of rotted teeth.

A third boy, having heard the exchange, turned away to leave.

"Where are you off to?"

"Back to my uncle's," said the boy. "I'll take my chances as a sailmaker's apprentice."

And with that the boy walked away, and three others followed him.

The talk among my fellows of such rough practices, to be sure, put me off, and not a little bit, but I was not swayed in my intention to set sail. What craftsman or merchant would take me in? There was not a blacksmith or ivory-tuner or limeburner or cordwainer or shipwright in the whole Caribbean who would teach me their profession and, what's more, I did not care to learn a polite trade. The sea, I knew, was full of men with secrets, and no pedigree was needed or desired to establish one's background and fitness. I laughed, ruefully and privately, at the recruits who had left—let them have their soft lives!—I was resolved to remain. A mulatto lad to my left cast me a knowing look.

"They may have futures on land, but our only hope is at sea," the dark-skinned sea-pup said to me in a soft voice, as if he was sharing a secret.

"I am from Ireland," I said. "Your tone seems to suggest there is some connection between us, when no such bond exists."

My skin, when kissed by the sun, invited such comments. The mulatto lad stepped away a few paces, and I looked out to sea. Soon, out on the cerulean expanse of Nassau Bay I spotted a small black dot growing. I nursed a quiet pride in my powers of observation that I noticed it first; now some of the other recruits were staring and pointing and talking about the approaching craft. The dot was small but growing and sported the red flag that we had been told to look out for. It was Calico Jack, rowing a longboat to shore. I hadn't expected him to be manning the oars himself; I imagined that he'd have at his disposal a grizzled, muscled, hardened crew, following his orders and doing the physical work while he focused on strategy and leadership concerns. But there he was, in the middle of the craft, an oar in each hand. I could see now that his face was red and glowing with the sweat from his exertion. He was rowing a heavy boat built for a dozen or more souls and doing it alone.

"Is that him?" said Baby-Bottom Face.

"I thought he was blond, like De Graff," said Rotten Teeth.

Calico was within shouting distance of shore. He laid down his oars and stood up in the boat, waving his arms and motioning for us to swim out to the craft.

"He's not as tall as De Graff," said Baby-Bottom Face.

"Nor as blond," said Rotten Teeth.

"You fools," said the mulatto lad. "You've never seen De Graff, none of you. You were both at your mother's breasts when he sailed these waters."

"Still," said Baby-Bottom Face, "I'm sure De Graff was taller."

"I think we should swim out to him," said the mulatto.

The mulatto waded into the drink, and a couple other sea-pups followed close behind. A few of the recruits hesitated—a number had brought with them heavy chests—but, since I had with me only a light leather sack, I dove right into the water. The Spaniards called the water 'round the Bahamas the Baja Mar, the shallow sea; and, indeed, I was able to wade a long way out before I had to begin to swim. The water near the shore is as clear as gin; beneath the water, with my eyes open in the stinging saltiness, I could see far out into the depths. A school of grunts flashed silver and a bright blue damselfish flitted past. Farther off, there were cities of coral, extending into blue shadows. A brown eel with gold stripes darted close to me off of my right shoulder but, lacking natural aggression toward humans, it soon swam off. Now I could see the bottom of Calico Jack's boat approaching. I raised my head above the waves.

I climbed into the boat; I was the third to emerge, a dozen others were straggling behind. Had I not paused to observe the wonders of below, I might have been the first. Still, I noted that the others were panting to catch their breath, and I, newly arrived, was already breathing with ease. Calico handed the oars off to the first two arrivals and he took his place at the fore. A few more recruits struggled into the craft and there were more still in the drink, but Calico gave the signal to depart.

"What of the others?" said one sea-pup.

"The swimmers who have not arrived," Calico growled, "would be better off drowning themselves now, rather than all of us later."

"But—"

"Listen, boy, and begin a new education: will not the bear, when caught in a trap, devour his own leg to escape?"

Now Calico was looking out toward the mouth of the harbor at the western end; not far out from the opening, a warship was anchored. I wondered what he was considering. Above, a flutter of pink flamingos passed by.

We kept rowing until the shore was no longer visible.

"Where is your ship?" I said.

"Our ship," said Calico. "And there she is . . ."

chapter 10.

Your first ship is always your first love no matter how many loves you have had before it. No horse, no carriage, no material thing that one rides or owns can compare. The *William* is a craft that I remember with my heart, and not my head, for every detail of her, from stem to stern, from her sails to her guns, is colored with vivid affection. She was a small sloop, with perhaps a single mast, but she is bigger in my memory, and with a larger crew. I remember her having more guns than she perhaps actually had, and she was perhaps slower in the water than she is in my recollections, but all lovers have a duty to be generous to those who share their emotions. Her hull was sturdy; it was made not of fir, which they use for frigates, or the cedar they use for even smaller craft; no, only heart of oak would do for the *William*.

Her ribs, too, were oak, and her keel a long straight stab of elm. In the sunlight, with a good wind, she did not ride on water, but sailed on the clouds. She was no mere assemblage of timber, this ship, but a giant oaken friend, who called out to you with rough invitation. The work was hard and the crew was tough, but the *William* and I, from the first hour, had a bond beyond blood. In the way that rank strangers can, in some circumstances, experience instant affinity, so, too, did this vessel, when I first stepped foot aboard her, seem to slap me on the back, throw a heavy arm round my shoulder, and take me into its confidences.

Life on the open water has always seem'd to me the very opposite of mere existence on land. All things seem possible when the breeze spreads every sail, the sun rides high in the sky, and the cool of sea-spray is in the face. There are no roadblocks or milldams, no buildings or monuments or marks of humanity to obstruct one's movement forward, ever forward. All is Poseidon's turquoise kingdom. There is, by my troth, a liberating sense that perhaps one can, at long last, grab hold of the greatness and opportunity that have eluded one on the land. Ahh, give me the stink of fish parts on the gangway, the coarse fulmination of seamen's voices bantering about the hardships of the voyage. Give me the rough camaraderie that comes when a group of men must haul together in order to survive each unknown horizon. How piteous must it have been for those sad folk who lived in that antique time when there were not such vehicles to transport us to New Frontiers. Can there be victory without challenge? Can there be life without newness?

To be sure, tho', the men of the *William* were not focused on such things philosophic. They were a lustful and gregarious bunch, wholly unconcern'd with the soul's interior. Tho', as far as the spirit and inner life is concerned, many seem'd to me to be nursing hidden grudges and, as men on account are wont to do, many seem'd to be concealing secret histories. Beyond some hints, however, they were a hard group to understand. For the main, the men of the *William* kept their true names hidden, so I had to make do with nicknames, tho' those monikers were often more revealing of character than proper surnames. Information, I decided, would come in time. The crew, over the first hours of our voyage, engaged in the long process of winging-out, which is when the bulkiest cargo from the ship's holds is transported, piece by piece and with much sweat, from amidships to the wales, to make the ship steadier in the water as she goes. As we worked, and in the days afterward, I gather'd biographic stories and anecdotes to learn more about the men with whom I was sailing.

The navigator, by the name of First-Rate, struck me as the most impressive of the lot. He was an officer and did not bear loads during the winging-out, instead directing it. The other hands were full of tales about him and the various adventures and tragedies he had seen in his career. Ranks, I found, were somewhat fluid on privateer ships, but he was consider'd by the men to be second in command to Calico himself, and, to be certain, it was clear he was a trusted and much esteemed adviser. He was an older gentleman, having seen some two score of years; with his balding pate, thin fishy lips, and a sharp, overhanging nose that dripped off his face like an icicle, he could not be described as handsome, but he was striking in his own wellpressed, well-dressed way. He had been an officer of some rank on a vessel in his majesty's navy and he still had a regal bearing that befitted his former station. I learn'd also that Calico had taken his vessel long ago and given his captive a choice—to either swear allegiance to the life of a privateer or suffer death by marooning. He chose, of course, the former, but carried with him, in his deep-set eyes, the haunted, lonely look of a man who had selected the latter.

Bishop was the fiend who served as boatswain, delegating day-to-day duties on the craft, meting out punishments, and supervising duels. He cut an arresting figure: he was bald and massively built. His face was color'd brown and weather'd much by the sea-sun and sea-wind, and the skin on his forehead, nose, cheeks, and chin were crack'd and peeling, like the ruins of an ancient fresco. Upon my first meeting with him it became abundantly clear that he was wholly unsuited to the task of managing and supervising other men. He counted himself pious, and he was given to quoting from the good Book, but his reading of scripture was like none I had encounter'd: Bishop's version had Christ our Lord slapping whores, mocking lepers, and betting on cockfights. In sum, his soul was rank with meanness, perhaps poisoned by the Father of Lies himself, and he cursed and hurled insults with a lustiness that was unsurpassed in its cruelty even by the standards of men of the sea.

"Go ahead, you shite-a-bed scoundrels!" Bishop could be heard to say, berating the hands on deck at their tasks. "You slabberdegallion druggels! You heirs of mongrel bitches! Remember what Christ our Lord once said: he who slows at his task is a he-whore catamite who should be buggered up the porthole! By God's wounds you'd best remember those wise words and work harder at your stations! Amen!"

Just where we were bound I did not know, but I had hopes it would be better than where I was. I took a place in a compartment in the lower deck; this was the place most of the ship's regular crew was established—Calico, First-Rate, and Bishop had slightly larger quarters toward the upper deck. Upon reaching my quarters, I slung my hammock (a ratty affair provided to me by Bishop) and encounter'd for the first time a number of other members of the ship's company, including a quiet lad with emerald eyes and woolly red hair named Poop (used like a woman, on occasion, by his fellows, he was given to frequently loitering on the poop deck near the captain's quarters, seeking protection) and, bunking some length away, Angel, a scowling, stoop-backed blue-eyed blond who served as the ship's master.

Angel was known as perhaps the most dangerous sniper on the seas, but he was also quite possibly the most foolish of all the children of Adam. He was a man with much anger in him, having been marooned for some time by his previous captain over what he deemed a triviality (three times he tossed anchors overboard without tying them to the ship). His ignorance was so vast, it looped back and almost appeared to be a kind of wisdom: when asked the simplest of questions—the color of the sky, the time of day, whether or not fish can swim—his brow knits, his eyes narrow, and he ruminates deeply, almost loudly, as if he were going through the most abstract theorems of metaphysics in his mind. He seems to understand the principles of mathematics—I've seen his lips move as he silently counts to himself—but when asked to add one sum to another, no matter what the original numbers, his answer will invariably be seventeen. And if the subject of the fairer sex is raised within shouting distance of the man, he will never fail to ask if any beard-splitting was performed. I was told by shipmates that when Angel was a child, an uncle remarked that he was dumb enough to drink gunpowder with his tea. Angel, mistaking, as was his custom, the metaphorical statement for an instruction, began to drink gunpowder with heated water every morning. Perhaps early on in this ritual, he may have had the sense to question it, but, after years of the practice, I have no doubt that all his doubts—as well as a substantial portion of his sense—have been laid aside.

Not all the men were easy with their introductions; in fact, in the main, most were rude, disturbingly boisterous, and vaguely hostile. One seaman, a Moor by the name of Zayd, kept his own counsel and his own company and utter'd not a word to anyone unless it was necessary for the ship's function and the performance of his duties. Despite his air of silence, he seem'd to carry about him a kind of learned quality. His gaze was always steady, his perambulations about the ship deliberate and seemingly directed. As it turned out, he was the ship's carpenter and surgeon. More than a few crew members charged, in muted mutterings well out of Zayd's hearing, that the good surgeon seemed to take some satisfaction in making his cures as painful as possible, and, in many cases, his treatments were only a little more bearable than the diseases they sought to minister.

Two other notably ill-willed shipmates were Hunahpu and Xbalanque. They had both originated in some once savage, but now settled, part of the Americas and their former way of existence was utterly laid waste. It was said the two, who were twins, identical in figure and face, were the last of their tribe, with no kin or community anywhere on this terrestrial sphere. They were of medium stature, well muscled, with high cheeks as smooth and flat as polished wood. Although the position of the man at the mast—a crew member designated for keeping a lookout for other ships, whether vessels to be pursued or escaped from—is usually a solitary task, the two brothers often performed the duty in tandem, and were deemed sharp-eyed as God in his heaven. The brothers were also incorrigible collectors of information and personal secrets, and their lordship over the ship's store of gossip was perhaps what gave them a dim view of their shipmates and a haughty sense of themselves. When the two came down from their shift at the mast, they seemed to still view their fellows from on high. The talk among the men indicated that in the main the twins were despised but also feared, and therefore tolerated. Because of my unique position on the ship, brought on by the secret of my sex, I took careful note of the brothers' comings and goings. I did not want to draw their ire or arouse their suspicions. Tho' I tended to change clothes in the shadows of the lower deck—I had discover'd an unused nook—I avoided disrobing, even in seemingly private situations, when Hunahpu and Xbalanque were off-duty and roaming the ship. Xbalanque was said to be ever longing for the restoration of his former land and its ways, while Hunahpu was in favor of establishing himself and his brother among the Europeans. I never heard either, however, express any such sentiments out loud, and if there was some way of telling them apart, whether through opinion or appearance, it was not apparent. They seemed to differ on nothing, and they both shared sharp eyes and even sharper tongues.

Happily, there were some in the ship's company whom I found to be quite agreeable in their personal relations. Chief among the friendlier sort was Sugar-Apple, the ship's cook. He had, during some adventure in his long-vanished youth, been in some sort of debilitating fire: the features of his face seemed slightly drooped as if made of melted candle wax; whitish hair sprouted from his scalp in sparse, random thickets; and his skin everywhere was the color of raw meat. In outline, he looked like one of his dishes: his plump, spherical body had the appearance of three dumplings, one stacked on top of another. When he spoke, it was with a Swedish accent as thick as a meat stew, but more often he was laughing, whether at some joke he had just shared with the crew, or at himself. Sugar-Apple was long past his fighting days: thanks to injuries sustained in the taking of some ship or other, he had only one and three quarter legs and just four fingers on each hand. One running joke was that if

Sugar-Apple had lost his digits while cooking, his dishes could only have improved in taste. Sugar-Apple's position, I reckoned, was part of his privateer's pension. In truth, Sugar-Apple was not too expert a cook—he consider'd his specialities to be burgoo (a horrid milkless porridgelike substance) and figgy-dowdy (a similarly repellent dish made by placing biscuits in a canvas bag, pounding them with a marlinspike, then dropping in bits of figs, raisins, and gristle and boiling the whole lot). But Sugar-Apple, despite his bonhomie, had his own secrets. When I mentioned that I was from Cork, his dancing eyes took on a faraway look, and his scarred smile faded. I thought I spied a look of suspicion, perhaps even fear, pass over his face. Quickly, though, his broad smile returned as our talk drifted onto other matters. Later, however, I found it impossible not to wonder about his strange shift in emotions.

The inward direction of the innards was a common complaint among the newer members of the ship's crew, and while the motion of the vessel 'gainst the waves was a primary culprit, Sugar-Apple's concoctions, no doubt, played no small part. Piss-tubs were allocat'd throughout the ship, but they were rank and rarely emptied, since Bishop was of the opinion that the contents would provide some use during the occasion of a fire. To relieve the bladder in other cases required one to scramble onto the nets strung about the bowsprit and to let loose in full view of the hands on deck—tho' none dared get too close if the wind was blowing full. In other cases, if speed was of the essence, one could position oneself over the bow, and the waves, if the sea was high, could provide a cleansing function as well. There was a plank with a hole set in the beakhead—it was also called the head—but it was invariably in use by one of the twins, when they were not at the watch.

Zayd provided for those whose constitutions were found to

be in variance with the conditions of the sea and from his medical chest—a great mahogany box with inscriptions in some Arab tongue—he doled out various potions and powders. These medicines included *Cassia fistula* (which was a syrup of senna, which is derived from the pulp of cassia pods) and *Succus Glycyrrhiza* (a blackish, brackish substance that, as it turned out, was merely licorice juice). When a sea-pup was taken with a large bowel, Zayd would take a more drastic step and apply hot towels to the fundament, and also advise the lad to balance on his head and hands and keep his legs spread apart. This last bit of prescription would be taken only if the sailor in question calculated that the laughter of his mates upon assuming such a position would be less discomforting than the ailment itself.

One time I spied lying upon his chest a wooden figurine about the size of a baby's fist. When I picked it up, it was heavy and fit easily into my palm. It was a well-carved thing, of a mother and a child; I could not guess its medical purpose, but it seemed related to fertility. It was smooth to the touch, as if it had been well handled. Along the base there were runes of some sort, etched into the wood in black. Whether this foreign object was a charm or a curse was beyond my powers of discernment. I had no time to consider the matter further, for I heard Zayd's footsteps in the corridor. I replaced the object on his chest and scuttled away before he entered. However, he may have sensed something amiss for, as he passed me in the hallway, he bore an expression that was difficult to read, as if his emotions had been written across his face in some foreign script.

"*Assalamu alaikum,*" he fairly spat at me as we approached each other.

"What?" I said.

"*Assalamu alaikum wa rahmatullahi wa barakatuh.*"

"I did not remove anything from your cabin, nor did I pick up the heavy figurine on your chest."

Zayd met my gaze and did not blink.

What sorcery was this? What spell did he mean to cast on me with his strange words? I walked away, my curiosity about Zayd and his work unsatisfied. Zayd's surgical arts, tho' sometimes painful for his patients, were said to have saved a number of crewmen, and it was generally held that he was far better at the task than was the last crewman to hold the post. That previous surgeon was a devoted acolyte of the technique of phlebotomy or venesection—which is also called bloodletting—and recommended and performed the procedure even on healthy men. He believed in the doctrine four humors—phlegm, blood, yellow bile, and black bile—and did, with regularity, attempt to bring these substances into equilibrium with the crew by sweating or introducing various liquids into the nose or ear. He also practiced the art of cupping, and would heat the mouth of a glass and clap it onto a patient's body until the flesh was sucked up and thereby purified. His arts, unfortunately, left the men bleeding, sniffing, and burnt, with the majority of the crew leaking two or more of the four humors from some orifice. In the end, the surgeon was left maroon'd on some isle by Rackam, and Zayd, with his sharp tools, replaced him.

Days and nights on the *William,* as on most sailing vessels, were divided into seven periods of duty (Sugar-Apple gave me his take on their relative merits):

Noon to four o'clock: afternoon watch. This was the easiest assignment, as the sun was up and sightings of target ships came more readily. Crew members who were just waking up would often down a mug of grog to take the edge off the lingering effects of the revelries from the night before.

Four o'clock to six o'clock: first day watch. Another plum period, in which the light was often good and didn't begin to fade until the final moments. A mug of grog was usually imbibed to toast the close of day.

Six o'clock to eight o'clock: last day watch. This was dinnertime, and grog was drunk to wash down the food.

Eight o'clock to midnight: first watch. When the sun was down and the moon was not yet up, disaster could strike if another ship crept up without being sighted. There was no good reason to drink grog during this session, but it was done all the same.

Midnight to four o'clock: middle watch. Perhaps the toughest time—many a man had fallen asleep, and faced whipping or worse for dereliction of duty. It was said that grog could help keep one alert, which of course was pure hogwash, but none could be found to argue against it, and so it was practiced.

Four o'clock to eight o'clock: morning watch. Attacks often are staged at dawn, so a sea-dog was well advised to stay vigilant. Grog helped to keep up the courage.

Eight o'clock to noon: forenoon watch. The mists of morning could sometimes obscure clear observation—another time to be wary if one was on duty. A mug of grog was usually lifted to toast the new day.

"Is there a time when the drinking of grog is not customary?" I asked.

"After your heart stops, and the angels take you, perhaps then," replied Sugar-Apple. "And if they're only serving milk and honey in heaven, I reckon most of this lot, if there's grog to be had, would rather be in hell."

My first assignment on the ship was being the man in the masthead for the upcoming middle watch, relieving Hunahpu and Xbalanque. It was customary for privateer ships at the time to keep a man at the lookout on the main masthead. I was to be station'd on the maintop gallant yard, which is the highest of the large wooden spars that cross the mast horizontally. Before I took up my new post—and I was eager to do so, tho' not so eager to have any truck with the twins—Bishop whistled all hands on deck. Sea-pups and veterans alike were mustered on the quarterdeck. Then the captain strolled in front of our rather ragged ranks and faced us, front and center.

Night had come and the stars were ablaze. On land, heaven's illumination is ofttimes obstruct'd by trees and the like; here, on the open sea, celestial glory stretch'd from horizon to horizon, uninterrupted in its brilliance. Polaris, the North star, shined particularly bright; we ignored her beckoning light, however, and continued in our course due south. Calico stood before us, his features and form clear and sharp in the starlight. He held in his hands a long roll of vellum.

"These are the articles of our pyracy, which all you fine ladies must sign," he said. "You may choose also not to consent to these articles, which is your right."

There was murmuring in the ranks.

"Yea, the Creator has imbued mankind with the gift of free will, and that attribute we do honor," Calico continued. "So choose to sign or not, and if not, to honor the almighty, by my troth, we will strangle you with a length of wire in such a manner that you will meet your Creator as swiftly as possible."

A bottle of ink and a quill pen were produced by First-Rate, and the vellum roll, along with the writing implements, was circulated among the assembled men. The veterans, whose names were already on the scroll, passed the materials on; the sea-pups, eager to seem unreluctant members of the crew, sign'd the articles with little hesitation or review. Most of the crew seem'd unable to read, given the blank way they scanned the document;

still, every new man managed at least to scrawl an X with the pen. Now the articles were given over to me: the vellum was sturdy and golden brown, like a quadroon's skin, and the writing on it was in fine black calligraphy. Having seen my good-for-nothing pater familias wrestle and contend with his share of contracts in his days as an attorney at law, I paused a bit in my turn and tried to read as much of the document as I could before giving it to the next man.

Article the First read: Every man has a vote on the affairs of the moment, but the captain is the final arbiter of decisions made in the heat of chase or battle. . . .

Article the Sixth: No boy or woman is to be allow'd amongst the company whilst at sea. If any man is found seducing any of the latter sex, or is found carrying a boy, girl, or woman to sea for carnal purposes, he is to suffer death.

Article the Seventh: To desert the ship, or one's quarter, in battle is punishable by death or marooning. . . .

Article the Eighth: There is tolerated no striking of another of the ship's company whilst on board; every man's quarrel is to be ended on shore, at sword and pistol, with the boatswain presiding. . . .

Article the Ninth: No distinction shall be made among the members of the ship's company in terms of treatment in regards to national origin or ancestry. . . .

This much I was able to read before putting down my name and then passing along the vellum, quill, and ink.

After Bishop collect'd the signed vellum, Calico addressed the group once more. "Pay you mind to part the fourteenth of the articles," he said. "The captain, his navigator, and his boatswain will all receive two shares of any prize, all others a share. Now, in the main, sea-bitches sail until they are killed or are caught. Not so we men of the *William*. I swear to you by

Aphrodite's snow white thighs that we will live to enjoy our spoils in this life and let the Creator take whatever retribution he might in the next."

The veterans cheered that line, and Calico continued.

"So mark you this: a hundred thousand pieces of eight shall we endeavor to collect, or its rough equivalent in treasure or tradable goods. Divided amongst us all, we happy seventy, that should be enough to comfort us all for the remainder of our days and make our hardship on the sea well worth the pain."

Now the veterans and the sea-pups cheered and there was much general backslapping and playful thumb-biting. I noticed that Sugar-Apple had made his way on deck and, with his cook's helpers, was rolling out barrels of grog. He smiled and passed me a mug of grog twice the size of any other.

"We Cork boys must watch out for one another," Sugar-Apple said in a brogue that I recognized as belonging not only to the Emerald Isle, but to my fair county.

Surprised to hear him speak in anything but his Swedish accent, my jaw fell open. Sugar-Apple put his finger to his lips and continued to distribute the spirits. The mood on deck grew considerably brighter.

"When do we sail 'gainst the Spanish galleon?" said one sea-pup, his mug of grog in hand.

The veterans 'round him burst into loud laughter.

"If I lied about the riches we will pursue, then pardon my poor mistruth," said Calico. "But we are all liars here—and thieves and roustabouts and scoundrels. It may be that the Spanish galleon is a myth. It may be that there is no golden treasure ship upon these waves that will suddenly provide for our fortunes. So for now, we hunt for what goods we can find. It's all about money, ladies, and it ever will be! Tonight we celebrate the riches that may come—and if they come not, we drink to the devil and curse heaven!"

Sugar-Apple, holding a mug aloft, began to sing (his Swedish voice had returned):

> *"To the mast nail our flag it is dark as the grave*
> *Or the death which it bears while it sweeps o'er the waves"*

At this, the veterans of the crew, with lust and abandon, joined in:

> *"Let our deck clear for action, our guns be prepared*
> *Be the boarding axe sharpened, the scimitar bared"*

In a brief enough time, the new recruits were so sodden with grog that any resentment, if there was any, toward the ruse that was used to get them on board was forgotten. For immediately following Calico's address, there commenced a period of revelry so untamed and wild as can be scarcely imagined. Freed from cultural boundaries associated with land and cities, my new fellows uttered oaths, cavorted about, and did such things that would pollute a draggletail's eye, nevermind the uncorrupted sight of a maiden fair. There was much quaffing of grog which, truth be told, is a horrible beverage, composed of rum much diluted with three times the amount of water, plus a little (mostly rancid) lemon juice to ward off the scurvy. But, in the midst of such a revel, the demonic mixture was the nectar of the gods.

> *"It shall never be lowered, the black flag we bear*
> *If the sea be denied us, we sweep through the air*
> *Some fight 'tis for riches, some fight 'tis for fame*
> *The first I'll not refuse, the last is a name*
> *For I strike for the memory of long-vanished years*
> *I shed blood where another sheds tears"*

How far away from me now seem'd that world of girdles and petticoats, curtseys and courtship! By my faith, I never felt my womanhood so intensely as when I became a man of the sea. In that pampered other world, tho' you'll never hear it said aloud, a woman feels all the lust and rude emotions as are experienced by men, a woman yearns, in her secret heart, to experience all the adventures and challenges that men embrace—and yet it is all denied, and all that desire is hidden in smiles and dimples. Let that world be damn'd! I lifted a mug of grog and drain'd it, and after hours had passed, and many more mugs besides, I climbed up to my new posting at the masthead and, with the whole of the ship and the sea and the celestial canopy spinning around me, I began my first watch.

chapter 11.

Ahhh, but how I wish you could feel the breath of the Chocolate Gale. I experienced it for the first time on my virgin night on the masthead. Ascending the fully erect length of main topmast was no small feat. My head and belly were full of grog. In my drunken state, the pole seem'd to bend and throb, and all the handholds were slick. A tipsy warmth had spread over my lips, my cheeks, along the flanks of my breasts, to the ends of my fingers and the tips of my toes. At that point in my career as a mariner, I knew nothing of spotting ships, and could hardly tell a schooner from a frigate. In addition, I, on occasion, transposed larboard and starboard, more often than not confused the boom with the gaff, and, I must admit, at that time I couldn't tie a bowline knot if all creation depended on it. However, I felt, despite my many failings as a man of the sea (the first being that I was hardly a man), I felt I was well suited for duty atop the masthead. Since, in that assignment, I was in the most favorable position to see and render judgment on what was floating on the waves, none down below would be able to gainsay my observations. My ignorance was thus well disguised as expertise. In any case, I was overjoy'd to be out of my dank, cramp'd quarters in the lower deck. The spirits made me perhaps more unmindful of the danger as I climbed the mizzen yard. At one point, I fell down the ropes a few lengths, regain'd my hold, and continued upward. I was, in truth, not merely intoxicated with the grog, but with ship life in its entirety. I was so happy I burst into loud song, a tune that I had often heard men singing while raising gourds of ale in taverns in New Providence:

> *"Drain, drain the bowl, each fearless soul*
> *Let the world wag as it will"*

I stopped my song and frowned at myself in the dark. I had been singing my tune in my maiden's pitch, high as a bird in flight. I hoped that the men in hearing distance were, like me, in such a condition as this would all be a dream come the morn. Adjusting my voice to adopt a more masculine level, I continued with my tune:

> *"Let the heavens growl, the devil howl*
> *Drain, drain the bowl"*

Ahhh—but my voice still had a feminine lilt, despite my attempts to lower its register. It seem'd my subterfuge was not expert enough to encompass song; in flirting with smooth-voiced Euterpe's craft, I was revealed. I made a promise that very moment that I would never sing again. This was no small thing since warbling is an expression of joy that increases the happiness it celebrates; many times afterward I sat in glum silence as fellows sang around me, my tongue eager to join the chorus. But, to maintain my manly artifice, I seal'd my lips and kept that oath all these long years, excepting one sad time.

So, dispensing with song, I had reached the maintop gallant mast, the small circular basketlike platform where I was to keep the lookout. I sat down and let my legs dangle through the railing. There is a calmness about the sea at night that can be found nowhere else and that serenity is undistill'd and unmatch'd in the post at the masthead, some two hundred feet above the rest of the crew, some hundreds of leagues from the rest of humanity. It is as alone as one can feel, and yet, you feel as one with all else. The men below had ceased their revels and either lay in the lower decks, recovering from their bacchanalia, or were bent over the railings, groaning and giving Poseidon his tribute. I could hear the soft splash of the waves 'gainst the oaken sides of the ship. A few of the men slept in pairs on the deck, holding on to each other for warmth, tho' the tropic night was far from cold. The oil lights along the *William*'s rails had been dimmed, and a soft golden glow came from them only. There was nothing to compete with the silver light of the stars and constellations. My eyes were open, and I was obeying my charge to keep watch for passing ships. But, in truth, I felt as if I was dreaming while awake.

"Do you feel it, lad?"

It was Sugar-Apple, drunk on his own brew, bellowing up at me from the gangway.

"Do I feel what?"

"Why, the Chocolate Gale, lad! And none other!"

"What?"

"The wind that rules the seas throughout the West Indies and waters of the Spanish Main is brisk and arrives prevailingly from the Northwest," said Sugar-Apple. "Sea-dogs have called it the Chocolate Gale, and the old tars say there is sorcery in it!"

"Sorcery? Of what sort?"

"At certain times the gust carries with it aromas, echoes, and eluvium of a most mysterious sort, tho' any land that might have originated such elements be far, far, far away. . . ."

With that Sugar-Apple stumbled away, mug in hand.

Perhaps it was just another ship's tale, but that very night I felt the gale. By my faith, I became aware of it wafting 'gainst my ear, arriving in kindly zephyrs, softer than baby's laughter. I smelled spices in the air—curry, pimento, escallion. I remember'd then the cooking of my neighbor Zed, how he would, in my youth, prepare me bowls of pungent pepperpot soup, or fry me potato fritters with sugar sprinkled on top. He would tell me stories of Jamaica, where he had once sailed, and relay legends of giant spiders and rebels hidden in the Blue Mountains. He would complete the tales he had only half-told the others, and whisper to me that wise King Gormund and Balor of the Evil Eye were both African rulers of Ireland in the misty mythic past, and that Irish lore confirmed it, even if the elders would not speak of it. Zed also spoke of Gaodhal Glas, ancestor of all Irish people, and how Moses cured him of a snakebite in Egypt, and as a result, Ireland is free from serpents forevermore. Even at that tender age I loved stories of daring-do and folklore and he had a seemingly inexhaustible supply.

It was then, lost in anamnesis, that it struck me how much I missed my parents. What a sad corsair I was, sitting among the sails and weeping for want of apron strings. We feel the absence of a thing much more than its presence; that, of course, is old wisdom. But the reason, I think, is this: when a thing is here, it is mere sensation, and then is skin deep. When a thing is gone, imagination takes over, and that goes deeper than bone.

I kept my watch and lost myself. Just as the surf erodes the shore, so, too, does the sea erase boundaries. The ever-crashing waves and the shifting winds make a mockery of maps and lines drawn by diplomats, kings, and queens. The wind courses over all, fills every sail, and belongs to no one. So, following suit, the other lines to which we are so accustom'd on land, fall away while shipboard. While the gale blew, I forgot time and distance, and various memories came rushing through me, as if they were immediate sensations. The gale also seem'd to carry with it the sound of Zed's voice, softly singing. I strained to hear the melody, which slipped in and out of the breeze. It was a sweet sound, diaphanous and sad and pure. Then I realized the voice was coming from below.

There was a shadow looming over quarterdeck on the starboard side (or perhaps it was larboard—I was still educating myself on nautical terms). I had no idea how long it had been there or who it was. It was a shadow darker than the surrounding gloom and therefore noticeable. It seemed to have a voice but no form. I wondered if I had fallen asleep and I pinch'd myself on the chin to assure myself that I was awake. The apparition continued singing in a tone of immense melancholy. Was it Sugar-Apple?

By this point I had grown extremely curious as to the source of this woeful voice. The song seemed to have no lyric, but was nonetheless, by means of pacing and pitch, laden with meaning: it seemed to both celebrate privateering and abhor it. Many of the men on board, I had come to learn, were victims of privateers themselves. Like First-Rate, they had, at some point, found their vessels taken by Calico and then were forced to choose between a life of infamy or no life at all. I could hear in this song the same sort of struggle—of a life lost and another found, of regrets and more than a little guilt.

And still the wordless song continued. It was too sad to be the joyful Sugar-Apple. Almost involuntarily now, I was standing up in the topgallant mast, leaning over the railing, ready to climb down from my high perch and to pursue and uncover the vocalist behind the song on the quarterdeck.

Then I saw something that stopped me. The sea was an immense darkness, from horizon to horizon. But at the water's edge there was a faint light, from unseen stars and the approaching day. Along this line, then, things could be seen in silhouette. And this came into my view: a dark spot 'gainst the light of the advancing morn.

My heart was set aracing.

I cried down to the decks: "Sail ho!"

chapter 12.

The day broke like a blister, spilling blood into the sky. The smell of sea salt was in the air, and of men's sweat, and the call of gulls was all around as the white-wing'd creatures circled our craft, sensing action, hoping for food. The wind veer'd to the northeast and east-northeast, and she was a fine gale at that, one that fill'd the sails, raised the spirits, and fired the blood.

"Rouse up, you sleepers!" the call went out. "Show a leg then! Rouse up, rouse up!"

The men of the *William*, but moments ago groggy from the revels of the night, now with much ebullition and resolution, attended to their stations. The *William* had not taken a ship in many weeks, more weeks than the men cared to admit or perhaps could even quite recall. Now, in these ravenous moments at the start of the pursuit, the ship herself seem'd almost to be grumbling and moaning in anticipation, like a hungry man's stomach growling at the sight of victuals. Men's voices, orders and answering shouts, grunts and bellows, virile laughter and booming work chants, resounded across the decks with the seabird screeches.

> *"Privateers bold and brave are we*
> *Who sail on the snowy crested sea*
> *Blow high! Blow high!*
> *We live and we fight, for plunder, no more*
> *We long for the sea and love not the shore*
> *Blow high! Blow high!"*

Calico was at the poop deck, First-Rate on his right hand, Bishop on his left just behind, and Poop lurking somewhere in the shadows in the far rear of the captain's deck, giving more credence to his nickname. Angel had taken to his gun-post on the starboard side, and was checking his powder and fuses, eager for a fight.

"How many shots do you have ready?" a fellow gunner called to him.

"Seventeen," replied Angel.

Zayd was also on deck, his cutlass drawn and at the ready, as if the boarding battle was imminent. Even Sugar-Apple had come up from his kitchen below and join'd the men on the quarterdeck.

"Hej pa dig!" he called out gaily.

Sugar-Apple was, of course, utterly unfit to join the battle given his one-and-three-quarters' worth of legs and eight fingers and his general and immense corpulence, but he was eager to witness in close proximity the works of grim-faced Mars. Smiling broadly, he join'd in with the lusty song of the other men.

> *"A broadside we send as we near the foe*
> *We board, we plunder and off we go*
> *Blow high! Blow high!*
> *And it ever has been, and will still be to me*
> *And the same to all sea-dogs bold and free"*

I wished I could see faces. From my high perch, I could view the ordering of the decks, and I could spy well the white sail of the prize we chased. And I could see clearly Calico's black-sleeved arms gesturing, exhorting, pointing toward the prey. But I could only imagine his brooding eyes, flashing like dark clouds bursting with storm; I guessed that in one hand he clutched his beloved black die with its blood red markings, twirling it in his fingers even as he ran through the odds of success and failure in his mind. Now his strong voice echoed up, hard and sharp as iron 'gainst iron. Our prize was on the starboard side, not dead ahead, and Calico meant to turn the ship hard and bear down upon it.

"Ready about!" he cried, preparing the craft for tacking.

"Stations for stays!" Bishop bellowed, calling the men to attention.

"Ready! Ready!" cried Calico. "Ease down the helm!"

Following his command, First-Rate, who, as helmsman, was at his place behind the wheel, pulled it 'round spoke by spoke and easily, rather than jamming her hard. This sort of conservation of force, it was explained to me later, results in a decrease in drag on the rudder, making a ship more maneuverable in pursuits.

"Helm's a-lee!" said Calico.

At this signal, the men let go the foresheet and the headsheets, allowing the bow to swing into the wind. This took away some of the power from the fore course, allowing the ship to turn in the wind and pursue the ship we covet'd.

"Ready! Easy down the helm!" commanded Calico. "Rise tacks and sheets! Haul taut! Mainsail haul!"

In the midst of this action, Hunahpu and Xbalanque join'd me at the masthead.

"You have an eye as sharp as Xbalanque's and mine," said Hunahpu, congratulating me on spotting the sail.

I nodded, a bit speechless from the unexpected compliment. Perhaps there was some difference in the temperament of the twins.

"The forenoon watch is ours," Xbalanque hissed. "Take to your hammock and let the sea-dogs with experience deal with the action afoot!"

By my reckoning, it was at least a full hour before their time to replace me at the masthead, but I offered up no argument. With nary a glance back—though I felt Xbalanque's scowl clawing at my scalp as I climbed down the maintop-mast—I left my place and occupied a spot on the quarterdeck. This is where the action was in any case. Sugar-Apple did me a kindness and, upon seeing me, tossed me my weapons for the fight—an elegantly cast pistol with a fifteen-inch barrel and silver butt cap, and a handsome cutlass with a curved twenty-seven-inch steel blade, an iron shell-guard, and an ornate brass hilt wrought to resemble a snarling dog. He winked at me as I caught the pistol in my left hand and nearly lost a finger on my right in securing the cutlass and slipping it into my belt. From watching the others, I was picking up a thing or two about handling small arms, but, at this point in my education, I was still more of a peril to myself than to others. Zayd, who now had a large battle-axe in his huge palms, regarded me silently as he stood nearby.

Could he sense my raging incompetence? Did he realize that, amid all these sea-dogs, I was as dangerous as a kitten?

"Wouldn't miss this for all the spices in the East Indies," Sugar-Apple said, drawing up to me. He was gnawing on a biscuit slathered with foul-smelling butter.

"What makes you so eager for the fight?" I asked. "It's not as if, in your state, you can join the fray!"

"The first fight, the first fight—there's where heaven in its glory resides," said Sugar-Apple. "The Norse had it right when they imagined Valhalla, that sweet place of constant battle and eternal strife! The initial engagement of any voyage gets the blood up—more than ale, more than whoring, more than anything to be found on land. You'll not feel this alive again—until you're dead and at Valhalla's banquet table!"

"'Tis only a fishing vessel," I said, as the craft we pursued came closer into view.

"Any catch is welcome when the fish aren't biting! These are trying times for men on account."

"How so?"

"The Governor drives us hard. A sloop such as ours lives off the sea—like a fisherman subsists off his haul."

"But we fish for men and gold and provisions."

"Aye, you've got it, lad. No honest port will take us in for careening and stores."

"Are we running low?"

"On everything—on water, on victuals, on ammunition, and lastly on patience, and that's most precious of all. So, to be sure, the captain will take this vessel."

"Sugar-Apple—the other day, when you spoke of Cork . . ."

"That was another life, and another job. To tell the whole story would take longer than it took to live it! Suffice it to say that there are some folks in dear old Cork who would like to see me skewered and roasted, and not because of my cooking. They want what's in my iron trunk, but they'll never get it—not while the *William*'s afloat!

"Why are they after you? Who are they? What's in the . . ."

I swallowed my words. Just then I noticed that while Hunahpu, up in the masthead, was tracking the vessel I first spotted, Xbalanque seemed to be tracking me. Had he heard everything? What would he and his twin make of it?

"Sugar-Apple . . ."

"Not, now, lad—look you windward!"

The vessel was now in full view, and we were in theirs. At such times, when one ship pass'd another on the high seas, it was common for the vessels to hail each other, and to perhaps exchange mail or news from their port of origin. Indeed, two figures had come on deck of the one-masted fishing vessel; one held a net in his hand and a fishing spear, the other waved agreeably with both hands as if to bid us good morn.

Calico sent the signal to hoist our colors. Red dawn had given way to gray skies, and against the expanse of morning unfurl'd our black flag—black as a moonless night, black as the shadows beneath a bed, black as laughter at a funeral.

By my soul, let me submit this full admission, to all who hear me and to heaven's company besides, that my heart fluttered with wild abandon, like a bird of the field unnaturally imprison'd in a golden cage and then set free, when I saw that black flag unfurl'd. Life is lived, by the most of us, in fear—of robbery, of violation, of the thousand evil and unfortunate circumstances that can harm the flesh and crush the spirit. Now, under the shadow of my black flag, I was, at long last, a woman of action. No more was I waiting for life to happen, waiting for events to take what toll they would; I was part of nature, one of the hard inescapable facts of the world, like sea and air and fire and rock. I was thunder, I was the quaking earth, I was a wave 'gainst the shore. I would change lives by the law of my desire.

We had closed the distance between our ship and the intended prize with some rapidity, and we could now see the faces of our soon-to-be victims. A fisherman and a young woman it was, and their eyes were focused upward at the black flag flying high above our ship. The female passenger—who was tender in years, no longer a child but not yet an adult—was, to be sure, the figure I had seen waving so gaily in the minutes before. Now her hands were limp by her sides, and her large eyes full of fright. I quickly sized up the scene, or imagined that I did: the fisherman, I surmised, was a man without sons, who had finally resolved to teach his daughter the trade. This, perhaps, was their first voyage, and, given her lack of experience, she had perhaps steered them too far away from land, and into waters rife with hidden dangers—including perils such as the men of the *William*.

Bishop was now beside Angel and whispering something low and nasty and nefarious into his ear. Both men were gazing at the fisherman's daughter as a wolf considers a fawn. Angel spat on his gun and polished the barrel, which pointed up at an acute angle. It was a medium-sized cannon, of perhaps three feet in length, made of bronze and mounted on a swivel. In twin sacks next to the gun, Angel had at the ready a supply of three-quarter pound shot. He also had his signature weapon: iron balls joined by a chain called Angel-shot. This ammunition, fired from a gun, hissed through the air and sliced off limbs and the like in its deadly trajectory.

"Split her beard!" Angel laughed, in response to something I did not hear. "Aye, split her beard!"

Calico bid Angel and Bishop to end their discussion and for Angel to fire a warning shot, as was custom, above the heads of the passengers of the fishing vessel.

Angel, eager for the chance to get a shot off, quickly followed his orders. A loud crack sounded and the crew cheered at the sound and the sight of the smoke.

"We're into it now, lads!" shouted Sugar-Apple.

The two passengers of the fishing vessel were now seemingly consumed with fright. Both were at the oars, attempting to paddle into the wind and away from the *William*. Members of our crew crowded against the rails of the quarterdeck. They were, one and all, armed with boarding weapons, half-pikes and axes, long knives and belaying pins. But for now the only weaponry they actually employed was sharp tongues, jeering and cat-calling and whistling at the entirely futile attempts of the vessel to outrun our clearly superior craft.

"'Tis a pity," said Sugar-Apple. "It goes hard on those who endeavor to escape a privateer craft."

"Will Calico have 'em killed?"

"Probably not. Old Calico's got a sense of empathy for those bound in captivity."

"But he forced First-Rate and others into service!"

"His empathy has its limits. Still, the captain's father was abducted by a press-gang, so he understands the situation."

"What's a press-gang?"

"It's a form of, shall we say, involuntary recruitment for the Royal Navy. Why join them when you can become a privateer and earn some real money? Anyway, they took Calico's father and now he sails for the other side. Look there! I spy there's a member of the fairer sex aboard the craft we pursue. It'll go hardest on her if Bishop gets his claws into her."

The fisherman and his daughter were now directly below our ship on the larboard side. I looked down from the railings and caught the eye of the daughter. She was pretty of face and pale of skin, with yellow hair cropped close, almost like a boy's, and with sea green eyes. Our eyes locked for a time, and I almost felt I could hear her voice, whispering some soft secret or heart's confession, but then the sound was lost in the general commotion, and the jeers from the men and the howl of the wind. Did she feel something akin to the fear I felt when I was assaulted by the neighborhood lads and lassies in Cork? I had longed to be the hunter and not the hunted, to be the dog and not the rabbit—but could I stand idly by, knowing the pain and the loneliness that I had felt when I was in her position?

In what happened next, it was almost as if I was watching myself from my perch on the masthead. In my reverie, I lost my balance and, falling overboard, grabbed at a rope along the side of the ship, and, finding purchase difficult on the slick side of the *William*, found myself swinging neatly onto the deck of the small fishing craft. I heard a cheer erupt from my fellows back on deck, who figured I had executed the move of my own volition. Quickly, I got my bearings. I was now on a bowsprit sloop or smack boat: a Bahamian workman's boat without much to recommend it. The keel length, I'd estimate, was a good twenty-five feet, and aft of the mast, I spotted a cargo hold whose top had slid off; the fish in the hold splashed and writhed and splattered trying to purchase their freedom through effort. Before I had hold directly of my natural sense, my cutlass was drawn and my flintlock pistol cocked. I had neglected to put any powder in with the ball, but I hoped I cut an arresting enough figure to make its discharge unnecessary.

"Listen well to my words," I said to the pair, as my mind raced to come up with something to say.

Their eyes opened wide, for I said these words not in my buccaneer's voice, but in the reassuring tones of a maiden.

"There are devils on board my ship that will make good sport of you," I said. "If you wish to live beyond this day that the Creator has made, cast your oars into the water and surrender all your possessions—your victuals, your sea-catch, and what other supplies or treasure you may have."

Within eyeblinks, other members of my crew were also on board the small craft, including Bishop, with a parched look on his face that seem'd to signal that only blood would quench his thirst. But the confrontation, in the main, was over. The fisherman quickly surrendered his catch, which consisted of seven angelfish and a stingray, which, tho' deem'd a delicacy by some, was considered a wretched repast by the men of the *Will*. The fisherman also readily revealed a hidden store of monies, consisting of five pieces of eight, three brass buttons, and something that was either a misminted shilling or a shard of cow dung. The admissions and submission placated our crew quite readily and they returned to the *William* to let the fisherman and his daughter continue sailing where they would, being of no further use to us.

Bishop had a more demonic purpose in mind. The fisherman's daughter was wearing a blue canvas dress that Bishop bade her to remove, and he cited a biblical passage in support of his cravings. I am no scholar of the Good Book, but I am reasonably confident that Jesus' parable of the shepherd and his lost sheep was not, as Bishop argued that day, a call by the Almighty himself for all virgins to submit themselves to those that board their fishing vessels. The girl, who I assumed shared my interpretation of the holy scriptures, refused his entreaty, and Bishop, being determined to see his will followed, began the rough process of removing the girl's garments himself.

The fisherman, startled by this sudden assault, stepped forward for the purpose of protecting his daughter. This, I judged, would result in trouble that would only lead to bloodshed and death. The fisherman, who was small and slight of build, had no chance against Bishop in a test of strength and, besides that fact, the men of the *William* all stood ready to intervene should the fight go poorly for our side. The fisherman, with an assault on Bishop, was about to seal his own doom, and that of his daughter besides. What could I do? I had not the strength of limb, nor the skill with weaponry, to thwart Bishop. And he was now too fixed on his carnal impulse to be persuaded by reason and eloquence. What could I do?

I stepped forward. With the flat of my cutlass I delivered, with great force, a blow to the forehead of the fisherman. Stunned, he collapsed and lay squirming on the deck of the ship as if caught up in some great apoplexy. Indeed, he resembled nothing less than some great sea creature, accustomed to breathing the waters of the deep, now dragged to the shore and suffocating on air. The men of the *William* laughed at the sight. Bishop, his assault on the maid interrupt'd, looked at the writhing fisherman and then at me, giving one last grunt before grabbing hold of a rope and climbing back to the ship. Laughter is the surest cure for lust.

I had never attacked a man before, nor struck another living being with violence. Having now performed the deed, I was not at all plagued with remorse. In truth, I was surprised at how good it felt—my assault was like an overdue sneeze that, when released, cleansed the body and focused the mind. I wanted to strike the man again, but could think of no good reason to do it.

As I prepared to depart, the fisherman's daughter tugged my sleeve and pulled close to me.

"I understand what you have done here," she breathed. "Sir or madam, you have my thanks."

I raised my cutlass to her throat and pressed it so close that a thin line of blood was drawn 'gainst her neck, which was white as sea-foam, and she gasped a little.

"Thank me not," I said, growling in my man's voice. "For if ever I spy you in these same waters, in this craft or some other, be assured that I will take possession of all you have, including your sacred honor and your very life."

Grabbing hold of her waist, which was slender, I press'd my lips to hers and she struggled in my arms. There was blood in my mouth, from where or what I do not know, her neck perhaps, but it had the strange effect on me of inflaming my senses. As she squirmed and her breathing grew hot and fast, I raised her skirt up past her thighs, which were flushed in color and soft to the touch. I looked her in the eye and saw a strange brew of emotion, fear, and confusion, yes, but also, perhaps, a long-buried yearning that had suddenly broken to the surface of her desires. I pushed her roughly to the deck.

I took from the boat what provisions they had—two salted hams, some rough dry'd beef, and a dozen bottles of Red-Streak Cyder. And after that embezzlement, I returned to the *William*. By my soul how I hoped she understood my lack of gallantry! For, it must be said, I was not entirely certain if I fathom'd my actions myself.

> *"Privateers bold and brave are we*
> *Who sail on the snowy crested sea*
> *Blow high! Blow high!*
> *We live and we fight, for plunder, no more*
> *We long for the sea and love not the shore*
> *Blow high! Blow high!"*

The revelry lasted through the day and long into the night. As I went below deck to take to my hammock, I felt a dull pain in my innards that I at first attributed to a mixture of the grog and the evening's excitement. It felt like scrivener's palsy, not in the hands, but the belly. I then noticed that I had a dry crusty spot on my breeches; reaching down between my legs, my fingers came up wet with blood. Was this some malady of the ocean? I had never experienced such bleeding before nor heard tell of it! I thought to ask one of my shipmates, but I held my tongue. What if this difficulty was peculiar to women that sailed the sea? I found a shadowy corner in the lower deck and scrubbed my breeches clean; finding rags, I stuffed some beneath my legs and tied them in place. Whatever pestilence afflicted me, I hoped it would soon pass. I fell asleep that night feeling somehow separate from all my fellows and I wondered if that feeling would ever pass.

chapter 13.

I am not one for dreams. My sleep passes in darkness, or rather in blankness. I see nothing, I hear nothing, and, upon waking, nothing is remember'd. If I do dream, if Hypnos has indeed granted me gifts in the night, visions of childhood, of the cliff-ringed headlands of Donegal, the moist low-lying meadows along the River Shannon, or the soft, insistent rains of a County Cork spring, that too cruel god of sleep takes back his presents with the passing of each period of slumber. Nothing remains when I rise, not even the rain.

Yet in the night that follow'd hard after the first fray, phantasms came to me on the wings of sleep and continued their grim visitations in the evenings afterward. Memories, mad, buoyant, and wild with color, floated along the river of my thought like self-slaughter'd Ophelia clutching her death-garland of crow-flowers, nettles, daisies, and long purples. When I was a child in Ireland, my father was a lawyer of some training and reputation. But before I was born, there arrived a time and a circumstance when his first wife cast him out. I have no, as it were, first-hand recollections of these incidents, being, I must suppose, too young at the time for such events to register. Relatives and neighbors would not speak of it, at least openly. But from stories overheard and whispers behind fences, I long ago pieced together the puzzle of my upbringing. My father was cast out for a tryst he had with my mother, a maid he encounter'd on one of his gambling expeditions. When the outrage was uncover'd, his reputation hung in tatters like the dead leaves of some tree infected with worms. His first wife, who was in possession of a goodly amount of wealth, divorced him, but later granted my father, whose practice had dwindled with the spreading news of his adulterous habits, access to a small allowance to support the son that they had had together. The son and the mother were both in poor health, and so the former had been placed in the care of my father. That son died before I was born.

Privateer life is long periods of drunken inaction punctuated by brief blazing moments of violence and celebration. So, between watches and sea-chases, in the time I should have been comfortably ensconced in my hammock, I instead crept around in the lower decks of the ship, in a futile attempt to outdistance sleep. I could not rightly understand why these particular visions had seen fit to make themselves known to me. There are so many beauties of recollection that I dearly wish'd would have come to me in the night in replacement. But the Creator, or perhaps he that rules below, did not bless me with those visions of that carefree earlier time. In their stead, I saw my father. Or rather I heard my father's voice, by some trick of the mind or some dreadful sorcery. His words were not mere sound, but utterance made flesh. I felt them touching me, like callused work-a-day hands; I could see them, flashing in the midnight of my mind as lightning storms. And I could smell their foul odor, like some beast of the field, butcher'd and then left to rot in some damp place. My father was ranting against women, as was his wont; against woman-kind in general and his former wife. The female gender was his downfall and his curse, the root cause of his failings in his profession and his emotional dissolution. God had taken a rib from man to give form and life to woman and, in my father's lifetime, woman-kind had returned to take possession of the remainder of the skeleton. And then he collapsed into piteous sobs. No river in Ireland was as comely, no castle so lovely to look upon, no garden as sweet to smell, as a beautiful woman. But, ahh, fruit while still on the tree is beautiful to admire; once fallen and given to rot, no odor is so repellent.

But none of it was real. I awoke in my mate's cabin. The room was dark and the wooden walls seem'd as close and tight around me as the sides of a coffin already sealed and committed to the earth and the almighty. Hunahpu and Xbalanque, who were both assign'd to my small quarters, were up and playing a game of dice in the flickering piss yellow light of an oil lamp. I could hear the creak of the ship's hull and the footsteps of crew members walking in the passageway outside and crisscrossing the deck above. One of the twins noticed me stirring in my hammock and fixed me with a stare that, surprisingly, lacked a portion of the usual malice.

"Join us in a game of dice, if you like," the twin said (by his affable inquiry, I judged him to be Hunahpu).

"I thank you, but not tonight."

"You were talking to Sugar-Apple on the gangway," said the other twin, whom I identified as Xbalanque by the scheming tone in his voice. "Something about an iron trunk."

"No," I said, "we were talking about an Irish wench."

"A wench?" interrupted Angel, who was bunked nearly half the ship's length away.

"We are far from wenches here," said Xbalanque.

"What this about a wench?" said Angel.

"I was remembering a woman I once knew," I said. "An Irish wench."

"An Irish wench!" cried Angel. "The lustiest creatures of them all! Forsooth, I pray you split her beard!"

"Yea, I split her beard."

"A good man you are, a good man!" said Angel. "Would you like a quaff of my gunpowder tea?"

"No thanks," I said. "I had a few musket balls for breakfast."

Now Xbalanque, skeptical of my answers, slinked his way back into the exchange.

"What was this Irish wench's name, and in what village did she reside?" asked Xbalanque.

But I was already out the door of the cabin. The passageways were small and tight and rocked back and forth with the motion of the ship. Straw was strewn on the ground to absorb moisture and give the feet some traction. A young sailor with a shaved head and missing ear bumped by me, babbling something about Salmagundi. May Poseidon preserve us. Salmagundi was Sugar-Apple's latest creation, a highly seasoned stew with ingredients that included all of God's creations: chunks of meat (reputed to be beef but most probably rat), pickled herring, hard-boiled eggs (from both chickens and lizards), vegetables (probably seaweed or fungus), plus liberal additions of wine (or cider since that was all that was readily available), oil, vinegar, salt, and pepper. I wondered if the young sailor with the missing ear was running toward the Salmagundi or away from it.

I wandered past the keeping pen, where the farm animals were. All manner of beasts were here: a horned goat roped to a heavy plank (his constant bleating was as sour as his milk), a dozen chickens (which delivered eggs reluctantly if at all), and several large lizards that Calico had picked up on some previous voyage (the lizards were generous egg providers, but their product was foul to the taste).

A few paces beyond, Zayd had his surgeon's facility: a cabin with no door, a wooden table stained dark with blood, and his large medical chest. Zayd had no formal training in the medical arts, I suspected, but, as the ship's carpenter, he was in posses- sion of the sharpest tools and thus duly outfitted for the posi- tion. I had another occasion, when Zayd was out of his quarters, to peek into his medical chest and, at that time, I cataloged the following with my eyes: a number of saws of varying lengths, a selection of knives, a mallet and a chisel, a dozen or so syringes, pliers (some caked with blood), and a variety of forceps. Next to the chest, Zayd kept a large decanter of mercury, which he would liberally pour on any injury or wound that fell to his care. The mercury was not necessarily to clean the hurt; instead, I was told, Zayd had discover'd that his patients were most likely to faint after the sharp sting of the mercury, making it easier for Zayd to go about the business of amputation. The one happy aspect to the surgeon's facility was that the screams of the dying and injured men were sometimes so horrendous as to cause the goats and chickens to fall silent and give the men in their ham- mocks a few moments peace.

I climbed the steps that led to the quarterdeck. Dawn was nigh and so, too, my turn on the watch. I was loath to return to my hammock, so I continued my rambling walk. I strolled to the poop deck; I could hear a trio of voices coming from the captain's cabin.

"We've raided this water until, like fields that were best left fallow, our finest efforts wither on the vine or else bear naught but small and bitter fruits," said the first voice, which was gruff and full of unchecked passions. "To perdition with farming. Christ our Lord said we should be fishers of men. Jamaica is where we'll find our catch."

"Jamaica would be the death of us all," said a second voice, calmer and more measured.

"But a glorious death," said the gruff voice.

"Great treasure is there, to be sure, but also great danger. All the privateers in the region have lately been drawn there, and so the island and its waters have been the central focus of a campaign against those who would live on account. Governor Woodes Rogers no doubt waits for us there, too, and, in addition, the forces of Sir Nicholas Lawes, his majesty's captain-general and governor in chief. To sail there is all death."

"What say you then?"

"We've lived off the sea longer than many others might, or have been able to. I say we set our sails for Brazile, or other lands situated in the torrid zone, from the equinoctial to the latitude of twenty-eight degrees south. There we might divide up what spoils we have and take our leave of this lifestyle while our lives we still have."

"Leave this life?" bellowed the gruff voice. "Never!"

Now another voice made itself heard, low and with a musical undulation, and the speaker relayed this story.

"I have more years than some of you, and thus can tell the tale directly. Port Royal, at its height, was a city of privateers and cutthroats, a place of drinking and revels, a sanctuary of unflagging commerce, where a working man might, at long last, profit from the sweat of his body and the ingenuity of his enterprise. It was, it must be said, a site more flourishing than Santiago de Cuba, Boston, or New York. Having escaped from a slavers' ship—which is, in itself, another tale—I found myself in Port Royal, in the year of our Lord 1692."

"How does this story relate to our current troubles?" said the gruff voice.

"Hold," said the musical voice, "and you will come into understanding. Port Royal is located on the tip of a sandy spit of land; the peninsula curls a bit, forming a natural harbor. This sheltered space was the chief source of the city's import. The water in the harbor was deep, right up to the land, allowing even the largest galleon to sail right up to the docks to dislodge its cargo and then, afterward, to careen and have its hull scraped clean of barnacles.

"The city was, from all appearances, well armed and most solidly built. It was encircled by a stone wall twice as tall as a large man and protected, at intervals of many paces, by a series of battle stations: Fort James to the west, Fort Rupert to the east, Fort Carlisle to the north, and Fort Charles standing tall to the south. Each fort had a commanding view of the land and sea and each boasted numerous large black cannons.

"I had been in Port Royal but for a fortnight or so, learning the lay of the land, and, in that time, unusual weather had blown in. It was a strange sky, the like of which I had never seen and, despite my experience, I have not seen since. The sun was bloody red, like the flesh beneath a freshly picked scab. The horizons echoed with the sound of stringed instruments striking wrong notes, playing broken rhythms out of time, snapping strings and then playing on, heedless of the discord. Intermittently, I could hear the mundane music of that cruel, great city:

the sad splash of slave bodies striking water as they were disposed, the cries of strumpets in the night, the dying squawk of a cock fallen in a streetfight.

"Now, all at once," continued the musical voice, "I heard a rumbling in the Saint Andrews Mountains in the North. The sound was far away at first; from this distance, it was not unlike a man's dry belly heaves, many times multiplied. A burbling, muffled by mounds of flesh. Then the roar grew closer and closer. It was like a thunderstorm passing through the ground. It seemed to me that the red earth grew redder, a deep shade of vermilion, as if flushed with anger or soaked in blood. The underground roar grew deafening, and my hands against my ears were no help; the noise sounded through my fingers, it shook my whole body, and I could feel the sound in my innards and in my bones. I fled, running through the gates of the city and heading for the hills, but the force of the noise and the movement of the earth threw me to the ground.

"The earth now moved as if it were a living thing," said the musical voice. "Now, from where I was lying, I could see the whole city. It seemed to me that the noise had become a vast music, great in rhythm and utterly lacking in harmony; it swelled up like a legion of deep-barreled drums beating in unison, pounding on toward some terrible crescendo.

"I looked toward the outer ring of Port Royal," said the musical voice. "The stone walls that circumscribed the city wiggled and writhed like eels. I saw the black iron cannons of Fort Charles and Fort James hurled into the air. The ground 'round the battlements rippled like the surface of a pond.

"Great fissures opened up in the streets of the city. The jagged chasms looked like greedy mouths, gobbling up the brick and timber-built houses, slurping in the court, and the warehouses, too. The gaps sucked in passersby, merchants and sailors, slavers and strumpets, stray dogs and pack mules. Almost immediately a great wail went up from the dead and the dying, the sufferers and the mourning. Still, the great vents went about their awful work, opening and closing like eager jaws, crushing and chewing their prey. A gray smoke issued from each of the vents.

"Almost no building was spared destruction—the Presbyterian church, the Quaker meeting house, the Jewish synagogue; all disappeared in bursts of splintered wood and shattered brick. The Anglican church was sucked down a dark hole, its tower bells jangling. The whorehouses and the prisons, the ramshackle market stalls, collapsed into the earth. Great clouds of plaster and powdered lime rose above the city.

"Half of the city rose up and the other half sank. High Street and Thames Street and Queen Street, all parallel to one another, now tilted up together, east side low, west side high. The whole city was like the deck of a ship submerging beneath the waves.

"There was another roar," said the undulating voice. "The water round Port Royal now swirled and rose up. The single-masted sloops and triple-masted frigates and big-hulled galleons careening in Chocolata Hole, at King's Wharf, at Waterman's Wharf, broke loose their moorings, riding high on the crest of a series of mighty waves before disappearing, one and all, beneath the fathoms.

"The HMS *Swan*, a great ship lately put to port, alone escaped this fate. One massive wave, taller tenfold than the highest building in Port Royal, carried the ship from the wharf and then over the city wall and then over the overwhelmed battlements and then over the tops of sunken houses. The *Swan*'s guns were torn away, so too its rigging and cables, and a hole was ripped in its hull where once the anchor was fixed. The great ship, now at the command of the wild waters, was carried by the flow straight onto High Street, where it sailed down the thorough-fare as if it were skimming down a great river. The ship finally came to rest atop the roof of a drowned house across the way from the fish market on Thames Street.

"Water was now the master of Port Royal. The fashionable merchants' houses on Thames Street and on Lime Street slipped beneath the waves. Water covered nearly everything, water covered Fort Rupert and Fort Carlisle, water covered Fort James and Fort Charles. Water covered all the alehouses and all the churches. Only debris moved on the surface of the sea— empty bottles of Rhenish wine, broken cart wheels, the yellow bodice of a strumpet, a great wooden chest, a cracked clay chamber pot—and bodies, black bodies that had been thrown into the sea by slaver ships the previous afternoon, along with the pale bodies of Port Royal residents who had perished that very day. Water took them all. The spit of sandy land that con-nected the town to the mainland was now one with the sea. Port Royal, once a peninsula, was now a sunken island. Streets were now rivers, ships now sailed the bottom of the harbor, and churches were entirely submerged with just their steeples jut-ting over the surface of the waves.

"I thought to myself then: the world is sand," said the voice. "Nothing lasts—not people, not ships, not battlements or cities. The streets are all sand and the stars are sand, too. We must know when our time is up. I agree with those who say we must consider an end to our voyage, and Brazile is as worthy a spot as any. Let us divide up what spoils we may, before we, too, are swallow'd up, like our fellows in that poor city of Port Royal."

A silence greeted these words. I could hear my heart in my chest. Did the former suggestion mean what I took it for? Might the men of the *William* lower the black flag?

"That's a long tale to make a philosophic point," said the gruff voice at last. "I've had shits that were not only of more substance, they were a good deal shorter as well."

Now a fourth voice—reasonable and commanding, unheard until now—introduced itself to the conversation: "Indeed these waters have grown hard. Within three days, we will run short of proper victuals. Within those same three days, we will run short of both grog and drinking water."

"For the men," said the gruff voice, "the loss of the grog will be the worst of it."

"Much consideration have I given to changing course," said the commanding voice. "These currents were plentiful in days gone by. But 'tis not treasure we now need but wood and water and food."

"So what's the plan?" said the gruff voice.

The words that followed next were softer and I could not hear them from where I stood, a few paces beyond the door. What plan could be afoot about the course of the ship? I crept closer and pressed my ear to the door.

Just then the door open'd and I fell forward, face first, into the captain's cabin.

Struggling to my feet I saw around me Bishop (a mug of grog in hand), First-Rate (smoking a long pipe), Zayd (sitting cross-legged on a wooden chair), and Calico (cleaning the muzzle of his flintlock pistol). Bishop was the gruff voice, First-Rate the voice of calm, Zayd had told the tale of Port Royal, and Calico was the voice of command. All four had grim looks on their faces at my unexpected intrusion.

"Let's crucify this one now," said Bishop.

"Stealth and curiosity are virtues for men of the sea," said First-Rate.

"We'll let him live—a night or two at least," said Calico, merriment now playing about his lips.

He offered me a hand up and pulled me to my feet. His hands were large and strong, I noticed. I have often passed trees that have grown around obstacles, locking them in a wooden embrace. My hand in his felt plung'd in oak.

"So what say you of our ship's dilemmas?" said Calico. "Come on now, raise your voice. You've signed on to the government of the ship's articles, so our troubles have indeed become your own, as surely as if we were married in a church."

Calico's voice was serious as he said these words but his eyes smiled a little. I noticed that his eyes were very much like a boy's, bright and touched with some levity, but worried a bit around the corners like a man who carries with him the weight of many years.

I swallow'd hard and found my voice.

"My opinion is . . ."

The men all leaned a bit closer.

"My opinion is . . ."

My underarms began to tingle with eddies of perspiration.

"My opinion is that I'll hold my opinion until I have more experience."

"Well said," smiled First-Rate.

Bishop sneered.

"But this I'll say," I continued. "The sea, it has always seemed to me, rewards men of daring. The fisherman must run the coral reef to catch the crevalle jack."

Calico seem'd lost in thought, and hardly seem'd to hear my words. He was bent over in his chair, stroking the sides of his well-polished boots, which he had removed.

"There are those who would judge a man by what he stands in," Calico said. "My father had boots such as these. His were not so polished nor well kept, for he had no money for repairs nor for replacement. He would work every day, or else look for work on the days on which he had none, and when he returned home, he would place his boots before the fireplace. Our hearth in those days was surrounded by gilded pictures of our relations. Soon the frames were sold, the portraits tucked away, and only the boots remained. We lost even the hearth, when we lost the house, which follow'd hard upon a press-gang conscripting my father in the night. But the boots remained. They were not dissimiliar, as I have said, to the ones I wear now—they had a square toe, as mine do, but also a large brass buckle, one that seem'd as big as my head when I was a child, and a tongue that curled up and out, like a black wave of leather. I remember well what my father wore."

Calico's face was full of passion but he mastered it. He slipped on his boots and stood up.

"So many have profited so much from these waters and we have yet to earn our fortunes," he said. "I recall when Port Royal was alive—bright like some glittering bauble hung between a harlot's breasts. Now that great port has sunk into the sea and another port, Kingston, has sprung up across the harbor. Cities rise and cities fall and still we have not earned our fortunes. How I hate the thought that so many fools and knaves and mountebanks have grown rich while we, full of intelligence and courage, labor on under the shadow of poverty and disaster! I curse God for it and all his angels, too!"

Calico motion'd the others to their feet.

"Our councils are at an end, for now," he said. "We will continue in these waters. But may the devil help us if our catch does not increase."

chapter 14.

The days grew desperate. Laughter died, conversations grew terse, and the men went about their appointed duties with a kind of flintiness—full of sharp edges and given to spark. The weather, she blew hard and dirty, with much rain and little sun. Over the course of the next two days, while sailing off the coast of Harbour Island, we encounter'd several more fishing vessels. Each of the craft Calico did the favor of relieving the crew of their nets and tackle, and, if there were bondsmen on board, he bade them to join us, and they invariably did. Then Calico would send the fishermen back on their course, wiser, but in the main unharmed. Bishop counseled that dead men would be entirely unlikely to reveal the whereabouts of our vessel, but Zayd advised it best for our ship to avoid the infamy and increased scrutiny that accompanies unnecessary cruelties. Calico took the latter's advisement, and so we sail'd on with hardly a fight.

With no great prize having been encounter'd, and no sea-battle to heat the blood, complaints and dissatisfactions ran their course on the ship, like the visitation of some great plague, and, indeed, the general mood among the men took on a sickly pallor. Everything seem'd to be running out: supplies, patience, time. The new recruits taken from the fishing vessels drained the ship's resources even more. The stores and barrels of fresh drinking water were very nearly exhausted. For victuals, Sugar-Apple offered the crew only iron-hard biscuits, which, when broken, were full of weevils with long black heads, jagged pinchers, and soft white bodies. The men, in search of sustenance in whatever form, sampled the weevils, but found them to be bitter in taste and, when swallowed, most times triggering an uncontrollable heaving of the innards. When duly criticized for his offerings, Sugar-Apple just shrugged and bade the men to catch and eat the multitude of rats that ran freely in the ship's hold, which men of the *William* did, judging the rodents to be a significantly more satisfying repast than the biscuit-weevils.

Calico remained distant from the fray. He dined among the men—when there was something to eat—but did not drink spirits with them. He would walk the decks and issue orders, but rarely would he pause for a conversation of any great length or depth. The men loved him, to be sure, despite the troubles, but none really knew him intimately. I approached him at various times over different matters, none of any great importance, and it seem'd to me that prolonged closeness almost seem'd to cause him physical pain. At first I attributed this to the burden of command, which must be particularly heavy in a time of scarcity and want, but, upon reflection I wonder'd what was at the root of his shielded character.

Most of the ship's company, and I count myself among this number, sought refuge from the ongoing troubles in the solace of routine. Indeed, there is a rhythm to the seafaring life that is orderly and unstoppable, vibrantly youthful and yet rooted in comfortably timeworn traditions. The bulk of the men on the ship who were not officers slept in cramped quarters below deck that at first inspired hostility and anxiety but, in time and by necessity, eventually conjured a certain familial feeling among the men. Our hammocks were strung so close together that only a slight shift while sleeping would rock several hammocks, one 'gainst another. Close by me was Poop, who mumbled passages from his prayer book each night before taking to his hammock. Once caught up in his rest, he was also given to sobbing in his sleep and calling out for his parents, much to the merriment and mockery of all the crew members within hearing range, who, given the close proximity of the sleeping arrangements, were plentiful. Angel's hammock was some distance from me, but he seemed ubiquitous: the fellow, when he slept, snored like Vesuvius issuing life-smothering ash on poor Pompei.

The ship's company was divided into halves, call'd larboard and starboard, in order to divvy up the tasks of operating the ship. I was designated a position on the starboard rotation. While one shift was on duty, the other shift was usually engaged in sleep down below, or in revels of some sort. While on duty, we all had places on the ship, fore and aft, with the more experienced sea-dogs station'd at or around the forecastle. Then, next in esteem, came the topmen, and the duties of the lower yard fell to them; following that group came the afterguard, who oversaw the after-braces, main, mizzen, and lower-stay sails. Next, and lastly, were the newcomers, and I numbered among this grouping. All the labor on board a ship is hard work, but the newbirds were assigned, by custom, the hardest, sweatiest, dirt-iest work of all, including watching and working the main and foresheets, swabbing the decks, knotting ropes, discarding waste into the sea, and whatnot. All these tasks I did when I was not sleeping below or not at my regular post on the masthead.

By some miraculous process, which amazed even the ship's officers, Sugar-Apple managed to keep the crew reasonably soaked in grog, though I noted, but kept to myself, that the beverage was becoming increasingly thin in consistency as the stores of drinking water were dissipating at a rate faster than originally forecast. But Sugar-Apple, canny as he was, under-stood that a privateer ship floated as much on grog as it did upon the sea, and so he kept the flow going, no matter how diluted. Still, with water and grog in limited supply, crew members were in a near-constant state of thirst. Tempers were short and phys-ical confrontations and contests were common occurrences.

In an effort to mask the modesty associated with beings of my sex, tho', I should say, little of that inclination naturally re-sides in me, I joined in heartily with the general spirit of compe-tition. It was yet another role for me to take on in the drama of my life, and I took to it as eagerly as Rosencrantz and Guilden-stern. While scrubbing the decks down with sand one afternoon I was questioned by Bishop as to the pace and forcefulness of my work. Tho' he was an officer, and I but a newbird, I cheekily put the query right back to my interrogator and asked him if he would care to wager a day's rations 'gainst the proposition that I could scrub a prescribed length of floor faster and cleaner than he, with an impartial man as judge. Bishop, a calm fury in his eyes at my impudence, docked my dinner one biscuit and con-tinued in his paces. But my point had been made with the rest of the crew: I was not the sort to back down from a confrontation.

I subsequently faced contests in rope-climbing, knot-tying, and unfurling the mainsail. I triumphed in the challenges I took on, or at least in a great many of them. But even in a rare defeat, the general level of respect for my labors increased among the men who worked beside me on the decks. These rough wooden planks were my proscenium, the sails my stage curtains!

The crew of the *William* ofttimes strove to give some ease to their travails by engaging in games of chance and other forms of mirth and diversion. At the start of the shortages, cards and dice were forbidden, by terms of the captain's orders, on the grounds that they were a prevailing source of combat between crew members. But the men, officers and newbirds alike, secretly continued in such play, the general view being that such entertainments were a natural and essential part of sea-life and thus should be tolerated, so long as fists, and not firearms or dirks, were used to settle disputes concerning them.

So, in the lower decks, the tedious hours were pass'd with such vagaries as Hob, Spice the Market, Dilly-Dolly, and Back-Gammon. Many hours were also whiled away singing and dancing, distractions that arose spontaneously under the influence of grog and the steady gaze of the stars. The men would twirl each other 'round and laugh, or else form kick-lines, all stomping their booted feet to a shared rhythm as flutes and fiddles played on. Each session of buffoonery and jocularity continued until the stars came out, or the sun went down, or the new shift began, or the grog ran dry, or the good nature of one or more of the men came to its natural end, resulting in profane taunts, bawdy challenges, the drawing of small arms, and a general agreement to dissolve the gathering to preserve the health and safety of all.

During such periods of jollity, I maintain'd a certain degree of control in my carriage, due to the secret of my sex and, in addition, because of the continuing interest in my affairs by those who seem'd to wish me no goodwill. Xbalanque, from his place at the masthead, kept an eye on my movements on deck, like some carrion bird tracking its prey from a treetop. Ofttimes, when I would look up, to spy a passing cloud to track the wind or note the patterns of the constellations, I would catch the glint of his eye from high above and he would hiss back at me like some serpent in human form. Bishop, too, was following my moves as well as actively asserting his dislike for me. Once, when he caught me engaged in a game of dice with Angel, with whom he regularly play'd such sports, he nonetheless took me to task for my transgression of ship's rules, tho' he spared Angel a similar punishment.

"By the devil, you've brought some curse onto this ship, tho' I know not what," Bishop said. "Meantime, you'll suffer half-rations for today, for the playing at games of chance."

"But . . ."

"Quarter-rations then," he said. "And not another word, or I'll put the matter to a general vote and see you maroon'd."

Happily, Sugar-Apple, that sweet sort-of Swede, ignored Bishop's order of quarter-rations and, more than that, he shared with me some victuals from his secret store: a basket of various fruits of a tropical origin.

"Worry often gives a small thing a big shadow," said Sugar-Apple. "Put it all behind ye and eat a little."

"You never struck me as a hoarder," I told Sugar-Apple, as I greedily tore into his gift of a rotten orange.

"I save all this not for myself, but as a safeguard 'gainst mutiny. Many a ship has turned bloody for lack of victuals. In my estimation, a ship's cook is second in importance among officers, before the quartermaster and the boatswain and behind only the captain himself."

"I did not know the cook was consider'd an officer."

"Well," said Sugar-Apple, winking, "in my mind at least."

"Do ya think any of the men capable of rising up?"

"Under regular circumstances, now, this lot ain't got the heart for it. But the stomach is a more powerful organ than the heart. I hear talk. At the very least, I could envision the captaincy being put to a vote."

"Who would vote 'gainst Calico?"

"Perhaps one of his officers—one with a grudge."

"What? First-Rate?"

"No, not him."

"But I've heard he was forced on board by the sea-dogs' choice."

"'Tis a lie, and a damn'd one at that."

"What is the truth of it then?"

"He had grown exhausted with the Royal Navy when he join'd us—some secret of his background or upbringing held him back in the ranks. Calico did him a great kindness by admitting him to our company. First-Rate would never turn against him."

"So who would rise 'gainst Calico?"

"Only a fool. But, like any ship on account, we've got a boatload of 'em."

"Bishop."

"Aye, he's a candidate. And if Bishop takes over the craft by vote or other means, it'll go hard on all the men, not just on you. Bishop's both smart and cruel, and that's a dangerous combination."

"What's his true name?"

"Yer full of queries! Well, as to his name, nobody knows, and I've never heard him tell the tale."

"Well, where did he get the name Bishop?"

"He was the chaplain of a ship, a French vessel she was. We took 'er on the open sea and offer'd her crew——"

"The sea-dogs' choice. Join or face the blade."

"Exactly. Bishop was, I'm told, a man of some piety before his capture. But after preaching so long 'bout the hereafter, he decided, when faced with the imminent prospect of it, that he liked the here-and-now well enough. He threw his prayer book overboard, I saw him do as much, and his vestments as well."

"Then he join'd the ranks."

"No——there's more of this vessel beneath the waterline! First-Rate advised the captain that threatening a man of God would bring the ship an ill omen. So, in the end, Bishop was allow'd to make his decision without coercion or enticement."

"So why'd he join?"

"Who knows why a man does this or that or the other thing? This, I do know——I saw Bishop's face that day, the afternoon he chose, of his own free will, to come on board this vessel and sail 'gainst heaven itself. I saw his visage and it was, I'd testify, like when a slug turns into a soft-wing'd butterfly, 'cept the opposite transformation took place. I tell ye true, his countenance, which, and this comes with the grace of God, formerly had a placid demeanor, like some mirror'd sea swept with no wind, by quick turns became wrought with some fierce distemper, like a rough zephyr blew hard an' dirty cross his soul. Truly now, my lad, I've seen events that would make dead men sweat and curdle mothers' milk in the breast, but even I turn'd away at the horror and melancholy of the sight."

As I mused on Sugar-Apple's words and gobbled down the sour rind of my orange, there was a shout from above deck.

"Best take to yer station," said Sugar-Apple.

"But I have yet to pose my chief query: what's in your iron trunk?"

Sugar-Apple winked again.

"All the riches of Cork," he said. "Now get ye topside! There's a chase afoot!"

chapter 15.

I have long found it entertainingly peculiar that although the articles and customs of seafaring folk prohibit the services of women on board ships, the vessels themselves are poetically and commonly understood to be of the female sex. I had long thought this latter tradition to be a mere illusion of some sort. After long fortnights at sea, and many days and nights spent outside the fair company of that gentler sex, it seem'd a reasonable thing to imagine the presence of women in that place where quite plainly none were present, just as a parched man, while traveling the desert, dreams up oases of water. And of course women, being thought of from time immemorial as creatures of many moods not all anchor'd in sense and logic, are quite easily linked to the vagaries of ships of the sea: the temperamental sails that get caught in the riggings, the leaky oak planks that cry and groan for the balm of pine tar, the clean beauty of the decks when they've been properly scrubbed. Ships, indeed, for every man, can become any woman: the jilted lover, the nagging wife, the starry-eyed daughter, the sluttish mistress, the unattainable goddess.

How absurd, some might reason, to regard a dead floating hunk of wood and rope as one would a living, breathing woman! And yet, I, too, began to regard the *Will* in just the same manner. I had felt a fanciful kinship with the vessel, yes, but what was inanimate had become inamorata. I no longer laughed so heartily when the boys called 'er the *Williamina*, a tone of caring in their voice. I no longer smiled so gaily when one of the old salts stroked 'er railings like he was caressing some maid's blushing cheek. By my troth, even as I felt the womanhood in me drain out, like the last draught in a drinking mug poured out in tribute to a fallen comrade, I simultaneously sensed a growing distaff presence all around me. She was under my feet, echoing in the hold; she was just above my head, billowing in the sails; she was in the gleam of the hull as the white waves crashed 'gainst the sides, her voice called out with the boom of every swivel cannon on the quarterdeck. Just as I once heard Bishop and Angel and First-Rate and the rest pleading, conversing, and cooing to the ship as if she were a mortal woman with understanding and emotion, so too, I, while sitting in my perch at the masthead during the hours of my watch, would ofttimes find my lips moving, engaged in some unheard discussion with my silent partner, my ship, my Willa, my lady love who never requited my passion for her in words.

And now, as I came up from the lower decks, I could feel 'er dander up.

"Ready about, ladies!" cried Calico, who was at his place on the poop deck. "Stations for stays!"

I could feel my heart in my chest. These are the moments that all should have—too many go about their lives, hardly ever feeling their arms and legs and innards. But, ahh, onboard a privateer vessel, when those calls go up—"Stations for stays!"—when the smell of powder is in the air—is any perfume so sweet?—you feel yourself as if for the first time. Those things that you forget in the day-to-day amnesia of living—the drawing of breath, the pumping of blood through the veins—one remembers again, all in a rush. You remember your body, which you had lost for so long. Aye, you remember yourself.

"Stations for stays!" Bishop called out.

This was the signal for one and all to move with alacrity to their designated positions, to see everything clear and to get the braces ready for running. The *William* was moving through the water nicely, neither jammed up so tight that the weather leeches of the sails were shaking, nor too far off the wind beside.

"Ready! Ready!" the cry went up. "Ease down the helm!"

Calico, Bishop, and First-Rate were at their usual posts on the poop; First-Rate put down the wheel slowly when thus addressed.

"Helm's a-lee!" cried Calico.

The hands on deck let go the foresheet and headsheets.

"Raise tacks and sheets!"

Ahhh—our prey was now in our sight. Like the wolf in pursuit of the rabbit, our jaws slavered in anticipation but we kept our eyes focused. She was a small vessel, boasting but two masts, and with a crew of perhaps twelve souls on board.

"Haul taut, you sea-bitches! Mainsail haul!"

And then, following hard on those commands, the words that filled our souls with wind: "Lift, too, the black flag!"

Now, our grim emblem flying, the crew of the ship we pursued took full notice of our vessel. We could see also their ship was loaded with goods of some sort—crates and barrels, containing what we could only guess. Whether provisions or treasure, we surely needed 'em.

"Halt your flight!" Calico bellow'd. "We sail under a black flag! Prepare to be boarded!"

The two-masted ship did no such thing. Instead, she hoisted sails and tacked into the wind, opening up some distance between our ships.

Calico was angry now. His fury spread to the other men, who grit their teeth and set their brows. Calico signal'd to Angel, who readied his canon. Poop, who was his powder-boy, scurried from the captain's deck to take his place at Angel's side on the quarterdeck.

Now, Angel was given his name not because of any resemblance he shared with those bless'd winged creatures of our Master's heavenly host, but because of his affection and copious use of Angel-shot, a form of ammunition in which a cannonball is sheared in two and the two halves joined by a small length of chain.

Poop took a cartridge, a flannel bag with some six pounds of powder in it, and rammed it down the muzzle of Angel's cannon. When Angel saw it breech, he let loose the cry: "Home!" Next, Angel pulled out his precious Angel-shot from a nearby barrel. This he dropped down the barrel of his cannon, followed by a wad, which Poop rammed home. Angel then lit a slow fuse.

"Fire!" he cried.

An explosion rocked the craft, like ten thunderclaps. The Angel-shot tore through the air with a piercing screech. The two halves of the shot spread out, the chain between them. The whole wicked creation now ripped through the crew of the opposing vessel, ripping off legs and arms and blazing a path of general destruction before thudding into a stack of goods on the ship's starboard side and setting them alight.

Next, a curious event transpired. The crew of the two-masted ship made no effort to save the goods that were set ablaze. Instead, they pushed and prodded them off the deck of the ship and let them fall, sizzling and sparking, into the waters of the Caribbean. What's more, additional crew members were emerging from the hold bearing what seemed to be crates of foodstuffs and barrels of water. These, too, they dumped into the water.

Calico signaled Angel.

"Fire on the down roll of the next wave," said Calico. "Let's hit 'em low, and put the threat of sinking in their minds."

Again, Angel's cannon boomed. This time he aimed at the opposing ship's side, piercing it with shot.

As the smoke cleared, we could see the men on the other vessel still going about their task of throwing goods into the sea.

Calico, alarmed, came to the railing of our ship and put a brass speaking trumpet to his lips.

"Are there any aboard who would trade their treasure and foodstuffs for their lives?" he asked. "We mean you no bodily harm, this we swear by the black flag we fly! Surrender your goods and then we will let you about your way!"

The crew members on the two-masted vessel seemed to be finishing up the work of throwing everything on board their craft overboard. I could see Calico's jaw grow tight. We needed those goods. It also seem'd to me now that the opposing vessel was sinking. It was still sailing at a good clip, however; we would never board it before it slipped beneath the waves.

"What say you to our offer?" said Calico. "Your goods for your lives!"

A man came to the railing of the opposing ship. He, too, put a speaking trumpet to his lips.

"I am the quartermaster of this vessel, now captain, since our former commander was laid low in your last barrage."

"My name is Calico Jack Rackam, and I am known for keeping my word."

The man on the sinking ship laughed. It was a sad, small laugh, but because both ships had grown silent in the tenseness of the moment, his laugh carried.

"Governor Woodes Rogers has sworn to hang you on the Palisadoes," said the man. "He, too, is a man of his word."

"And yet, here I am," replied Calico.

"Rogers hung twenty and five of your brethren at the wharf in Nassau after you sailed out. His word is proven, yours is not. And Rogers has promised death to all those who submit to pyrates. He has been granted full cooperation in his campaign from His Excellency Nicholas Lawes. The two governors mean to make the Caribbean, in its entirety, a haven for settlers and their families. Rogers has said this: he does what he does for the children."

Now the man's ship was starting a quick slide into the sea. The deck had tilted noticeably, and the waters were beginning to lick the deck on the fore.

"I say this to you pyrates—I die, but I descend to that other world knowing that you will soon join me, and meet your punishments there. What a sad lot of barking mongrel dogs you are, with no port, no race, and no nation to call your own! This is a ship of slaves and whether you are white or Moorish, you shall be treated like poor servants, one and all, when you are caught! The governors are on to your scent. Woodes has already posted along Bay Street notices announcing the planned method of your execution."

The ship was at a sharp angle now, and the water swallowed up half of it. Still the man continued.

"Weights will be piled upon your chest until your lungs cease their movement and your heart expires. Next, to be certain that you are dead, a cord will be twisted 'round your neck until your eyes bulge. Then your bodies will be hung in cages put in public display, for the purpose of moral education and crime prevention."

The man's crew had deserted the ship. They splashed and scattered about; the weakest swimmers were already slipping beneath the water. The quartermaster was the last soul on board his ship, and he stood on its very tip, the last portion visible. The men of the *William* did not jump in the drink to save the stores. Drowning men are dangerous adversaries; wild with the fear of death, they will pull down anyone who swims near.

I looked at Calico, and, so, too, did the eyes of all the crew of the *William* turn to the captain. We had just lost a prize that we dearly coveted. We were dangerously low on food and water. And now this news that we were all marked men.

Calico just smiled.

"You're nobody," said Calico. "'Til somebody kills you."

At his words, so confident, so commanding, the gloom that had settled over our ship seem'd to lift a bit, and there appeared to be some small hope.

The man on the sinking ship, who was so full of mockery before, now for the first time appeared full of fright. He drew a pistol from his side holster and, with surprising speed, got off a shot.

His aim was well wide of Calico, but it caught Sugar-Apple full in the face. There was a dull thud as the shot struck skull.

Calico drew his own weapon and returned fire. The quartermaster fell from the tip of his vessel and, along with his craft, slipped into the depths of the sea.

Now all turned to Sugar-Apple. He lay on the deck, his arms spread out, his one good leg twitching and then still. A pool of blood grew around his prone form. That sweet face was now a mush of bloody pulp and white bone. Zayd set down his small bag of surgeon's tools and kneeled down beside him. He attended him for a few moments and then laid down his works and bowed his head. Sugar-Apple was beyond medicine. He was gone.

"*Inna Lillahi wa inna ilahi rajtun,*" said Zayd, in a voice that was no more than a breath.

"What are those words?" I said, my voice rising to a shout. "What devil words do you speak?"

Zayd turned to me.

"We are from Allah," he said. "And it is to him we are returning."

I could hear Poop sobbing somewhere. I could feel hot tears in my eyes. I didn't even see Sugar-Apple come up to the quarterdeck. It was beyond belief that he could be taken so quickly, in a single burst of smoke and sparks.

Calico betrayed no disconsolation. He walked back to his captain's cabin.

Before closing the door, he issued a command over his shoulder at First-Rate.

"Set a course for Jamaica," he said.

PART THE SECOND

Sea-Changes

chapter 16.

Ahhhh—now where was I in my tale, my darling one, my love? For a woman of age am I now, respected in the town and throughout the parish, and yet the wisdom and store of knowledge I have built up over all these long years has faded and grown wispy, like the gray hair upon my head. I remember so little of what made me so wise and well regarded! It is a trick of time which the Almighty plays on us all, that the more we are known, the less we know. Even as we accumulate memories, like piles of leaves in autumn, they blow away as we gather them in. So where was I in my tale?

Perhaps something to awaken my senses, which, in my advanced state, are as behind a veil or a darkened glass—I see shadows and suggestions of life but not always the thing itself. Yes, perhaps something to awaken my senses and bring the young life back, if only for a moment, if only for the length of my story to you. Ahh yes, my tea has grown cold and I have barely touched it. Sweet of you to offer to refresh my cup, my sweet bird, my kind one. But indulge me this—while in the pantry, in the top cupboard to the left of the window. Ahhh—you've found it. That's coffee, my dear, straight from the Blue Mountains of Jamaica. Finest brew in the world. Oh—what's the trouble, my dear one? No matter, my pearl, that you are too small to reach what I requested, I'll fetch it myself. Ahhh—now my vision returns. In my mind's eye only, my darling, in my mind's eye. Like two tall trees the masts of the *Will* now sprout up before me.

The sublime exultation of one's first leagues out from land soon gives way to the grim reality of life at sea. The far-flung waters can be a lonely place; there is no canyon, no desert, no snow-swept plain, no dense forest echoing with the howls of beasts and creatures unknown that is as lonely as the open sea. So, night after night, I was at my post on the masthead, closer to heaven than to the ship below, and yet my proximity to God and his heavenly host offer'd me little respite and, like others on the crew, I felt a crushing lack of hope. The very air appear'd alive with the absence of angels. We felt forsaken by God and abandon'd by the devil. It seem'd Governor Rogers had us tripped up and outwitted at every turn and move, like a canny player pressing hard his position in a game of chess. The small inlets and islets we sail'd by and at which we may have taken refuge and restock'd our provisions at an earlier time were now, thanks to the good and intrepid Lawes, guarded well by man-o'-wars flying the colors of England and the standard of the Governor.

"De Graff, that blue-eyed sea god, would never have been pressed so," Xbalanque hissed in my ear (I had become expert at telling one twin from the other). "There was a man worth a score of Rackams."

"Close your damned porthole," I replied. "Or else I'll tie a turk's head knot round your throat, you scoundrel!"

So we sail'd on. Rackam drew deep into his stock of expertise, built up over long devotion to the sea, and he studied hard his charts, many obtained at bloody cost, and yet there was no place for the *Will* to careen and water herself. So we sail'd on. We had gone too far to turn back and yet we knew not what awaited us in the outstretch'd waters before our helm. And so we sail'd on.

In my perch, as shy dawn spread her gauzy red veil across the sky, all the world seem'd water, and I felt alone, more than I have ever felt with solid earth beneath me. Below, I heard the groans of the men who were hungry and without water. In the distant past, one and all had cursed the foul concoctions that Sugar-Apple had, with temerity, called victuals; with his passing, and with every man left to himself to find and prepare his own grub, Sugar-Apple's preparations seem'd akin to the finest feasts cooked up by the greatest chefs of the capitals of Europe. The food that remained was tasteless and rotting: scraps of bread and dried strips of rat flesh. Lemon rinds were prized delicacies and fistfights broke out with regularity for the right to suck milk straight from the teat of the one scrawny, coughing goat that remained tied up in the hold. Bellies grumbled and rumbled and almost howled with complaint over the unfairness and hardness and inhumanity of it all; the ship's hull, leaking and barnacle covered and in sore need of repair, creaked back as if in answer, as if all the men, the tragic passengers of this doomed voyage, travel'd the blue expanse in the empty gut of a starving giant.

One afternoon, 'round or about this time, a man who had been station'd on the forenoon watch fell hard from his perch on the mizzentop and broke his skull. I was beneath deck in my hammock, but the reverberations of the impact tore me from sleep for it sounded like a melon, fired from a cannon, striking its target. I went quickly up top and Zayd was already attending the poor fellow, who, with his last energy, made the sign of the cross and then gave up the ghost. If ever God had his gaze on our ship, he, with the utmost certainty, seem'd to have averted his vision now. The men, who had gathered in a circle 'round the accident, looked on with hard secular eyes. Neither fortune nor heaven was smiling on this journey. Xbalanque pushed by me, all sneers and sibilance, and climbed the mizzenmast to begin his watch early. Hunahpu followed after, looking upon me with more felicitous eyes.

The singing, the reveries and revelries, they were all in our wake. There was hard work to be done. The men put their faith in their hands, hoping that physical labor could distract the mind from lamentation and redirect the body from dissolution. The ship itself was in no happy state. A shot from the last ship we had opposed had scored true, breeching the hull, and we men, being unable to repair the damage given the current state of supplies, made do with coping with it as best we could. A team of hands worked day and night pumping water from below, where the breech had occurred, up and out of the ship, lest she fill with ocean and take all souls aboard to the briny bottom. At times, when I was not in my perch, I shared the labor and it was hard. Already we suffer'd chores without adequate and fitting amounts of water to drink; the pump crew's thirst increased as the salty spray from the breech found its way into the eyes, nose, and mouth; and all the while the work put an ache in the shoulders, a burn in the belly, and a stiffness in the neck.

And so my watch became even more important. Even after my stints at the pump, even as my eyelids grew heavy and sleep courted me hard, I dared not let sweet slumber's arms wrap themselves around me. Much was riding on the watch—our chief hope, forsooth our only hope, rested in the taking of another ship, one well-stocked with provisions and the like. By bringing misery to others, we would be freed from it ourselves. We had started this journey with dreams of gold and jewels; we continued it now with our thoughts focused on more mundane stuff: meat and water and bread.

I stared out at the blue, searching the horizon for a sail. The sea was stagnant, the sky was stale, and nothing was in my sight save the boat below and the endless blue-green of the sea. A spray of porpoises surfaced off starboard; the happy creatures seemed to mock the crew with their white bellies and crooked smiles. They leap'd up from the water a great height, and when they slid back in, they made nary a splash. We had no tools to catch 'em with or else we would have eaten every one, white bellies, crooked smiles, and all.

The days passed to night and the nights passed to day and no calendar was kept and time slipped away. Still I looked for that elusive sail. I was dreaming in daylight now, perhaps a quarter mad from thirst and hunger, perhaps a quarter more mad with boredom. Phantasms came to me, like waking, walking dreams. Floating in the cloudless sky I saw the image of a young boy. He looked of my own blood—he had my self-same olive skin, the same crimson curls of hair and high cheeks and full lips. I saw the light of mischief in his eyes, burning like tallow candles.

I imagined at that moment that I had a doppelgänger of some sort, a twin or some sibling of opposite sex but similar countenance, hidden from me all these long years for purposes unknown for a design unreveal'd. I saw my father lead the doppelgänger by the hand through the streets of Cork, down shady Shandon Street, down puddle-lined Mallow Lane. I hear his voice—it's a high voice, all treble strings—cursing all the women in his life, my ma and his ma and the God who made a world ruled by women and underpinned by money. He is gripping the hand of the little boy tightly, too tightly, but the boy does not cry or struggle or whine tho' he looks all too uncomfortable in his clothes—a too tight red coat matted with dried mud, brown breeches cut off just below the knee, stockings that were once white but now brown with dirt and dust, and leather shoes with large square buckles and loose soles that had nearly flopped their way off.

Then the vision faded like a ring of tobacco smoke. Through the haze of my thoughts I saw a square of white. A sail. A sail! A sail! My heart leapt up like a child called from some punishment back to the table to share in dessert. I called down to the poop deck.

"A sail! A sail!"

Rackam near sprinted to the bow of the deck as the men took their positions and set the sails for pursuit. We caught a strong gale of wind at southwest, and we made our way quickly toward our quarry. Now I could see 'er more clearly. She was a man-o'-war, Dutch in origin it seem'd, with a good dozen guns on deck; Rackam was intent to take her no matter what colors she flew or what arms she was arrayed with.

"Haul taut!" Rackam ordered. "Let go and haul!"

Angel was at his gun, peering intently over the rail. His eyes, like those of a cat, were bright slits, his countenance was grim. He looked back at Rackam, ready to fire at command and waiting for a signal.

"A shot of warning then!" came the cry. "Fire!"

So we fired a gun for 'er to bear down, but, instead, she continued to give us the chase. We ran at a right good rate, there being smooth water, and eventually, we outbore our consort and drew close, spotting 'er off our larboard bow. Now, at this distance, we could more easily see the condition of the ship and the state of its crew. The vessel's sails were in tatters and hung from the mast like dead vines from a tree in winter. As for the crew, there was but one figure apparent: a man of medium build, youthful in age, and dressed in brown leather pants, a white shirt with sleeves rolled up to his elbows, and a brown vest. Around his forehead was tied a red scarf. He was now standing up straight, but slightly to the side. The language of his posture had a laughing arrogance to it.

We pulled alongside the strange ship and, seizing her with grappling hooks, we prepared 'er for boarding. A roar went up from the crew. At long last, after many hard days and nights, we had captured a prize.

I could see the face of the man now. He was blond, blue eyed, and clean shaven. A smile played about his lips, which were full but cracked and somewhat whitened. He held a long wooden pipe in one hand and on occasion, and in a leisurely fashion, he would put it to his lips, take a slow drag, and then blow smoke rings into the air.

"Hoist the black flag, you sea-bitches!" cried Rackam.

The flag was flown.

Rackam, with long deliberate strides, went to the railing and hoisted a brass speaking trumpet to his lips.

"Hoy there—we fly under the black flag!" Rackam shouted.

The man said nothing, but, perhaps in way of reply, blew another smoke ring.

Rackam continued: "We would take your ship and all its goods. Do you yield, or must we broadside your vessel?"

The man met Rackam's gaze for a long moment. Then he extinguished his pipe, put it in his pocket, and drew a cutlass from a scabbard with his left hand and a pistol from a holster with his right hand. I thought he might have smiled a bit more, but the line of his mouth moved but a little.

"Take my ship if you will," said the man, whose voice was high but rough. "But honor me and humor me only in this—send your men 'gainst me one at a time so that, in single combat, I may send them one by one, one and all, to the boneyards of the depths, where, with their mothers in their company, they may discuss and make repayment for their sins in this world. Come!"

A hoot rose up from our crew.

"Come now," said Rackam. "We have lost both the patience and the taste for such sport. We are on account and in need of supplies. You are vastly outnumbered—unless you have some hidden hands on your ghost ship that remain unseen. I say again—will you yield?"

The man spat on the deck. A look of anger now crossed his face, like a gray cloud 'cross the sun.

"Overwhelm me if you will, but live with the knowledge that I, alone in number, challenged your pride and your manhood and came out the better. Ha! I thought more of the Brethren of the Coast, but clearly I was in error."

The men aboard the *Will* were now in a state of much agitation—merriment, mostly, but mixed with some anger. Who was this stranger to boast so?

"Come!" said the man. "If you are proud of your profession, attempt to take me, one after the other. Your mothers wait for you in hell!"

Rackam met the man's gaze across the railings and the water. Then the captain began to unhook his shirt to prepare for, it appeared, close and brutish combat.

First-Rate put his hand on Rackam's shoulder.

"He's not proven he can contend with the likes of you," he said. "And he's not shown that he's a man of his word. He may ambush you with fifty men if you cross over there."

"What is your counsel, then?" said Rackam.

"I'll take him," growled Angel.

"Go on, take my life!" shouted the man. "I an't happy here!"

The ships were now but a few feet apart. Angel stripped off his tan shirt. He revealed a torso that was of a goodly build and bronzed by the sun and roughed by the elements. Indeed he was built far sturdier than his opponent; in this battle he was like a castle opposing a wattle house. Angel had a pistol in one hand and a cutlass in the other. He stood at the railing for a time menacing the solitary stranger across the gap and, with much alacrity, he leapt the distance between the two ships, over the railing, over the watery divide, and onto the opposing deck.

Angel landed ten paces from the stranger, but he stumbled a bit, and that proved to be his undoing. The man was on him quicker than a shadow. With his cutlass, he disarmed Angel of his pistol and it spun away down the deck. Angel recovered his bearings to strike the man with his fists, but too late—with a crack, the man fired his pistol and at close range. Angel stood for a bit, amazement in his eyes at the speed of his defeat. He turned on his heel, walked a few paces back toward the *Will*, and then tumbled over the railing into the blue water.

"Rest in peace, sea-bitch!" the man said. "I only regret your death wasn't slow!"

Now, my blood was up. Several men were ready to mount their own challenges, Rackam chief among them, but I was the quickest of all. I leapt the expanse between our ships, a cutlass in my grip. Rackam called out to me, reached out to restrain me, but I was already in the air; all I could hear was "Revenge! Revenge!" and my ears were ringing with the sound like the belfries of churches on Sabbath.

Would that Rackam had succeeded in his efforts to restrain me! For, in truth, my skill with the sword and pistol, tho' improved, was akin to a seven year old's prowess with pen and ink.

My feet were, and not for the last time, running far in front of my head. So how should I tell this tale, and yet retain some measure of heroic drama, which, it is said, is the very soul of any story?

Should I say then that our swords rang like music? As with his attack on Angel, the stranger was on me even as I hit the deck. I had certain parries and thrusts that I had learned from Zed, and from watching men in duels and in fisticuffs. I moved through them deliberately, but with grace; I was like a dancer, going through his paces, moving sweetly to a familiar refrain. My opponent, however, was something else entirely. He reminded me of something wild, unpredictable, unchoreographed. Animals, too, have their dances and courtship movements. But they require no music, they adhere to no known rhythm.

Should I say, then, that our swords struck again and sparks flashed where the blades met? Now I faced him. I could smell his breath, which was curiously sweet—like leaves of mint and rue. Looking close at him, he had a distracting, manly beauty. He was not large, but he was stout; his countenance was stern but not unyielding, and his movements were decisive but flowing, like a strong river.

If this was a hero's tale, I would say again that our cutlasses rang once more. Ahh—this was the music for this gambol, and our hearts were pounding out the rhythms. The song was a duet of steel 'gainst steel. Cross the quarterdeck the deadly dance went, along the gangway, and down the forecastle. There I jumped down to the head and he pursued me. I could not feel my limbs. This was not due to any accident or exertion, but because of a wild emotion that built up in me as we fought on. I could hear the cheers of the men, waving and stomping their feet. No doubt Xbalanque was taking bets—and laying odds against me.

What a tale this could have been! See now how the grave sky gave way to rain, like a woman, heavy with child, when her water, after months of burden, at long last breaks. The ship on which we fought rocked as a tall sea buffeted it with much force, to and fro. Yet all this commotion, the other men, the sky and the sea, the shouts and the roars, all of this had no effect and was of no import to me. I saw and I heard and I felt only him as our swords crossed and recrossed across the ship's deck, back and forth, thither and yon. His blue eyes blazed through the rain, like harbor lights seen from the far-flung fathoms; his breathing came heavily now, and his nose curled up like some snarling passionate beast sniffing out its prey. I saw the flash of his tongue and he seem'd to me mouthing words to himself, whether prayers or curses, I knew not. But we fought on.

I parried and thrust at him, and he hacked at me; my forays were made carefully and with an economy of motion, his strokes were wild and bold. Now, I changed my stratagems for the moment and took a cruder swing, bracing my feet and putting the bulk of my weight into the attack. My blade struck his and the man, being unprepared for such a forceful cut, stumbled somewhat and released his blade. I was unable, however, to reap benefit from his misfortune; I, too, lost my bearing having unleashed too wild a stroke. I found myself tangled in loose rigging. In finding my feet once more, I lost my grip on my cutlass, which, along with my opponent's blade, slid across the deck, clattering all the way.

We both stopped short, startled by the strange turn of events. He readied his flintlock, and I brandished mine, but—alas!—the rain had wet the powder in both pistols, rendering them useless for our aggressions. Again, I paused and he did as well, and before long we found ourselves again and flew at each other, each with the mind to tear at the other with bare hands, having neither blade nor pistol to accomplish the job otherwise. Together, we tumbled to the deck.

But, in truth, this was not how the battle unfolded. Our swords never rang, and our pistols were never brought to bear. The only element of my story that's true is the tumbling. When first my foot landed on the quarterdeck of the ghost ship, I remembered my fear, remembered that my skills with side arms were suspect, and suddenly had a clear, terrifying image in my head of being gutted by a cutlass. Having lost my concentration, my heel slipped and I fell. My attacker tumbled over me, losing his footing and his weapons. We then grappled like schoolboys, tangling ourselves in the rigging, until Rackam, leaping from the *Will*, came between us and pulled us apart. We paused on either side of him, chests heaving. A length of cord was still tangled about my waist.

"It seems we are at a draw," I said.

"Don't it?" the man growled back.

Rackam put his hand on my shoulder and turned to the stranger.

"You have proved yourself," Rackam said. "Will you join us?"

The man's eyes were cauldrons of rage. Then, like the night turning to sweet morn, the fellow's demeanor changed. All that was fierce was, with alacrity, affable; it was the same sky, but brighter. He laughed and took Rackam's hand in his, shaking it with vigor.

"Prithee," I inquired, "by what name are you known?"

He drew a knife from his boot—and I stepped back, readying a defense. The man laughed and, stepping forward, he cut the rigging from around my waist, freeing me.

"Call me Read," he said.

"And call me Bonn," I replied.

chapter 17.

The morn arrived with fresh gales of wind from the west-southwest to the northwest with some small rain. The zephyrs continued to blow into the forenoon watch; accordingly we got down our fore-yard and reef'd our mainsail and our foresail. There came a great sea, and the ship took on a fair amount of water to leeward but we sailed on; as the day wore on, the weather turn'd toward moderate. In the late afternoon, a man died of the Bloody Flux and, after Zayd had a look at him, we threw the corpse overboard. No prayer was said, and the fatality contributed to the general mood of turgidity among the crew.

Read, however, seemed fill'd with much vigor, and upon establishing a hammock in the ship's hold (he took Angel's bedding spot), he immediately began to explore the ship to familiarize himself with its crew and its affairs. Having left his previous ship with little or nothing to represent himself, he challenged a baker's dozen of the crew to a game of Nine Pins. His prowess at the game was equaled only by the charm he show'd with each victory, expressing much empathy with the loser and good humor at his own success and, after the series was completed and his prizes and money collected, I dare say that I may have been the only person, save Read himself, who noticed that he won his tidy fortune without having entered any original stake.

The men, for the most part, overlook'd the loss of Angel and welcomed Read quite readily into their company, in part because the life of the sea is hard and violence and competition are necessarily expected, and also in part because of a general recognition that every hand was needed if the crew was to survive our present circumstances. A search of Read's ship had revealed nothing in the way of valuables—it was a ghost craft, with no maps, no charts, no crew, and no foodstuffs of any sort. Read offer'd no explanation but had seem'd eager to set off from his former vessel with as much haste as could be muster'd. The *Will* still needed supplies. We remained desperately on the hunt.

Short, hard squalls were common in these waters, and, after one blew through hard, agile hands were needed to adjust the rigging and reset the sails, some of which were torn and loosened from the blast. Although tired to the marrow of my bones, I answered the call. Now, rigging a schooner is rough, sweaty work—such vessels have two tall masts that rake aft, and a long bowsprit, which points out at a small angle. On the bowsprit and the jib-boom, along with five other hands, I helped set the staysails and jibs. Then, already exhausted from that work, we hung on the foremast a square sail, next, abaft the foremast, we positioned a gaff foresail and, finally, panting to catch our breath, we stretched out a gaff-topsail on the top-mast and let out a cheer, one and all, as the breeze caught it and puffed it full.

The early evening produced a change in fortune and helped secure a place in the men's hearts for Read. Xbalanque and Hunahpu were on the watch and, as in the previous day and the day before that, they had seen nothing; Read, however, employing a spyglass he had won from one of the men, spotted a sail and sounded the call from a place on the quarterdeck. It was a small craft, with one mast and a crew of three, but we boarded her anyway, as we were in such a state that no fish was small enough to throw back, even the minnows. Read leapt first onto the craft and found a store of salted beef and three kegs of rum; the latter prize was greeted by the men with as much enthusiasm as the old explorers must have greeted the discovery of the Americas. After relieving the ship's crew of their goods, we sent them on their way—Rackam told 'em to get his name right when they reported to old Governor Rogers—and then, despite the fact that the captured store was likely to last little more than a few days, we commenced a period of revelry to celebrate the find.

Read, who by appearances had consumed more than his finder's share of the kegs, climbed high into the riggings and called out to the men. Evening had come and most of the men were sleeping, tired, or drunk. At Read's voice, tho', a cheer went up. Read acknowledged the huzzahs with coruscating eyes and a swirl of his hand and began to sing a song. No, it was not so much a song as its opposite: he spoke in words shot through with appetency as storm clouds are pierced with lightning. His verses had no melody attached to them, but were, instead of tuneful, pure bolts of rhythm that sparked the heart to beat faster and fired the senses. He chanted in a high voice, but one that was clear and strong and that penetrated the night. How I wished my vocals could intertwine with that spiral of sweet sound without revealing my true gender! How I wished circumstances had not dictated that I wainscot my heart! After a verse or two other crew members joined in with abandon.

> *"Come with me*
> *We'll ride on the ink-dark sea.*
> *Don't you long to*
> *Ride or die?*
> *Fah-fah-fah-fah-fah-la-la-la"*

"Ride or die!" Read shouted, raising his mug from his place high in the rigging. "Those are words to live by—and perish by! Curse the devil, spit in the ocean, and raise a mug high you sea-dogs! Ride or die!"

"Ride or die!" went up the cry from one and all—save two: Bishop, who took an early rest, and Xbalanque, who remained snarling in the shadows, apparently enraged and ashamed that the sail had been spotted on his watch, but not by him. Hunahpu seem'd as taken as the others with the newcomer and cheer'd as lustily as any, but his twin had the look of a fierce mongrel trapped in some corner, his soup bone taken away.

I must say that, tho' I did not share in Xbalanque's particular emotions, my spirits were not as light as the ones that had floated Read to the upper riggings of the ship. I had no quarrel with Angel, one of our latest casualties, and a man, at least to me, who seem'd to have done his job with some degree of reliability and vigor. Now he was dead, and at Read's hand. I had also developed no small affection for Sugar-Apple, regardless of the shortcomings of his culinary art; since his loss, I had been increasingly aware of the fact that I had no close companions aboard the ship, no mate with whom I could unload the contents of my heart or discuss the events of my watch. I was without friends and family, bereft of a mother and a father. Who would press me to their bosom? Who would whisper to me words of affection and camaraderie? The instantaneity with which the crew had taken to Read left me with an ugly enviousness that I tried to bury deep inside myself, like some miscarriage ashamedly interred in a midnight cemetery.

And yet there were stirrings in the dirt. How different Read was from myself, how much more agile in his relationships! The men gathered 'round him as he told stories of his many scars—he had been shot seven times, by seven different shooters on seven separate occasions, and the marks on his arms, legs, stomach, and back testified to his words. I stood to the side, mute, my body unmarked, unremarkable, and utterly unrevealable. The men were under his spell, I was under a curse. Read was quick to laugh, whereas I preferred to offer only a grudging smile, and then only on occasion. He was full of anecdotes and tall tales, some true, some perhaps not so true, but all entertaining; in the opposite, I was given to merely lending an ear and not wagging my tongue.

My growing resentment for Read was bolstered by his unfettered affection toward me. Time and time again, when we spotted each other on deck, he would bellow a hearty well-met if he was far away, and, if in closer proximity, he would slap my back with manly enthusiasm or else drape one of his well-formed arms 'round my shoulders. Often he would lean close in and whisper some secret joke about one of our fellows, only for my hearing; other times he would playfully toussle my hair and give me an affable kiss on the cheek. I offer'd him no encouragement in his affections; indeed my response to him was just short of Hyperborean, and yet, like a born native of some icy land, he drove forward into my wintry blasts.

Read had also fallen in tight with Rackam, and the two

would often pass the afternoons playing chess on the poop deck. They played on a checker'd board, with pieces made of ebony and sculpted whale bone. I had a passing familiarity with chess, but no deep intimacy; with much spying, I managed soon enough to master the rules. The two were evenly matched, and won and lost games in roughly equal amounts. Read was given to launching bold attacks, slashing with his queen, capturing pieces at will with his knight; Rackam's approach was to engineer complex gambits that put his positions and pieces at risk in order to lure his opponent into a hidden trap. Both pressed attacks ruthlessly—but I sensed they both had weaknesses. After some thought and careful study, I devised an opening by which the offense could be sharpen'd if more care was placed in the defense.

The crew was hungry, thirsty, tired, and yet Read seem'd to bring with him good humor and good luck, and the stink of our former mood seem'd to blow away, as if carried by a fresh, clean wind. Three days after he join'd our company, yet another sail was spotted, and immediately the call went up to give chase. The sail was located on my watch and my cry went up simultaneously with Read's from the deck below.

As we pressed the pursuit, Rackam was of a mind to fly the Jolly Roger and thus strike fear into the hearts of our prey, perhaps spurring them to surrender. Read, who over the last few days had gained the captain's ear if not his heart, offer'd an alternative. It was early in the morn, and the sun's full light had not yet entered the sky. The ship in our sight had not yet altered her course and, by all appearances, was not yet aware of our presence. She was a formidable foe: a three-masted vessel with some twelve guns mounted on her railings, and perhaps more mounted on deck. Read argued that we use the element of surprise and that we dispatch two longboats, crew'd with seven hands each and that the men take out the opposing crew at the mounted guns before the *Will* initiated an open attack. Rackam and the crew put the plan to a vote and not a man was in disagreement, tho' I failed to raise my hand for either the negative or the affirmative and Xbalanque crept away before the tally was taken. I did not see how Bishop voted.

Our longboats were of West Indian construction, being made of two cedar trees hollowed out, with three oars on either side. First-Rate took command of one vessel and Read took possession of the second, with Rackam left behind to command the *Will*. I was of a mind to sit out the proceedings, but Read grabbed my hand, pulled me aboard his ship, and slapped my back.

"Who wants to live forever?" he said, smiling like a skull.

The morning was still gray, and a mist hung over the black water. As we set out, with only a quarter of an hour left before dawn, we immediately became aware of a difficulty. The ship we were pursuing had increased its speed and would not easily be caught. If we did not catch the ship before the sun lit the sky, our longboat would be an easy mark for her mounted guns. Read, who had been navigating the craft, pushed aside one of the crew and took a seat at the oars next to me. We rowed with all our might and quite soon our clothes were soaked with sweat. Alas! The ship we pursued was clearly on the move now and had caught a full wind.

"Row harder, sea-dogs," Read said. "Row, or this boat, come the dawn, will be our coffin."

And so we rowed. Read had a natural air of command and the growl of his voice encouraged the men. The wind must have heard him, too, for it died and then changed direction. Soon we had caught our quarry and we crept up astern. She was a fine ship, of French construction from the look of her. We scaled the sides and surprise was ours—the ship was better built than captain'd and all hands had been dozing through the night, without even a man in the masthead. We took the men when they were in their hammocks and the captain, short of stature and faint of heart, surrendered after the promise was made that no harm would come to him or to a cabin-boy of whom he had grown fond, and that in raiding his ship's stores, he would be left with at least one crate of his precious Madeira wine. The former we granted, but the latter we wholeheartedly denied, tho', once we broke open his store of spirits, we offer'd him a glass to toast the demise of his captaincy and craft.

So now, well stocked with newly captured victuals and other supplies, yet another night of revels commenced. God rested but once after shaping the heavens and earth in seven days; in the week since Read join'd our company, we had so far had occasion to take our pause twice in the same span. But, ah, if I could have but cried "Avast!" to the celebrations raging around me, the cauterwauling, the backslapping, the chorus singing, and carrying-on. We make our own time on board ships, no matter what the calendar declares: so while it was a springtime in the hearts of the other men, in my mind it was an icy December of the soul.

Even as the men celebrated, I went below deck, to a secret space that I had found insulated from sound and sight, from laughter and smiling eyes, from the pounding of dancing feet and the screech of the fiddle. I was still plagued, every month as surely as the cycles of the moon, by a bleeding between the legs and it was here, in my hidden chamber, that I washed myself, scrubbed my breeches, and stored my soiled rags. I had also transported Sugar-Apple's iron trunk here for safekeeping, but I had yet to peer inside of it to learn its secrets, for my sadness at the loss of that sweet soul was too fresh. Instead, I used it as a bench and now, gloomily, I fairly collapsed upon it. In the darkness, a decanter of spirits my only company, I put my head in my hands and I wept. The source of my melancholy, I knew not; it was a deep dark well with no bottom in sight and full of the echoes of my own voice. So I wept into this well as if I could fill it with my tears. I felt all around me, even in this enclosed space, a stiff, chill wind. I was without companions, without direction, without a ship of my own. I was alone on the waves, buffeted to and fro, driven to what sea or what shore I knew not.

It was then that I became aware of another presence in the room. I cried out for the stranger to identify himself, and then, with a laugh and not with words, he made himself known. It was Read, having left the revels above to seek some solace below. He had a bottle of Madeira wine clutched in one hand and his breath was sweet with the drink. He cozied up beside me in a cloud of spirits.

Ahhh—I could have spilt his heart's blood at that moment. There is a sanctity of private moments that should not, must not be interrupted or else all the days of our lives are spent in shallows and in misery. We require small, quiet moments set aside in our days and nights to find the true meaning of what we see and experience. Most people, based on my private observations, do without the reflective moments, and so, without them, they simply follow the footsteps of their lives, never guessing that the path they follow is truly one of chaos, a road that leads in circles, or worse, over a precipice. I, however, safeguard my moments of introspection, checking the charts and maps of my soul, as it were, before continuing on the journey of my life. But, ahh, I am not some philosopher king, given to spending his time remarking and reflecting on the metaphysical and the mysterious; I am but a mariner and I will leave such introspections to more erudite folk.

But, by my faith, it must be said that I did not welcome Read into this time I had earmarked for my soul's self-reflection. I felt an anger in me escape its bonds, like some shark, a hook caught in its jaws, that snaps a line and swims free. All the rage and resentment I had harbored was now on the loose, ready to confront he who had implemented my torment. This ship was mine; I had joined her crew long before we had come upon Read and his phantom ship. I was filled with fury that bravery, which came to me only by accident, by tumble and by heel slip, seem'd to be his natural state. He was so unlike me, and yet how much I longed to be like him! How I hated him for being what I aspired to be! The fingers of my hand, almost of their own volition, got hold of the dirk in my waistband. Now was the time, perhaps, to finish what I started on that afternoon when we first fought. How good it would be to plunge the dagger deep within his breast! How satisfying it would be to feel his hot blood spill out upon my hands!

What happened next was as unexpected as the sudden surfacing of a whale, or the happy leap of a flying fish. Before I could react, or say but a word, Read had taken me in his arms and press'd his lips to mine. My first move was to pull back, but not too far. Indeed, his lips were fuller and softer than I might have thought, and certainly not as rough. I could taste the wine on his lips and the tip of his tongue; I felt a kind of intoxication, tho' I could not say if it was from the wine or his sudden kiss. His arms were sturdy and strong and held me firmly in their grip, tho' not unpleasantly so.

But now, my sense came back to me, even as all around me seem'd to welter away. Did Read have a notion of my true gender? No, his kiss and his approach seem'd not that of a man toward a woman, but of something, perhaps, in between. What should my reaction be? At that, I'll admit, I lost hold of my thoughts, so fired was my blood at his continued embrace. But enough! I recover'd again and thought of my place on the ship—romance of whatever form would open my secret to my shipmates and leave me vulnerable to marooning or simple execution.

I shoved Read away and stood up. He considered me with a look of bewilderment—not just over my actions, but it seem'd he appeared a bit confused about his own as well. Had his kiss surprised him as well as me? A look of shame passed over Read's face, follow'd hard by his familiar affability. He clapped me hard on the shoulder, as if his previous action had been simply part of the general manly celebration occurring through the ship. Then he quickly left the small corner and I remained behind, in the darkness.

In the morning, when I began my watch, I was left to puzzle about the previous night's events. What exactly was at the core of my encounter with Read? Had his heart guessed at my true nature, prompting him to act as any man would left alone in the presence of a maiden? Or had I had too much to drink that night and imagined the closeness and intensity of his embrace? Indeed, now, in the light of the day, the kiss we shared seem'd all blurred, hard to remember and harder still to interpret.

At the end of my watch, Read was waiting for me on the quarterdeck. He smiled at me and clapped my arm with much familiarity; his touch, on this occasion, seem'd softer and less brusque than in our earlier encounters. Later, in the afternoon, as I did my part with several other hands to unfurl the mainsail, he came up beside me and spoke for a time. He also spoke to other hands on deck, generating his usual bonhomie, but, with me, it seemed he reserved particularly gentle tones of affection.

Later, as I lay in my hammock, I could not willingly go into the arms of sleep, so alarmed was I with my unexpected predicament. I could not pin down what Read's feelings were on this matter; nor could I accurately chart my own. All I did know for certain was that we were both sailing on a dangerous sea. This was a hard ship, the *Will*, as all privateer ships were. I had survived this long because I had suffered no breech in my hull; romance would cause all the water of the world to spill into me and take me to the fathoms below. This I could not allow.

But, nonetheless, as my hammock swung in the dark of my quarters, I imagined rocking back and forth in the safe harbor of his arms. I thought back once more to the unexpected sweetness and softness of his lips. I had been alone for so long, like one maroon'd on some isle, I had forgotten even what I had forgotten, I had no words for what I had lost, and now unnamable emotions and needs were flooding back into my soul. Ah— how I loved men! I had forgotten my affection for the sex, even though I had been working among them. I loved their strong, safe touch, the scruff of their faces, their thick hands, their hard eyes turning gentle with love like a high sea turning smooth. I was a maiden who had guarded my chastity and surrendered it to no one, and yet, in my dreams, more men had passed through my bedchambers than passed through that of the Queen of Sheba.

I decided I would take action. I had to get away from Read, remove the source of temptation. I would transfer my shift from starboard to larboard; while he slept, I would work, and while he worked, I would sleep and we would meet only in my dreams. Yes, this fantasy could be only fantasy. I would see the captain about my shift come the morn.

chapter 18.

At dusk I heard the singing once again. The voice, like milkweed seeds caught by some summer breeze, drifted up to my perch at the masthead. I had come here after my sleep, and now I had finished my shift and was preparing to see the captain. But the voice distracted me, and now, with the coming of the light, I was determined to identify the singer and query him about his song. As Xbalanque and Hunahpu ascended to take my place, I climbed quickly down, looking for the source of the monody.

The voice, however, was elusive. It seem'd to come from every corner, and then to fade when that corner was turn'd. It echoed across the deck and seem'd, at times, to issue from the holds below and even from the waves that crash'd 'gainst the ship's hull. I squinted my eyes and tried to follow my ears to the sound. A shadow I saw, a shade that seem'd to sing aloud; the dark shape flickered as it sang, like some ebon flame, and then, as I open'd my eyes to gaze upon it fully, the figure disappeared, like a match extinguished. I was left, then, with only the faint echo of the strange song in my ears.

"Come back!" I cried. "Who are you and what is your song? I only wish to converse, nothing more! Come back!"

But then I held my voice. In my wanderings, I had lost sight of my surroundings. I found myself in front of the captain's cabin, standing before his very door. At the sound of my voice, he had come to his doorway, and he heartily bade me to enter forthwith.

Rackam's accommodations were far short of glorious; his room was at best ten feet wide and twelve feet long, and with a ceiling that would make a tall man stoop and a short man doff his hat. His bed would have tempted old Procrustes to ready his scythe, and his sheets and blanket were in need of darning and washing or perhaps outright removal. A small mahogany desk in the corner was cluttered with various tools of navigation—a sandglass, charts, and the like. The walls of the cabin were, in the main, bare, except for two small portal windows on opposing sides, and a small painting of a mermaid locked in an embrace with a man with a fish's head and fins for arms.

Rackam himself was seated at his desk bent over a chessboard, which he focused upon with much concentration and some obvious consternation.

"By Aphrodite's arse, he has me hard-pressed," muttered Rackam.

"Read?" I said.

"The very one, the very one," said Rackam. "His play is all feral, all emotional, but beyond his visceral forays and blunt sacrifice lies a canny strategy. To underestimate him is to not give the wolf his due—such creatures being savage, and yet capable of stratagems to catch their prey. And, indeed, I am nearly caught."

I drew close and studied the board. Curious it was, that although I had studied the game for some days now, and had come to some understanding of the rules and stratagems, I had, I learned, been mistaken as to the craft that had gone into the pieces. I had previously thought the set to be made of ebony and whale bone; I now saw that one set was made of the most exquisitely crafted ivory, and no doubt purchased at a hefty price, and that the other set, in sharp contrast, was made from ordinary lead. Ahhh—I had discovered the move that had eluded Rackam. I picked up a black rook and captured a white knight. Rackam at first shook his head and then, after a minute of pondering the move, let loose a wide smile.

"An unexpected move," he said. "A wise move—a daring move. We pin his king and his opposing rook while threatening his queen. Brilliant! Had I another lifetime to ponder my move, I can say, with all confidence, this same move, no doubt, would have also naturally come to me! Ha!"

Rackam got up from his desk and flung himself on his bed.

"Now, I may take my rest," he said. "But first—what brings you to my quarters? Not to complain about the rations, I hope?"

"There is not enough food for me to complain about the quality, and the food we have lacks quality enough for me to desire additional portions."

"It is the shares you worry about then? None are to be apportioned until we accumulate a hundred thousand pieces of eight. I keep all the shares for your own protection, lest, when we hit port, your gold winds up between a slattern's legs."

"I come not to talk about finances."

"Then what then? I know you—you're not given to flapping lips and loose words. Nor am I—so we have that in common. Where do your people hail from?"

"Ireland," I said, "by way of Carolina. My father resided there, though he has lately removed."

"My father was a farmer. He raised cats, whose secretions were used in perfumery."

"What a curious occupation!"

"He had, it must be said, a streak of fatal whimsy. He was ever in pursuit of wealth, which, like a gossamer slip caught in the wind, ever eluded him. He also fancied himself a horticulturist—I believe that is the term of the day—and had been cultivating a kind of gray rose, but was unable to grow it, perhaps because of the dull climate. We had a modest estate in Colchester for a time but when my father's accounts went bankrupt, he removed to London, where he instituted a bear garden."

"A bear garden?"

"There were two others—one at Marylebone Fields, and another at Tothill Fields, Westminster. In each, a bear was chained to an iron ring fixed to a stake; butchers and others with a mind to exercise their dogs, or at the very least, have an afternoon's sport, would set loose their mongrels to worry the bear for the amusement of spectators."

"How did that venture fare?"

"Verily, it flourished—until one of the beasts broke loose its mooring and mauled the daughter of a prominent attorney. What a bloody sight! Afterward, my father was plagued by lawsuits: for money owed to a shipping concern, for arrears of payment to a linen draper, and the like. He searched for other employment—as a tobacconist, as a snuff-maker, as a soap-boiler—but guild restrictions being what they are, as a man of some years, he was never taken on as an apprentice. When he was, at last, stolen by the press-gang, he owed more pounds than he was likely to earn in five years and twenty."

"What became of the family?"

"My mother removed at last to Whitefriars, a monastery that, by custom, serves as a sanctuary for debtors. I will not trouble you to describe the hell in which she descended in order to make our accounts right, but it killed her, even before they put her in the ground in an unmark'd grave. After that sad event, I, at last, took to the ocean."

"And your father?"

"He died at sea, I think. But when we amass our hundred thousand, I will build myself a comfortable home, and I will grow a whole garden of gray roses. And once I have that house, and that garden, I'll clip me a bushel of gray roses every week and place them above my fireplace! How does Jamaica sound to you as a place to make one's retirement?"

"You won't need a fireplace in Jamaica."

"But I will build me one nonetheless! And I'll chop wood every day to keep it burning!"

Rackam laughed.

"Let us get a head start on our relaxation," he said. "A game of chess, perhaps?"

So we stopped speaking and started playing. Or perhaps we were speaking through our playing. Locked in combat with him, I felt we were continuing our conversation, but in a differing form. His pawns were anecdotes, his opening gambits were monologues, his sacrifices seemed, to me at least, to be confessions of some sort. With every move, I felt our minds were in communication, not just about the stratagems of chess, but about other things as well. Our game lasted for what could have been hours, and soon, my advantage was overwhelming—he had but a king and two knights and I had my king and two queens.

He considered the board, both hands propped up behind his head. He stood up, paced about the cabin, and sat down again. He reached for one piece, drew his hand back without touching it, reached for another, and then pulled back again.

"You are . . . formidable," he said. "Before you and Read, I'd not been beaten at chess, nor even challenged. But ahh— here's the move to foil your plans!"

And then a curious moment: his eyes flickered from the board for a moment and locked with mine briefly before settling back on the board. What did I sense in his eyes? Embarrassment? Surprise? These were all uncharacteristic emotions for so worldly a mariner. And then I realized that he had been reacting to something he saw in my own eyes—that, almost due to a force outside my will, I had, for all this time, been fixing the captain with a look of the most intense longing. There are moments in life when one feels one's emotions play nakedly on one's face but cannot by any means control them; in part one wants desperately to hide whatever feelings are on display, but, in another part, one wants them to be seen for some reason only the Divine Providence greatly understands. I struggled to compose myself but found that I could not. Was I some lovesick maid? No! I was a sea-dog like all the rest!

I jumped to my feet.

"Must you go now?" said Rackam. "'Tis your move!"

"I need a few winks before my next watch," I said, turning quickly to the door of the cabin. "I have to go."

I left the cabin. Were there holes in my ruse? Had I let my guard down overmuch? My original purpose forgotten— asking for a switch from the starboard shift to the larboard— I went immediately to the lower decks to get my bearings and consider the strange signals and statements I had been presented with that day. I did not return to my quarters, knowing that Xbalanque would be getting off his shift soon, and I had no wish to have truck with him. Instead, I went to one of my newest hideouts: the sail room. This was the area where the spare sails were folded and stored; the light was dim and the quarters were tight, but the area was quiet and clean. Ahh—here was a place where a man could get some solace.

Alas, not tonight. When I arrived at my place of refuge, Read was already there before me, waiting for my arrival.

chapter 19.

The room had been dark when I entered; the sail room, by custom and regulation, is kept in such a state, with no lamp lit, to protect the sails from any spark or conflagration. Suddenly, an oil lamp's glow came before my sight—I heard the striking of the match, smelled the sulphur—and its illumination spilled onto Read's face. Ahhh, his visage! In this light, what had seemed rough and tumble before now took on a kind of beauty, like some rugged peak illuminated by a morning sky. His blue eyes, which seemed hard as gem stones before, now reminded me of something fragile and fair, robins' eggs perhaps. I started to speak, but I found I could say nothing save in my high-pitched maiden's voice, and so I said nothing.

Read too, said nothing, and betrayed little with his expression. He neither smiled nor frowned. He took a step forward and I gasped a little. He paused and set down his lamp, a safe distance from a stack of mizzen-top sails. Then he quickly closed the distance between us 'til he was standing so close I could feel his exhalations on my face.

Read was breathing hard, as if he had just completed some task of physical exertion, as if the simple act of walking toward me and standing close was a labor of Hercules. Even in the dim light, I could see that color had come into his cheeks, and his broad chest heaved like a swimmer surfacing after long moments in the deep fathoms. His eyes did not look directly at me at first, but were focused mostly on the floor, and he shifted his feet a bit from side to side as if he could not get his bearings.

Now, he took my right hand in his left and he brought our clasped hands up to his face, almost touching his lips but not quite. He closed his eyes and his breathing steadied a bit, and his feet stopped shuffling and found their stance. His hand was surprisingly gentle; he held me firmly, but not too hard, and his hands were not as calloused and rough as I might have imagined them but rather soft and small. Now, with his free hand, he stroked my left cheek a little and then held my face. Now I found myself experiencing the most intense emotions. My own breathing was arrested, and I could feel a hot flush arise in my face. I wanted to turn and run, but found that I could not move. Read's eyes looked up from the floor and met mine. His gaze was steady now, like a ship running under full sail under a strong wind. There was silence in the room save for the pounding of an immense drum, which I soon recognized was the sound of my own startled heart.

Read leaned forward and kissed me; at first his lips barely grazed mine, like some doctorbird buzzing 'round a blossom; then his lips found mine again and his arms drew me in entirely, and he kissed me with passion and force and almost a kind of desperation, the way a man forgets all manners and tears at food, having been denied victuals for a lengthy period. His lips were hot and his cheek was smooth; I would not have expected a man who fought so fiercely and lived so roughly to have such supple skin.

I must say, at that time, I gave no thought to safeguarding my virtue and modesty, so caught up was I in the emotion of the moment. Ahh, the fire in my blood had been stoked and now was raging in a manner that was most uncontrollable. I felt as if I was between worlds—the land and the sea, between maiden-hood and manhood, between chastity and the devil's sin. I was floating on air, like some spirit, the winds of chance blowing me where they would. He embraced me and I stroked him in turn and my hands began to explore the mysteries of masculinity, the secrets of which had haunted me these many years.

But what was this? As my hands explored his body as eagerly as any conquistador ever explored the Caribbean, I came across an unexpected region. Now, tho' I had made a study of men, I nonetheless lacked firsthand experience, as it were. And yet, based on the instinct given to us by the Creator who resides in the blessed realm of heaven with his host, I had some notion that something was not as it should have been.

I stepped back a pace, out of his embrace.

His look at first was one of concern, and then of understand-ing turning toward mirth.

"Come now, my sweet. Be not concerned that the physical commerce in which we are engaged is, by some means, unnatu-ral, or in deviance with the laws of the Divine Providence."

Read opened his canvas shirt, grasped my hand, and placed it on his breast. I then had confirmation of what I had suspected, for his bosom, hidden from the eyes by the bulk of his clothes was, when touched, rounded and full, and not unlike my own.

His exhibition of battle scars for the other men, in which he had shown much but clearly revealed little, was part of an exuberance that served to distract from what I saw now—Read was so forthright about what he wanted that he had convinced the world to take him for who he wanted to be. I was shocked, but somehow not surprised. That is to say, the revelation that he was a woman was certainly a momentous thing, in that it would perhaps change the relationship that existed between us, but at the same time I saw how it laid the groundwork for all that had passed thus far. There is a secret connection that exists among members of my sex, contained in soft glances, muted laughter, and flitting hands. We learn to conceal our feelings and thoughts from the prying eyes of men, reserving our communications for one another. The sweet songs of birds may be only breakfast music to some, but to the creature of the air, it may be poetry, conversation, and the very substance of information. Now, with our disguises pierced, I saw that, all along, Read and I had communicated and connected as only two of the fairer gender could.

"Now you know my secret," she said. "There is nothing to keep us apart. We are as opposite in gender as Adam was from Eve, Orpheus from Eurydice, or Antony from his Cleopatra."

She kissed me hard again, and, by my faith, the sensation was not unpleasant and, in the unreflective instant, seem'd far from unnatural. What was the measure of a man? I wondered. Was sex to be found in attitude or in flesh? For, in truth, Read was more of a man, and less of a woman, than any man or woman I had ever met. And yet, to some degree of truth, the opposite was also accurate. But, ahhh, I am no philosopher, just a mere mariner, and such questions of the heart and head are perhaps best left to others with schooling in the arts of metaphysics and the like. So again I stepped back.

"Are you not pleased?" said Read.

Now she had to be told my secret. This time I grasped her hand and brought it to my bosom. She smiled at first and then, as realization set in, her blue eyes widened. She stumbled back a bit, and fell upon a pile of sails.

"Like Actaeon when he came across fair-limbed Diana bathing in the wood," I said, "I fear we have both gazed upon that which our eyes should not have witnessed."

"What is this tale you tell?"

"Actaeon was a youth who, in the ancient tales of Ovid, came across Diana bathing in her secret pool."

"I know this tale, tho' I have never read it. The goddess, in her fury, changes the boy into a stag and sends his own hounds after him in the chase."

"Yes—and Actaeon is ripped, flesh from bone, a meal for dogs."

Read smiled. "But we are two Dianas here. And there are no dogs in sight."

At that, I smiled, and so, too, Read began to laugh with much gusto and I joined along with her. She pulled me down to the sails with her and we held each other and lost ourselves for the moment in the frivolity and jolliness of our situation. She kissed me first on the forehead, and then on each cheek, right and then left, and then she pressed her mouth to mine. We lingered in that kiss for some time and then we stared into each other's eyes, wondering what would come next.

It was then that Rackam, who had been in the shadows watching throughout this entire encounter and had seen all and now understood all, chose to step out of the dark and into the oil-light.

chapter 20.

Sleep took my hand, leading me away from shore and wading into a sea of imaginings. A dream I had then, one that was turbulent and filled with ill portents. Many questions I had, about Read, about Rackam, and, most certainly, about my own future on board the *Will*. Now that my secret was known, and Read's as well, I remember'd with some foreboding the clauses and regulations that were contained in the contract I had signed when I first join'd the crew; I thought, as well, about what punishments I might soon endure, with drowning, marooning, and execution by pistol among their number. It was not death I feared, but disgrace. No, perhaps that does not quite capture it—I dreaded revelation, the dissemination of information that would separate me from my fellows, and permanently brand me as the other, despite all my hard work. But how could it be avoided now? All these questions and quandaries floated about my sleeping head, like dead things in fetid water, but soon I was plunged into the fathoms below, drowning in the currents of my own mind, the concerns and queries of my day left far behind on the surface.

I woke up to the sound of song. The words were different, the melody altered, and the voice lower—but something in the essence of this tune reminded me of Ma, and I had a clear vision of being suckled at her breast. The sweet amen smell of mother's milk was in the air. I arose from my bed. I knew not whether it was night or day or what the watch was; my cabin was dark, and as I left the lower decks to go to the main deck, all was bathed in a half-light that could have signaled either dawn or dusk. The soft melodious voice that I had heard on previous occasions echoed across the quarterdeck. The music seem'd to have no words. It was a song in a series of clear and direct tones, each one bright and full. Then, in a shift as subtle as leaves turning from summer's green to autumn's tan, the melody seem'd to reorganize, and words were made distinct, but in a language I could not recognize.

What were the words? The music conjured images of infidel ships from the African coast, crew'd with turban'd men with dark brows and serene eyes. I saw bright blades falling and rising again, soaked in crimson. I saw gold-filled Spanish galleons broken open like eggs. I saw flames reaching up into the night like drowning swimmers as coastal Caribbean cities burned. Did I imagine these things or were they wrapped up in the true import of this song? Hard as I would listen, this song seem'd to have no theme, or its particular meaning seemed always just beyond my reach. But what things I saw in it nonetheless! And what sadness and sweetness and violence was wrapped up in its cryptic strains! I followed the sound, determined, this time, that I should uncover the identity of the singer. It spoke to my soul—so intertwined with loss and conflict—and now Hark! I saw a long shadow at the forecastle, and the shade was lost in the ecstasy of performance. Drawing closer, I saw that the singer was the ship's surgeon, Zayd. He was kneeling on a rug, his eyes bowed and his hands open at his side. He was stripped to the waist, and I have never seen before or since a man of his exquisite musculature. His muscles were lean and black—a blackness so dark, he seemed to be cut out of the night sky and poured into human form. Indeed, the lights of the sky were reflected on his shiny, smooth muscles, as if his very being was a map of the constellations.

Zayd hardly moved, but seem'd as still as any figure ever carved in granite. He moved his hands up, gradually up, as if reaching toward heaven, and the starlight danced on his muscles in a dazzling show of white fire. It was a cool night, and yet his skin was slick with sweat, and tendrils of steam seemed to rise from his body, curling upward like fallen angels fighting their way back into Paradise. There was a rich, musky scent in the air as well, like pimento logs burning in fire, or some grand soap purchased at an Oriental shop. It was an aroma that both awakened the mind and quieted the nerves.

Gazing upon Zayd's form, I was filled with the most curious sensations and emotions. Although I had not exerted myself, I felt my breathing grow labored, as if I had been in the midst of a long sprint. Next, I felt a warmth spread from my bosom throughout my body, as if I had drunk a pot of warm tea spiked with Jamaican rum. My body felt buoyant, as if it was ready to cut its tether to the earth and ascend to the celestial realm. My hands became small birds and they fluttered about my body, alighting here and there, but never perching for long.

An enormous unnamable need welled up in me, like a giant dark wave taking shape off a battered coastline. I wanted to cry and laugh and scream and so, caught between actions, I was near-paralyzed.

Still the music continued, and its fashion and form were both sacred and profane. There were words and no words, like a monk's chant that perhaps once had definition but now has only meaning. Images and sounds and feelings came to me and I felt as if I was being carried, once again, into the visions that come with slumber, only now I was caught in a waking dream. The sharp smell of a lemon rind, a line of black ants marching across an open palm, a severed finger in a pewter bowl. The images were meaningless to me, and yet filled me with terror. The slick muscularity of a horse's haunch, the burble of a mountain stream passing over rocks, a girl's tongue licking the edge of a sword, the smell of barbershops. Enough! I wanted to escape these things, but I felt confined, grown over, like something knotted in the trunk of an old oak. And still the dread tune continued: the chill that comes with an approaching rain before the first drops fall, the silence between the flash of lightning and the crash of thunder, a black ship riding on a tall dark sea.

Suddenly, Zayd paused and his eyes met mine.

"So at last we talk," he said.

"We have conversed before."

"Only in passing."

"What is the song you sing?"

"Do you know my song?"

"I would not have asked if I did."

"The melody is an old one from my homeland. The words are verses that I have fashioned, and they tell the story of Laurens De Graff."

"The greatest privateer of them all! What do you know of him?"

"He was, as you say, supreme in these waters. Where others commanded single ships, he led a fleet; twenty and two ships at its height, and three thousand men."

"Three thousand!"

"Aye, and fully armed. On one expedition, De Graff led a force of privateers—Dutch, French, even English and Irish Jacobites, supporters of James the Second of England who had, at that time, recently been deposed from England. De Graff set upon the eastern tip of Jamaica, landing at Cow's Point and ravaging the island. He made a feint toward Port Royal, and when the English sent troops to meet him, he used the opportunity to return to his vessels and escape, the holds of his ships heavy with loot. It was a magnificent operation, and no privateer has staged its like since."

"Does your song sing of what he looked like? His flashing blue eyes? His blond hair, like the locks of some god?"

Zayd laughed.

"Is there some hidden jest in my words?" I asked.

"De Graff was born in Holland, but his hair was not blond, rather dark and woolly, like my own. His eyes were not the blue of the sea, but the black of the night. He suffered in servitude on the Canary Islands under the Spanish before winning his freedom and joining the brethren of the coast."

"But the stories . . ."

"The stories are untrue. The Spanish, the English, and the French spread tales so the slaves still under their control would not be inspired to revolt. If De Graff's true identity were known, would not the eyes of every slave look out to the ocean and see freedom bobbing on the waves? Would not the hands of every bondsman reach for a blade or a blunderbuss? Would not the hearts of every servant beat the rhythms of revolution? Surely I need not explain such things to you. Surely you, too, once saw liberty in the sails of every ship you spied from the shore."

"What do you mean?"

"*De Griff* is an old term for a person of three-quarters African ancestry. Is there not some of *De Griff* in you as well?"

"W-w-why . . . why do you say such things? How do you know such things?"

I did not wait for his answer. And I do not know why I did what I did next. By my faith, I do not even know how I did it, as my body seem'd entirely out of my control. With Zayd's song ringing in my ears, I crossed the quarterdeck and walked straight to the captain's cabin. I paused not even to knock— I opened the door and walked in. Rackam was in bed, caught in some dreamless sleep, and sat up startled when I entered, a cutlass in his right hand.

"I have been considering our previous encounter," said Rackam. "Indeed, no sleep worthy of the name has come to me tonight while I wrestle with its meaning."

I said nothing in response.

"Heaven's work is truly extraordinary," said Rackam, "that two such creatures as yourselves should be on board a single ship."

"Perhaps there are more of us than even we can imagine," I said.

"Perhaps."

"Perhaps all the ships at sea, and those at dock as well, are teeming with us."

"Perhaps, but I think not. 'Tis a thing, even with this double proof, hardly to be believed, except that it is true."

"On the contrary," I said. "'Tis only common sense that two hands in similar circumstances would find each other and, having been located, investigate each other's natures."

This time, Rackam was silent.

I noticed that on the table to his side, our chess game was still laid out, and it was my move. His last turn had put me in a tight position. But, after contemplating the positions open to me, I formulated a response.

I took a step forward and moved my piece.

"Queen to king seven," I said.

Then, Rackam, without considering the board or making a move in response, sprang up from his bed with great violence, toppling the entire board and all the pieces upon the floor of his cabin. He took me into his arms roughly and kissed me hard; so filled with violence was his embrace that my lips bled, for he press'd them so, and I tasted blood in my mouth. I pushed him back and wiped the blood from my mouth and soon discovered it was not mine, but his. In my passion, and I know not how, I had opened up a gash on his cheek, which now ran red and unchecked.

Memory, not modesty, prevents me from detailing the ecstasies that followed these initial embraces. But I would have it known, even if the light from that first flame has dimmed in my mind's eye, neither time, nor distance, nor lovers since, have cooled that fire's heat. My life-long study of men, conducted, up to that point, for the most part, from afar, and with some sense of dispassion, reached a new stage, and, I thought, some sort of a conclusion, tho' I would later learn it was yet another beginning. There is a kind of commingling of souls that takes place when the flesh is join'd, or so it seemed to me in the blossom of my experience, which I now, with age, know to be the romantic illusion of youth. Like a dance between two partners, or a duet of musical instruments, or the planets in measured orbits 'round one another, one seems to sense another soul for the first time, and in the darkness in such transactions, one sometimes seems to hear the other without speaking. Language peels away, like the skin off a grape, and the sounds given to us before the Divine Providence granted us language—the sighs and grunts, the exhalations and moans—suddenly carry with them tides of meaning, as if they were the form of language themselves.

Those who have progressed past the virginal to the knowledgeable know that in all but perhaps the case of True Love, if that poetic thing exists, the real second self we sense in the bedchamber is but our first self counted twice. We create the perfect partner, and we have congress with it, we imagine that person's soft thoughts, and we accommodate them, we read meaning into the imagined self's touch, when really the meaning in question is just one of our own imagination. We close our eyes when we kiss, I think, so even as we love solid flesh, our souls can dream the true love of our hearts into being.

There is a story that Ovid tells—and that great man relays the myth better than this rendition by his poor servant—the tale of Tiresias, a man who, while following the flights of bees and birds, comes across two copulating snakes and ventures to kill them both but, having launched the blow and failed in his double murder, finds himself transformed by the beasts into a woman. After his seventh year of womanhood, desiring to return to his former sex, he strikes the snakes again, and finds himself turned back into a man.

One day Jupiter, king of the gods, idle and drinking ambrosia, launches into a discussion with jealous Juno, herself blissful with divine nectar. In Jupiter's reckoning, as the conversation went, women invest but half the labor in the affairs of the flesh, and yet receive more than their fair share of pleasure, which, by his calculus, was numbered at nine tenths. Juno mocked his godly math, and declared that only a soul who had lived in a woman's body could truly understand that gender's particular condition and pleasures.

Jove, laughing, announced a solution: he called for Tiresias to be found and the question put to him. The mortal, soon discover'd, and perhaps ignorant of the sad fate of humans who come in the middle of divine contests and arguments, readily presented his answer: woman, he declared, received nine tenths of the pleasure when it came to matters of the flesh. Hearing this, angry Juno struck the mortal and blinded him. But kingly Jupiter, winner of the wager, took pity on unlucky Tiresias and, tho' blinded forever, granted him the gift of insight—and made the events of the future known to him, as if he could see them with his failed eyes. And so that story ends, tho' it continues in other ways—it is Tiresias who first predicts Narcissus' tragic fate.

Even as John enter'd me, deep as powder and ball rammed in a musket, I thought of my fair Read and I remembered Ovid's ancient tale.

chapter 21.

The days passed by like white-winged sea-birds; all through the afternoons, I longed for the evenings; I counted the whistles 'til the end of my watch, prayed for the sun to find its place in the horizon's bed so I could, once again, find my place between my darling Rackam's sheets. By my troth, I had never felt more entirely like a man than when I lost my maidenhood. A new vigor coursed through my veins, and my ship's chores were performed more readily. I felt more than the equal of all around me now that the mysteries of their gender had been revealed to me in intimate form. Even when my love was not immediately in my sight—and from my perch on the masthead I saw most and heard much—I could taste him on my tongue like a just-completed meal; I could smell his heavy man's musk on my fingers, see his dark gray eyes in my own mind's eye. I would, at times, open my mouth to catch the sea-spray and imagine it was sweat licked from his chest; by my faith, salt never tasted so sweet.

Yet there was a cloud on his brow. He would not discuss it and he would not make any grim portents known to me, but I could sense he was carrying with him some burdensome concern. In our games of chess, he would press his advantage and then grow distracted, as if he was engaged in other games in his head. He exploded into sudden anger one morn at Poop over some petty indiscretion; he later grew calm, and threw an affable nod at Poop as if by way of explanation or apology, but his outburst, however brief, was a striking break of character. I wondered if his distress bore any relation to Read, but Rackam refused to speak of the matter, feeling it best to continue as before and to regard Read as another sea-dog and member of the crew. I, too, decided to renew my camaraderie with Read and to carry on as before.

One night after our encounter in the sail room I walked up to Read as he leaned over the railings on the quarterdeck and looked out into the ink-dark sea. Sea-foam sprayed our faces, the stars effervesced overhead, and an invisible night wind tickled the hair on our arms. The deck was quiet save the sound of nature. I found my place beside him.

"There were more weevils than usual in the biscuits this evening," I said.

"Close your eyes and pretend they are cashew nuts."

"And that works for you?"

"No," said Read, "for I have a supreme distaste for the cashew nut, and, if I had to partake of one or the other, I would prefer to eat a weevil. But it may work for you."

So we leaned into the dusk together, flank to flank, and, after a time, Read abruptly turned away.

"I must take my leave," he said. "I'm set to work the deck on the morning watch."

"One question before you go . . ."

"What?"

"Oh, 'tis nothing. Forgive me, and go your way."

"What? Out with it!"

"'Tis a strange sea malady: every month, I bleed."

"Where?"

"Between the legs."

Read laughed loudly, and continued for a great while.

"Why do you laugh? Is there a simple cure? Some medicine?"

"I have heard of women who take Manus Christi—a mixture of powdered pearls, gold leaf, sugar, rose water, and the yolk of an egg—to induce such bleeding. But I have heard of none that have either sought, or succeeded, in doing the opposite—in curing it!"

"Why would a woman want such an affliction?"

"'Tis the curse of Eve, my friend. In Germany, they call it a visit from the red king; in France, they say one has gone to Montrouge; in your Ireland, they say a lady is in season. 'Tis nature's way of saying you are ready to bear children, and thus must bear the burden of all women, brought down by Eve's ill-advised apple bite in Eden."

"I am with child then?"

Read laughed again.

"No, but if the bleeding stops for more than a month, then that is a sign you are with child."

"What should I do?"

"Do what I do. Stuff rags between your legs to absorb the discharge—tho', by observation, unless you have grown a new organ, I see you are doing that already. Two things more: when the bleeding comes, clean yourself in the head, and throw the soiled rags overboard with the other refuse. And, lest the red king visit you unexpectedly, wear black breeches."

With that, Read kissed me on the forehead, and strolled away, whistling.

*T*he time had come to open Sugar-Apple's trunk. I went down to my secret space below deck, taking care that I was not observed or followed. I removed the shroud I had placed over the truck and found—and should I have been surprised on a ship full of felons?—the lock had already been picked. Perhaps Xbalanque or one of many of the rogues on board had already gotten to the contents. I open'd the trunk. The lid was heavy, being made of iron; the rusted hinges groaned like sick grandparents as I pushed the top back. I peered inside. The trunk was filled with papers.

Whatever thief had peeked in first was no doubt disappointed—few of this lot could read. I began to sift through the contents. The story that they told was this: Sugar-Apple, in his other life, had been a record keeper in County Cork. From the appearance of things, he had been a privateer long before he took to the seas—transferring lands held by wealthy families to poorer ones by altering wills, deeds, and the like. Some of the funds no doubt ended up in Sugar-Apple's own pocket. There were other records in the trunk as well—he seem'd to have grabbed what he could before he was run out of town—including papers documenting the arrival and departure of ships and what cargo they transported in their holds and so on.

A few of the documents made reference to the DeDanann Land Holding Company, the business venture that had supposedly helped make my father rich. The company's real estate was primarily in Jamaica. DeDanann, judging by the records, had been operating for years, primarily with the funding of wealthy backers in Ireland.

It suddenly struck me. Da had probably never been bankrupt. He had merely been relocating his money. His whole life was a swindle.

If I found Da in Jamaica, there would be a reckoning.

*A*nd so the days passed. We sailed the waters of the Caribbean and made our way to the current off the coast of Jamaica, and yet, tho' we drew close, we did not take port. We had gone some days without taking another prize and, once again, our supplies had diminished and were in sore need of replenishing. There were several scuffles among the sea-dogs and Zayd kept busy dressing wounds and bandaging them. After a time in which the crew did much speculation as to the nature of our next endeavor, Rackam called the lot together on the quarterdeck and let them know his mind: his boast, made in the bar of New Providence, was true, and he did have a great prize in mind, which carried with it great risk. He was of the opinion that we should lead a raid on the Madrid galleon.

"Yes, there is a Madrid galleon—'tis more than rumor and myth, it is a real thing, and, indeed I have indications of its course," said Rackam. "Before, it might have well have been a lie, so difficult a task is it to make its capture. But now we have sail'd into desperate times, and, in such days, hard things must be attempted. So what say you?"

At this announcement, there was much murmuring among the men; First-Rate raised an eyebrow and seem'd to embark on making calculations in his head. Read, for his part, caught my eye, smiled, and winked—he was clearly ready for action, no matter the peril.

Bishop, however, gave a loud snort at the announcement.

"'Tis a mad attempt, and ill advised," he said.

"Why say you?"

"The black galleon is a vessel of the first rate, said to boast a hundred to a hundred and twelve guns, with fighting men numbering eight hundred or more."

"The numbers are well known to me."

"She has never been taken, tho' bigger ships than ours have tried."

"What you say is true."

"There have been seven attempts, if reports are to be believed—all have met with failure."

"Verily, you say."

"We are but seventy souls," concluded Bishop. "I say again: this is a mad attempt and will meet with ruin."

There was, following Bishop's statement, much talk and debate among the men about the correct course of action and the merits of each choice. I thought briefly about Rackam's father, and his flights of fatal whimsy, but said nothing. As the discussion continued around me, Read stepped forward and, putting two fingers to his mouth, let loose an ear-rending whistle that caused many of the men to cry out, startled, and prompted Poop, who was standing nearest to Read, to yelp and wince in discomfort and cover his ears.

Read addressed the crew in a strong voice.

"A fine idea has been put forward," Read said. "Men of the *Will*—who will follow?"

Several of the men called out in the affirmative, but others were silent and some shook their heads.

"It is a mad attempt," said Bishop.

"Madness is required for such times! The good Governor Lawes expects us to restrain ourselves, and to hold to smaller prey. No doubt, in these waters, every sloop and schooner will be manned by agents of his employ."

"So with the minnows guarded, we attack the whale?" said Bishop. "The Madrid galleon is the prize of prizes. It carries, below its decks, the treasure of the New World—the bulk of the gold and silver brought forth from the mines of South America for this year."

"It is precisely because the galleon has never been taken that it will be vulnerable. It is because the Governor would never imagine that we would take the risk that we should try."

"It cannot be done!" boomed Bishop.

"Hear me now!" said Read. "By some coincidence, the captain and I are on accord with this plan. I tell you this: the ship on which I rode came within a brace of shakes of taking the galleon last year, had the passengers aboard been but bold enough. Instead, one by one, they turned against each other and only I survive. I have seen that craft, I have seen her crew, and she can indeed be taken, by men that are bold in their boots. With one strike we can make our fortunes and, even if we fail, we can establish our names. So what say you all? Ride or die!"

At such rousing words, all aboard, save Xbalanque and Bishop, called out "Aye!" and raised their weapons above their heads to support the cheer. Rackam, much pleased by Read's words on his behalf, strode toward him and clapped him on the back.

So we resolved to remain in the waters off the north coast of the island of Jamaica at a certain latitude and longitude that Rackam's spies indicated would be the route taken by the Madrid galleon. The hands who staffed the masthead were particularly informed that the galleon would fly a black sail and would have a wide hull, like a vessel pregnant with another. Rackam instructed each and every man aboard the *Will* to be of increased vigilance for men-o'-war dispatched by Governor Lawes set sail to capture us and see us hanged.

"The good Governor Lawes no doubt has the gallows built and the nooses tied," said Rackam. "I have no plans or desires to see my life's journey conclude on the end of a rope in the Palisadoes. So stay vigilant all!"

We sail'd in an easterly direction, in close proximity to some of Jamaica's main cays and natural harbors. We passed Negril Port, where the water is so clear one can see the sea floor, even at several fathoms deep; we glided through the blue-green waters of Montego Bay, where the palm trees on the shore seemed to dance and wave like friendly maids; and we continued past Platform Bay, where the breeze carried the smell of flowers and fruit, making the mouth water and the heart sing.

As we sailed, I noted that Read and Poop, quite against my expectations, had struck up a kind of friendship. The two were assigned the same watch and so spent days and nights together; they combed and plaited each other's pigtails, they mended and washed each other's clothes, they took meals together in the mess, and they slung hammocks together side by side. This was not seen as at all unusual; most of the men had partners in such fashion. Sea-life was long and hard and it was borne more readily in pairs. Still, in Read and Poop, I sensed a closer tie than most. And because I knew of Read's secret, I wondered to myself the true extent of their connection.

Curious, I put the inquiry to him as he cleaned a deck-gun one afternoon. Read had taken command of the cannon that had formerly been assign'd to Angel and had, as gun-head, appointed Poop as the second member of the squad. They were an odd pair—Read in all his blunt, coarse beauty, with his strong words and bold moves, and Poop, pale and most times silent, reluctant to act, given to remaining in the shadows.

When I asked Read about Poop and whether there were any boundaries attached to their friendship, Read just laughed, throwing his head back and grabbing his belly in his mirth. He then hugged me and kissed me on both cheeks. Finally, after a wink, and without saying anything by way of explanation, he turned his back to me and returned his attentions to his cannon.

Xbalanque, from his post on the masthead, had also taken note of the connection between Read and Poop, and I heard him whispering sly poison about it to Bishop, who, word had it, was offended that the two had dared to take possession of Angel's gun. Bishop was also stung that, tho' he was the more senior member, Read's words had managed to have more sway with the crew. Already, by nature, a cruel man, he began to bark orders at Read with an increasing ferocity. His glances at Read seethed with anger, and, when he addressed him on whatever matter, he made no attempt to disguise the disdain in his voice.

Although Bishop was a giant of a man, well muscled and frightening to behold, with his peeled face and many scars from combat, Read betrayed no intimidation. Whenever he was addressed by Bishop, he smiled; whenever he was given a task by Bishop, no matter how difficult, he laughed; whenever Bishop's name came up in conversation, even when Bishop was within earshot, Read bellowed with jocularity.

"Let him challenge me, if he dares," Read told me. "'Tis not size that makes the warrior, but skill."

Indeed, Read's prowess as a fighter was well known throughout the *Will*. All had been impressed by his sword-work when I dueled him that day on his phantom craft. Since then, I had seen him wrestle to the ground men twice his size and I once witness'd him, using a broom handle, disarm two drunken crewmates fighting with cutlasses. He was quick and deceptively strong, and, word was, an exceptional pistol shot as well.

"Did you slay those aboard your previous vessel as you suggested?" I asked him one day as we leaned against the rails, breathing in the fresh wind off the Jamaican coast.

"Where did you learn that tale?" said Read.

"Why from you, you fool! In your address to the men, you said your former crew dispatched themselves through combat, with only you remaining."

"That is a tale to tell children to frighten them," said Read.

"Then what happened?"

"My previous ship, it could be said, contain'd those who would take advantage."

"I see your lips moving but cannot, by my troth, figure your meaning."

Read smiled, but there was a shadow on his face.

"My dear Bonn," he said, "I am who I am and will brook no evidence to the contrary. There are those, aboard ships at sea, who would treat a woman as a woman, even if she, by any reasonable standard, is of the opposite sex. But I have means of defense and I put them to use. But—ahhh—this is all a horror I cannot tell just yet. When we have made our fortunes, and we sip coconut milk on some Caribbean shore in our dotage, then will I spill the secrets of my youth to you, and you will respond in kind."

Read continued to laugh off Bishop, and Bishop, his attempts foiled, began to watch Poop more closely. Poop, being of a tremulous nature, became all the more nervous and excitable with a watchful, baleful eye focused on him. Bishop, sensing at last that his pressure was resulting in some ill effect, began to follow Poop all the more, like some wolf stalking the smallest member of a flock of sheep, or a no-see-um buzzing 'round the ears on a sweaty day.

Bishop pushed on in his efforts at annoyance and intimidation. He critiqued Poop harshly as Poop scrubbed the deck, tho' the deck, after his efforts, was nearly like a mirror; Bishop hovered around Poop as he folded the sails, berating him to repeat each attempt again and again until Poop grew flustered and tearful. And when Poop reacted thus, Bishop berated him directly, attacking not only his skill at tasks but his very person, assaulting the boy's physique, which was slight, and his general lack of comportment.

After such sessions, Read would take Poop aside and whisper words of encouragement in his ear. Read also began to teach him the skills of fighting—the pistol, the dagger, and the sword—but Poop seem'd a reluctant student, with little natural ability in the martial arts. When Read pushed too hard with his training, Poop would retire to a small dark corner below decks, cover his ears with his hands, close his eyes, and shake, as if afflicted with some sudden chill.

"Get up!" Read would tell his charge. "You must become a fighter!"

"Perhaps it's not his nature," I said. "Perhaps it's not in him."

"None of us know what is in us," Read replied, "until our guts are spilled."

One afternoon, after a full hour in which Bishop mocked Poop's manhood in full sight and hearing of other crew members, his insults raining down like a plague of frogs, something in the lad snapped. A small dagger—one that he had used in his training sessions with Read—found its way into his hand. Bishop, seeing the flash of metal, snarled and drew his own weapons, a cutlass in each hand. The two circled each other, and the crew gather'd 'round to witness the slaughter. I watched this transpire from the masthead and began to scale down as quickly as I could, with a mind to save Poop before he was hacked to pieces by the larger, stronger man. Read, I knew, was below deck and so it would be up to me to take some action.

But I was too late. First-Rate stepped between the two and called an end to the confrontation, which, if left unregulated, could have spread throughout the ship. He suggested a formal combat to settle the differences between the two, and soon word was passed around the *Will:* the ship would lay at anchor off some small islet and the duel would take place in the morning.

That night, Poop lay in Read's hammock, crying softly against his shoulder.

"You can let no man rule you," Read told him in a quiet, firm voice. "If your life is not your own, it is not a life."

I was put off by the sight, because Poop's weakness seem'd to forecast doom in the coming duel. If only I had been faster scaling down from the masthead! The sadness and futility of it all was too much for me to take. I left the sleeping quarters and ascended to the quarterdeck to take in the night air.

Bishop was there, bent over his weapons, sharpening their edges.

chapter 22.

It was a day in which the sun never rose. The canopy of the world, instead, faded from the black of night to a sickly gray, with only a pale patch of sky the color of a long-dead corpse to denote where in the heavens the sun had hidden her face. As the morn dragged on, it seem'd to me that the ceiling of the world had fallen, for a moist, white mist had descended, enveloping the ship in its entirety, and floating along the surface of the water like the pale breath of angels.

I was on the morning watch, and, just as the morning turned to white, I was surprised to be joined by Read, who took a place silently beside me. For a long time, we said nothing to each other, for the masthead is small and cramped and the mere touch of his shoulder 'gainst mine was communication enough between us.

Our eyes looked out to sea, studying the flatness of the water, the changing shades of the sky, the shifting mist. I was glad to have him there beside me. With strangers, we often struggle to make conversation; with acquaintances, the dialogue comes easily because of shared pursuits and interests; with true friends, language once again falls away, and shows her face when required.

The mist was clammy and cold, and, as I had begun to shiver, Read put an arm around me and held me tight to him. It was then that I noticed that Read had begun to speak, but in tones so tranquil that his words had mixed almost imperceptibly with my thoughts. Read was talking about his love for the sea, and for high adventure, and of his service on other privateering vessels before this one. I decided to pose a question that had been much on my mind.

"When the men took advantage of you on your last voyage . . ."

"Must I repeat myself like the seasons?" Read said. "I do not wish to speak of it again."

There was a silence between us, and then, at last, he spoke.

"My mother, when I was a child of fewer years than I could count on both hands, came under assault by a group of sailors put to shore. They killed my father, and, as he fought, my mother dressed me in boy's clothes. The attackers, ignorant of my true sex, spared me and bade me to watch while they went about their business with my mother. I remembered that these fellows were each branded by a similar tattoo, that of a bull snorting flames, perhaps obtain'd during some shared drunken revel. As fortune had it, having kept an eye out every day for all these long years, I came upon a few of these fellows, the remains of this gang, on my previous vessel. I ended their voyages early."

"You killed them all?"

"Grace O'Malley would have done no less."

"Grace O'Malley?"

"You know the name?"

"Very well. I am surprised that you do."

"Of course! It is a legend I know intimately. I am British-born, but even as a young'un, I took interest in the fairy stories of your Irish folk. My mother would sing the song."

Read sang in a strong voice these words:

> *"Grace O'Malley is coming across the sea,*
> *With soldiers armed and strong,*
> *Neither French nor Spanish but Irish,*
> *They scatter the attackers"*

"She is no legend," I said. "In Ireland we called her Grainne Mhaol. She was a sea-dog, like us. Before the time of your grandmother's mother, she ruled the waters off western Ireland—King Philip the Second of Spain paid her one thousand pounds for the right to fish in her territories, even Queen Elizabeth petitioned her for a treaty of cooperation."

"Ha! So the song is true!"

"I will not sing it now, but, when I was a girl, I would hear children in the streets of Cork sing her ballad, '*Oro Se Do Bheatha Bhaile*,' in our tongue."

I spoke these words:

> *"Grainne Mhaol ag teacht thar saile*
> *Oglaigh armtha lei mar gharda*
> *Gaeil iad fein's ni Frainc na Spaninnigh*
> *'S cuirfidh said ruaig ar Ghallaibh"*

"That song gives me heart!" said Read. "Here's to Grace O'Malley! Like her, I will resist all powers. I will kill before some man passes, unbidden, between these thighs. I will die before some brat, unwanted, issues out of them. The men on my last vessel failed to understand that, and they paid a heavy price. No man will ever rule over me!"

For a long time, it seemed, we were alone together on the masthead, and whether a week had passed or a quarter hour, I could not say. But, at the assign'd time, Xbalanque and Hunahpu came up to relieve me of my duty, and as I climb'd down along with Read, Xbalanque tossed me another of his nasty sneers. But he reserved his real venom for Read.

"The men have cast their wagers ten to one 'gainst your friend," Xbalanque said to Read. "By tonight, he'll sleep not in the hammock next to yours, but on the seabed."

"Ten to one? Those are fine odds! Put me down for a ten-shilling bet cast 'gainst my charge. Either way, then, this fight will result in my good fortune!"

Read laughed as he said this, and appeared merry, but after he passed Xbalanque, his true mood bobbed to the surface and his countenance turned grim.

All hands had gathered on the quarterdeck, and most were in a boisterous mood. One might think that, aboard a privateering vessel, the men would see enough blood in the normal course of action, but duels always aroused a special interest. Rackam stood waiting along with the men and his face did not betray whether he took any joy or displeasure in serving as the master of the grim ceremonies. First-Rate stood beside him, checking on his gold pocket-watch; looking up, I saw Hunahpu at the masthead, his eyes out to sea as was his duty, whilst Xbalanque, by contrast, watched the proceedings below with much interest and exchanged signals with his seconds down below about the progress of the wagering.

The two combatants themselves were, at first, nowhere to be seen, but, in fair time, both came on deck. First arrived Poop, who struck me as rather rabbitlike in his demeanor—his brown eyes were wide with emotion and darted back and forth in his head; his nose was twitching as if he could sniff out the approaching calamity and thus escape it. He had always seem'd a smallish boy, but on this day he seem'd positively minuscule, more punctuation than man, and once he walked into the center of the crowd of onlookers, it was hard to pick him out again, as his tiny comma was lost in the alphabet of full-bodied mariners.

Now came Bishop, and his approach was like that of a mountain. At his base he wore massive black leather bucket boots, square toed and flaring at the top. He was clad in leather breeches on his lower half, and the muscles of his legs could be seen bunching and tensing even through the thick material. His torso, broad and sunbaked, was bare. At his summit, his ruined face was sunburnt and red, and his eyes smolder'd like the smoking vents of Vesuvius. His mouth, filled with broken, craggy teeth, was set in a deep scowl that fell down his chin like an avalanche of scorn. When Bishop stood over Poop, the boy was lost in the giant man's shadow.

Just then, Rackam made an announcement that stunned us all—save Read.

"Another has challenged Bishop," said Rackam in an even voice.

"I'll have time enough for the next after I finish with the first," said Bishop.

"The new challenger is Read," said Rackam. "And he asks for the right to proceed with his challenge first."

Now Rackam turned to the crew.

"I put the vote to you all: should Read's challenge precede the prior one?"

A general cheer went up. Privateers, after all, are fair folk when they aren't engaged in thievery or debauchery, and a duel between Read and Bishop seem'd more sporting.

"I've been shot seven times by seven men," said Read. "This is no challenge to me, just another scar."

Bishop pushed Poop aside and strode toward Read.

"First, I'll dispatch of you," he said. "But know this before you die—I will, after cutting you to the quick, return for your companion, and he, too, will join you in perdition."

"Xbalanque!" Read called up to the masthead. "Double my bet 'gainst myself!"

"But this is my fight!" said Poop, in his seldom heard, small, thin voice.

"It is mine now," said Read.

Poop started to draw a sword but Read grabbed his wrist, disarmed him, and kicked him backward. Poop stumbled into a bucket of suds, slipped, and splayed out on his back.

The men, all around, including Bishop, broke into loud laughter.

"You may be many things," Read said to Poop, "but dangerous, you are not."

At this, Poop regain'd his feet and scurried from the quarter-deck.

"I am dangerous!" Poop called back, over his shoulder. "You'll see!"

And so he was gone, and the proceedings continued. Read selected me as his second and Bishop selected Rackam, not out of friendship, but due to every crew member's respect for the captain's sense of fairness. A pirogue was launched with the quartet of us aboard. It was a silent ride, save for the sound of the oars that were manned by Rackam and by me. But as the oars lapped the water, there soon arose a serpentlike hissing, growing into a wolflike growl. It was Bishop muttering something under his breath that sounded like a cross between human speech and the wild sounds of the forest. Bishop, who was staring right at Read, who stared right back, continued to mutter and his voice grew louder and louder until he was shouting his monologue so all creation could hear it.

He was engaged in a prayer of sorts. His words seem'd to be drawn from some psalm, but his tone was obstreperous rather than solemn, truculent rather than kind. He said:

> *"Do you indeed decree what is right you Gods?*
> *Do you judge people fairly?*
> *No, in your hearts you lie.*
> *Your hands deal out violence on earth.*
> *The wicked go astray from the womb.*
> *They err from birth*
> *Speaking lies*
> *They have venom like the venom of a serpent*
> *Like the deaf adder that stays its ear*
> *So it does not hear the voice of charmers*
> *Or the cunning enchanter*
> *O God, break the teeth in their mouths*
> *Tear out the fangs of the young lions, O Lord!*
> *Let them vanish like water that runs away*
> *Like grass let them be trodden*
> *Down and wither*
> *Let them be like the snail that dissolves into slime*
> *Like the untimely birth that never sees the sun.*
> *The wicked will rejoice when they see vengeance done;*
> *They will bathe their feet in the blood of the righteous.*
> *Amen."*

If the delivery of this redoubtable sermon had any effect on Read, he disclosed few signs. After staring down Bishop, who, in time, looked first away, Read fix'd his gaze out onto the water, and then, looking back at me, gave me a confident wink. He mouthed the words "ride or die," and then smiled and winked again. Despite his bravado and confident gaze, I did notice beads of sweat building on his forehead. As the mist-filled day was not overly hot, I attributed the perspiration to be a sign of some inner anxiousness that he had, for the most part, successfully concealed.

The mist parted, like a white curtain drawn open. We pulled the pirogue up onto a small islet. It was little more than a bar of sand, really; treeless, rising only a few feet above the waves and certain to disappear with the next great swelling of the sea. The ground was rocky and color'd steel gray; a few paces in, tho', it exploded with color: some cousin of the passionflower flourished along every visible surface. The passionflower grows as a vine, largely along fences and walls; here, it ran along the rocks like moss, in varying shades of scarlet. Indeed, the earth seem'd ablaze with the five-petal'd flower, and the air was filled with the redolent perfume of its blossoms and the sweetness of the small, nectar-fill'd fruit the plant bears.

There were no animals here, no wind, and no sound save that of our footsteps as we headed to the center of the islet. When we reached that place, John handed each of the combatants their choice of weapons; Read, a cutlass; next, Bishop, with his selection—a broadsword and a boarding axe, both of which were massive in their dimensions and newly sharpened. Read and Bishop stood a few paces apart with Rackam between them. A soft rain began to fall, and, all at once, the mist broke entire and the sun filled the sky like an immense and golden smile.

"Let the combat commence!" cried Rackam.

Bishop launched the first blow, charging forward and swinging his axe as tho' he meant to fell a whole forest. Read easily avoided the blow, which struck the earth and sent splinters of rock and shreds of flowers flying 'round the air. Before Read could make his own attack, however, Bishop displayed unexpected quickness and dispatched another swing with his broadsword. Read parried the blow, but his weapon betrayed him, and, giving way to the ferocity of Bishop's attack, the blade broke into a thousand glittering shards. One piece grazed my face, burning like a lit match. I put my hands to my cheek, looked at my fingers, and saw blood. Seeing Read weaponless, I drew my own cutlass to join the fray. Rackam stay'd my hand.

"This fight is not your fight," he said.

Bishop was pressing his advantage against his weaponless foe; he reared back mightily once more and brought down his boarding axe, and when it descended, it was like a tree falling to earth. Read, however, used his speed and rolled to the right, evading the blow by the width of a whisker. Then he jumped to his feet and, even as Bishop prepared another blow, he set off arunning. Bishop quickly join'd the pursuit, and, thus engaged, the two circumscribed the islet, like Achilles pursuing Hector 'round the walls of Troy. Read was, indeed, fleet of foot, but the rocks were sharp and treacherous and tore at his heels; his blood was soon mixed with trodden flowers. Bishop, the slower of the two, seem'd impervious to the pain, and also untiring, and, even as Read slowed down, Bishop continued his pace, unflagging. Once again, I gripped my own cutlass, considering an intervention, despite Rackam's previous admonition. But again, Rackam held my wrist, sensing my thought.

"I have to do something."

"A man must fight his own battles," said Rackam. "Or he will war with those that denied him."

At last, the pursuit neared its conclusion. The light in the sky had faded, moving from a lighter shade of gray to a darker hue, that near-black that comes just after the setting of the sun but just before the stars come out in their silver raiment. As the dusk arrived, Read stopped short in his tracks and so, too, did Bishop pause.

"Thirty times have I pursued you 'round this island," said Bishop. "Thirty times have you evaded me. What trickery do you now employ?"

"I will run from you no longer," said Read. "I am weapon-less, and you are in possession of both a broadsword and a boarding axe. As a man, I ask that you allow me to die a fighter's death: lend me but one of your weapons in which to defend myself with honor."

Bishop grimaced and, in response, readied himself for a final blow.

"Then grant me only this," said Read, and I could see his eyes were bright with tears. "Provide only that I be buried properly, in the Blue Mountains of Jamaica, which is a place that is dear to my heart, or see that I am interned in some green field in Oxfordshire, England, which is the place of my birth, and the region in which my parents resided, tho' I have not been there in many a year. Just see to the disposal of my corpse and I ask nothing else of you—for the one thing I fear, I'll admit, is being food for some pack of wild beasts on the land, or for the sharks and slimy things that haunt the deep."

But Bishop's face was grim, and his heart did not show pity at Read's last words.

"No mercy did Samuel show the Philistines when the men of Israel marched from Mizpeh and smote the armies of their enemies in Bethcar," said Bishop. "No quarter did the men of Belial show Naboth the Jazreelite, when he blasphemed God the Redeemer and was therefore carried out of the city and stoned. No clemency, then, will be granted unto you. And now I read from the book of Acts chapter twenty-seven." With that, his weapon still in his grasp, Bishop lifted his eyes toward heaven and said this by way of obsequies:

"Now when much time was spent, and when sailing was now dangerous, Paul admonished them,

And said unto them, Sirs, I perceive that this voyage will be with hurt and much damage, not only of the lading and ship, but also of our lives.

Not long after there arose against the ship a tempestuous wind, called Euroclydon.

And when neither sun nor stars in many days appeared, and no small tempest lay on us, all hope that we should be saved was then taken away.

Amen."

As if struck by the ecclesiastical words, Read dropped to his knees and bowed his head, exhausted and agape in the shadow of his great and unvanquished opponent. Sweat was pouring down Read's face like rain off a leaf after a shower; his white shirt was soaked with his effort. This was no longer a duel, but an execution. Bishop dropped his boarding axe on the rocks, and it fell with a mighty clang. He raised high his broadsword, and, it seemed to me, in the dying rays of the sun, that flames ran down the blade.

Just then, even as Bishop lifted his weapon, Read grasped the sides of his own shirt and, pulling them apart, ripped his sweat-soaked top down the center. At that moment, his bosom was exposed, which was full and womanly, with pale flesh and nebles as red as blood drops. Bishop's eyes grew wide as hens' eggs, and in his surprise, his swing went wild. Read reached into his waistband and, in a blink, pulled forth a small dirk and thrust it into Bishop's heaving chest, puncturing his heart. Bishop now fell to his knees, clutching at the wound. With an easy gait, Read walked over to Bishop's broadsword, caught hold of the huge hilt with both hands, and, with one swing, cut deep into Bishop's neck. And yet still Bishop would not die. Tho' his head was half sever'd, he held it on both sides with his great hands, keeping it in place, tho' all logic said death was inevitable with such a mortal wound. Dancing 'round his foe, Read swung again, and with this cut, he lopped Bishop's head clear from his shoulders. The giant's body, spurting its essence, collapsed onto the rock and, recumbent, watered the passionflowers.

Read paused for a second and, it seem'd, sobbed a little, overcome by emotion. But he quickly regain'd himself, tying his shirt in place and bursting into loud song, which he continued as we walked back to the pirogue to make our way back to the main ship, where fires were lit up in celebration of the duel's victor. Here went Read's song:

> "Hail! You are welcome home!
> Hail! You are welcome home!
> Hail! You are welcome home!
> Summer is fast approaching!"

It was "Oro Se Do Bheatha Bhaile," rendered in the English tongue. When we reached the ship, the men grieved not for Bishop, who drove the fellows hard, and without humor, but instead took up with Read's tune, which was known by some of the men and quickly learned by the others. How those notes thrilled my soul! Yet I held to my oath and did not sing, tho' the blood in my veins pounded along to the rhythm of the song.

> *"Welcome O woman of constant sorrow!*
> *To our grief you've been shackled,*
> *Your great lands possessed by wrongdoers*
> *You yourself sold into slavery*
>
> *My greatest wish would be to see*
> *Even if I died a week after I saw it*
> *Grace O'Malley and her mighty warriors*
> *Declaring banishment to the attackers*
>
> *Hail! You are welcome home!*
> *Hail! You are welcome home!*
> *Hail! You are welcome home!*
> *Summer is fast approaching!"*

Given his canniness and skill with a blade, the men were not surprised that Read had come back the victor. There were a few murmurs as to why we were singing such a song by way of celebration, but any inquiries were washed away with grog and soon the ship's company was belting out other merry tunes as well. Poop did not join in; after being informed of the particulars of the fight, he scurried off to sulk in the bowel of the ship, shamed that he had not fought his own battle. His absence was hardly noticed. On and on the songs went, making sport of death and of capture and of heaven's inevitable justice. The revels, as are their custom, would have continued until the last draught was drained, but Xbalanque rushed down from the masthead to deliver a message that he would only whisper into Rackam's ear. The news spread through the ship soon enough:

Spanish colors, off the larboard quarter!

The black galleon, at last, had been spotted.

chapter 23.

The sail had been spotted about five leagues distance to windward, bearing south by east. The decks were alive with sea-dogs scurrying to their stations. Rackam took to his place on the poop deck, and First-Rate stood beside him; Rackam motion'd me to take the place formerly fill'd by Bishop at his other side, while Read and Poop mann'd their gun. Rackam twirled his black die about in his left hand as he consider'd the situation and measured the variables. By Rackam's reckoning, the black galleon had not seen us as we lay in her way, and so he thought it best that we maintain distance until nightfall; there would be a full moon out tonight and plenty of light to steer our course. Surprise and speed, tho', would be of the essence. First-Rate issued the command to add a sail to the foremast, and thus gain the needed celerity. "Up top, a-hoa!" he called. "Lace on your bonnets, and keep 'er sharp!"

At that, First-Rate turned to Rackam.

"She draws more weight than us, and yet she's the faster in the water," said First-Rate. "She's the biggest game we've yet to hunt—and the most dangerous."

Rackam smiled, and yet his look was still one of firmness and resolve.

"If we catch this prey," he responded, "we'll not need to hunt again."

We chased the ship through the day, keeping 'er on the horizon but not out of sight. Then night came and it was clear and the stars were out and the moon was bright and we continued to keep 'er in our sights. The light was all silver that evening, and it lent all a ghostly feel. 'Round midnight, a fleet of flying fish off larboard flashed argent and violaceous hues and kept the night watch fair company. Rackam and First-Rate remained vigilant throughout the dark hours, leaning on the rails and discussing various stratagems for taking the vessel come the morning.

The day came again, and it was bright with no clouds and a fresh gale of wind at southeast by east, but despite the breeze it was violent hot. The sun was already a quarter up in the sky when we gave chase leeward. Rackam ordered every item not essential to the chase at hand to be thrown away—books, trinkets, broken and unfixable weapons, refuse of any sort.

"Lighten the load, you sea-bitches!" he howled. "All you fine ladies will replace what you lost soon enough!"

Rackam's eyes were bright, his mouth was set, and he was clearly eager for the contest to commence. The men, too, were full of energy and emotion and threw away their unneeded flotsam and jetsam with nary a complaint or whimper. The black galleon! This was the stuff of legend; taking her would make this voyage worthy of a song. A sea-dog's life is lived in hope of taking possession of great wealth; hope, however, differs greatly from the facts of the matter, which are that a sea-dog's existence is most typically an impoverished one, with the bulk of the prizes taken being such things as victuals and other basic supplies. Ofttimes the most a privateer can hope for is seizing hold of a store of wine so that, in the last, he may drink and dream of someday capturing finer things.

But now, sailing in the wake of the black galleon, the prospect of real treasure—the gold of the Indies, the jewels of the Aztecs!—made the heart of every hand on board pound as if that organ would burst through the walls of flesh and bone that confined it. The black galleon! We had no idea exactly what baubles we would find on board, but we knew our reward would be great. It was almost not to be believed that on this wide sea, we had found our prize!

"Haul taut! Mainsail haul!" cried Rackam.

The yards on the mainsail and crossjack were, accordingly, swung around together and, with as much alacrity as could be mustered, braced up sharp for the new tack. We were bearing down hard on 'er and we had the element of surprise in our favor. Now I could see her colors in full: the flag of Spain and the ebon sail of the black galleon. Ha! Well, we had our own dark colors to display. Now, closing still, we hoisted the Black Flag. She flew high and strong and flapped in the wind. To our surprise, the opposing vessel, at the sight of our approach, came to immediately, and signaled that we could send over a boarding party at our first convenience.

Now, I had been told it was the custom of and policy of certain ships to submit to another craft flying the Black Flag rather than to run the risk of conflict and casualties. Not every captain had the stomach for sea-battles, and loss of stores was often seen as preferable to loss of life. But I assum'd such policies were more common with vessels of a smaller size, and ones less able to put up a defense. For so grand a vessel as the storied black galleon to give up so readily seem'd to defy sense and explanation.

Rackam, First-Rate, Read, and I went aboard the vessel and were confronted by a man in official uniform, with many medals and ribbons festooned 'cross his chest. He was a Spaniard with a long, flowing mustache and an air of supreme arrogance, despite his ship having just submitted. He spoke English well but with a trace of an accent, one that may have been almost undetectable had we been unaware of his background and the colors that his ship flew. He strode toward us in long, insolent strides.

"Is there any among this rabble with authority to have dialogue with me?" he said, in a voice that dripped with condescension.

Rackam stepped forward out of our number.

"I am captain of this vessel."

"The great Calico Jack Rackam," said the man, executing an extravagant bow.

Rackam nodded and ignored the affront in the man's tone.

"Your countrymen have promised a reward to the man who brings you in that you might dangle at the end of a yardarm," said the man.

"You're not the man to bring this man in," said First-Rate.

"And who is this that dares address me?" said the man. "The traitor who left his commission in the Royal Navy to take up with pyrates? I speak not to traitors or dogs of any sort!" The man then spewed forth poisonous vitrolic words at the Judaic religion of First-Rate.

At that, First-Rate started to draw his sword, but Rackam stayed his hand.

"What is your rank?" said Rackam to the Spaniard.

The man smiled.

"I am the captain of this vessel, financed by proprietors in Madrid, and bound for a port in Cadiz."

"Her course will now be our decision," said First-Rate.

"Governor Rogers said you were boastful men," said the Spanish Captain. "He neglected to mention that you were also impertinent."

"You conversed with Rogers?" asked First-Rate.

"Oh, my dear, damn'd, dirty traitor. Your presence in these waters is well known," said the Spanish Captain. "Did you think we would allow you to take us so easily? Know this: you will be pursued until you are caught. Rogers knows where you are, and what you have done. He means to make these waters safe for the families of honest folk. His excellency has said——"

"He does what he does for the children," said First-Rate. "We've heard."

"He will be gracious if you submit of your own volition, but cruel if you foolishly choose the course of escape," continued the Spanish captain. "I now offer you these terms: surrender now, to me, and I will grant you your lives."

"You're giving us terms?" said First-Rate.

"We will let your crew disembark, without arms, on an uninhabited portion of the coast of Jamaica. The weather is pleasant, the native inhabitants, except for the Maroon tribes in the interior, mostly subdued, and a man, if he is willing to sweat, can earn a living off of the land. As for you, Calico Jack Rackam, you must submit to us, and give yourself to my first-lieutenant as prisoner, and journey back to Kingston to face the charges that Governor Rogers, through his associate Governor Lawes, has prepared for you, while we collect our much-deserved reward. You will be granted your life, but must, publicly, confess your crimes, submit to the lash, and swear allegiance to the Governor."

Rackam seem'd lost in thought. If Governor Rogers and Governor Lawes were indeed marshaling all their forces against us, and had succeeded in recruiting foreign mariners in their cause as well, then indeed our journey seem'd hopeless. Privateers relied on stealth, and, if our ship and crew were well known and expected, then our eventual capture was an inevitability. So this is how it would end! Without honor, without treasure, and living a life at the whim of the hated Rogers!

"Don't be a fool," said the Spanish captain. "Surrender now. Trade your dignity for a little life. It may be that, after your confession and punishment, and if you survive the lash, that we may find a place for you here, among us, as a cabin-boy or such, to assist us in the capture of other illegal privateers. What say you to our terms?"

"Your terms we reject utterly," Rackam said suddenly. And at that, Rackam, with the back of his hand, struck the Spanish captain with a blow to the cheek that resounded so loudly that it sounded like a cannon shot. The Spanish captain lay on the ground, holding his jaw, which, from its askew position on his face, seem'd shattered.

"You fool," he said, and with the words issued dark blood from the corner of his mouth. "You'll be begging me for quarter soon enough. And your entire rabble of traitors and mulattos and Moors and savages will be clapped in shackles!"

It was then that we saw two more black sails on the horizon.

chapter 24.

We are closest to the void at the beginning of our lives and near the end; at that moment when we first leave our mother's belly and in those final days before our own children slip our corpse into the womb of mother earth. At the close of our lives, we fear death the most, perhaps because we have seen life and know all too well the difficulty of its proper maintenance, and it thus becomes more precious to us. At the start of our lives we are half in love with death, for it represents the one time we were truly safe, when we were swaddled in the flesh of our parent, and had no fear or want for anything. What delicious contradiction that those who have the least of life hold it most dearly, and those who are so full of life, the young, treat it with the least care!

In my youth, death was my constant companion, and he was not an unwanted one, but a beloved, invited guest. By my faith, when the twin galleons were spott'd, my heart soar'd when I realized there was a battle afoot. Existence, to me, seem'd too ordinary to bear without the challenge of mortality. Great things required one to risk greatly. "Ride or die, sea-dogs!" went Read's cry, and I smiled at the thought of confrontation with our foe.

"Time is running out," said First-Rate to Rackam. "We must hold council and decide on a course of action."

And so, after locking the galleon's crew in a hold, Rackam and his officers debated strategy. There was little time for the ordering of the battle, and even less time for fear. Our cause, of course, was hopeless: there was little a schooner such as the *Will* could muster 'gainst the two mighty craft that were bearing down upon us. From the size of them, each of the black galleons probably boasted one hundred guns, and crews of eight hundred men or more. They looked like vast floating, fortified cities, populated by legions of armed residents. We were outgunned and outmanned—but perhaps not outmanuevered. Zayd joined our ship's councils and made it known that he had something to say.

"Surgeon," said Rackam, "your skills are not yet required—but they surely will be."

"It is not the medical arts I have come to discuss," said Zayd. "I have some experience that might be of use in our current situation. I served on board a vessel under the command of De Graff in his later years."

"De Graff!" said Hunahpu, who had been listening in on the councils. "The blond, blue-eyed sea-dog! The greatest privateer of them all!"

I smiled at Hunahpu's words. So Zayd served with De Graff—
that was how he knew the truth of the privateer's woolly hair
and dark eyes for his song. Zayd, as it turned out, also had a
plan, which he shared with the men. He said it was a combat
scheme outlined once by De Graff but never employed in battle.
It was a bold proposal, and laden with peril. It is certain Zayd's
approach would have been rejected had Read not championed
his strategy.

"The chances of Zayd's plan working are slim," said Rackam.

"The chances of us perishing without it are greater," answered Read.

"I am inclined to take wise risks, not wild ones," said Rackam.

"Time is running out," said First-Rate. "We must decide on
a course."

Then Read made his move. Approaching Rackam, he swiftly
pried the captain's familiar black die from his hand and threw it
into the drink.

"Chance be damned!" said Read. "We rule our own fate this
day. I say we follow Zayd's plan. Only ingenuity and courage
will save our hides this time."

So, after this exchange, Zayd's approach was adopted and set
into action.

The first, captured galleon was sent back in the direction of
her sisters, her colors raised, her crew and captain imprison'd in
the hold. The Spanish captain muttered what seemed to be oaths
and curses as he was ushered below, but, because of his broken
jaw and his Spanish, he was not understood by me and likely not
comprehended even by his own men. Rackam, Read, and I,
along with a skeleton crew from the *Will*, stayed on board the
Spanish ship to man her. First-Rate went back to the *Will* and
sail'd her northwest, away from the other two Spanish vessels,

which were fast approaching. As the *Will* sail'd off, we fired a few shots at her, being careful not to actually strike her.

"If our ruse works," said Rackam, "they'll think the *Will* turned tail."

"And when we sail up to them in one of their own ships, we'll broadside 'em both!" said Read.

"But if our subterfuge is recognized," I said, "we'll be sunk for sure."

Rackam said nothing, but Read laughed at the thought of our destruction.

"Do you want to live forever?" Read said, and he kissed me playfully on the cheek.

"Stations for stays!" Rackam cried out.

Our small crew of men scrambled to find their places on the unfamiliar ship.

"Ease down the helm!" said Rackam.

The Spanish ships were now approaching; one would pass starboard, another larboard. They were monsters, both of 'em, floating castles of wood, clad partially in iron armor, their thick masts rising from their decks like a mighty grove. I could see members of their crews scurrying about the deck, tending to their chores, the rigging, the shrouds. The wind had picked up and their sails blew full.

We sailed still closer; Rackam displayed not a hint of anxiety as he held the wheel and stood at the helm. I wondered: could the opposing crew, at this close distance, see that we weren't Spanish? We had not had time to strip the officers of their uniforms and so we manned the ship in the more flamboyant garb associated with privateers. My mind continued to speculate: did the trinity of ships have some secret code by which to communicate distress, or whether the craft in question was friend or foe? We had not press'd the Spanish captain for details on his hailing procedure and thus were relying entirely on instinct and guesswork. Read had taken his station at a cannon and, as we approached still closer, Rackam gestured for me to take a place at a gun as well. As I went to my position, I noticed Rackam's knuckles as he grasped the wheel were very white.

"Man your guns," he said. "Ready for my signal."

Closer now, we flew high our Spanish colors as we sailed between both ships; we leaned 'gainst the railings and, with broad smiles, we waved merrily at the crews of the other two vessels and, with much cheer, they waved back. Rackam held his hand up—his signal would come soon. Ah—the faces of the crew on the passing ships were showing signs of incredulity. A few crew members called out strange phrases to us in Spanish, and we did not answer, unsure of what was said and what the response should be. Our clothes, no doubt, were as suspicious as privateer colors; our faces, too, would seem foreign to these men from Madrid. I could hear that voices were beginning to be raised on either ship. Rackam quickly called for crew members of the *Will* with origins in Spain to take their places at the railings, show their faces, and call out to their countrymen in their native tongue. Ahh, there was hidden strength in the patchwork nature of this motley crew!

"At my command!" said our captain.

At that, Rackam brought his hand down. We fired all our guns, starboard and larboard. The air was filled with cannonfire and, following that, the screams of men. By my faith, it sounded like sweet music to me! In the smoke and confusion of the moment, we employed our grappling hooks and pulled both the ships within boarding distance. Now the *Will* had turned about and was joining the fray. After laying down boarding planks,

I was the first aboard the ship to larboard and, as I stepped on deck, I drew my cutlass and my dagger. I hoped that bravado would be worthy substitutes for my lack of skill.

"Ride or die!" I cried as I charged.

There is a poetry to combat that is wholly unknown to those who have known only the prose of peace. The world moves to a different meter, and time slips its usual boundaries. For cowards, I reckon, the moment seems stretched and unbearable, and the dangers overly prolonged. For the brave, battle is like the act of love, in that it seems to last forever and yet not long enough. Details appear'd to me in the struggle, as in a still life closely observed: the craftsmanship on a sword-hilt, the sound of the footsteps of a man attacking from the rear, the sea green eyes of a Spanish soldier who had been shot through the throat. The first man I assaulted by feinting to his left and slashing his right arm; he dropped his weapon and yielded—I kicked him in the shoulder and he toppled over into the water and likely drowned. Next, I parried the attack of a bulky deckhand who swung at me with a wooden board from behind; I slashed at his eyes and, when he dropped his plank to tend to his wounded face, I ran him through the belly. The third man I killed was readying his musket when I hacked his right leg and then plunged my cutlass through his chest. I looked him in the face as he bled, grievously, and was surprised to see no hatred there. Indeed, tho' I held him on my weapon stuck through like a pig, his thoughts seem'd far off, and I was invisible to him.

"*Mi carino . . . mi amor . . .*" he said.

Who was he calling out to? I wondered if he had family of some sort or if he was in the grip of some death vision that made him spout nonsense. A fly buzzed by my ear at that moment and I focused anew on my task. I turned my blade, and thus shredded the Spanish sailor's heart.

The Spanish fought hard and with some honor, but they did not fight long. The ship was designed for intimidation and, once boarded, its crew lacked fighting discipline and strategy. Our men were well tutored in the fighting methods of the Spanish, but our opponents were confused and frightened by the myriad approaches the members of our versicolored crew took to the battle. Rackam also made it known that the crew of the first ship was held hostage, including the captain, and that they would all be slaughtered in a most unmerciful fashion if resistance continued. This sway'd a goodly portion of the second and third crews. Rackam also made 'em the sea-dogs bargain: those who would join with us, would share in a portion of the booty we stole. Had the Spanish fought us, and continued hard, there is some chance they would have prevailed, being in by far the greater number. But in his last argument, Rackam was persuasive.

"Come now!" he shouted. "Join us and share in the toil of your sweat! In your ships you have the treasure of kings and yet you return to Spain to live like pawns! I am John Rackam and I am known as a man of my word! Join us and live as kings— or fight us and die like dogs!"

And thus the battle soon ended, with a number of casualties in the opposition, but no deaths on our side, save two hands who fell from the riggings. When Rackam announced the battle was finished, and had the privateer's Black Flag run up the poles of all three ships, a cheer went up from the men of the *Will*, and a fair number of the Spaniards, both the wounded and those few who had come over to our company, joined in the acclamation.

Our haul was bigger and grander than we had hoped or even imagined. Gold bullion, precious stones, and silk were all among the cargo. There were thirteen chests of gold coins, eight hundred pounds of wrought gold, and twenty-six tons of uncovered silver. There were also many dozens of hogsheads and puncheons loaded with spice and a variety of precious contents, and many barrels of wine, beer, rum, and other spirits. The men walked through the holds of both ships amazed, laughing, crying, bursting into spontaneous jigs and dances, giddy with our good luck. Rackam clasped Zayd's hand in congratulations and, deeming that form of laudation insufficient, subsequently took the Moor into his arms in a full embrace.

Even as the goods were being transferred from the Spanish ships into the hold of the *Will*, the celebration commenced. The men, having waited so long for such a prize, fell almost immediately into a celebration so wild and unrestrained that even Rackam found himself unable to check their passion and, instead, lifted a bottle of Madeira wine and saluted his men with a long quoff. 'Twould have been easy for the Spanish sailors, their guards soaked with wine, to have mounted a mutiny or escape, but the bulk of the captured men, having been pressed hard by their officers while in service, now reveled in witnessing ordinary men enjoying spoils and join'd the jubilee. Even First-Rate, normally a reserved soul, participated in the merrymaking, dueting with Read in a loud and boisterous song.

"His majesty's Royal Navy denied me my rightful rank because I am of the tribe of Abraham," cried First-Rate, his usual cool reserve melted away. "Now I will have the life I want, and damn the ignorance of the world!"

As for Xbalanque, his reaction was most peculiar and unique. As he and Hunahpu passed by me on the forecastle, Xbalanque suddenly bowed his head and burst into sobs.

"I have been a wretch," he said. "I have treated you without honor."

"Perhaps there is blame and provocation to be found on all sides," I said.

"Because my brother has always been content, even eager, to establish himself among the powers that conquered our land, he is of an even temperament. But I cannot help but think of the slaughter of our people, and it has twisted my soul. I can now make a new start. No more will I plague men. When next we dock, I will leave this life."

"We will establish a business of some sort," said Hunahpu.

"But we will do something peaceful and true," said Xbalanque, "and we will live as our fathers did before us."

"I wish you well," I said. "Both of you."

I walked up close to Rackam and, when it seem'd we were unwatched by the other men, I rubbed his neck with some affection. He closed his eyes as my fingers pressed his skin and he let out a deep sigh. Then, running his hands 'round my waist, he pulled me into the shadows and pressed his lips to mine.

"The men!" I said.

With several quick cuts of his sword, he cut down a sail, which fell over us both. The world went white.

"Let them be damned," said Rackam.

*T*ho' the moon had set, the stars were out and a man hanging in the rigging would have been treated to quite a sight as there, on the poop deck, we engaged in the transit of Venus. Rackam spread out part of the sail beneath us and, thus equipped, we set sail on our own private sea. The urgency I felt in Rackam the night he took my maidenhood was gone, replaced by a tenderness I had never seen openly in his demeanor before. All of his movements were gentle and blithe; he kissed me as if the night would last as long as the year. I stroked his arm and his belly and his broad chest until he moaned loud enough for the man in the masthead to ask if there was trouble below and we both laughed a little and Rackam called out that all was well. Afterward, we lay together for a time, the sail pulled around us like a blanket.

"I sense a change in you," I said.

"As captain," he said, "I cannot let my guard down even for an instant."

"And now, in the wake of such a grand success?"

"Perhaps, my sweet. But I've seen weakness destroy others, and I've held the lesson close to my heart."

Rackam told me he had begun in the privateer's life after taking over a ship when its commander, a Captain Charles Vane, refused to board and fight a French man-o'-war; Rackam, then a quartermaster, led a mutiny and was voted captain and took the ship into outlaw waters.

"Why did Vane refuse the fight?" I asked.

"There are many reasons why a man declines to fight; each is a shade of the same color—fear."

"Hadn't he faced such circumstances before?"

"Vane had recently brought his wife aboard the ship— a wench from Wales, as I recall. Her presence made him weak; when we were attacked, he feared for her safety."

"So he feared not for himself, but for others."

"Whether he worried for himself or for others, the result was the same. No anchor should hold a privateer's ship at port; we must be ready to sail with the wind. I have been encumber'd before and each time I have cut loose. Sometimes the love one develops for one's fellows . . . but, I must not speak of such things. I cannot be anchored. It must be so while I remain in this life."

There was a silence between us as I reflected on his words.

"You said, once, that you would leave this life when you had accumulated a certain level of funds," I said. "You have surpassed that, and ten times over."

Rackam said nothing.

"Before I joined the ship's company," I said, "I saw the body of a lad who had been hanged in the market in New Providence. It had been said he would die in his shoes, so he kicked 'em off before he dropped. Is that what you want? To die in your shoes?"

Rackam said nothing.

"Rogers will come looking for us."

Rackam pointed up at the sky, which was full of stars.

"Would that old Governor Rogers was a constellation," Rackam said.

"Why?"

"Then, from any place at sea, I could see him scowling at my success."

Rackam and I kissed again, and I held his face. He buried his head in the crook of my neck and I felt him shudder. I stroked his hair and touched his cheek gently and felt a wet warmth; I could not tell if it was sweat or tears. He kissed me again and we fell asleep, letting the kiss last 'til first light.

I did not know then that that kiss would mark our last victory.

chapter 25.

There are islands off the north coast of
Jamaica that are of a tropic and pleasing climate
where sea-turtles journey to mate and to spawn. After
the *Will* successfully took the trio of Spanish galleons,
Read, who was better traveled than he commonly revealed, recommended to Rackam that one isle in particular would make an
excellent site for the men to continue their revels. Read went on
at length about the beauty of the location, which he said was
covered with yellow banana flowers. Many of the turtles to be
found there were, he said, excellent eating and very sweet of
flesh and larger and tastier than any similar creatures to be
found in Europe or the English colonies.

There were three varieties, he said: one sort of turtle was as
big as a longboat, he claimed, and of a similar elongated shape,

weighing several thousand pounds. The flesh of this giant, however, was slimy and of a nauseating flavor. There was a smaller variety as well, the size of a man, with bright red shells—these, too, were edible, but their flesh was loose and stringy and full of oil. The third kind, a variety of about four feet in length on the average, was the best for cooking—the flesh was sweet and fat and delicious, and, when salted and spiced, it was a provision that could last many months at sea and yet retain some flavor. I have never been an admirer of eating the flesh of creatures that the Divine Provider Who Rules in Heaven has seem'd to cast out of his glory, like turtles and snakes and bugs of any sort, but, by my faith, Read explored in such detail the charms and succulent tastes of these creatures, my mouth watered for them as if they were made of sugar.

Read asked Zayd to join us, but he declined.

"Alas, such sojourns give me little joy," Zayd said.

"Why?" I asked.

"I would not burden you with the troubles that plague me."

"We have already nearly died together," said Read, "and there are no doubt more perils in store. I have also heard your tale of Port Royal and the disaster that befell you there, so you know more than most of the fragility of the corporal. Let us get through what private revelations we have now before death cuts short our tales."

So Zayd, agreeing, was thus convinced to tell his story.

"*I* was born in the fair Republic of Sale, which is in Africa," said Zayd. "It is a country of corsairs, and the like, but it is well-govern'd and it has been, as long as memory, a democracy, with each able-bodied man contributing his vote on who should rule, and on major decisions that affect the nation entire.

"On the coast of my fair land, there is a pool, sheltered by the arms of sandbars, that was much beloved by the citizens. The waters in that pool, because of the purity of the coastal light and the refined quality of the underlying sand, were, upon the surface, like a mirror. When a boy in that country reached three and ten years old, he was taken to that curious body of water, which was known as the pool of Sidi Abdullah Ibn Hassun, to peer into its mirror, look at that face that stares back, and thus take measure of his own future. Nearly all who participate in the ritual give the same reply to what they see, and, accordingly, they learn the trade of a corsair. When it was my time, I saw a different future, and so dedicated myself to the healing of the sick.

"As years passed, I took a wife, and had one son, and, for a long while, lived happily in Sale. It is a place whose beauty was unmatched in all the world. Spires pointed the way to heaven, and from the mosques, calls to prayer from the muezzins rang out five times a day across the winding streets and alleyways. There were gardens everywhere in Sale with roses, herbs, and cypress trees for shade. Cafés sold mint teas, yogurts, saffron rice, and canary wines. The air smelled of spices and the calm salt breeze from off the ocean.

"While on a short trip to Cadiz, my ship was taken by slavers. All my fellows were killed or transported to be sold, but upon learning of my profession, I was spared and kept on. The voyage of this ship, which was poorly managed and grim, stretched on for months and years, until at last I escaped when we anchor'd off Tunis, but, instead of traveling directly home, I was forced by circumstance to remove to France, and from there to Port Royal—and you have heard my adventures in that luckless city—before securing a place on a ship bound to my home country.

"My journey back to Sale was long and arduous, and when I arrived, I found the city had been laid to ruin and the republic had fallen. But my heart had not felt its last blow, for I discovered that my wife, whom I married for love and not for any monetary or familial arrangement, had remarried, and my son had taken the name of the man he believed to be his father. I had been gone, without explanation and with no way to send word, for seven years, and so could not lay blame for this turn of circumstance on my former family. Faced with the fall of the city, and the near-certainty of my death, my wife had made a new union, feeling it in the best interests of her son. Now, upon my return, she was tormented with guilt and, after confessing her love for me, sought to prove it by drowning herself and our son in the pool of Sidi Abdullah Ibn Hassun. She succeeded in both her endeavors.

"For seven nights I looked for their bodies. The pool, so lovely in the days of my youth, had grown rank with misuse and then disuse and the surface was stained with a foul-smelling algae. At last, on the seventh day, as the sun rose, I leaned over the side of my small boat and, despairing that I would never find the bodies of my wife and son, and mourning also for the ruin of the city that I loved, I wept, and my tears mingled with the water. In the moments afterward, it seem'd to me that the pool regained some of its former luster, and I saw my reflection in it, and thus my fate. Accordingly, I gave up the search and I join'd up with De Graff, that grand corsair who figures in so many tales, and together we set ourselves on attacking cargo ships, particularly slavers, taking gold and silver and other booty as our compensation, but invariably setting captives free. Alas, no treasure, and no adventure, could ever distract or compensate me from what I had lost in Sale."

*A*fter Zayd completed his melancholy tale, Read once again proffered his invitation for the Moor to join on our sojourn to the island of the sea-turtles.

"I pray, come with us," Read said. "You have earned the right to relax a little."

"Leisure time leaves my mind awandering. I think of my lost ones, and know that I will leave no heir behind. Go on without me."

"We will talk again on these matters," said Read. "And I mean before the angels above or the devil below takes us to our rest."

*S*o Read and I gathered together our things for the trip. As we readied the longboats, we spoke about the affairs of the *Will*.

"I have heard talk that Rackam may disband the company, in light of our recent prize," Read said.

"We have discussed it," I said.

"We should discuss it more," he answered. "There are more than turtles on this island. Here also resides a pair of privateers, dangerous and fabled. My intention is to seek their counsel about our endeavors."

"Who are these privateers?"

"You will meet them in good time."

As we approached the island, the water shimmered with many sparkling hues, turning from dark violet to medium green to almost clear blue. Read leaned over the railings and pointed out, in the waters beneath us, huge passing shadows, which looked like they were from clouds, but the sky was clear. The underwater shades were turtles, massive and swift; the creatures fed on the sea-apples that grew beneath the waves—that submerged crop is said to be sweeter than any fruit that grows on terrestrial farms.

We launched longboats for the men to take to shore and Read and I were among the first to disembark, with Poop traveling in our company. Ahhh—Read's description of this place as a paradise did not do it justice! The beach where we landed was as white as a fair maiden's breasts, the wind was calm, and the sun hot but not unbearably so for these parts. Read laughed and pointed out two turtles, each seven feet in length, coupling on the beach.

"Their congress seems . . . slow," I said.

"Don't it?" said Read. "Their copulation lasts several days. Would that men could endure as long, or women."

Poop, who was walking a few paces behind us, giggled and blushed at such rude humor.

Read and I unloaded a pair of marlinspikes from the longboat and went walking along the shore. We took off our boots to feel the sand beneath our toes, which was soft and warm and pleasing to the feet. We were alone, save Poop, since the other men who had come to shore had not disembarked near our landing. We walked hand in hand down the beach and, from time to time we would show signs of affection to each other: Read would stroke my hair and caress my brow or I would kiss him lightly on the nape of the neck or the back of his hand.

As we strolled the beach, female turtles dug pits in the sand and laid their eggs. The eggs, as we saw after close observation and handling, were not brittle shelled, like those of a bird, but soft and covered with only a thin membrane. Read said they were not good to eat, but provided the warning too late for Poop, who gagged and spat out the remains of an egg he had attempted to consume as a midday snack.

"You are fortunate the mother did not discover you eating her young," I said to Poop.

"No matter," said Read. "These mothers do not care much for their eggs once they are laid. In that, they bear similarities to many parents."

A few paces on, we came across a turtle of the edible variety which, tho' heavy, all three of us managed to flip over. The creature lay on its back, its stubby brown legs fluttering helplessly.

"They do not possess the power to right themselves," said Read. "If left in this manner, they would survive for a short time, but then succumb to the elements and perish."

To put the creature out of its misery and provide for our supper, Read and I simultaneously drove our marlinspikes into the creature's soft underside. To my surprise, it let out a sound that was not unlike a baby's cry. We twisted the marlinspikes to bring its end more swiftly, and it called out again and then one last time before it ceased its movement and then seem'd to die.

Night was coming hard on and so we built a small fire on the beach near the water. We had slaughtered the turtle by this time and stripped it of its shell. We impaled strips of turtle flesh on the end of pimento sticks and held them in the fire for roasting. The aroma was pleasant and promised good eating to come. The beach around us, while in the main pristine, was also littered, at a few points, with the wooden planks of shipwrecks, mostly privateer vessels that had been captured by Rogers and, the crew having been taken into custody, left to crash into the shore. Other crew members having set up residence for the night at other spots along the beach many paces along now announced their presence by starting bonfires with the ship wreckage; the strip of white beach looked like a group of stars a god had pulled from the firmament to blaze its glory directly on the earth.

"I'm saddened that Zayd did not join us," said Read, looking 'round at the night sky. "To endure so many troubles! And yet he is unbroken. I feel there is a joy in him, hidden by melancholy, that longs to come out."

"To lose a child and a spouse is a calamity beyond all calamities," I said.

"The first is more tragic than the second," said Read. "We can forget former lovers and learn to romance others just as well. But the heart never falls out of love with a child."

Poop had drifted asleep, and so Read and I held on to each other as we sat 'round the fire and roasted turtle meat. The fire reached up and pushed back the night. Read's strong but gentle hands kneaded the muscles of my shoulders.

"You have the softest skin of any privateer I know," he said.

"I know not whether I should be insulted or pleased. I like to think, at least, that I have the muscles of a privateer."

"These bodies," said Read, "are perhaps what we are, but not who we are."

Read, reaching from behind, traced his fingers along the line of my neck. I had unbound my bosom and loosened my shirt and my upper torso was exposed. A large bead of warm sweat dripped from Read's face into the hollow between my breasts. The perspiration mixed with my own and trickled down my belly, disappearing between my legs.

"I want to kiss you," he said. "I want to kiss you as Rackam kisses you."

I leaned forward, away from Read, and his hands fell from my body.

We did not speak for a time.

"Where, by my faith, are the fabled privateers we are to meet?" I said, at last, when we had both recovered ourselves.

"We will see them in the morning, at first light," said Read.

"Who are they?"

"They are a duo of much experience, who have fought many battles and who will bring us guidance. Their labors are the stuff of legend, and of song."

"Why do you seek to convince me to remain in the life? Surely a noose awaits us if we tally in this profession past our time. I have convinced Rackam that the moment has come to turn respectable."

"Respectable! I was that once—and married too," said Read.

"You were married?"

"To a Flemish lad, who, like me, was an officer in a Regiment of Horse. We retired after several engagements, and I made the tilt toward housekeeping, and together, as a means of finance, we managed an inn under the sign of the Three Horse Shoes."

"You were married, you served in the army, and you served as the maid of some comfortable country inn? I don't know which of these things is the more surprising."

"My husband died soon after we opened our establishment; then, the Peace of Reswick being concluded, there was no resort for me in the service. Looking for adventure, or, at the least, relief from the boredom of central Europe, I took passage on a ship that was bound for the West Indies. When it was taken by privateers, they took me for a man and I was offer'd the seadog's choice, and thus began my run in my current profession."

"How does all this relate to our current circumstances?"

"Ride or die, that is my shibboleth. To stop moving is to perish. My time rooted in place at the Three Horse Shoes was the unhappiest and most calamitous of my life, costing me a mate, a profession, and nearly my life. But—thank the stars!— it did not cost me my youth. That is the very definition of when growth is possible, and all paths are clear. If one does not attempt actions that are reckless and revolutionary when one is still young enough to dare them, one might have well have been born old. And most men are born old."

"But not you."

"No," said Read, "I was, like most, born old. But I will die young."

We sat in silence for a bit, and Read poked the fire with a stick. Hot embers floated into the air and merged with the stars.

"Governor Rogers—" I began.

"Will pursue you whether you stay in the life, or leave it."

"Why?"

"Rackam and the Governor have had some business."

"What business?"

"It is better not to speak of it."

"Tell me."

"It is better—"

"Tell me what you know."

"Rackam and Rogers had some business. I know only that they served together on a vessel named the *Duke*, which traveled with a companion ship the *Duchess*, and embarked on a privateering voyage."

"What? The good Governor was a pyrate?"

Read spat.

"Nothing so common for the Governor. He was a lawful crook, his plunder was done with the permission of her majesty, Queen Elizabeth. A letter of marque he bore, to give official sanction to his slaughter. I know not the particulars, but on the voyage or afterward, Rogers and Rackam had some business and it ended badly. And Rogers's lapdog, Governor Lawes, has sworn to bring about his master's retribution."

Read spat again, this time into the fire, and sparks flew up into the heavens.

"I know not the particulars. I only know this: Rogers will pursue Rackam until one or the other is dead."

"You harbor a secret."

"You know me too well, my love."

"Tell me your secret."

"I cannot, for it is not mine to tell. Either Rackam, or the Governor, must tell you this truth or it is not to be believed."

We paused in our conversation, and, in the quiet, the voices of other crew members of the *Will* drifted into our ears—our fellows were chanting and singing choruses. Our fire was dying now, and all along the beach other fires were going out. The voices were fading, and soon the soft, rhythmic slurp of the surf against the shore was louder than any song.

"Kingston will be the end of it," I said. "We will quit this life."

"Humor me only in this," said Read. "Let us meet the privateers first. See them, and make your decision."

"And when will we meet these legends?"

"At first light."

So when morning came, and the turtles had all left their eggs and slipped back into the waves, Read and I walked down to the water's edge to meet the privateers. He told me, as we walked, that these privateers were bold and strong, able with the sword and accurate with the pistol; that they had braved many battles together and evaded capture at several turns.

"So where are these privateers?"

"Smell the air!" said Read.

"What?"

"The air!"

I breathed in the morning. The scent of fresh mangoes was in the breeze, succulent and sweet.

"There is no such air in London or in Paris, nor in New York besides," said Read. "Perhaps you could have filled your lungs with the perfume of such freedom in Sale, but that city is forever lost! On some day many mornings hence, when you and I are old and these firm bodies give way to slackness and wrinkled flesh, you will remember the smell of mangoes and you will remember this time. Let no man change you! This air, this life, this is who you are!"

"But I'm the one that wants to leave this life, not Rackam. I convinced him."

"No, he convinced you to convince him."

"What?"

"Men fool women into thinking that they are following the second sex's commands when, in secret and in advance, they have already mesmerized the women into issuing commands that the men wished to follow in the first place."

"I thought that was a stratagem that women employed."

"Women have a reputation for the tacit manipulation, but it is undeserved. Their spirits can be so malleable, they oftentimes unknowingly adopt the hopes and desires of their mates even when it is counter to their original interests. Their lover's goals then become indistinguishable from their own."

"Enough of this talk."

"So when women tell men what to do, in some secret way they are actually following the man's commands. In this interpretation of human behavior you may invest in me your trust. When it comes to emotional subterfuge, men are, by some wide distance, the biggest women of them all."

"Ahhh! Enough!"

Read fell silent.

I surveyed the horizon.

"I do not see a sail," I said. "Where are your bold privateers?"

"Look at the sea. The privateers are there."

I looked into the water, which, in this light, at this time, like that fabled pool of Sidi Abdullah Ibn Hassun, had the sheen of mirror. I saw my face for the first time since I had set sail—it was bronzed, and perhaps as dark as Zayd's, and my hair, unkempt and free, was a red tangle like a blazing bonfire. My journey, and the elements, had brought my secret history to the fore. There was some wild blood in me that I had not taken measure of before. Baltimore lived within me. All this time I thought of myself as an actor, a charlatan, some sad jester rendering an impersonation, an approximation, a weak lampoon of other men. The anger I felt, the rage that ruled me, the glint of the she-wolf's eye that bore down on me still—I thought all these things were buried within me somehow. But I have long believed that our faces, eventually, reflect who we really are, and the lives we have led. The soul is a kind of cartographer, sketching our life's journey on the vellum of our visage. I looked closely at myself in the sea's mirror.

"Do you see the privateers?" said Read.

A breeze blew across the face of the waters and my reveries came to an end.

"I see only myself," I lied.

I looked down the beach. Poop had built a city of sand beside the surf, with high barricades fortified with seaweed and sticks for spires, and now, as the morning faded, the lapping waters eroded its foundations into silt and sea-foam.

Hand in hand, Read and I walked back toward the longboat.

PART THE THIRD

Dead Reckoning

chapter 26.

In the voyage of our lives, there is a shadow-line, before which our thoughts are focused more on opportunities to be gain'd, and beyond which our concerns are ever after more concentrated on dreams that have slipped from our grasp. And so our ship sails on, carried by a sadder wind than it was before it transversed the divide. Ahh—the people we could have been haunt us like ghosts; we see ourselves with other lovers, in other countries, kings and queens of nations of our own imagination. There can be little joy in living when one resides in a graveyard of passed lives. All we need, by my faith, is this: to have a life that's worth a story. For who are we but the tales we tell? Bodies wither, wealth erodes, the things we build inevitably fall to ruin, and the inventions we devise are eventually surpassed, for such is the nature of things scientific. Only stories last forever, or at least as long as there are voices around to tell them, which is plenty long enough.

So where was I in my narration? I need a sip to refresh my spirits, my darling, my sweetness. Behind where you fetched the coffee there is a compartment—ahh yes, you've found it! A fine burglar might you have made, my sweet one! That's Jamaican rum, saved from the store of the Spanish galleons we raided when I was young. Now that I have lost a step, the rum has but hit its stride. You can put the coffee back, my dear. Yes—pour a mug. That's for you, I'll sip straight from the bottle. Ahh, it does bring a flush to the cheeks, does it not? Trust me on this advice, my dear one, and keep it close to your heart—a good, strong bottle of rum, when the heart is shattered and lonely, is always ample substitute for a lover's touch. How I wish I had a strip of turtle flesh and a roaring fire to go with my refreshment! But where was I in my tale?

Jamaica! Ahh, the days slipped away in that tropic place. Yesterday was tomorrow and tomorrow was yesterday and each day passed like the day before. Jamaica! Every season is summer and all is everlasting emerald. There are no golden leaves tumbling in cool autumn air, no icy lace falling from above. Time, in that place, never seem'd to pass, and the summer seem'd huge and eternal. Every morning's bed-rising repeated the last in its glory and its comfort. It was the very opposite of our life among the brethren of the coast. The *Will* had been scrapped and sold; John and I watched her three masts stripped naked. The crew had scattered to the four winds; John and I were content to let them blow.

"Do you miss the sea-storms, Captain Rackam?" I would tease John.

"Not a bit."

"Do you miss the taste of salt in your mouth?"

"Coffee will do."

"Do you miss the combat and the roar of muskets?"

"I have not thought upon it."

"Do you miss the stench of men in the crew quarters?"

"Perhaps a little," he joked, "but then the moment passes."

John and I lived snugly in a gray hut on the crest of a brown hill. The walls of the hut were made of bamboo, cut after it had ripened so it would harden as it aged and not rot. The roof was thatched with the tops of sugarcane stalks, the long narrow leaves plaited in a tight crisscross pattern to keep out the wind and wet. Those times seem ever present. Rising from my rest after a long gentle night, I gaze upon my surroundings as the mists of morning pull back from the land like a billowing sheet. The green hills, rolling, voluptuous, are revealed naked in the light, like lovers in a bed savoring the last of slumber. Purple-crested doctorbirds hover above the pale yellow blossoms of cashew trees, long-legged egrets ride serenely on the rumps of cattle. The shadows of clouds pass over the cedar trees of Fullow's Wood, the white waters of One Eye River, the swaying grasses of Grave's Valley. The sun rises higher, changing color and heat, passing from warm red to yellow hot.

"Get up my love! Get up and greet the day!"

John rises beside me, and makes his presence known with a soft kiss on the nape of my neck. He strolls to the front of the hut, as he does every morning, to check on his beloved gray rose bushes—they have yet to bloom in this unfamiliar climate, but he is optimistic that they will blossom soon. He laughs, and goes to the back of our hut. A pawpaw tree grows there and every morning he scales the trunk, climbs into the branches, and picks a fruit and a flower. He jumps to the ground, tumbles onto the grass, regains his feet, and comes up smiling. He eats the yellow-orange meat of the fruit with a squeeze of lime, offers me a bite, which fills my mouth with sweet juice, and then he gives me the yellow-orange flower he has just plucked for me to wear in my hair. He has work to do, and fields to till, but it is violent hot, and so we take a stroll along the coast, walking in the shade of the trees at the edge of a forest that overlooks the sea. The tips of the branches of the trees are dotted with blossoms of cream, pink, and emerald. The breeze is light and the cries of gulls carry in the air. In the waters below, schools of fish travel in darting clusters of gold and green and silver. Farther out from the shore, I can see dark, unexplored continents of coral beneath the shimmering blue waves.

"There is a fair wind this day," says John. "South by southwest."

"Our sails are folded, and stored away in the sail room," I say.

"So they are."

As the cool of the late afternoon comes, we return to our land; I pull up seven cassava plants, cutting off the roots—which look like fat fingers—and leaving the green stalks behind. I return to the hut and peel the rough brown skin off of each root, exposing the white flesh beneath. I slice the flesh of the roots into thin strips and then cut those strips into even smaller pieces and place the diced bits in the center of a square of muslin cloth. I twist the cloth tight, squeezing out the poisonous juice. Then I open up the cloth and knead the pieces of cassava root, along with a sprinkle of salt, into a lumpy mash. I am making a bammy. I light the cooking fire behind our hut and put the mash onto an iron plate. After the edges of the bammy begin to blacken, I pull it from over the fire. I bite into the bammy when it is still warm. The inviting, bready smell fills my nose. It pleases me, and I know it will also please John.

"Remember Sugar-Apple and his dishes?"

"Too well," says John, his cheeks bulging with bammy. "His companionship was a treasure, but I do not miss his food!"

So this is the life we lead. We reside in the parish of Clarendon, a few days journey from Spanish Town, also called St. Jago de la Vega, and the Blue Mountains tower in the near-distance. Our ship's company had long since been disbanded and, with much celebration and less haggling than might be expected, the journey's treasure was divied up with each man receiving an equal share, tho' John, privateer that he is, saved a diamond brooch for me as a token to mark his affection. After the breaking of the ship's fellowship, John and I, bidding good-bye to Read, Poop, First-Rate, Zayd, and the lot, pushed a little way into Jamaica's interior, which is rich and loamy, and he purchased a modest tract of land on which to do his farming and live as a man retired from a life of turmoil and strife on the unpredictable sea. From time to time I would think of my father and wonder where in this land he resided. When travelers passed by, I would query them about his whereabouts, or whether they had heard of him or seen a man who matched his description; but whether he was living in the open or under some pseudonym, I did not know, and, in any case, there was no news of him.

Soon enough, John and I contracted with a team of men—whites, blacks, and mulattos almost the same shade as me—and they aided in clearing a sizable space of land of weeds and tree roots, and together we also began the construction of a great house. The new domicile was as grand as any home in which I had ever lived, or visited—its walls were of cedar wood, its roof wide and sloping, its many doorways seem'd to smile a happy entrance to all visitors. All around and on every side, growing naturally and well matured, there were fruit trees—

ackee, jackfruit, banana, grapefruit, citron, and lime. But growing in most abundance were the mango trees, their leather leaves shining as if wet with rain, the red-gold fruit hanging, ripe and ready for plucking, tender and savory to the tongue.

While I cooked and worried myself with things domestic, John took to the fields, shirt off, pouring sweat, hacking with his hoe, churning up the red-brown earth and laying in donkey manure to make it all the richer. I would join him when my chores were done and we would, kneeling side by side in the earth, dig holes and lay cuttings for yams. 'Round the field we planted peas, which attract snails and other blight and distract them from doing injury to the main crop; as soon as the pea vines sprouted up from the soil, John and I set up poles in the earth for the new growth to run up on.

When the night came, for our supper, I would prepare Stamp and Go, which is codfish flavor'd with onion and garlic and black pepper and other spices, rolled in a golden batter and fried. On other nights, I would ready pepperpot soup, which is a stew made of callalloo, hale, pepper, and other ingredients, and is very hot. Or perhaps I would make ackee and codfish or oxtail and beans, depending on my mood and John's taste. Near the hut and house we had begun a grove of pimento trees, the product of which is called allspice in these regions. After our evening meal, John and I would sit among the trees of the grove taking our rest in hammocks slung between the trunks, the aroma of the trees in the air all around us. He liked me to dress as a man, and to talk as a man, and so, since that was consonant with my nature, I would wear his breeches and canvas shirts, and together we would talk in the rough cadences of men, even as we shared sweet intimacies. We would lie there as we sipped pawpaw juice squeezed into calabash containers; on occasion, John would light his pipe and I would burrow into the crook of his arm, and we would look up into the night sky, which was full of stars and very clear. Sometimes I would think of the *Will*, her proud masts disrobed and desecrated, and a gray gloom would tinge my meditations. At other times I would think back on the face of the man I stabbed through the chest on the Spanish galleon and I would wonder again if he had any children, and the memory would take hold of me like a mantis that bites off the head of its mate and then it would pass just as suddenly and I would be filled with relief that I had left that life of death behind.

The troubles came with the summer rain.

chapter 27.

The past is always present. Throughout my life I have seen my history spread out before me, like some well-trodden road in some dark wood beckoning me to take its course. When I dreamt at night, during those days in my well-appointed house in Jamaica, I dreamt of things gone by. I felt the cradle-rock of the waves, I heard the rude, thrilling cries of the men, and I felt, once again, the breath of the Chocolate Gale. My dreams were not visions, I saw nothing but a darkness visible—no, even beyond Milton's poetics, I saw a darkness invisible, which is to say a nothingness beyond the absence of light. There were other sensations in my slumber—I could feel that sweet zephyr ruffling the small hairs on my arm and on the back of my neck like fingers made of air. Children's voices danced around me, fluttering like autumn leaves. The wind grows stronger now, running its small hands around the hair on my head, tousling it, tugging it, tickling my ears, whispering things I only half-hear and quarter-understand. Remember: the salt taste of sea wind, the sweet stink of man sweat. Remember: the burn of a rigging rope running through your hands, the sound of a whistle marking the end of the watch. Now behold: the afternoon sun above a white sand beach, the flat sea stretching from horizon to horizon, the topgallant sail blowing full of wind, looking up at a blue sky full of white clouds from my perch on the masthead with no man in the world between me and the Divine Providence.

John will not tell me his dreams. And yet he is haunted by some revenant of whom he will not speak, or perhaps cannot name. He calls out in his sleep in many tongues: Portuguese, Spanish, French, and languages that I cannot identify and which I did not know he spoke. His voice, at the times of these utterings, is hoarse with fear and tension as if he were undergoing some trial, the outcome of which is either life or death. On some nights, he whispers a name that I recognize—Woodes Rogers— and says it as softly as a priest ever read a psalm. On occasion, his forehead pouring sweat, his limbs writhing, his brow furrow'd mightily, John mutters some phrase in English, spit out like a curse, but taking the form of some command.

"Way aloft, topmen!" he would call out. "Take one reef in topsails!"

Or another time: "Stand by the booms! Trice up! Lay out and take one reef!"

Or another: "Light out to windward! Light out to leeward! Toggle away!"

On one occasion, midway between midnight and morning, I woke alone in our brass bed in our big house. We had imported the bed all the way from England, and yet John had never slept soundly in it a single night. Now I found him disappear'd and surmised that his nightmare had been of sufficient power to drive him entirely from his sleeping place. With much alarm, I gathered my nightclothes about myself and went in search of him.

The night was full of rain. There had been showers before, enough to fill the Traveler's Tree—named so because its hollow leaves store cool rainwater to slake the thirst of passersby—and enough to keep our small farm flowering and fruitful, but the rain had never come like this. This storm had been ceaseless—it had been going on more days than we cared to count and it threatened to continue longer than we could predict. The effluence came down at first like spears of water, then like mighty columns, and finally like walls of unending wet. It seem'd as if the sky and sea had switched places, and the latter was falling back to its rightful location.

The rain turned the sky gray in the daytime and hid the world behind a blurry veil; at night, the stars were washed away and the whole of heaven was submerged in the deluge. The spray had fists: it punched at you like a thousand pugilists, and it tugged at your clothes and pulled at your shoes. The downpour had a voice: it howled incessantly, like a pack of wild dogs baying at a full moon. At times, it seemed the rain had a spirit as well and, in the whip and whirl of the cascade, one could almost imagine a figure, vast and spectral, many armed and full of fury, performing a kind of violent, magic dance in the inundation.

I stood at the doorway to our home and I called out to John and received no reply, not from him, nor from any other soul; our estate, once staffed with people, had been emptied because there was no work. The fields, once filled with hands, were empty because the rain of St. Swithin made planting and harvest impossible; so too, the main house, once surrounded by builders, had been left half-finished because the rain prevented further construction. And yet we remained living in it, and the rains came down.

I turned from the doorway and searched our home: the great bedrooms that had never seen a guest, the kitchen that was now empty of food and cooks, and the dining room with its table for twenty and places set for two. Finally I returned to the doorway and looked out into the gray rain, whose voice now seem'd to roar obscenely in the ear, mocking and profane, louder with each passing moment.

Into the rain I went, instantly soaked to my skin but pressing ever forward, calling John's name out into the falling river, hearing naught by way of reply save the million-throated voice of the rain. And still the rain came down. I called out over the ruined fields, into the surrounding pimento trees, out into the ruined shacks where our workers once resided. I walked on and called out to where John and I had cleared ground for the con-struction of a sugar mill, I yelled down into the depth of a newly dug well, I yelled into the branches of a tall cedar tree. I heard nothing and I received no reply. And so the rain fell, gray and wet and interminable.

It was in the grove of mango trees that I finally saw them. At first I thought it was the rain, performing its mocking rigadoon. Then I thought it was some wild beast, a boar perhaps, off-course on its way from the tangled slopes of the Blue Mountains and now wandering here, lost and uncertain. Then, even through the rain, I thought I heard a man's voice—not words, but mut-terings—and, with the instinct of my profession, I reached for my cutlass and then cursed myself silently that I was foolishly unarmed and now, here I was, confronted by rank strangers. My heart was beating again in the old way, and I both dreaded the sensation and wished it would never stop. Tho' I had drowned myself in pleasure in this place, tho' I had tasted every taste, heard the sweet songs of birds and felt the soft caress of a true lover, my eyes and skin and ears never came alive like this in that place, as they were in that moment. There are some that grow attached to opium and, after partaking of a puff, while away their days, ever afterward in the service of that sweet narcotic. I have never smoked the stuff myself, and yet I felt I knew its ways, for no anodyne could be as transporting as action. Ahh, for a cutlass at this time! I broke a branch off from the cedar tree, peeled back its tip to make it sharp, and then turned once again to the figure behind the curtain of gray rain.

"Speak, stranger!" I said. "Say your name!"

I heard nothing in reply.

Now I saw two figures, and they were crouched over a third. Was that my John on the ground, subdued? With a battle cry I ran forward, brandishing my cedar branch and offering, in my heart, my whole estate for a sword.

Then, as I approached, one of the two figures looked up at me. Ha! I dropped my makeshift weapon and hugged him tight. It was Read, come again after a long absence from my eyes.

chapter 28.

Read and Poop had journeyed from St. Jago de la Vega, three days journey over land, to find us. They had been lost in the rain when they had come across John lying face down and motionless in the muddy patch of earth beside the mango grove. They did not know why he had fallen, whether because of some unknown ailment or at the hand of some unseen assailant. They had stooped to the ground to offer him some assistance when I made my arrival.

Carrying John on our shoulders, we return'd to the main house, and, after drying off, and being given a mug of hot coffee spiked with rum, John recovered his senses. His bearings came back gradually, and, for a time, he seem'd to be immersed in another world. His eyes look'd past me, beyond his guests, and focused on some far-off vista. He open'd his mouth as if to speak, but said nothing. He reached out as if to take hold of some prize, but grasped at air. Finally he stumbled to his feet and fell into his favorite chair and would suffer no inquiries about his condition.

"Why have you come?" John said at last to Read and Poop.

"Are you not glad to see us?" said Read.

"You are well met," said John. "But I sense an ill omen."

"I do not sense it," said Read. "Perhaps it is the rain you hear."

"Indeed, it has fallen in such a constant manner as to make a man mad," I said. "But, come, tell us why you have come."

"My dear Bonn," said Read. "Surely there is happiness in your heart upon our arrival."

"There is joy there. But there is also an inquiry."

Read laughed and clapped my shoulder.

"We've come for gold," said Read.

"You'll find none here," said John. "I've not buried my wealth in the ground, or in some hidden cay like the privateer legends of song. My treasure is bank'd, and therefore well protected."

"All you'll discover here," I said, "are wet fields, rotten mangoes, and unending rain. The coffee we all drink ranks among the last of our supplies."

"We've not come for your gold—we've come for more gold than you possess, or than we all possess or than can be imagined."

John's eyes narrowed as he heard this news, and my heart beat faster. Read lift'd his mug to his lips, paused like any showman on stage, and continued his dramatic monologue.

"The gold we seek is not here—it is in Dry Harbor Bay, near Port Negril. And it is waiting for us to seize it."

Now Read spoke his peace. He had been frequenting drinking establishments located on the north coast of the island, in such places as Porto Maria Bay and the like, when he had been so fortunate as to come across some information of a certain value. He had been playing Back-Gammon in a bar, and his opponent lacked the funds to support his wagers. Read had drawn his cutlass, ready to run the scoundrel through, when the man in question offered up a tale to pay his way.

"Why should I trust the word of a man who has lied at wagering?" Read told the man. "Come, a sword point's too romantic for your end. Accompany me outside, so I can finish you with a musketball."

"Listen!" cried the man. "There is a ship that sits in Dry Harbor Bay. . . ."

And the man told this tale. Typically, as all mariners know, a hull is cleaned by burning off the barnacles (which slow a vessel and make it difficult to steer), caulking the rotten planks, and swabbing the hull with a mix of tallow, oil, and brimstone, ingredients that resist the spread and return of the vermin of the deep. One vessel, in particular, that had been brought in to careen at Dry Harbor Bay was much more than it seemed.

"This vessel is outfitted like any common fishing craft," said the man. "But within its hold sits treasure bound for Portugal. The gold in its hold far exceeds the wealth to be found in possession of a dozen Spanish galleons."

I interrupted Read's narration and spoke thus: "By what means, dear Read, have you ascertained this tale's veracity?"

"Because at the conclusion of this story, the man produced a letter that told of the plan, marked with the seal of the good Governor Rogers himself. He may be at war with privateers, but, regardless, and on account of sea-dogs like those gathered here, merchant ships still sail in trepidation, and have been advised to travel in disguise to better hide those things worth hiding. I have spread the word—I want to gather the old crew together and take this prize, if it can be taken!"

"We have gold enough," I said. "Indeed, more than we can spend."

"You can never have too much wealth, just as one can never have too much air, or too many kisses. It is a thing without limits, like the sea or sky or the appetite of fire."

From his seat in the corner, John let out a sigh. He was not one for sighing, and the utterance had the effect of a shout. We all turn'd toward him to hear what he had to say.

"I feel I must tell you both this, so, in making your decision on this matter, you have the whole truth. Firstly, Governor Rogers, and his agent Governor Lawes, will not rest until he sees me, and whomever are my companions at that time, hanging from a noose at Gallows Point. Mark you those words, for they are true and factual."

"Why do you say this?" I asked.

"I know because I have heard him, from his lips, swear to carry this out."

"Why?" I asked. "What drives him? These seas are full of scoundrels."

"To understand the Governor, one must first acquaint oneself with his daughter."

So then John told his story.

Governor Woodes Rogers's daughter, he said, was full of spirit and in possession of a comely figure, a white breast, and full blushing cheeks. At the time of this incident she made her residence in London, leaving to her father the affairs and politics of the new world. She was innocent of all men and had, in consultation with her mother and her priest, made the decision to enter a convent and thus betroth herself to the Divine Providence and forsake the things of this earthly sphere, and, accordingly, was bound on a voyage to a port in France.

John, in his first expedition as the captain of a privateer vessel, took her craft at sea and gave all aboard the sea-dog's choice: to join his crew or be put to sea in a longboat, and, thus equipped, to face the storms of Poseidon. Most aboard, being men and women of station, accepted the latter—the rich often reason with optimism, figuring that, since's life breaks have broken for them favorably thus far, there is no reason to believe luck will not continue to support them in all things. The Governor's daughter, however, accepted his invitation to remain, tho' the choice of joining the crew was, in fact, only offered to the men. This was a woman who had a spirit of adventure, and yet had never known challenge; she found herself drawn to the sea-life with the same intensity she was formerly drawn to chastity and prayer.

So she join'd John's crew, not as a man, as Read and I had done, but as a woman. This proved a mistake. John and this woman soon became loyal, and John, being more reckless than his more mature self, enjoyed her charms openly and with abandon. His crew, a wild collection of convicts and roustabouts, grew jealous and resentful, having no members of the fairer sex to satisfy their carnal needs.

One day, as John went ashore to obtain supplies, a full complement of the crew, perhaps a score, came to John's cabin to enjoy his new charge and the pleasures of her flesh in the same way he did, but with more roughness, and some blade work. John, upon his return, slew all the men responsible, each one in their turn, but his love's spirit was lost. She was like some pluck'd flower, wilting and never to regain her former freshness and blossom. He return'd her to London and later, through contacts, he heard that she had died in her father's house, in her mother's arms, after confessing to a loose-tongued priest the complete tale of her misadventures and of John's part in them.

"Now I am haunted by dreams of this affair," said John, "enough to remove my senses and leave me prone, as you found me."

"So can there be no mission?" said Read.

My heart sank, as if my chest had been tied with iron chains dropped into a deep river. Our mission was aborted even before it started. John caught my eye and no doubt read my disappointment. I truly was my father's child after all this long while, for dirt, and farming, were to be my future. Ahhh—in every relationship, something in someone dies, and it is almost invariably within the woman. When two souls meet, one must give up its former habits and adapt to the other. The only hope is that the new life at least has some charms to rival the old. But damn to hell our fields and fruit trees—how could they ever compete with the spray of salt sea in the mouth and the wind at one's back? I would never smell the sweet aroma of the Chocolate Gale again. I could feel tears coming on, but I fought them back.

"We must stay here," I said. "For Governor Rogers, and his agent Nicholas Lawes, will be ever vigilant."

"I see the wisdom in such caution," said Read.

"On the contrary," said John quietly. "We must go."

"What?" I said. "Have I missed the point of your tale?"

"Entirely," he said.

"I must confess," said Read, "I, too, have lost the sense of the thing."

"A ship on the move is hard to board," said John. "If we stay still, the Governor will find us."

"Is that your tale in its entirety?" said Read. "I am someone who has left his share of yarns half-told himself, and I sense you have more to relate."

"That is all I have to say."

"Then our course is clear," I said, my blood rising up to the new challenge. "We must do what the governors least expect—strike!"

And so we packed what supplies we had and all of us, John, Read, Poop, and I, headed out into the rain. John checked his garden of gray roses one last time as we left our farm. No flowers had taken root. All that was there was mud.

chapter 29.

I cannot say what drew us back into the life. Was it the love of gold or the thirst for such enterprises that stir the blood? Or perhaps it was some strange infatuation with death, whose sweet perfume, danger, could not so much as be whiffed in our comfortable landlock'd country life. Then, too, perhaps we were drawn by that same force that sets the patterns of storms, and gives rhythm to the tides, draws sea-turtles to their spawning grounds with each season, and placed the constellations in their eternal vectors.

But ahhh—I do not believe in fate. Cassandra whispers her prophesies in my ear and I laugh, as if her words were merely riddles for the amusement of children. I did not argue with John, nor with Read, because I did not want to; there were a legion of reasons I could have muster'd in an argument to remain, but I did not sound the battle cry. When one has a skill at a certain thing, it is hard to set aside that talent. If we are true to our souls, we must follow our facility even if it dooms us. Proficiency applied makes us feel unburdened and free; ignored and unused, it follows us like a lead shadow, dragging on our lives interminably. I did believe, at one time, that I was playing the role of my life, like smooth-tongued Viola searching for her drown'd brother in Illyria. I knew my lines, but the question was begged: who was the actor beneath the costume? Now, in my return to action, I at last recognized the truth of it: unlike some thespian, I understood I was not slipping into some part, but slipping out of a character, such as wrongly besmirched Hermione or sad-eyed Ophelia, and finally leaving the stage for the honest streets. The role was real.

*I*t seem'd, at first, that the heavens smiled on our journey. As we took the path toward our destination, the rain, which had fallen these many days, stopped. Next the sky, which had been somber, faded from gray to a happy blue, and the sun came playfully from its place of hiding and danced across the sky, shining brighter than a newly minted doubloon. We walked carrying only light leather packs, pistols, and cutlasses, with John at the head, Read and me following, and Poop trailing.

We continued on, passing Scots Cove and Hudson's Hole and Parrot's Bay. The forests shifted from scattered groves of trees to denser thickets, and soon we were beneath a high canopy of branches that blotted out the sky. The ground was matted with decayed fallen leaves. The earth here was springy and spongy and seemed to add bounce to the step as we walked. The trees, however, seemed engaged in a struggle to gain footing in the loose soil, which sagged away even as their roots reached out to take hold of it. The roots of the trees—which looked like the gnarled hands of crones—were, in most cases, naked and exposed; the loamy earth around them had been washed away by flood or blown away by wind. Many of the trees were of Olympian stature, and their root systems were the size of houses. Not long into our trek, our small party passed underneath a huge, ancient cedar tree whose exposed roots spread out on either side of us, leaving enough space for all in our party to walk through upright.

Near the close of day, we came to a waterfall. The foliage of the forested land near the sea had proved to be thick and very near impassable. We had therefore continued our trek a bit farther inland, where the trees and scrub were less dense. But we had encountered an unexpected obstacle. Before us now was a vast green ridge, stretching for miles on either side. The ridge was a near-vertical slope and covered with trees. To climb this ridge would be more difficult than scaling a mountain.

Still, there might be a way. In the center of the ridge, a waterfall cut through the trees. The water had eroded the rock, making the slope of its stream more gentle than the ridge around it. The fall was long, extending many feet upward. The top of the falls was shrouded in white mist and spray and merged with the white sky. The waterfall, then, seemed to flow straight from heaven and down to the earth.

In the end this was what was decided: being the nimblest climber of the group, I scaled the falls in the lead, with a rope tied around my waist. Next came Read, holding the rope, and then followed Poop, with John taking up the rear. In the early going the current was a mere trickle of water on the rock. Soon, it was a flood, crashing all around. Spray flew in our faces and into our eyes. The current was less swift at the sides of the fall, where the water cascaded over the rocky earth alongside the forest. So we scaled up the sides only to find that the rocky ground there was slippery with slimy moss. I found it difficult to gain sure footing and harder still to hold on to the rocks ahead and pull forward.

The flood crashed down around us as we went farther up the sides of the waterfall. The current grew even stronger. It was a roar in the ear, like a thousand dogs howling in rough chorus. It was hard to hear anything else but the roar of water, hard to think on anything else but the water. It seemed to fill the whole world with spray and foam. The falling flood soaked the clothes to the skin and tugged at the arms and legs, pulling us all downward even as we strove to climb upward.

But soon the top of the falls was in sight; I could see it ahead through a curtain of mist. Read lost his footing and Poop began to go down with him, but, finding a toehold on the rock, Read maintain'd his grip on the rope and pulled them back up.

"Why did we come back to this life?" I shouted to Read.

"I did not come back for gold, or for glory," he hollered back. "I came back for you!"

At last I reached the top. I waded through the rushing water to the bank of the river that fed the waterfall and waited for the others to come to the summit. The sun was setting now and the last light of the day was shining through the mist at the summit of the fall. The air was filled with rainbows. They danced in the air. I looked through the rainbows and the mist and over the crest of the waterfall. The forest was spread out before us.

Through the mists and colors, in the distance, I could see Dry Harbor Bay.

chapter 30.

We reached the harbor in the late afternoon. Seabirds floated above the drink like white petals thrown into the wind; below, vessels of varying sizes glided along the water, gentle as prayers. Farther out to sea, dolphins splashed and played, arching over foam-tipped waves. Read, holding his cutlass in his left hand with the tip toward the harbor, pointed out the treasure ship. The *Adventure*, her name was, and she was a two-masted vessel with all her sheets down, lying anchor'd in the water.

"We'll need a boat to take her," said John.

We left our packs buried under the sand in a strip near the harbor and carried with us only our light weaponry—pistols, swords, and the like. We swam out to sea a short distance and came upon a fishing vessel with one mast. I boarded first, being the strongest swimmer, and I told the crew that their craft was taken; Read and John climbed on board hard after and, with their drawn weapons, echoed my claim and gave it additional force.

I then recognized both members of the fishing duo.

"Hunahpu? Xbalanque?"

"Yes, it is I," said Xbalanque, my old foil.

"I see you still practice the profession that Xbalanque and I have abandoned," said Hunahpu.

I looked upon the twins with some amazement. Xbalanque's face was much changed: where before there was sinister intent, there was now placidity; his mouth, which had been set in a sneer, was fixed in something resembling the beginnings of a smile. His eyes, once full of mischief, now regarded me with what seem'd to be a bit of pity. And Hunahpu, always the more genial, seem'd even more friendly than in our days on the *Will*.

"We ply an honest trade now," said Xbalanque. "We are fishermen, like our ancestors."

"We used our privateer winnings to establish ourselves," explained Hunahpu.

"You are both well met," I said, "but we are in need of a vessel."

"We have no valuables aboard this ship," said Xbalanque.

"And no fish either," continued Hunahpu. "We have caught naught but a single bluefish all day and, in my opinion, they are horrible eating. Surely there are better catch for privateers in these waters than the likes of us."

"Put your mind at ease," said John. "We give you our word that we will give you back your boat when we have concluded our business. You know my word is good."

With that, Read took the oars from Hunahpu and steered the boat toward the treasure ship.

"You know the Governor is looking to hang you," Xbalanque told John. "Rogers hung a privateer every day this month. Whatever mission you're on, abandon it. We're all better off fishing."

"Or trying to fish, anyway," said Hunahpu. "We have caught nothing sizable or salable for two weeks."

"Come with us and you'll have a catch you can boast about," John replied.

Now the treasure ship came into view. The *Adventure* was a sleek vessel—two elegant masts, a sturdy oak hull, an elegant carving of a mermaid on the prow—but, as Read had predicted, the ship was clearly undermanned. There were just two hands aboard her deck, and one of the men lay under the forecastle, his cap slid down over his eyes and a loud snoring in the air around him.

John motioned for us to creep up astern. There were ropes dangling from the vessel's hull. John took the lead and Read and I follow'd him while Poop, hands shaking, watched the fishermen, a pistol in his unsteady grip. Xbalanque look'd amused by the proceedings, but in Hunahpu's face, I saw the lacertilian look, which I remember'd from his brother's visage when I knew them on the *Will*, slowly slither into his features and his eyes.

"Will you join us?" asked John.

"Let them go their way," said Xbalanque to his brother. "It'll lead to no good."

"What's my share?" said Hunahpu.

"Same as ours," said John, "if you can still hold a pistol."

"I can, indeed," answered Hunahpu. "And I can fire one, too."

"Don't be a fool," implored Xbalanque. "If you go with them, and they get caught, the Governor will hang us both."

"Do you want to stink of fish parts your whole life?"

"This is how our fathers lived."

"Our fathers are dead!"

"They live through us."

But it was too late—Hunahpu was already standing up in the boat. Rackam offer'd him a gun, but Hunahpu drew his own pistol from his waistband.

"You seem ready for action."

"You might say I've been waiting for you," said Hunahpu.

Hunahpu shimmied up the ropes after us. Xbalanque, shaking his head and sighing in resignation, pulled a long flat knife from his belt and followed his brother up the ropes.

Now all six of us—Rackam, Read, Xbalanque, Hunahpu, Poop, and I—stood on the deck of the ship. The two hands who had been asleep at their watch had woken up and regarded us with surprising calm.

"This ship is taken," said John.

At this, Poop put his fingers to his mouth and let loose a sharp whistle.

"What are you doing?" said Read. "You'll be heard!"

"I am dangerous," said Poop. "I told you I was."

The deck quickly filled with fighting men—dozens pouring from every doorway and hatchway like some ant mound disturbed with a kick and now on the march. One of the crewmen kneeled, aimed his musket, and fired. Xbalanque's throat was blown out and he fell to the deck, clutching at the wound.

"No!" screamed Hunahpu, followed by another utterance in his native tongue.

John, amidst this commotion, pulled his pistol and fired— but no shot sounded, as his weapon was wet from our swimming. He reached for another pistol off his bandolier.

"Throw down your arms!" shouted one of the opposing crewmen, taking aim.

"We'll kill your companions first," said another. "We've got orders from Lawes!"

At that, John paused.

"Don't you halt the fight on our account!" I said. "If we are to die, it'll be as men!"

But it was too late—John, head bowed, had let his weapon slip from his hand and had fallen to his knees in surrender.

"Lawes and Rogers want me, not you," said John. "We're finished."

At this, Read let loose a battle-whoop and, running forward, brandished his pistol and fired it—and when it, too, failed, he drew his sword and waded into the crush of men flooding the deck.

"Ride or die!" he shouted.

I drew my cutlass and found my place beside him.

I do wish, with all my heart's blood, that our final battle was worthy of a song. Ahh, how I desire that I could relate to you that the length of our battle was such that the sun was well above the skyline when we began our fight and that the moon had shone her face ere the conflict was concluded. How poetic it would be, if I could but report that the ship's deck was slippery with blood, and that the air was filled with the cries of men and the smell of gunpowder and yet still we fought on!

Alas, moments after I had drawn my sword, the thing was decided, and I was fallen, wounded, on the deck. I never saw the gun flash that struck me, nor did I hear its report. I saw only Poop standing over me, pistol smoking, tears running down his cheeks.

chapter 31.

After an initial period of imprisonment in Bridewell Prison, which is in the ruin'd city of Port Royal, I was taken by an armed escort of one score and six soldiers of his majesty to St. Jago de la Vega, which means "St. James on the plain" in Spanish; the town is also called, by the English who now rule it, Spanish Town. I had not seen John in many weeks or perhaps months; I did not know the exact time because I had lost sight of the sun and the moon during my incarceration. Accounts of the whereabouts of my fellows—most notably, Read—had also been kept from me. All I knew was this: Rogers and Lawes, once a few of my former crewmates had fallen into their snare, had been able to expand their search and catch nearly all who served aboard the *Will*.

I now shared a cell with First-Rate, who had, some weeks before, spurned an invitation from Read to join the mission, explaining that he had a flourishing business as a saddler. Now his establishment was seized and he shared our fate.

First-Rate sat in the corner of the cell we shared, his arms limp at his sides, his face as blank as a piece of parchment. The guards had cruelly beaten him, and, in wide red strokes, they had painted a Star of David across his bared chest. I waved my hand in front of his face and initially received no response. Then First-Rate began to cry.

"Pull yourself together, man," I said. "You've faced worse."

First-Rate, still crying, began to laugh.

"I weep not because I fear for my life," he said. "How I hate the established powers of this world since I was denied my rightful commission in the Royal Navy! When first I heard of your mission with John and the others, my heart longed to follow, wherever it led, whatever its fate. But I clung to respectability and now it is my downfall. Shamefully, I was taken without a fight. Had I just been captured with a sword in my hand and blood on my blade, I would have gone to the gallows with a smile on my face."

"First-Rate," I said, "you are a man of courage and honor. When we see each other again, in hell, I'll be proud to call you comrade."

With that, the cell door was thrown open and I was taken outside. I look'd up at the sky to see its sweet face again, and found the sight to be strange. The sun was bloody red, like the flesh beneath a freshly picked scab, and the heavenly expanse all 'round the dim orb was cloudless and dull—gray on gray. Still, the day was quite warm, and my guards would allow me no water, nor food.

"They're sayin' yer a witch," said one flat-nosed soldier,

who seem'd to be the leader of this lot. "Being if that's so, you can work yer magic and enchant yerself a luncheon."

So the secret of my sex was laid bare and it was mandated that I be moved to another facility. St. Jago de la Vega is some thirteen miles' journey from Port Royal, and, after an hour's march through a forest and along a dirt path, we came to our destination. The town sits at the top of a green slope, where the Rio Cobre winds its way 'round the foot of White Marl Hill. It was a grander place in its earlier days, before the English came and razed it because the locals would not reveal where their treasures had been hidden. The houses—there were several hundred left, and some had been rebuilt—were made of tile and wood, some others of brick, and still others of strips of sugar-cane tied together with hemp rope. Few of the domiciles were constructed above a single story, due to the fear of hurricanes, earthquakes, and other natural disasters that afflict this region.

The sun, now, is blazing hot, and remains red and angry. We cross the Rio Cobre and walk to Barrett Road. Heat rises with the dust off the sandy streets; heat drips down the sweaty shoulders of shirtless sailors unloading crates of codfish and herring and salmon on the docks. The heat plays tricks with the eyes and makes the breezeless, lifeless air seem to move and oscillate. Even squat buildings in this strange light seem to twist and sway like coconut palms caught by a high wind. In the distance, above and beyond the city, the St. Andrews mountains dance in the heat, like images seen through the flickers of flame. On the streets, pedestrians keep to the shadows, seeking to avoid the direct fury of the sun's gaze, which looks down on the city as if it were God's great eye.

We pass by the red-brick tower of the cathedral of St. Jago de la Vega, the tallest building in town; perhaps it risks the threat of disaster with its height because, as a place of God, its architects felt that it would be exempt from nature's wrath. As we walk up Red Church Street, strumpets strut on the side of the avenue, hawking their fleshy wares. They come in all shades—white, mulatto, quadroon, octoroon. Some are dressed in clothes of the country—a red-and-white bandana, or tie-head as it was sometimes called, wrapped around their hair, a plain apron around their waist, bowed on the side. Others were dressed in more elaborate styles not too many years removed from the drawing rooms of Europe—evening dresses with close-fitting bodices and full frilled sleeves, silks skirts gathered in pleats at the waist and hanging in folds to the ground. The harlots' costumes were third and fourth hand, worn in places and patched in others. A goodly number of the slammerkin themselves seemed similarly well traveled and worn.

"Why, that's Anne Bonny!" one whore, who was large of body, called out. "What other woman would require such an escort! Tell us your tale, Bonny!"

"Too good for the strumpet's life?" another shouted at me. "I hope they hang yuh high and bury yuh shallow!"

The harlots surrounded me and pulled at my garments. My hands being chain'd, I was unable to beat them off, and my guards, laughing, did little to restrain my attackers. The slammerkin clawed and bit me, slapped and punched me, and I fell to the earth before being pulled back up again, roughly, by my manacles. I realized that they were trying to disrobe me, and I tried to hold fast to my clothing but it was for naught. Soon, I was standing naked as African cargo on the deck of a slaver, and the laughter of the harlots rained down on me. I had not appeared in public as a woman for a considerable period. Tears came to my eyes and I choked back a sob.

"Now she knows her place!"

"The Governor does what he does for the children!"

"You'll get what you deserve!"

"Ha!" said Flat-Nose. "You look like a woman now."

"Give me a sword and we'll see who's a man," I said.

We arrived at Parade Square, a green expanse that was surrounded on all sides by large white buildings that were built in a flowing Spanish style. I was marched past the ivory-columned grandeur of a building marked as the Supreme Court to a low beige building located directly behind it.

"Middlesex and Surrey County Gaol," said Flat-Nose. "Here's your new home, witch."

"If you have any honor, you'll lend me a coat, or some covering."

"They'll provide for you once inside."

"Why was I transported to this place?"

"Weren't you told?" said Flat-Nose, laughing. "The trial of you pyrates starts with the morn and Lawes means to see you hang'd."

chapter 32.

In the morning I was taken from my prison cell at the Middlesex and Surrey County Gaol and escorted by guards over to the Supreme Court. The walk was a short one, but the trip, on this occasion, took a considerable amount of time. The distance was filled with gawkers come to attend the trial, or at least loiter in the general vicinity of such an infamous affair—there were strumpets, sailors, farmers with dirt from their fields still smudged on their faces, young girls holding aloft privateer dolls with nooses sewn 'round their miniature necks, local merchants selling sugarcane sweets and calabashes of rum, well-to-do men and women from the sugar plantations with their opera glasses out and delighted to finally be putting them to some use in this uncultured region.

"You'll hang for sure, witch!" one girl with bright red hair shouted at me, twisting the neck of her privateer doll.

"I'm a reporter for the *Boston Gazette*!" cried a brown-haired young man with a shiny face. "Can you give me a quote for our readers? How do you feel about the separate trials?"

I was ushered into a wooden courtroom and a guard chained me to my seat.

"Your day of judgment will come later, m'love," he said to me. "Today, Calico Jack will get his comeuppance."

Indeed, John was led into the courtroom moments later. He was with ten other men, all from the ship, including Zayd, Hunahpu, and luckless First-Rate, who had the misfortune to be linked to our unhappy band. Even Poop was there among the accused; his treachery had won him only a chance at the gallows with the rest of us. I felt no hatred for him, only the sadness one feels for a fool. The men all seem'd gaunt, and they were unshaven and dirty. They were, every one, in chains and the spectators in the courtroom hooted as they were dragged in. In addition, rotten food and other refuse was hurled at them. I tried to get John's attention but could scarcely be heard over the din of the mob. He stared straight ahead, his eyes dark and sunken.

Next, the court crier came before those assembled.

"There will be silence upon punishment of hanging!"

All fell quiet at these words, for it was known they were backed with force of law.

"This being Wednesday, November the sixteenth, the year of our lord 1720, a court of admiralty is held before his excellency Sir Nicholas Lawes, his majesty's captain-general and governor in chief in and over his majesty's island of Jamaica and other territories thereon depending in America!"

At this, Lawes swept into the courtroom and took his seat at the front. He was a tall man, proud in bearing, with a large sharp nose and piercing gray eyes. His pallor was closer to that of a statue or graven image than that of a living being, and he did not blink much, nor smile at all. Upon taking his seat, he laid his hand upon the Good Book and swore an oath in a deep voice, then, having finished, he nodded for the court crier to continue with the opening proclamation.

"All manner of persons that can inform this honorable court, now sitting, of any pyracies, acts of terror, or robberies committed in or upon the sea, or in any haven, creek, or place in or about this island, or elsewhere in the West Indies, where the admiral or admirals of our sovereign lord the king hath or have any power, authority, or jurisdiction, let them come forth and they shall be heard."

John and the rest were led to the bar and were told by the register to listen to their charges, and the register, as directed by Lawes, read the articles exhibited against them.

"Articles exhibited in a court of Admiralty, held at the town of Saint Jago de la Vega in the said Island, the sixteenth of November, in the seventh year of the reign of our sovereign Lord George, by the grace of God, of Great Britain, France, and Ireland, King, and of Jamaica, Defender of the Faith, by virtue of a commission, from his said majesty King George, under the Great Seal of Britain, bearing Date, the third day of April, in the fourth year of his majesty's reign, issued pursuant, to an act of Parliament, made in Great Britain in the eleventh year of the reign of our late sovereign lord King William the Third, since made perpetual, entitled An Act for the More Effectual Suppression of Pyracy, for the Trying, Hearing, Determining, and Adjudging of all Pyracies, Felonies, and Robberies Committed in or upon the Sea."

The language used was so intricate that I often had trouble following the thread of whatever meaning was at the core of each statement. But like a ripe fruit that, once bitten, reveals itself to have meat rotten and infested with worms, so, too, did this proceeding have a putrid core. After the ornate opening statements, there then followed such a cavalcade of lies as can scarcely be believed. John and my fellows were accused of things that they had not done and were alleged to have said things that they did not say. Perhaps there were crimes that we did commit, but to be charged with base offenses that were petty, and besides, not of our doing, was some felony in and of itself.

"Charge the first: that Calico John Rackam and his fellows, on the first Day of September, in the Seventh Year of the reign of our Lord the King, upon the high Sea, in a certain Sloop of an unknown Name, did Solemnly and Wickedly consult, and agree together, to rob, plunder and take, all such persons, as well as subjects of our Lord the King, with force of arms upon the high sea, in a certain place distant about two leagues from Harbour Island in America, and within the jurisdiction of this court, did pyratically, feloniously and with great terror, attack, engage and take seven certain fishing boats and there piratically, and with great terror, did steal, take and carry away the fish, the fishing tackle, of the value of ten pounds of current money of Jamaica.

"Charge the second: that afterwards, to wit, the fifth day of October, in the year last mentioned, that the said Calico Jack Rackam and his fellows and every one of them, in the said said pyrate sloop being, by force of arms, etc., upon the high sea, in a certain place, distant about three leagues from the Island of Hispaniola in America, and within the jurisdiction of this court, did pyratically, and with great terror, set upon, shoot at, and take two merchant sloops, then being sloops of certain persons, subjects of our Lord the King.

"Charge the third: that they, Jack Rackam and his fellows and every one of them, in the said pyrate sloop being, afterwards, to wit, the nineteenth day of October in the year last mentioned, with force of arms, etc., upon the high sea, in certain place, distant about five leagues from Porto-Maria-Bay, in the said Island of Jamaica and within the jurisdiction of this court, did pyratically, and with great terror, shoot at, set upon and take, a certain schooner, of an unknown name."

The charges continued—all false, lies upon lies. I wondered what the purpose of such falsehood was, and why the court did not proceed with a case built upon the facts, some of which, I must admit, could have possibly been viewed as against our favor. The richest of our prizes, among them the Madrid galleon, were not listed among our crimes or even mentioned. All our ill-gotten goods—or at least the treasure we had not spent—had certainly been collected by authorities by now. So where were all the riches we had stolen? Then, observing Lawes upon the bench in his finery, I was struck by a revelation—the courts were, by far, the cleverest pyrates of all of us. These crimes they accused us of, no doubt, took place—but they were, in all likelihood, committed by persons under Lawes's employ or by privateers sailing under a letter of marque. We, who sailed under no country's banner and who lacked a treaty with any territory, were being made to pay for crimes that were filling the coffers of King George in Britain as well as those of Lawes and Rogers. The treasure we had stolen they would steal back. The riches of the Madrid galleon they would surreptitiously confiscate. And there would never be any record of their wrongdoing. And no one would put stock in the protests and ravings of convicted pyrates.

And thus have the affairs of this world ever been conducted. The slavers sail on, the cat-o'-nine-tails cracks, and a waltz is played. The city of Kingston was rife with crime, and so, too, were the streets of New Providence. Port Royal, the city lately wracked by earthquake, was still maimed by that event, with little evidence of public works to aid its recovery. Human cargo was rotting in the holds of ships in violation of every dictate of decent conduct. And yet the concern of the government was ever on pyrates, and their efforts were bent on directing citizens to mind the public hangings and the directives toward the suppressions of pyracy, rather than to focus on the felonious official activities in front of their own faces. And so the slavers sail on, the cat-o'-nine-tails cracks, and a waltz is played. Every nation needs a good pyrate—to give citizens a reason to fear, to provide soldiers an enemy to fight, and to grant kings and queens, governors and generals a villain on which to pin their own acts of plunder and pyracy. What fools we were! The boldest pyrates run nations and do not command mere single ships!

The charges having been read, the prisoners were questioned by the register: "What do you all have to say? Are you guilty of the pyracies, robberies, and felonies, or any of them, in the aforesaid articles mentioned, which have just been read unto you? Are you guilty or not guilty?"

Whereupon John stepped forward and brushed his matted hair out of his face. He met Lawes with a steady gaze and the Governor leaned forward in his high chair and returned the stare.

"I speak for all," said John. "We are all not guilty. You are all the guilty ones here and you are twice guilty, for the Lord hates hypocrites and oath-breakers more than he despiseth a pyrate or a thief."

The crowd broke into loud hooting and John and the rest were pulled back by the chains. The trial then continued.

One by one, the register did call and produce witnesses to prove the said articles and establish the charges against the prisoners; each witness, having been duly sworn in, was examined by His Excellency the Governor.

Thomas Spenlow, of Port Royal, a rotund man and a mariner on the island of Jamaica who was said, by the court, to have been the commander of a schooner alleged to have been taken by John, deposed thusly: that to the best of his remembrance, on or about the nineteenth day of October last, Calico Jack Rackam took his ship by force and took out of his said schooner fifty rolls of tobacco, nine bags of pimento, and kept him custody for about forty and eight hours.

Then Peter Cornelian and John Besneck, two other witnesses, were produced, but, being Frenchmen and not speaking English, one James Burr was sworn in as interpreter, and the two Frenchmen testified that the prisoners who stood accused had taken them off the shore of the island of Hispaniola in America where they were hunting wild hog, and then, afterward, forced them to sail with him.

Now, before God, I had never seen these two Frenchmen in my life, not aboard the *Will*, nor on any ship or shore in the West Indies. At their testimony John, who I knew to have been schooled in some French, shook his head, which I took to mean that the witnesses were not being translated in a way that was accurate to their original meaning in their own tongue.

After all the witnesses had been examined (there were two score or more of them, and if we have robbed them all in truth, we would have been several times richer than we were), His Excellency the Governor asked every one of the prisoners if they had any defense to make, or any witnesses to be sworn on their behalf, or if they would have any of the witnesses, who had already been sworn, cross-examined; and, if that were the case, what questions would they propose?

Whereto they all of them answered that they had no witnesses, that they had never committed any acts of pyracy, and that their design was always from the start against the Spaniards who were his majesty's enemies.

After a brief period was taken for the Governor to consider the evidence, the prisoners were taken back before the bar, and the Governor pronounced his sentence on each of them, one by one, ending with John. The court, they were each told in turn, had unanimously found them all guilty of the pyracy, robbery, and terror charged against them. They were then each asked whether they or any of them had anything to say or offer about why the sentence of death should not pass upon them for their offenses.

John just looked at Lawes and smiled.

Lawes did not smile back, but instead said these words: "You, Calico Jack Rackam, along with your fellows, are to go from hence to the place from whence you came, and from thence to the place of execution, where you shall severally be hanged by the neck, 'til you are severally dead. And God of his infinite mercy be merciful to every one of your souls."

The Governor's business being thus concluded, the court adjourned till twelve days hence, morning nine of the clock in the forenoon to hear the case against me and against Read. As for John, his execution was set for the evening of the day after next.

chapter 33.

It was Friday, the eighteenth day of November, and the church bell was tolling nine of the clock of the forenoon. The bells of the Cathedral of St. Jago de la Vega were loud and strong and I could hear them echoing over the town square, over the roofs of the low houses, and through the walls of the jail. Hard after, a voice slithered into my ear through the door of my cell.

"Your precious Rackam's gonna get 'imself hung today," said the voice. "Old Governor Lawes will hang him on the tip of the Palisadoes he will, when the clock strikes noon."

"Take me to him!"

"You'll be seeing 'im shortly enough, missy—whether in this life, or in the next."

I tried to sleep, but could find no purchase in my slumber.

In my mind's eye, I imagined the noose 'round John's neck, and the hard gray eyes of the Governor upon him. I grabbed hold of the bars of my window and pulled them, but to no avail; next I threw myself against the door of my cell and, being granted no success, did so again with increased vigor before collapsing on the stone floor.

We had escaped hard situations before; there had to be some way out, some means of changing our fate. I closed my eyes and thought of Read: perhaps he was planning something, a jail break or a daring escape or a clever bribery.

"Guard!"

I heard footsteps in the outside hall.

"Guard, I know not your name or your financial position. But you should know this: I have treasures beyond your dreams that are yours for the taking if you would only but loose me from this place."

"My name is none of your concern," said the jailer, whom I did not see but heard through the walls. "As for your treasure, every privateer tempts me with such dreams, and I dismiss them, at each turn, as the products of fantasy and desperation."

"But—"

"Your Calico Jack will face his end today, missus, and there is nothing that you, nor I, nor the Devil himself—whose cause you served—can do to stop it. Reflect on God and your crimes. Your end approaches as well. Now be silent!"

I heard his footsteps head off down the hall.

"Guard! Guard!"

There was only silence as an answer to my entreaties; I pounded the door with my fist until my hand turned bloody. Next I sank to the floor again and buried my face in my lap. I tried to clear my thought; surely reason could find a path out of this place.

The bells of the Cathedral of St. Jago de la Vega tolled ten times.

Perhaps John had a plan, or Zayd or First-Rate. They were all able men, and had fought and thought their ways out of many a tight corner. Ride or die! None of them feared death, that was the truth. Therefore, each and every one of the men imprison'd would be free and clear-minded to focus on eluding the end that Lawes had set out for us, one and all.

By my faith, this was not the way it was meant to end! I thought back and wondered if there were things that we could have done differently. But, ahhh, none of us could have changed our spirits. I was already dying a slow death trapped in domestic tranquility; if we hadn't been pulled back into the life for this operation, it would have been another, or some other outlaw action down the line.

I wondered if John was thinking of me. I wished there was some way I could send word to him, to let him know that I was still alive, that there was still hope. There had to be some way of reaching him, that needed to be my focus. This region was full of privateers, and most of the citizenry supported our cause, and not Lawes. Perhaps some bystanders could be recruited to avert John's grim sentence. Yes—that was a course of action.

"Guard! Guard! Guard!"

The footsteps again.

"You must have some need, some thing you want. Come—tell me what in the world would suit your desires and, to merit my release, I will fulfill it."

Silence.

"Come now, guard! Time is awasting! Tell me straight!"

A voice answer'd, but it was an unexpected sound.

I recognized the voice. It was Governor Lawes.

It was then that His Excellency Nicholas Lawes, Governor of Jamaica, told me John's secret. He told me out of spite, out of jealousy, and perhaps out of the fear that he could never fill the place in his master's heart in which John once resided. Once the secret was told, I knew it was true, and I did not question it. I fell silent and listened to Lawes's footsteps fade down the corridor. I thought of the sweet times in Clarendon parish when John asked me to dress up in men's clothes and together we made the transit of Venus and, after those recollections of joy, I wept bitter tears.

The bells of the Cathedral of St. Jago de la Vega tolled eleven times.

The door to my cell swung open suddenly and Flat-Nose and his fellows burst in, clapping chains on my hands and feet and leading me roughly out into the hall and, with rapidity, out of the prison.

"Where are you taking me?"

"To see your sweet Calico Jack," said Flat-Nose.

The mobs ringed 'round the prison had increased in size and had multiplied in their passion. There were many hundreds of people massed at the doorway, women and men, adults and children, well-to-do and not-so-well-to-do. Their voices, at first, did not seem like human voices to me—I heard a parrot's caws and dog howls and the squeal of cats and the calls of other beasts. Newspapers were shoved roughly before me bearing crude renderings of my likeness.

The day was violent hot and there was no wind. I was escorted down the narrow strip of land that is the Palisadoes. I could see black rings of crows circling in the sky far out ahead of me.

"They've already hanged six and four more," said Flat-Nose. "Calico Jack was saved for the last."

Now I was close up and could see the awful sight. Zayd, First-Rate, Hunahpu, and several other crew members from the *Will* were hanging from wooden gallows that had been set up in a rough line at the end of the beach. A crowd circled all 'round the scene; some in the mob were laughing, others singing, still others had fists upraised and were baying for more blood. Near the back of the crowd, mounted on a great white horse, was a tall figure in a great purple coat. By his bearing and the honor guard accorded him, I took him to be Governor Woodes Rogers, come to see his nemesis meet his final reckoning.

Rogers's face was a horrible contradiction. He might have once been judged by some as handsome: he had large eyes, a strong nose, a high forehead, and long sloping cheeks. But because of a musketball that had pierced his left cheek in a seabattle, his upper jaw was mangled, a large section of his top lip was peeled away, several teeth were missing, and his red gums were exposed. He looked like a corpse, skillfully prepared by the undertaker, which had subsequently been feasted upon by vermin.

The bells of the Cathedral of St. Jago de la Vega tolled twelve times.

John had not arrived. His execution time had come, and he had not been brought before the crowd. Could he have escaped? Did he win some pardon? No, no, no—I could not allow myself to feel hope. I could not permit myself the luxury of anticipating anything but grief and blood. I tried to beat down with fists the feeling surging within me, triumphant, like the surf hitting rocks on the shore and leaping toward heaven, that there was a chance John had evaded his death sentence. But why couldn't I hope? Why shouldn't I hope? John had eluded tragedy before, so many times, too many times to enumerate. Why couldn't he do so again? Why shouldn't he do so again? The bells had tolled. His time had come and he was not here. Why shouldn't I dare to imagine us together again, in a house, some small home in the Blue Mountains, eating sweet fruits and counting clouds, or perhaps sailing on the waves again, with a new ship and a new crew and a new life and the breeze at our backs. John was not here. I could hear the talk among the throngs who had gathered. Murmurs ran through the crowd like the wind through a field of long grass. John had escaped. John had been pardoned. John had been granted a letter of marque. There were rumors, there was gossip, there were whispers and shouts and pushing and shoving and the pointing of fingers and everyone had an opinion but nobody knew anything.

The bells of the Cathedral of St. Jago de la Vega tolled once.

Now I saw John. When he arrived, hope left. The execution had simply been delayed, not abrogated. John was unshaven, his hair was wild, his clothes unkempt, but his eyes were calm. On his feet, he wore his square-toed boots, which his guards had let him keep, perhaps to show they caught him in action, or perhaps so his footwear, in its finery, could mock, by contrast, the wretchedness of his condition. Beside John was Poop, clad in rags and slippers and choking back sobs. They were both led up the stairs of the gallows. They were to die in succession.

My feet were bound, so I could not run to my darling John; my hands were chain'd and so I could not wave out to him. I called to him, but I could not be heard above the din of the mad crowd. And now a chant was going up, started by the men who owned the whores and then carried on by the whores themselves: "For the Children! For the Children!"

But, soon enough, the chant had transmogrified into something more direct: "Blood! Blood! Blood!"

I often wondered, in later times, what John might have said had I been able to converse with him that last time on the Palisadoes. I do not think he would have said any of the sad, small things that doomed lovers say in fairy books, nor would he have performed some show of comforting bravado, nor would he have bared his heart in the way that lovers sometimes do when both realize that their current moments together will be the last that this life allows them.

No, I do not think he would have told me that secret that was unreveal'd until his final hour, the one that Read surmised and I guess, in some way, I always knew. He would not have told me that he never romanced Rogers's daughter, and that the story was a front, a ruse, a lie, to cover another deeper deception. He would not have told me that he and Woodes Rogers, on some voyage long ago, shared those things that men sometimes share on sea-voyages, when one comes to know one's fellows in a way one never would on land. To John, all flesh was flesh, and this episode was just one of many; but to Rogers, it was a moment of deep ignominy, of weakness, of sin, and it was his drive to purge himself that drove the Governor on his campaign to destroy John and all who sail'd with him. John was ashamed only that he had picked a companion so recklessly. But, by my faith, John would have said nothing of all this.

"Blood! For the children! Blood!"

Now Poop had begun to sob openly, tears running down his cheeks.

"Look at the pyrate! He cries like a woman!"

The crowd jeered and laughed and hurled dead lizards and chicken heads and other refuse and bade him to cry more. John bent down and, with intensity, whispered something to his young companion. Poop swallowed hard and ceased his sobbing.

Now John was moved above a trapdoor and a noose was placed around his neck. He stood for a moment, motionless, silent, his face white but shining, like a cloud lit from behind by the sun.

"Blood! Blood! Blood!"

"Look at the mighty Calico! He'll die in his shoes!"

Then, insolent to the last, John kicked off his square-toed boots. One flew into the crowd, over the heads of the mob, 'til it was lost in a sea of converging bodies; the other fell right at the hangman's feet. Poop, his face wet with tears, stood straighter. John smiled and met the eyes of the spectators.

At the back of the crowd I saw Rogers raise a long arm and bring it down.

And so the order was given: John dropped through the gallows' trapdoor, and, with a loud crack, his neck was snapped. Poop was hanged next, and his body flung into an alley at the end of Thames Street, where it was stripped by whores and devour'd by dogs and rats. Later, soldiers under the command of Nicholas Lawes carried John's body to Plumb Point where it was hung on Gibbets in Chains as a public warning to lawless privateers. The last time I saw John, crows were stripping flesh from his tongue.

chapter 34.

I had, that night, a dream of the most peculiar and disturbing character and, like phantasms of that particular sort, upon waking, I could scarce remember the contents of my fantasy. However, another sight greeted my eyes, which, at first, seem'd to me the product of some cruel mirage, like a vision of some green oasis to a traveler who has been on a long trek through the sands of some parched desert. Read stood before me.

I had scarcely embraced him before he tumbled, near lifeless, into my arms. A sort of flux he had, and his skin was hot and damp, and he called out things that made no sense. His legs and arms were mark'd with scratches and wounds as if he had been the subject of assault. In addition, some guard had done Read's hair up in pigtails and smeared cosmetics across his lips and cheeks in crude red strokes. Wetting my fingers, I wiped off the cruel gesture, and removed the ribbons from his hair.

"Read!"

His eyes fluttered open and they seem'd to meet mine, and he caressed my cheek as you would that of a lover.

"A thousand waves roll over me," he said. "I feel crabs scuttling sideways across my mind."

We had scarcely a moment to spend together ere the guards clapped us in chains and conducted us toward the courtroom. As I was marched through the crowd, a copy of the *Boston Gazette* was thrust before my eyes. An article that purported to be about my predicament quoted me as having said to Rackam: "If you had fought like a man, you hadn't a been hung like a dog." By my troth I would never have uttered such words!

"Say what you will!" I cried. "I'll see you all in hell or on the high seas!"

The courtroom, on this morning, was packed to overflowing and Lawes, having entered, quickly moved the proceeding toward its start.

The register made his familiar cry: "Articles exhibited in a Court of Admiralty, held at the town of Saint Jago de la Vega in the said Island, the twenty-eighth of November, in the seventh year of the reign of our sovereign Lord George, by the grace of God, of Great Britain, France, and Ireland, King, and of Jamaica, Defender of the Faith," etc.!

The register then read the charges that accused us, both Read and myself, of things that we never did and recounted things said that we never uttered. After all was read, we, the prisoners, were asked by the register what we had to say.

"Mary Read, alias Read, and Anne Bonny, alias Bonn, are you guilty of the pyracies, robberies, and acts of terror, or any of them, in the said articles mention'd, which have been read unto you?" it was asked. "Or not guilty?"

Whereupon we both answered "not guilty" and I was much pleased and grateful that Read had found his senses for that one utterance.

The witnesses were subsequently called and, by my troth, I had never seen even one of them in all my life before these trials began and they recounted such lies that would make him that rules the world below choke on the words.

Dorothy Thomas, a maid of adult age and stout, deposed that she, being in a canoe at sea, with some stock and provisions, at the north side of Jamaica, was taken by a sloop commanded by one Calico Jack Rackam who took out of the canoe most of the things that were in her, and she further said that the two women, being Read and myself, were then onboard the said sloop and that we wore men's jackets, and long trousers, and handkerchiefs tied about our heads; and that each of us had a machete and pistol in our hands, and cursed and swore at the men to murder her, and that they should kill her to prevent her coming against them, and Dorothy further said that the reason of her knowing and believing us to be women was by the largeness of our breasts.

And then the same Frenchmen who testified at Rackam's trial were produced as witnesses, being John Besneck and Peter Cornelian, and they came to the bar and were sworn.

These next two witnesses, meaning the Frenchmen, declared that the two women now in shackles, meaning me and Read, were on board John's sloop at the time that their ships were taken by John and his crew. They went on to say that the women they saw were very active on board and willing to do any thing, and that I, Anne Bonny, handed gunpowder to the men, and that when we saw any vessel, we gave chase or attacked, and we wore men's clothes and, at other times, we wore women's clothes, and that we did not seem kept, or detain'd by force, but remained of our own free will and consent.

During this testimony, Read began to writhe and to moan slightly, and pulled at his chains as if meaning to escape, and yet I could see his actions had no logic or reflection behind them. He carried on as if there was a pain in his innards and so I rubbed his belly a little and, in doing so, I realized he was in possession of a secret. I reached down between my legs and, remembering Read's words about Eve's curse, it occurred to me that I shared the same secret as my fellow. I kissed him on the forehead and I smiled.

The witnesses had now finished their testimony and His Excellency the Governor asked the prisoners, me and Read, if we, alone or separately, had any defense to make, or had any witnesses to swear in on our behalf, or desired to cross-examine any witnesses that had been so far heard.

I answered for us both and replied that we had no witnesses that had not yet been heard and we had no questions to ask of those that had appeared and we had nothing to say other than the fact that all who had addressed the court were damn'd liars.

Lawes asked that the last of my words be stricken from the record and Read and I were taken away from the bar and put into a small room for custody while the Governor considered the evidence. I held Read in my arms and I rocked him a bit, as if I was holding a babe; he closed his eyes and made small sounds in his throat.

Then, after a time, we were brought back before the bar. Governor Lawes fixed me with a grim stare and said that the court had unanimously found "you guilty, both you, Mary

Read, and you, Anne Bonny, of Pyracy, Robbery, and of acts of Terror. Do you have anything to say, or to offer, why a sentence of death should not pass upon you for your said offences?"

I said nothing.

Read, with his last strength, open'd his eyes and took his feet. He waved aside my support and met Lawes with his eyes.

"If I have been silent, it is not because I am weak, but because I am temporarily afflicted," he said. "As for the gallows, I do not fear it, nor do I think it cruel because, if not for that kind instrument, all cowards would become privateers and would, as a natural result, so infest the seas that men of courage would die of hunger."

After this proclamation, Read stumbled and fell back into my arms.

Lawes paused for a moment after Read's statement and issued his reply.

"Then, having said nothing," he said, "or nothing worthy of report, I declare this: you, Mary Read, alias Read, and you, Anne Bonny, alias Bonn, are to go from hence to the place whence you came, and from thence to the place of execution; where you shall be severally hang'd by the neck, 'til you are severally dead. And God of his infinite Mercy be merciful to both your souls."

After judgment was pronounced, I stepped forward and informed the court that the sentence must be stay'd.

"Prithee why?" said the Governor. "This verdict is not for you, but for the future of the children of this island. On that principle have I staked my honor."

"If, indeed, you care for children," I said, "verily, you must let us go free."

I informed the court that which I had only lately learned: that Read and I were each quick with child and so, having no other options, we were forced to plead our bellies.

The Governor retired to his chambers for a short while. A murmur and several cries of shock arose from the gallery as the news of the reason for the delay spread. The Governor then emerged and rendered a new judgment. His Excellency the Governor, after considering the weight of public opinion and the scrutiny of newspaper scribes, decided to charge us with the punishment that we were never to sail again, under pain of death. We were to be fined the amount of twenty thousand crowns for our previous sea-transgressions, but, that fine having already been paid, we were, after processing, to be set free the next week.

The gallery erupted, equal parts cheers and howls.

"Who—who paid our fine?" I asked.

The Governor returned my question with a sneer.

"Why, your father, of course."

chapter 35.

I am going to see my da.

With Read at my side, I am leaving Port Royal. He is weak and leans against me for support. We walk down Thames Street. From here we can see the water. It is flat and gray and dead, with nary a wave or ripple. From this distance, the harbor is a clouded mirror, reflecting nothing, revealing naught of its own features. Ships brought into the wharf lay motionless in their moorings. I see a three-masted ship flying British colors, recently brought in to careen, laying nearly on its side in the shallows of the stale water. The great ship's foremast, mainmast, and mizzenmast have been stripped of their sails and jut out naked from the tilted deck, held down by blocks and tackle. The vessel looks like the skeleton of some vast sea creature, washed up, rotting on the shore, or come from some other world to haunt the living. A half-dozen seamen moved about its hull, burning off barnacles and slimy sea growth, applying pitch and caulk to rotten planks, and swathing on a mix of oil, tallow, and brimstone to help ward off further incrustations.

We climbed the hills that ringed the city and trekked out to the lands beyond. The landscape grew gentler as we passed through the rolling green fields of the sugar plantations. The stalks of sugarcane, twice as tall as Read, danced in the warm afternoon breeze. Read ripped out a stalk, peeled back the green leaves, and sucked on the stringy sweet innards. He coughed a little, but smiled at the taste. Following his lead, I pulled up a stalk and chewed on the tough, sugary core.

Set at intervals between the vast green rhomboids of sugar-cane crop were the great houses of the plantations. I had never seen homes of such grandeur, not in Cork, nor Dublin besides. They were like giants with many eyes and many mouths crouch-ing in the slopes. They had tall, flat sides and wide, gently slop-ing roofs. The front lawns all boasted large, generous gardens bursting with red and yellow and blue flowers. Nearby, each of the homes had either a towering wooden windmill or a large stone waterwheel set in a stream. By custom, and necessity as well, Read said, the houses were located a musketball's distance from the barracks of the slaves' quarters.

One of these great houses belonged to my da.

As Read and I continued to walk, we noticed that some of the fields, and some of the great houses, were on fire. We could see black smoke swirling into the air. We saw, too, a brown-and-white windmill with its spinning vanes on fire. We could hear the beat of drums echoing across the fields.

"Those are *burru*," whispered Read, his voice cracking from the fever and from the exertion of travel. "Talking drums."

Read guessed that there must be some sort of slave insurrection ongoing in these parts. Slave masters would never allow their charges to beat their drums so openly, so loudly. I imagined slaves, shackles 'round their ankles, sprinting through the lush fields. The sweetness of the cane was still on my tongue.

The dirt path away from Port Royal now faded out and became mere trample marks on the soft grass. The grass path we followed was lined on either side with flowers—the white blossoms of the ramgoat rose and the elaborate beauty of the crane flower, with its bright orange petals and stalks bent at right angles. Read was taking note of some of the vegetation. In particular, he seemed fascinated by the bladderwort, a squat, carnivorous plant with wide leaves like two hands pressed together at the wrist, palms open. The plant, with seeming innocuousness, lured insects between its leaves, which were joined at midrib, and then closed them tightly around its unsuspecting prey. The strange plant mesmerized Read, as if he had found a kindred spirit. Read stuck his finger between the leaves again and again, smiling each time the plant's jaws closed tight.

"The plant, I've heard, when eaten fresh, is good for fever," Read said.

He plucked off the bladderwort's head to keep in his pouch, but its leaves went limp as soon as the plant was decapitated. So he plucked another one and ate it then and there, even as the plant's jaws quivered.

Read belched.

And so we walked on.

I also picked as I strode along, gathering ingredients for the preparation of a midday meal. I picked peppers and chocho and other edible plants I found growing wild. As I continued along the path, crouching from time to time to uproot some new vegetable or spice, I grew wary. It seemed as if there were eyes on me, although there was no watcher to be seen. I thought I could feel a stare on the back of my bare arms, on my legs, running across my limbs like the light touch of fingertips. Footsteps, too, I heard; the crunch of stones beneath paws, the snap of twigs. I looked quickly around—nothing could be seen but grass and trees. But the air seemed warmer, unnaturally so.

I looked at Read. He nodded. He could feel it, too.

"Do you have any tinder?" he said.

I pulled a small leather pouch out of my breeches. After searching through it, I handed him some strips of juniper tree bark.

"I need four."

I raised an eyebrow and passed him a few additional strips.

Read crouched down on the grass path.

"In these parts, they believe we each have two spirits," he said. "After we die, one goes on to judgment."

"And the other?"

"It stays on this earth and haunts the trees. They call such spirits duppys."

He lay four strips of bark in a small pile in the center of the path.

I gave him a quizzical look and pointed toward the tinder.

"Duppys can't count past three. If they see four strips of bark, they will count and count and recount them. If a duppy's on our trail, this will stop him."

He stood up and we continued down the path.

As we walked on, it seemed as if the air returned to a more normal temperature. Duppys, according to Read, throw heat when they approach, so he took the cooling temperature as a sign that perhaps the thing that had been following and watching us was falling behind or gone entirely. We allowed ourselves to feel some relief. But now the black smoke from the burning sugar fields was growing thicker. My da's house was close. We were both weary from the long walk, so I thought it best to stop and eat a proper meal.

We halted and I lay down my pack. I had been carrying some cooking supplies—tin pots, dried meat, and the like—and so I decided now to put them to use. We had paused near a Traveler's Tree and I broke off a few of the leaves and drained the water into a pot. Setting the pot of water over a fire, I mixed in dried kale, salted pork, okra, callaloo, and some of the other wild vegetation I had found along the path. It was the recipe that Zed, my old African neighbor, had taught me. When I was done, I allowed Read to take the first taste. The aroma was pungent and inviting and he greedily slurped down nearly half the pot. Then, a few seconds later, the seasonings caught up with him and his eyes bulged and his face turned crimson.

"It's called pepperpot soup," I said. "Its spices are strong for some."

Read got to his feet and ran toward the Traveler's Tree and drank deep from more than a few of its hollow water-storing leaves.

*W*hen we resumed our journey, the heat returned. It felt like the warmth from a just-scratched rash. It faded every time Read looked 'round trying to uncover its source. When he stopped searching, it returned, hotter than the time before. The heat seeped beneath the skin and made the muscles throb and the bones ache. My eyes and tongue felt dry; my chest and arms were damp with sweat. Read kneeled down and lay a pile of bark strips on the path. He would have left even more but I felt it best to spare a few for less supernatural tasks, like lighting torches and sparking the cooking fire.

We continued on, this time walking at an even quicker pace. The trees around us grew taller and more numerous. Tall Royal Palms, with sloping trunks and wide leaves, crowded the path. Small lizards—red, blue, and yellow—jumped from tree to tree or scampered before our feet. Read stopped me and cautioned me to let the lizards pass.

"If a croaker bites you," he said, "you must reach water before the croaker or the bite is death. At least that's the belief around these parts."

I let the lizard pass and looked up.

We had come to my da's house.

chapter 36.

There were vast fields of sugarcane and beyond them a great green lawn and in the middle of
that a large white house and further still, I could see the
brown shacks of the slave quarters. The day was all but
over and yet the night had not yet come. I could see shapes
moving against the bloody sky, and hear shouts and some screams
as well. Read unsheathed his sword and held it unsteadily as he
was still shaking with fever; my blade had already leapt into my
hands. Smoke rose from the fields, and I could smell the sweet
stink of burning crop.

I saw a shape move at one of the upper windows of the white
house. The barrel of a musket emerged, tracking us as we moved
up the walk. Then the musket was pulled out of the window and
the front door was swung open.

It was my da.

He was as I remembered him. Shorter perhaps, than in my recollection, and thicker around the waist. His hair, too, was gray where once it had been black, and he was bald on the crown of his head.

He considered me, and in his eyes I read his thought: has my daughter returned a son? He was dressed as I was, as if we were each standing before a mirror, unsure which was the reflection and which was the real—but knowing one of us had things backward. My privateer clothes had been seized during the trial, and though I was still clad in garb that aligned with my nature, it was of a sort that was less conspicuous to authorities: a gentleman's three-cornered hat of a dark blue, a man's waistcoat of the same coloring, and gray leggings. These same articles he also wore, and in the same colors. Only the shades, perhaps, set my wardrobe apart from his, and the fact that he wore his hat not on his head, but held it in one hand.

Waving his musket, my da bade us to come into his house.

Inside the house was all manner of finery—carved chairs and tables, paintings and sculptures, gold and silver baubles of various sorts, silverware and chandeliers. Yet the interior was in disarray, with benches and cabinets piled up against the doors and windows, as if to brace the portals against some siege. A hoard of weapons was collected in the center of the floor— swords, guns, spears, and the like.

"Welcome to the war," said my da.

I did not wait to ask him what I needed to ask him. I had not the time to hesitate, for the purposes of decorum, or to reestablish those familiar bonds, which, once connected, allow one party to ask another questions of an intimate nature. I was not that little girl who threw balls down the forest-shrouded trails of our village that had no name. I was not that daughter who wept bitter tears for as many weeks as I can remember when Da left home, without explanation, without indication of where he might be bound or when he might come back. No, I was a sea-man, and I had seen many things, and done many things, and had put that old me behind me, like the landscape in the rear of a racing carriage.

"Your face . . . your hair . . . your clothes," my father said, gazing at me. "The stories I have read in the newspaper are true!"

I could wait no longer.

"Why did you pay to set us free?"

My da smiled an awful smile.

"I always wanted a son," he began. "But my son is dead."

So he told me why he left us. Or, rather, he gave no explana-tion, but described the path that took him from the Old World to the New, from one island to another, from Ireland to Jamaica. I will not trouble you with the details of his chronology. With the sounds of insurgency raging around his mansion, he told me of the events that followed the Game of Bowls in our village.

All these long years Da had nursed resentment. He had sac-rificed his first marriage to be with my ma. When his first wife had died, and his son by his first wife passed on as well, he had dressed me up in boys' clothes to pass me off as his dead son to collect money from his first wife's rich family. And so I began my life in deceit. Ma had been a maid when they met, and Da put his standing at risk with their union. He had suffered much to establish his new family—he had gambled, he had lied, he had broken blood ties. Ma, he said, repaid him with a knife in his back. He did not want to believe that I could be another man's child, not at first. But then the legacy of Baltimore became clear, if not to others, at least to him. He saw it in my skin, in my hair, in my love for adventure and action, even in my push to join the Game of Bowls. So Da planned his revenge. He bought land in the New World, prepared a new life, and left Ma with nothing but old debts. In the night he had fled, convincing Zed to join him under some ruse or another, or perhaps just appealing to that old corsair's long subordinated love of the sea. As he boarded the ship, Da had claimed Zed as his slave, and, following various adventures, and having landed in Jamaica and established a farm, he had put him to work in the fields. It pleased him that the man who had cuckolded him was now his servant.

But when he heard of my exploits, fresh anger burned within him. He saw that Ma, and Zed, still lived within me. And so he paid for my release. It was no easy task to bribe two blood-thirsty governors. The payment had ruined him—he now had no money for overseers, for crops, for fresh water, or even for food, and the ongoing insurrection was the result.

"Where is Zed?" I heard myself say.

"In the back acres," said Da. "Beneath the sugarcane, in a place that is not marked."

So Zed was gone. The sounds from outside my da's house were now inside my head. I walked to the window. When I looked forward, I saw myself staring back, stronger, older, darker, hair in tongues like fire, eyes bright as planets. There were voices from the outside, rough and talking in terrible tongues that I somehow understood or had at least heard before; there were screams, too, and exhortations, and the thunder of gunfire, the clatter of swords, the rumble of crowds of running feet. My sword was in my hand, my fingers gripped tightly around the hilt. I could taste blood in my mouth and I saw red, like a scarlet curtain had been pulled before my vision.

So he was gone. Sweet Zed, who had taken me in that night after the Game of Bowls, when my father had not. Who had protected me from the wolf, when my supposed father had not. Zed, who had taught me the technique to throw balls, who had shared with me recipes from the West Indies, who had shown me how to hold a sword and how to stand up straight. I remembered now the songs he would sing me, when my father was away, and how he would point out the ordinary things of life—cows, trees, fields—and give them new names, strange names, names that mystified me with their sounds and thrilled me when they tripped off my tongue. Yes, I remember now, how it was when I was younger. How sometimes I would see Zed and my mother share a smile or a look or a whisper. What were they talking about? Did he tell her of his years on the run, living in hills and caves, until the local population came to trust and rely on his healing foods and potions? Did she tell him of Da's rages, his wild gambling, his drinking, his wandering eye? Perhaps it was around that time that the old Moorish corsair, alone in this land, and the young Irish woman, a stranger in her own bed, came together. Maybe that is why, when I am exposed to the things that he loved—the sea, the sun, the salt-spray—my secret history comes out. Is my hair his hair? Is my skin his skin? Do we share the same dreams?

"You abandoned Ma," I said to Da. "You disowned me publicly in Charles Town. Why then did you pay my fine?"

My question hung in the air, unanswered.

"I paid for your release," Da finally said, "because I wanted to kill you myself."

I turned to face him. His musket was aimed at me.

"It is time to kill the past," said my da. "I have cheated and I have lied. I have enslaved men and I have killed them. I have raised a child that was not my own. I created this thing you are now, half-man and half-woman. You were too young to remember it, but I dressed you up as a boy when you were a little girl. My first wife's family accepted you as my lost son and paid handsomely. Now the world buys the ruse. It ends now. Tonight I bury the past."

There was a flash of a blade. Da's gun slid across the floor. His right hand had been hacked off. He dropped to his knees. Read stood above him.

"She is not the past," Read said. "He is the future."

There was a crash, as something, a burning something, broke through the barricaded window and it shattered into a thousand shards. The shouts of former slaves could now be heard more clearly. The curtains caught fire, and bullets cracked and whizzed through the air. My father got up and ran, locking himself in a room that was already ablaze.

I turned my back and left, with Read at my side. Even as I exited the front door, dark shapes rushed by me. The air was filled with smoke. The fields burned. My father, my true one, was buried somewhere beneath the burning crop.

chapter 37.

And so, my darling, my loved one, this, then, is the story of how you passed from this world. Read and I established ourselves in a small house in Kingston, with wattle walls and palm fronds for a roof. Steady employment was lacking, and within a few weeks I had exhausted what monies I had on hand. Read had grown even more ill, as the pregnancy had caused him much distress, and so I needed cash to maintain his care.

Our cupboard was bare and Read's anguish weighed heavily on my soul. Whores beckoned me to open my legs, accept my lot as a member of Eve's strain, and join their company, but I cursed them and their keepers and said I would enter their places of business as a paying customer or not at all. But Kingston is a hard town, and there seemed no way for a woman to earn her keep without paying tribute to Captain Johnson. I would not take that tack. With nowhere else to turn, and looking to submerge my sorrows, I took to raising a mug at the many establishments in Kingston constructed for such a purpose. By my faith, that was a stroke of luck. I found that my tales of the sea so entertained the patrons of taverns in the region that I reasoned that there must be gold in there somewhere.

I contacted the *Boston Gazette* about work but found there to be little interest in employing a creature of my sex, and my notoriety was seen as more of a hinderment than a boon. Several other publications offered me employ writing wedding and birth announcements and the like, but the positions described did not fire my blood and thus were of little interest to my way of thinking. All the while Read grew weaker.

By chance, while draining a draught in the Double Snake, a representative of a publishing house in New York overheard one of my tales and asked for me to relay the story to him in fuller fashion. Initially, I thought his approach to be of an untoward kind, and drew my dirk to gut him from chin to belly, but he assured me his interest was genuine. Over the course of several nights we met at the tavern and, at each encounter, I recounted for him some salty story or another, and, at last, he presented me a fair sum to write a book about the sea-life, which would be entitled *A General History of the Most Notorious Pyrates,* or something of the like. He thought publishing under the name of a woman would be scandalous, and so I picked a false name—Captain Johnson, if you please—and I began my work, excited at the task.

I would have composed the book for free, so thrilled was I to take up the agendum; I also appreciated the distraction. Read, at this point, was beyond the skills of medicine to bring him back to good health. My only hope was that, after childbirth, Read would recover some of his vigor.

But it was I, in the end, who suffered the first physical calamity. I woke one morning to find that I had passed a clot, and, with that sad event, you died before you had ever lived. I had fought in many battles, but this stroke wounded me more than any blade or musket ball. No death, not that of a friend, or a parent, or a sibling, or a lover, is as tragic as the passing of a child. For with that small demise is wrapped up many murders: love dies, hope dies, and all children that child might have had, and their offspring besides, are lost to eternity—and so one plot became a graveyard of lost possibilities.

And so I buried my future. I wept, but I did not immerse myself in my own melancholy; Read needed my aid and I turned to him. In due course, Read issued waters, deliver'd a child, and then died. I cut the cord with my knife, and even as the baby began wailing, the color drained from Read's cheeks like the blush leaving the sky at sundown. Ahh—I cannot dwell overmuch on that event because it is too sad.

"Sing me a song."

Breaking my oath 'gainst vocalizing, I sang him a song whose words I had first heard from him. I sang it in my maid's voice, which is high and light. And I used Zayd's melody, which was shadowy and sad.

> *"Come with me*
> *We'll ride on the ink-dark sea.*
> *Don't you long to*
> *Ride or die?*
> *Fah-fah-fah-fah-fah-la-la-la"*

I fought back my tears with all the ferocity I ever did an opposing swordsman. Read smiled and, taking note of my distress, he gather'd himself and told me this tale.

"So you have contracted to tell our story, and that of our fellow brethren of the coast. Well, listen close, you old sea-bitch, for I have one last tale to tell, so hear now my discourse on how I came to carry the child I have recently delivered. No, I will not save my strength, for there is nothing else I wish to apply it to, and there is too little time left to be miserly.

"After our capture during our abort'd final mission on which we were all betrayed by Poop—curse him, and me, for sharing affection with him—and I was imprison'd in Bridewell Prison, the same facility in which you and our other fellows were caged. I called out to the air, hoping for a response, but whether the bulwarks were too solid or our shipmates too timid, I do not know, but no answer came. My cell was violent hot in the day, but at night came the true discomfort, for the walls of stone, and the melancholy of my predicament, made me shiver and moan with chill.

"It was then that I heard a consoling whisper, coming from the adjoining cell. My neighbor would not identify himself, perhaps because of the shame of the wretchedness of his condition. So on the unidentified voice went, softly but unstoppably, like a river that, after long centuries, carves a path in rock for its bed. Even as the frigid breeze blew through the cracks in the stone, turning a tropic day into an arctic night, the wall whisperer told stories of the wind, of all the gales he had known, from gentle squalls to raging hurricanes. My mind was redirected from the suffering of the present and instead transported, by the feather'd wings of thought, to the four corners of the world.

"Spoke the whisperer: 'The Greeks, in their mythology, have Boreas, the north wind, and so also have Notus, the gale of the south. Off the coastal beaches of Mexico, which are warm and lined with swaying palm trees, there blows the Cordonazo, or, in common parlance, the Lash of Saint Francis, which summons the cyclones and drives even frigates to their doom. In France, in travels through the Rhone Valley, with its many castles, good wines, and pleasant rivers, I've felt the snap and sting of the penetrating wind that natives call the Mistral; and on the Aegean Sea, I've been kissed, lightly on the neck, by the Elesian, a summer breeze that carries off the Mediterranean, bringing good cheer. And so, too, are there places where the sea goes flat as a just-made bed, and those regions are called the doldrums along the equator and the horse latitudes to the north and south.

"'But in my estimation, after traveling this whole world, and many places more than once, the greatest and most formidable of all winds is the Harmattan, a hot, relentless gale that blows from off the Sahara onto the northwest coast of the continent of Africa. It is proceeded by dancing jinns, twirling spirits of smoke who conjure a kind of red fire that burns the eye and the face and lashes the hands. The Harmattan is laden with sand, but of a type whose grain is more minuscule than the kind found in tropical places. This sand is as fine as sugar, and it enters the nose, the ears, or any space that is presented to it, even soaking the skin as if it were liquid. It lingers in the air like mist, and is therefore taken into the lungs with every breath, and it does not disperse when the wind subsides. And rarely does the great Harmattan flag; it continues, without ebb, for days, weeks, and so the world around disappears because of its power, for one cannot see even an arm's length to the side, front, or back. All is dust and wind and heat.'

"Even as my stranger-friend murmured this description to

me, and we continued in our anonymous discourse, I felt the winds of his words whipping around me. The walls fell away, like a leaf caught by a breeze, and I surrendered to the storm. Below me I saw the houses and constructions of the people of this world, until finally I soared out to sea. As I continued, I thought, how like the wind are the things of this life. We give the world names, but what distinguishes one wind from another? All are individual yet indistinguishable, invisible and yet somehow apparent. As I thought these things, as I flew on my imaginary current of air, my body was engaged in its own work and my hands found a block of stone that separated my cell from the stranger, and I pushed. I was filled with a sudden desire for this person, who had talked me through to midnight on the saddest evening of my life. The stone fell away and I crawled through into the chamber of my new friend, dearest storyteller.

"It was you, my dear Bonn, it was you. We did not speak. Because of the lingering chill, I sailed quickly into your harboring arms and you into mine; because we did not know, given the prospect of execution hanging over one and all of us, how much time we were given, we dispensed with preliminaries and explanations and let our instinct and emotion rule us entirely. So I kissed you, as I had longed to do all these many years. Your lips were rough, but as our passion continued, they became soft and moistened, and were exceedingly well cushioned. Soon we disrobed and I kneaded the long sleek muscles of your back, which heaved like an unquiet sea.

"Even as I enumerate the ecstasies we two shared that night, they spring alive again, in my mind, and I feel those pleasures again, coursing through my dying flesh. A veil seem'd blown away from the world during that evening, and like a curtain part'd by a summer's wind through an open window, I saw through the fantasy that is flesh, all those sad illusions that assign us to ourselves. In that cell, on that evening, you and I shared the kisses we should have shared, stroked the strokes we should have stroked, and did all those things that chance and custom and a devilish serendipity prevented. An immense joy rose in me then, for I had finally tasted of a possibility for which I had longed, and, simultaneously, a huge disappointment bore down on me for I knew that the time was fleeting and that my waking dream would not last. But for that brief sojourn, the ramparts were as nothing, and despite my imprisonment, despite the walls circumscribed around me, I could see the fires of Kingston, and all the stars, and a cloud passing before the face of the moon. There was no you, there was no me, there was only an I and an I. Then it passed; I could see the town no more, nor the night sky, and your apparition departed, and I was alone again with the Moor on the cold stone floor."

Read never spoke again, nor open'd his eyes. I held him in my arms as he went, and his body, hot with fever, grew cold ere he was plucked from my arms by the undertaker. Read asked to be buried with his sword, and I did him one better. Before dirt was thrown on that sweet form, I threw my cutlass into his grave as well, so that our twin blades would always be crossed, even in the next world, wherever that realm has its location.

Even so, with that lachrymose event, I did not cry, for now Read's progeny was in my hands, and, putting aside my own difficulties, I commenced my care for the child to see that it would grow into adulthood in happiness and in wisdom. Read's child was dark, like Zayd, and shared his brooding eyes. A baby had freed them both: Read from prison and Zayd from oblivion. I named the baby Will. I cleaned him and I dressed him; I told him stories of the sea and of privateers. He would not sleep at night unless I lay down in bed beside him; he would not stop crying in the morn until I gave him a breast to suck. The first time he called me Ma was the first time that I felt needed in all the years I have been on this earth. After the death of my child, I thought motherhood was forever lost to me. With Will, I got my second chance at my last chance.

I turned back to my writing. My book was published under a false name, and it was a sensation, resulting in the issuing of several editions, in both England and America. Not all the stories in the volume were true, and my editor, eager for sales, added sensation and sentiment to several of the chapters to further excite the gentle reader, but, on the whole, I was much satisfied and fulfilled with my efforts.

But, ahhh, by my faith, I could never forget you, my precious one. Even tho' you are not here, you hear; even tho' you cannot be seen, I hold you in my mind's eye. Every afternoon I see you dancing in that plot of land where I buried you; it is now overgrown with flowers, and I see you bend to breathe in the sweet perfume of the blossoms. Read's child whom I have taken as my own is now in the meridian of life, and a parent several times over, and yet you, my joy, my heart's blood, have remained ever a child, immortal and innocent, undead and unchanging. I wish you were at peace with your father, John. But it has been sweet, over these brief decades, to have you here with me.

As I approach the end of my life's journey, I see you more clearly, waiting at the end of the path, smiling and waving and beckoning me on. You have my emerald eyes, and my fire red hair; my sight has dimmed and my locks have turned to gray, but in you I see my youth and it is preserved. I imagine you, playing along the beach as I once did, feet splashing in the surf, pausing from time to time to pick sea-grapes, frowning and laughing at the sour taste, and then sprinting on, as fast as adolescence.

Do not pause to look in the water, my darling! For we are not our reflections, we are not these false things we see in mirrors, in newspapers, or even in the eyes of others. Read saw himself true, and so could look. I tell you truly to look within to see yourself. For the flesh is false, and inheritance is not the sum of ourselves.

Whisper to the flashing water your real name, write your signature in the sand, and shout your identity to the sky until the answer returns to you in thunder. The whole world conspires to tell us who we are, every nation assaults us with amnesia, and so we must do those things that will never be forgotten if we are to preserve our souls. Did I do wrong? Yes, but tho' blood stains, it fades and sometimes washes off. Could I have chosen another path than the one I took? Ahhh—as a mariner I have learned, over these long years, to take whatever wind blows, and then bend it to one's will. By my faith—we steer by the stars, they do not steer us! The end comes to all of us whether we be governors or sailors, harlots or craftsmen, scoundrels or monks. But the end comes quicker to those who do not live their lives as they choose. If your life is not your own then in what way is it living?

Ah, my darling, my loved one, my voyage is far from finished! Wave to me from the farthest shore, for I have pulled up anchor and I sail again. I bequeath my body to the beach for the tide to take. Read is at my side, and we are young, and the sheets are full of wind. I taste sea-salt in my mouth and it is as intoxicating as Jamaican rum. The water below, the swift warm current of the Caribbean, is as clear as tears, the kind happily shed after a healthy laugh or a loved one's return. Read claps me on the shoulder and starts to sing, and, smiling, I lift my cutlass to the sky. All ships in sight will quaver at the fear of our coming!

Together, we raise the Black Flag.

AUTHOR'S NOTE

The main characters in this novel—Bonn, Read, and Calico—
are real people. Their trial, held in 1720, was one of the most
infamous events in the history of the West Indies, drawing attention in newspapers from Boston to London, and inspiring
plays and ballads. The surprising ending to the trial is also a
matter of record. For the most part, the public has forgotten
their story, but their exploits are still celebrated in museums in
the Bahamas and Jamaica, and in historical tomes about the history of pyracy and female mariners. As a native of Jamaica, I
first heard bits of this story when I was a child.

The many period works I'm indebted to include: *A Cruising
Voyage Around the World* by Woodes Rogers, *A Trip to Jamaica
(1700)* by Edward Ward, *A Discourse of the State of Health in the
Island of Jamaica* by Thomas Trapham, *A Voyage to the Islands
Madeira, Barbados and Jamaica* by Sir Hans Sloane, *The History
of the Isle of Providence* by John Oldmixon, *A New Voyage Round
the World* by William Dampier, *The Buccaneers of America*
by A. O. Exquemelin, *The Pirates Own Book* by the Marine

Research Society, *Gems of the Cork Poets* by various authors, *The History of Jamaica* by Edward Long, *The Tryals of Captain John Rackam and Other Pirates* (*1721*), printed by Robert Baldwin, *A General History of the Robberies and Murders of the Most Notorious Pyrates* by Captain Johnson, and Daniel Defoe's novels *A Journal of the Plague Year* and *Moll Flanders*.

Contemporary books I found useful include: *Life Among the Pirates* by David Cordingly; *Pirate Utopias* by Peter Lamborn Wilson; *Seamanship in the Age of Sail* by John Harland; *Boarders Away* by William Gilkerson; *Port Royal* and *History of Jamaica* by Clinton V. Black; *Buccaneer Harbor* by Peter Briggs; *A Short History of Kingston* by H. P. Jacobs; *The Capitals of Jamaica*, edited by Adolphe Roberts; *Port Royal, Jamaica* by Michael Pawson and David Buisseret; *Black Roadways* by Martha Warren Beckwith; *Historic Nassau* by Gail Saunders and Donald Cartwright; *The Diligent* by Robert Harms; *Irish Cities*, edited by Howard B. Clarke; *Discovering Cork* by Daphne D. C. Pochin Mould; *A Dictionary of Cork Slang* by Sean Beecher; *Atlantean* by Bob Quinn; *The Story of the Irish Race* by Seamus MacManus; *The Black Celts* by Ahmed Ali and Ibrahim Al; *Charleston! Charleston!* by Walter J. Fraser, Jr.; *A Short History of Charleston* by Robert Rosen; *The Monster City: Defoe's London, 1688–1730* by Jack Lindsay; *Bold in Her Breeches*, edited by Jo Stanley; *She Captains, Hen Frigates: Wives of Merchant Captains Under Sail*, and *Rough Medicine: Surgeons at Sea in the Age of Sail* by Joan Druett; *Iron Men, Wooden Women: Gender and Seafaring in the Atlantic World, 1700–1920*, edited by Margaret S. Creighton and Lisa Norling; *Women Pirates: And the Politics of the Jolly Roger* by Ulrike Klausmann, Marion Meinzerin, and Gabriel Kuhn; *The Book of Pirate Songs* by Stuart M. Frank; and *Men-of-War* by Patrick O'Brian.

In researching this work, I traveled to Ireland and the Bahamas and used material in the Jamaica Archives in Kingston, the Public Records Office in London, and the New York Public Library (the Schomburg Center for Research in Black Culture in Harlem was particularly helpful). Rick and Erin Borovoy, Tara Harper, Aisha Labi, and my agent, Caron K., gave me invaluable advice and support, and, of course, my terrific editor, Rachel Kahan, also deserves my gratitude. Two of my Jamaican aunts, Hyacinth Anglin and Rosalie Markes, aided my research on the island's history and culture. Finally, I'd like to thank my parents, my wife, Sharon, and my son, Dylan, for general and infinite inspiration.

A Conversation with Christopher John Farley

Q: You say in your author's note that, as a native of Jamaica, you'd heard stories of Anne Bonny and Mary Read when you were growing up. Are they still part of the cultural imagination in Jamaica and the Caribbean? Does your version of the story differ at all from what you'd heard?

A: I heard a lot of Jamaican legends and stories over the years—about Anancy, the trickster spider of myth; about Nanny, the warrior queen who fought British colonists; and about the pirates who made Jamaica their capital during the eighteenth century. Pirates still are very much part of the cultural imagination of Jamaica and the Caribbean. You'll find them in museums, on bottles of rum, in the insurgent attitude of citizens, in the lyrics of reggae songs.

My version of Anne Bonny's story differs from the conventional version—which is not to say that it is in variance with the truth. *Kingston by Starlight* is a novel, not a straight history book. Much of Anne's story, as historians know it, is drawn from Captain Johnson's book *A General History of the Robberies and Murders of the Most Notorious Pyrates,* published in 1724. Nobody really knows who Captain Johnson was (he may have been Daniel Defoe, author of *Robinson Crusoe,* or he may have been, as I speculate in my novel, someone else). Nobody really knows where Captain Johnson got his facts. Fact-based writers—"journalists" may be too kind a term for them—in the eighteenth century often made up facts and embellished tales (and the tradition still survives, and perhaps flourishes, in the twenty-first). Ben Franklin, for example, frequently made up stories under pen names and published them in his newspaper, and he was one of the more honest newspapermen. I did try to remain faithful to the historical record I believed was true, but I also recognized that other parts of the record were probably flawed. So if an event could have happened and felt true, I followed it.

Q: Did your research into the lives of Bonn, Calico, and Read uncover anything unexpected?

A: I was fascinated to find how easily lines of race, sex, and class blurred on pirate ships. Paupers could become buccaneer kings; aristocrats sometimes tired of their pampered lives and joined the brethern of the coasts; black slaves and white slaves found freedom afloat; and there are more then a few stories of women who became successful pirates in the Caribbean, Ireland, China, and elsewhere. The cultural backgrounds of Bonny and her shipmates are not entirely established in the historical record; the past I created for Bonny represents the tenor of the times, as well as the guidance of the voice I heard as I wrote the book.

Q: In what way do these characters' lives reflect the stories of the people who lived in the eighteenth century West Indies? Are they typical of their time or were their lives extraordinary?

A: The pirate tales I tell in this book are true ones. Port Royal was once a pirate capital that was swallowed by an earthquake. Lawrence DeGraff was a pirate of African descent whom the press falsely portrayed as European-looking. There really was a Grace O'Malley who ruled in Ireland as kind of a pirate queen. And African pirates did play a role in the early history of Ireland.

Q: Were these characters extraordinary or typical?

A: Extraordinary people are often deemed so because they are representative. They carry, in the stories of their lives and the thrust of their actions, the spirit of their age. Bonn, Read, and Calico performed some amazing exploits, but there were others who did similiar things, although they did not shine quite so brightly.

Q: You write very passionately about both slavery and piracy in the West Indies. In what ways do you think those "trades" ultimately shaped the culture of the Caribbean, both in the 1700s and in the present day?

A: Slavery helped enrich Europeans and European-Americans while it simultaneously devastated the economies of African nations and native communities in the Americas. The shock waves of slavery continued to impair the economy of post-colonial governments in the West Indies long after emancipation. Slavery also, of course, took a toll in blood and bodies. Bob Marley, the reggae poet of the Caribbean, on his very first major label release, featured the song "Slave Driver," a track whose lyrics provided his album with its title, *Catch a Fire*. The legacy of slavery is a real one for Caribbean singers, poets, novelists, and others. But, in many ways, rather than weakening the culture of Jamaica, all of this has made the soul of the region stronger and more resilient. It helped stir the embers of a fighting spirit. Revolutionaries and provocateurs of all sorts, from Marcus Garvey to Claude McKay to Kool Herc (one of the fathers of hip-hop) were natives of Jamaica.

Q: When you were working on this novel, how did you—a Jamaican-American male author of the twenty-first century—find the voice of an eighteenth-century Irish girl? In what ways was it easy—or difficult—to imagine her life and capture her voice?

A: I had to search for Anne's voice—I looked in museums and libraries; I paged through history books and memoirs. I finally found it when I returned to Jamaica. I left Jamaica when I was a baby and became an American citizen when I was a teenager, but I do return to Jamaica whenever I get a chance, which is quite often. My connection to the island is familial and intimate—my grandparents and my mother are from Jamaica. I have other relatives that live there. And one of my brothers, Jonathan, who is a Harvard- and Oxford-trained mathematician, accepted a post to teach at the University of the West Indies in Mona, Jamaica. Because there is so much mystery about the real Anne, I spent years researching the established facts, using them as the skeleton of my story, and then used my imagination, guided by my study, to fill out the rest of my tale. It is perhaps impossible, I think, to create a fully alive fictional character solely with one's conscious mind. It seemed when I was first writing this book that I was part of an elaborate masquerade: a man passing himself off in his fiction as a woman who is passing herself off as a man. I did not start writing the book until, after all my investigation, I felt Anne herself was telling the tale through me. I was on a beach in Kingston when I thought I heard her voice. I was not far away from where some of her shipmates may have been hanged. The first sentence of *Kingston by Starlight* came to me as if it had been whispered in my ear: "I believe I will begin at the end." So my novel is, in some sense, a ghost story.

Kingston by Starlight
by Christopher John Farley

Reading Group Guide

In an adventure story rich with the salt of the high seas and the mystery of hidden identities, *Kingston by Starlight*'s spirited narrator tells of a life lived always on the outside. Abandoned by her father, Anne Bonny seeks her fortune in colonial Nassau, where a bold deception lands her aboard the pirate ship *William*. Dressed as a man, she discovers that she fits in rather well at first. Anne Bonny's male alter-ego "Bonn" is a bold, adventuresome lad who enjoys the seafaring life. But Anne is, of course, a woman coming of age, and even as she becomes an accomplished sailor, she finds herself drawn to two men, the witty and cynical captain of the *William*, Jack Rackam, and the tough, athletic Read, both of whom are harboring secrets as shocking as Bonn's. When the three men and their crew are arrested and taken to Jamaica for trial, Bonn's life takes a stunning turn when her past comes back to haunt her in a way she'd never imagined, and one last secret is revealed—a revelation that will forever change her life. Christopher John Farley's sweeping tale touches on gender roles, race, religion, history, forgiveness, and revenge with an almost Shakespearean intensity. This guide is designed to help direct your reading group's discussion of *Kingston by Starlight*.

QUESTIONS FOR DISCUSSION

1. The narrator notes that though real names are rarely if ever used on the *William*, the assumed names by which her crewmates are known are more expressive of their various characters. She herself changes the name she uses for the captain throughout the book; at times he is "the captain," at others Calico, Rackam, or John. What does this say about the character of their relationship at these times? The name "Anne Bonny" is only revealed near the end of the book. Do you think this is the narrator's real name?

2. It is clear that much of society disapproves of Anne's father's marriage, her mother's position, and her own appearance and background. How does Anne herself feel about these things?

3. How does Anne's experience on the slave ship affect her? When her father rejects her, does she fully understand why?

4. Anne's reluctance to enter into prostitution to earn a living is understandable—but she doesn't appear to regard murder as a similar breach of "virtue." Why do you think this is? When faced with a choice essentially between piracy and prostitution, what is it about piracy that appeals to her?

5. What role does spirituality play in the story? Discuss Bishop's biblical "quotes," Zayd's prayerful meditation, the "Praying Mantises" on the slave ship, and Read's growing superstition as examples of the role of faith in the characters. What opinion does the narrator have of religion?

6. From time to time, the storyteller seems to interact in a very real way with her audience—in requesting and then sharing

refreshment, for example—but at the end of the book it is less clear that her audience is a living person. To whom is she relating her narrative?

7. Is Read and Bonn's relationship more like the friendship of two women or of two men? Their mutual affection is largely a result of the extraordinary experience they have in common, but how much do they actually share—in terms of character, experience, and gender identity? By the end of the novel, have their personalities become more alike or more unalike?

8. Discuss Anne's relationship with Calico Jack Rackam. What attracts her to him, and vice versa? What do you think of her reaction to the story of his alleged affair with the Governor's daughter? Is her lack of jealousy a sign of faltering affection, or merely a world-wise acceptance? How long do you think their relationship might have endured if they had lived peacefully in their new home instead of setting out again?

9. What is the nature of Anne's passion for men? Does it have at its root a search for a father figure? Or is it merely the romantic feelings of a young woman? What else do you think might be at work in her desire not only to learn about men, but to live as a man among men?

10. Is the revelation that Zed is Anne's true father a surprising one? Others have clearly known or suspected all along—has Anne truly been blind to the fact that she has African blood? How does her experience contrast with the much-repeated story about the pirate De Graff and Zayd's revelation of De Graff's true identity?

11. What does the narrator learn through the course of her story? Is she wise at the end of it, or merely experienced?